FOUR WEEKS

'Your dear Gran ty
of romance and o a.
So after I'd sold as
Cook's . . .'

Thus Abigail Langley and her two sceptical and irrepressible daughters came to Venice. Abigail had been born wealthy and had enjoyed a fashionable season, but now an impoverished widow, she meant to give her girls this one chance of meeting eligible young men. For she knew, secretly, that she would soon go blind . . .

And Grandmother was right! The magic of Venice once again brought romance, but hardly in the way Abigail had intended. And she, too, found her life miraculously changed . . .

RICHMOND HERITAGE

Ninety thousand pounds . . .

It was a staggering blow to the Richmonds. When Old Adam, Jim Richmond's father, died unexpectedly, he was still the legal owner of Milton Mains, the farm which was the family heritage. Jim and Mary had to find death duties of ninety thousand pounds. They had lived lavishly for small farmers. Their riches, their inheritance, had been in the land. The only way they could raise the money was by selling the lovely old Georgian farmhouse, and the land, and settling in something more modest.

Mary's mind was in a turmoil. Not an hour ago she had made preparations to leave Jim – and now this had come like a bolt from the heavens . . .

Also by Susan Sallis

A SCATTERING OF DAISIES
THE DAFFODILS OF NEWENT
BLUEBELL WINDOWS
ROSEMARY FOR REMEMBRANCE
SUMMER VISITORS
BY SUN AND CANDLELIGHT

and published by Corgi Books

SUSAN SALLIS OMNIBUS

FOUR WEEKS IN VENICE

RICHMOND HERITAGE

Susan Sallis

CORGI BOOKS

A CORGI BOOK 0 552 13613 1

FOUR WEEKS IN VENICE and RICHMOND HERITAGE
first published in Great Britain
by Corgi Books a division of Transworld Publishers Ltd

PRINTING HISTORY – FOUR WEEKS IN VENICE
Corgi edition published 1978

PRINTING HISTORY – RICHMOND HERITAGE
Corgi edition published 1977

Corgi Omnibus edition published 1991

This book is set in 10/12pt Plantin
by Busby The Printers Ltd, Exeter

Corgi Books are published by Transworld Publishers Ltd, 61–63 Uxbridge Road, Ealing, London W5 5SA, in Australia by Transworld Publishers (Australia) Pty. Ltd, 15–23 Helles Avenue, Moorebank, NSW 2170, and in New Zealand by Transworld Publishers (N.Z.) Ltd, Cnr Moselle and Waipareira Avenues, Henderson, Auckland.

Made and printed in Great Britain by
Cox & Wyman Ltd, Reading, Berks.

FOUR WEEKS IN VENICE

CHAPTER ONE

Abigail did not close the shop until the last possible minute in case a stray customer should chance by. But 'Langley's Gowns' was not in a fashionable part of the town and in any case Abigail's clientele were a faithful band who had appointments for fittings and rarely dropped in casually.

So at three o'clock she threw a dust-sheet over the light-grey afternoon dress on the dummy in the tiny workroom, placed her smart straw hat carefully to the front of her still dark and lustrous chignon and secured it with the diamond hat-pin which had belonged to her grandmother. And *she* had had it from the Prince of Wales after her coming-out party in 1885. Abigail could remember her grandmamma clearly as an upright old lady of seventy-two giving her the hat-pin – with other jewellery – on Abigail's twenty-first birthday. And her words.

'We haven't much money any more, Abbie, my dear. And probably if there is another war with Germany what we have will be valueless. But if you're in difficulties – a real emergency mind you – you will have these special pieces. And more than that, child. You have breeding.'

Breeding. Abigail smiled at her reflection a little mistily. It was such an old-fashioned word used in the way Grand-mamma had used it. Even so . . . she checked that the hem of her natural linen suit was straight and drew on the summer gloves that matched her hat. Breeding or no, Abigail Langley of 'Langley's Gowns' must be her own advertisement. The only advertisement she could afford.

Her smile deepening at the thought, she at last hung the

sign in the window which read, 'I regret we are closed. If you can call back in the morning we shall be open at nine o'clock sharp.' Both Abigail's daughters had hooted with laughter when she wrote out that sign in her old-fashioned copperplate, but as she had told them – with great dignity – politeness costs nothing. They had laughed even more at that and Christine had said teasingly, 'Darling Mother. D'you mean to say if politeness was a penny a time you'd give it up?'

Abigail had tried to look reprovingly at her dear girls and Susan had hugged her and said, 'If it was a pound a word you'd pay up, wouldn't you, Mother? You're from a different age somehow. In spite of everything that's happened you still believe in – in – being a lady!'

Christine said, 'It's more than that Sue—' They loved analysing their mother as if she weren't there at all. 'Not just surface politeness. It's a code of courtesy she believes in. She's a gentle-lady.'

More laughter. But Abigail had smiled without reproof. She had known it was a compliment.

She locked the shop door and stood peering at her tiny window display; a blouse in cream shantung, exquisitely hand-tucked. The sleeve ought to be lifted slightly to show the fullness, but there wasn't time now. And some dark red backing would accentuate the delicacy . . . she stepped back and cannoned into a woman shopper.

'I'm so terribly sorry—' Automatically she clutched her hat as she turned. It was a young woman, unhurt and uncaring.

'You want to look where you're going,' she said tartly and walked on without enquiring whether Abigail was all right.

Abigail stood where she was for a moment, her grey eyes suddenly still. Then she shook herself impatiently and started off towards the park. Her appointment with Stephen was for half-past three.

*

2

Abigail Langley, *née* Carruthers, had been born fifty-eight years before, a silver spoon firmly between her pink baby gums. An only child, she was the pride and joy of the Carruthers family, and parents and grandparents spent a great deal of time discussing her future. There were to be no more wars, and in the shining new world which Abigail was to inherit she could have anything she wished. She went to an expensive finishing-school in Switzerland. Her needlework was excellent, she could play the piano quite well, sketch and paint watercolours and make herself understood in French and German. She would have liked to have gone to an Art College and learned dress design, but that was not to be. Instead there was a coming-out party, her presentation, her London season, and then the wait for a husband.

Unfortunately by this time the Carruthers' money had depreciated for one reason and another. Abigail was only qualified to be a rich man's wife. The men she met were certainly rich but she couldn't seem to fall in love with any of them. There was plenty of time. Mamma assured her there was no hurry. Papa borrowed some money on his town house and they managed another season.

Denver Ritchie came into her life. He managed his father's estate in the West Midlands and he was comfortably off and wrote poetry in his spare time. They fell in love instantly and it was such a highly suitable match everyone was delighted. Abigail would be a marvellous squire's wife; she could ride to hounds, run the Women's Institute and entertain tranquilly. Yes, she was certainly qualified to be Mrs Denver Ritchie.

They were engaged when she was twenty-two. It was 1939 and Denver joined the Royal Air Force. He was killed in August 1940.

So Abigail drove an ambulance. Lots of girls did and as she had no nursing experience and the women's forces would have taken her away from her parents who were quite incapable of coping with ration books and identity cards, it seemed the only thing to do.

In the grim years that followed, Abigail learned to cope quite well. It didn't show. Her hands never blistered or grew rough, and her long lustrous dark hair rarely escaped from its chignon and she never lost the innate courtesy that was part of her. But she looked after Mamma through her long last illness, and when Papa told her at the end of the war that there was no more money at all, she started dress-making in earnest and supported both of them in a small respectable flat near Paddington station.

Then something marvellous happened. A friend of Papa's came to call one winter afternoon just as Abigail was wheeling in the trolley with the anchovy toast under its silver cover and the teapot on its tiny methylated flame. He was younger than Papa, no more than fifty, and he was a shy, gentle man, frightened of women and quite resigned to staying a bachelor all his life. He had an accountancy business near Mincing Lane; he called it a 'counting house'. Mr Carruthers introduced him as 'my money man, Abbie. In the days when we had money, of course.' And of course in those days he would never have been introduced to the daughter of the house.

He saw before him a curious mixture of girl and woman; chestnut-coloured hair – masses of it, very clear grey eyes – he felt he could see into her soul, good skin, the long lines of a racehorse. She was only about thirty-two or three but in many ways looked older. Of course the war had done that to a lot of women. When her father introduced them, she looked straight at him and her rather firm mouth curved into a half-smile that was unexpectedly mischievous.

'Have some anchovy toast, Mr Money-man,' she said.

His real name was Ambrose Langley.

He fell hopelessly in love with Abigail Carruthers and hesitantly, almost fearfully, she let herself love him. They were married on her thirty-fifth birthday after two years of patient wooing. It was a September day of falling leaves and deep golden sunshine and that was how their short marriage was. Darling Papa lived long enough to hold baby Christine in his arms and as he looked down at the wide blue eyes so strangely like Ambrose's, he asked a tentative question of his daughter.

'Abbie. Dearest Abbie. Do you mind very much that you will never be very well off? That you will never have the position in society which you deserve?'

Abigail laughed joyously. 'Papa – I can never be poor because of Grandmamma's jewels. And as for position in society, I don't really know what that means. I am me – Abigail – whether I am washing up in my own kitchen or entertaining guests for dinner.'

Her father had one more question. 'And do you mind very much my dear . . .' his voice faltered and he held Christine close. 'Do you mind that this is not Denver's baby?'

Abigail's smile became wider if anything. 'When Denver died, darling, he became part of many people, surely? He certainly became part of me. Therefore – in a way – Christine *is* his baby.'

Papa smiled too. Old Grandmamma Carruthers who had known the old King when he was Prince of Wales, had been right. Abigail had breeding.

It took all her breeding to manage when Ambrose died in 1962, a week before their tenth wedding anniversary. His heart gave out quite suddenly on the way to Mincing Lane. His much younger partner was kindness itself and saw Abigail through all the business of death, though after her parents she should have been used to it. His wife looked after Christine and Sue for a couple of days – Christine was eight and Sue was five. Later she offered to adopt them and for years afterwards the girls behaved atrociously when visitors came in case another offer should be made.

It was this offer which made Abigail realize how desperate the situation was.

'You see, Mrs Langley—' Ambrose's partner fiddled with his pen, terribly embarrassed. 'Your husband took me on to try to pull the business out of the bankruptcy court. And I haven't done that yet. It wasn't that he couldn't get accounts . . . I don't know . . . I think perhaps he was so happy with his family . . .' it sounded like a criticism and the young man flushed.

But Abigail understood only too well. Ambrose had declined to join any kind of rat-race. He had been articled before the First World War and his methods were from that era. It was one of the things that attracted him to Abigail; they were both born out of their time and in each other they had found a refuge.

She missed him in many ways but there were the girls to think of. She started dress-making again. There were still relatives who remembered her way with a needle. They brought other customers with them. When the girls were old enough to be left alone for short periods, she saw a shop to let in the old part of town. It had a workroom and a nice little display window. Of course there wasn't enough money to have a proper coming-out party for Christine or to give her more than a secretarial training. But there was a candle-lit supper in the flat the day before she took up her first job and there were boyfriends and a lot of laughter.

Baby Sue was all right too. She insisted on leaving school at seventeen and joining the County Repertory Company who did Shakespeare and Pinter at local schools and kept going on a grant from the Arts Council. She was called the assistant Stage Manager; it seemed to mean making the tea and repairing costumes. But she was happy and there were also lots of boyfriends. No-one special of course. Abigail hoped there would never be anyone special from the Rep. Company or from Tillingham's Department Store where Christine was a secretary. Like Mamma and Grandmamma Abigail wanted someone special for her daughters. She couldn't exactly describe the young men she had in mind, but she was certain they would not be found backstage or in any department store. When Christine talked about David Blake who ran the antique side of Tillingham's she had been horrified.

'What on earth do you mean, darling – he tried to "chat you up"?' She had gazed wide-eyed at Christine who was obviously rather flattered by this approach from the staff's most eligible bachelor.

Unexpectedly Christine had fidgeted with embarrassment.

'Nothing, Mother. I'm the new girl and he had to try it on. He's got a reputation to live up to.'

Abigail had sighed deeply. '*Now* do you girls see what I mean? You're always giggling at my old-fashioned ideas, but men like that – dilettantes we used to call them. They're just irresponsible. If only I could afford to give you a proper London season – or take you to some fashionable watering-place.'

'Sounds barbaric to me,' Christine replied shortly. 'Like a slave market.'

Sue, trying to learn some lines to understudy the leading lady that evening, remarked peaceably, 'Don't worry so, Mother. There's plenty of time and something will come up.'

When Abigail had visited Stephen Crawford, Ambrose's friend and doctor, just three weeks before, she had guessed something was coming up. And that probably time was running out.

She paused by the gates of the small sunlit park and looked around her with that wide clear gaze that was so typical. It was August but already there was a smell of autumn in the air; autumn when things seemed to happen to her. Meeting Denver, marrying Ambrose . . . the funeral with the leaves falling gently. She smiled to herself. Life had been good to her and she had faith that it would go on being good. The trees, the sunlight, the birdsong – these were things she could hear, smell, feel.

She walked briskly down one of the paths leading to the lily pond. He was already there. Stooping a little, unmistakably a doctor even without his bag, he was gazing into the cluttered water, lost in thought. The girls said he was 'past it' and would most certainly have wanted her to visit a specialist if they'd known. Someone who would have seen Abigail as an eccentric old woman without enough money to be a private patient and would never have agreed to meet her in a park by a lily pond.

Following her own line of thought Abigail laughed as she greeted her old friend.

'What did I tell you Stephen? It's much nicer out here than in your stuffy office, isn't it? Look at those chrysanthemums. Really, I must try and find the park-keeper and congratulate him. I've never seen such good blooms.'

Stephen Crawford said, 'Abigail.'

She took his arm. 'Let's walk as we talk, my dear, shall we? Neither of us gets out often enough these days and we must make the most of this weather while it's here.'

They skirted the pond slowly while Abigail exclaimed on the tamarisk trees and the asters.

Stephen said, 'Abigail, I didn't ask you to come and see me to talk about the flowers.'

'Of course not.' The smile she gave him was bright and untroubled. 'You've got the results of my eye tests, I realize that. But our affairs seem very small when we view them in perspective, don't you agree?' She sighed as she read his troubled face. 'Tell me then, Stephen. I won't interrupt you.'

He began to talk, wondering as he did so whether she was really listening. Often she would stop and cup a flower in her gloved hand, then she would nod at a passer-by or lift her face to the sun. He ploughed doggedly on.

'The trouble is progressive, Abigail,' he concluded, trying to maintain the objective tone he used with all his patients. 'I believe an operation has been performed in America, but its results are still uncertain. I'm sorry, my dear. I can give you no hope.'

She said briskly, 'In any case, Stephen, my money would not run to America.' They had reached the children's playground and she watched a small girl thrusting herself into the blue sky on a swing. 'How long before I cannot see at all?'

He hesitated with the usual medical man's reluctance to give times and dates. Then his hand covered hers.

'Three months. Perhaps four. But I must warn you that before that you will get periods of lost vision—'

'Blindness you mean.' Abigail drew in her breath. 'My goodness d'you think that child is safe on that swing, Stephen? She's very tiny to be going so high.' She watched anxiously until the swing began to slow down, then she turned to her silent companion. Again she smiled reassuringly, 'Oh come, Stephen. Don't look like that.'

He swallowed. In the face of her complete acceptance, any kind of sympathy would be trivial so he said instead, 'What will you do, Abigail? Will you tell the girls?'

'Heavens no, not yet. Why depress them? They'll have to know later so let us enjoy ourselves in the meantime.' At her gentle insistence they began to retrace their steps. 'As a matter of fact, Stephen, I've been thinking about the girls and their future for some time. Christine is twenty-four and Sue's nearly twenty-one. Time they were thinking of getting married.'

'You can hardly expect them to consider marriage at a time like this, Abigail—'

'That is why they mustn't know, my dear. And why it is so urgent to encourage them to meet some suitable young men. This has brought the whole thing to a head. I won't be put off any longer.' Her beautiful grey eyes, no longer seeing the flowers, were determined. 'In fact I'll take a taxi at the park gates, my dear. It's only just gone four o'clock. I can have the whole thing arranged by the time they get home from work.'

She would say no more and Stephen had to be content with a promise of a telephone call when 'everything was arranged'. Meanwhile Abigail rode back to the flat in style and went straight to the dressing table in her bedroom. As she opened her jewel box she was staring at the photographs of Ambrose, her parents and her grandmother which were ranged along the polished mahogany top.

'You do understand, don't you?' she said lovingly. 'After all this is a real emergency.' And carefully she dropped the matching set of emerald necklace and earrings, dress clips and bracelets into her handbag.

The girls came in together that evening. Christine's cornflower-blue eyes were unusually bright and it was obvious she had been chattering all the way up the stairs. She stopped abruptly at the sight of her mother in the kitchen.

Sue said, 'What's all this then? The shop caught fire – no, some rich man came in and offered you ten thousand for the stock.'

Abigail laughed as she dished up fried chicken and vegetable salad. '*And* there's banana fritters for pudding,' she announced triumphantly at the girls' astonished faces. 'This is by way of being a celebration. Enjoy it and then we will go into the parlour. I want to talk to you.'

They knew better than to question their mother about some coming announcement so they sat down and obediently enjoyed their meal though Christine was noticeably silent and Sue talked even more than usual as if to cover up for her. Abigail smiled and nodded rather abstractedly and toyed with her water glass and when the meal was finished she actually suggested leaving the washing-up for once.

Knowing that something really big was on the way, the girls took their places in the tiny room overlooking the street which their mother always called the parlour. She clasped her hands and began to pace up and down. Christine whispered, 'Enter Lady Macbeth—' But Sue shook her head. 'Portia. Mother is a schemer all right but she wouldn't go so far as murder. I hope.'

Abigail said sternly, 'Now be serious girls.' She stopped for a moment staring at them as if she was seeing them for the first time. 'I want you to listen to me properly. This is no laughing matter.' She resumed her pacing. 'As you know, I am not at all happy about your prospects . . .' The girls sighed. 'All right, I might have mentioned that before. Which is as well because you know my feelings.'

Christine broke in hurriedly. 'Before you go any further, Mother, this seems a good time to tell you. Without any help from some ghoulish marriage market, I've got a date. A proper one this time. Dinner and the theatre. Just the sort of thing you'd approve.' She cast down her eyes demurely. 'I hope you're pleased.'

Abigail was temporarily nonplussed. 'Oh.' She stared at Mamma's rosewood piano, also as if she'd never seen it before. 'Dinner . . . hmm. And the theatre. With whom?'

Sue rushed in. 'Someone very nice. I met him at the bus stop the other night when he was chatting up . . . I mean, talking to Chris. And it's obvious to me he's given everyone the wrong impression—'

Christine said quietly, 'David Blake.'

There was a small silence. Abigail faced her daughters. 'Darlings. I know what you think, but bear with me. If –

if this young man is serious, Chris, my suggestion may well help to prove his intentions. It's only for four weeks. And if he's *not* serious, well – who knows – you may well have met someone else by then in any case.' She sat down and took Christine's hands. 'Give my way a chance. It's old-fashioned I know but new ways aren't always best. And your dear Grandmother always said Venice was a city of romance and only the very best people stayed at La Paloma. So after I'd sold the emeralds I went straight to Thomas Cook's and they're arranging it all. A whole month in Venice, darlings. At La Paloma.'

There was another silence, this time electric.

Then Sue twittered, 'Do I gather you've flogged Granny's jewels?'

Abigail nodded without reproof at her daughter's turn of phrase.

Christine breathed, 'And blown it all on a holiday in Venice?'

'Not all of it, darling. We shall need clothes. And taxis. And a little nest-egg to come home to in case of . . . eventualities.'

'Like a posh wedding to an Italian count?' Sue said, awed.

'Or someone similar,' Abigail agreed calmly.

Both girls stared at their mother, marvelling. It seemed crazy after years of living carefully to sell the jewels for this.

Christine said slowly, 'It must mean a lot to you. Getting us married off to suitable men.'

Abigail stood up and went to the window. 'You're reproaching me, Chris. I don't want to marry you off at all. I want to give you the kind of opportunity I had. Oh, I know mine didn't work out because of the war. But I had my chance – try to understand, my dearest girls. This might be the last thing I can do for you.' She added a little laugh to take the solemnity out of her words.

Sue glanced at her sister. Frankly she was having a thin

time of it at the Rep. As she had said privately to Christine only the other evening, 'For Assistant Stage Manager, read General Dogsbody.' She had inherited her mother's enterprising spirit and the thought of a month in Venice filled her with excitement. Anything could happen. But what about Chris who was almost convinced that David Blake was no casual Casanova after all?

Christine read Sue's thoughts as if they were written on her forehead. She grinned at her mother's back and shook her head wryly.

'Well, if it's all settled there's not much to discuss, is there?' she said. 'One thing, Mother. If we don't get hitched—' Abigail shuddered ostentatiously. 'Sorry. If we don't find suitable suitors—' Sue giggled. 'May I bring David Blake to the flat for supper one evening?'

Abigail whirled round, glowing. 'Naturally, darling. You can't lose, can you? Either of you? And it will be so wonderful for me to have you all to myself for four whole weeks. It's going to be such *fun*!' Christine nodded reluctantly, and Sue made some cheeky remark about her mother playing gooseberry to all the rush of 'suitable suitors'. Abigail was in full spate. 'I remember Mamma describing a trip she took one evening in a gondola with Prince Luizanni,' she clasped her hands and paced more energetically. 'He wrote a poem to her – composed it during the time it took them to glide the length of the Grand Canal. Of course it was in Italian so she didn't understand it then, but when she came home she had it translated and—'

Sue said, wide-eyed, 'Maybe if we took a typewriter it would help?'

They all laughed, the holiday mood overtaking them. Then the girls listened properly as their mother expounded plans. She was – or should have been – an elderly lady. Her life had not been easy. Yet there was an innocence, an adventurous gaiety about her that had little to do with years or disappointments. Her grey eyes were as clear and untroubled as a mountain stream as she listed the things they must do before leaving in September. The shop must be closed, leave had to be arranged from the theatre and from Tillingham's. And of course, there were clothes . . .

Two weeks later Venice glowed golden in the September sun. The peace that belonged to the island city where the chug of motoscafi was the only mechanical sound lay like a blanket over the onion domes and palazzos at that hour of the day. It was siesta time.

In a quiet square with pigeons strutting by the steps of a narrow canal, Frank Morrell, industrialist from Detroit, Michigan, was attempting to paint a moored gondola. The gondola, tugging against the striped barber's pole to which it was leashed, made a perfect silhouette against the glittering water. Unfortunately the gentle movement of the water continually pushed it behind Frank's easel. For the fourth time he moved his camp stool and tried again.

The small boy who was watching him spoke in Italian.

'You are rich. That much I know.'

Frank frowned at the twitching gondola. 'And how do you know that, young man?'

'Because every time I carry your painting things you give me lire. Poor painters carry their own stuff.'

Frank barked a laugh and went back to filling in the background. How in God's name was he supposed to paint water?

The boy continued thoughtfully, 'And you're American because I hear you talking to other Americans in the hotel. But you are Italian too, because you talk my language.'

'My name was Morrelli if that's any help to you. And why all this curiosity, Dino?' Frank painted out the highlight he'd just done and sighed deeply. Steve had told him to take a holiday back in the old country and try to paint, and from a peculiar kind of cussedness he was doing exactly as he was told. He knew it was supposed to make him feel warm – here in his native Venice where so long ago he'd been glad to earn a few lire carrying painting gear. He could tell anyone – for free – it wasn't working. No-one remembered Francisco Morrelli any more and the folks who had heard of Frank Morrell of Morrell Mechanics were sycophantic slobs who saw him as a meal-ticket. He was alone here, just as he was back home. Isolated by his money and the unmistakable and irritable authority it gave him.

The Italian boy spoke in English, hesitantly. 'I not curious, Signor Morrell. I want to know about you because I like you.'

Frank turned and stared at the dark-haired boy. He said abruptly, 'Why aren't you in school, Dino?'

'It is the vacation, signor.' The boy grinned. 'In the vacation I carry easels and bags for money—'

'To go to America and become rich? Is that why you like me?'

'Ah no.' Dino's grin softened. 'I never leave Venice, even when it sinks in its own mud.' He pretended to throw something for the pigeons, but they weren't fooled. 'I get money for Mamma. Soon she will have another bambino and can no longer do her work in the hotel.'

Frank's cynical expression changed for a moment. Hadn't he left Venice for that same reason over forty years ago? Yet another bambino, another mouth to feed, and though he hadn't wanted to go, America was the land of opportunity, of work. And all those bambinos, those brothers and sisters – and his parents – wiped out in the war before he had time to send anything much home for them. The war . . . that had made him rich when there was no longer a reason for being rich.

Frank unpinned his painting and with great difficulty ripped it in two.

'Come on, Dino,' he said brusquely. 'You take this and I'll carry the portfolio.' He thrust the easel at the small boy. 'Let's have a cool drink back at the hotel, and you can go on guessing about me.'

Dino picked up the torn painting and gazed at it in astonishment for a moment. Then he hurried after Frank.

'One thing I know for sure, signor—' His grin nearly split his face in two. 'You are not an artist!'

Frank looked down at the young face bobbing beneath his elbow. OK, so the kid clung to him like a fly for the few lire that came his way. But hadn't Francisco Morrelli done the same thing? He managed to return Dino's grin. It was the first time he had genuinely smiled since Steve had said, 'Look, Dad. For God's sake get out of it! Go back to the old country and take up painting or something. Get off my neck and give me a chance, will you?'

Together, both laughing, the man and the boy climbed the wide steps of La Paloma hotel and sat down on the sun terrace.

La Paloma had seen better days. Forty years ago it had given shelter to nobility and before that there had been a carefully fostered rumour that the poet Robert Browning had composed a number of stanzas beneath its roof. Now, its situation on a small quiet canal just behind the Grand waterway still attracted the package tour organizers, and there was rarely an empty room. It suited Frank in his present mood. He had got his secretary to book him in here because he was unlikely to meet anyone who knew him. Of course the manager was wise to him and had tried to give him a room overhanging the canal with private bath and shower but Frank in his grim mood of martyrdom had insisted on a cubby-hole at the back of the building looking out on the airshaft which also served the kitchen. It suited his cynicism to be among tourists and yet to opt out of tourism. Painting gave him something to do while he observed and derided. Venice had been his home. Now, empty of his family, he saw it as a sham. A big con. A charade.

After Dino's departure he stayed on the sun terrace watching some young people in the hotel pool. There was nothing to do until dinner. He looked at his watch. It was only six minutes since he'd looked before. Time was endless in Venice. It always had been.

He got up and went to his room and wrinkled his nose at the smell of spaghetti sauce from the airshaft. He sat on the edge of his bed and stared at the carpet and wondered what in hell he was going to do when he retired if he couldn't even take two little weeks of holiday without wanting to crawl up the wall. Except, maybe, it would be better if it wasn't enforced. Not that Steve had exactly twisted his arm, but he'd done the next best thing: pinched his pride.

Trouble was, he'd been so goddarned right. Sure, Frank believed no-one else could handle the reins of Morrell's Mechanics like Old Man Morrell himself. And sure he thought he was indispensable. He couldn't deny it even to take away some of the white tension from Steve's face. But when his son – his own son – had turned round and blurted, 'Frightened I'll prove you wrong, Dad? Scared I can manage as well as you?' – that was a challenge. That was the kind of thing those old English knights used to do when they threw down a gauntlet.

Frank made the impatient sound he made at so many board meetings, a cross between a growl and a hiss. So what was he trying to prove? That Old Man Morrell *was* indispensable? Did he really want his son to fail – to come through on the phone and beg his old dad to go back? And if he didn't want that – if he actually wanted Steve to cope – didn't that mean there was no longer a place in the firm for the Old Man?

Frank grunted again with frustration. One way or another he was banished to Venice for at least two more weeks. And it seemed like eternity already.

He tried to think of something else. What else was there besides Steve and the firm for Pete's sake? Oh . . . Virginia. After all, without Virginia there would be no Steve. Except that Steve was the only good thing to come out of his long-dead marriage. No, Virginia was no alternative for his thoughts; he'd had a letter from her just before he left trying to up her alimony to pay for her wedding to a man twenty years her junior. It was pathetic. But no more pathetic than coming back to the old country to look for some nebulous meaning to life. Why else had he fallen in with Steve's pat suggestion really? Dammit, he could have gone to Palm Springs or Rio . . .

He stood up suddenly. He didn't have to stay in this mausoleum, did he? One thing money did for you, it gave you freedom to move around. And that's what he'd do. He opened a cupboard and got out his pigskin luggage and began to hurl his clothes out of drawers. He couldn't wait to go. Too late tonight, but first thing tomorrow morning . . .

He picked up the phone to book a flight. No reply of course. The girl on the switchboard was doubtless hanging over the counter laughing with some of the guests. That was the trouble with Italians, too darn friendly. Irritably Frank went across to the manager's office himself. Rezzonico was a flapping fool whose smile was practically coin-operated. Frank watched his face fall at the cancelled booking.

'You are dissatisfied, signor?' The liquid dark eyes were strangely like Dino's. 'There is a vacant room with a view—'

'No, I have to get on.' Frank felt contrarily pleased at turning down the more expensive room. 'First thing tomorrow. Let me know which flight and lay on transport.'

He did not say please. Manners were usually meaningless and took time, and time was money.

He ordered a beer and took it out to the steps wondering if he might see Dino. Sheer sentimentality of course. He could leave lire for him at the desk and that was all the kid wanted after all.

A motoscafi appeared along the canal. It was a welcome relief for Frank's thoughts and he watched it as he had watched the tanned girls in the swimming pool. People did not really interest him, they all had their axes to grind as he'd discovered years ago when he married Virginia. Even Steve wanted his father out of the way so he could take over the firm. No, people were simply a diversion, like animals in a zoo.

The motoscafi chugged to the hotel's mooring-pin sprouting its stripes from the side of the riva, and the boatman sprang ashore and held his small craft steady. A great deal of female laughter floated over the water. Frank did not usually enjoy hearing women laugh. It reminded him of squawking hens. This was different; this laughter was full of excitement. Like kids on their way to a party.

The three women who rather totteringly stepped ashore were by no means children. In the cut of their clothes and their natural assurance Frank smelled money. And yet . . . indefinably there was a freshness that did not go with the rich people Frank knew. Mostly money tarnished. And these women were bright. Bright as new silver dollars.

First there were two girls. One was fair, one was dark, and they wore slacks that made their legs look very long. They reached into the boat's interior and helped out another female even taller than they, thin, nearly angular, wearing a green linen suit and a very large hat. Plenty of leg again, and in sheer nylons they were very good legs. Yes, extremely good. Frank moved his dark glasses further up the bridge of his nose to scrutinize this older woman. She had class, he'd give her that. Used to having her own way. Not much younger than himself probably, but the hair that showed under the brim of the hat was still luxuriantly brown.

The boatman surrounded the females with bags while the older woman produced a parasol and without haste opened it above her hat. The girls seemed to have difficulty in controlling their resurgent laughter and the woman said something to them. They both swallowed visibly, stood up very straight and tugged their jackets over their hips. Only then did the woman open her bag and pay off the motoscafi. She must be a duchess at the very least. Yes, most certainly a duchess with that unconscious air of command and that grace, that – what was the word? Panache. She stood for everything Frank disliked most. He watched.

The small craft drew away and the three women stood amidst their luggage turning themselves slowly to look at the whole scene with evident pleasure. They were waiting for a porter. No-one came. Of course the whole kit and caboodle were ushering people in to dinner now, asking how they'd enjoyed their trip to the lido. That was the trouble with the Italians. No-one was going to come. The Duchess and her two handmaidens were going to have to carry their own bags. Frank almost grinned for the second time that day.

The women finished surveying the scene and looked helplessly at their cases. Frank mentally rubbed his hands. And then the Duchess glanced right at him and walked over on those racehorse legs of hers. Unbelievably she inclined slightly over him. He stared up into her clear grey eyes, hypnotized by astonishment.

'Do you understand English? Inglese?' Her lips moved exaggeratedly. Did the blasted woman think he was dumb? Or even deaf?

'Naturally,' he snapped.

Her face, which reminded him suddenly of old rose petals, flowered into a radiant smile.

'How *very* lucky.' She turned and spoke over her shoulder, 'Darlings, I told you everything would go well for us. I've found someone.' She came back to Frank and tactfully avoiding staring at his painting trousers murmured, 'I can see you're not actually on duty at the moment, but would you mind terribly . . .?' She indicated the bags with a deprecatory wave of her hand. 'I'll go on in and find out the number of our room.'

She did not wait to see what he would do. She swept along the patio, her parasol twirling gently, her green-linen rear-view even more impeccable than her front. Frank fumed.

The smaller girl, dark with a sassy look to her, smiled widely as if Frank was now sharing the special in-joke that had been amusing both girls for some time.

'Don't bother. We can manage. Mother is living in the past,' she said cheerfully as she began to hump the bags. 'Chris – if you get this one under your arm, Mother's hat box can go—'

'It's no bother,' Frank said sulkily, surrendering to the inevitable and slightly intrigued by the feeling of intimacy that grin had given him. Incredibly he was standing up whatever the reason, he was taking the darned hat box and another two bags that must weigh a hundred pounds each. He was saying as Francisco Morrelli might have said, 'I'm kinda used to this sort of thing.'

He followed the Duchess and the twittering girls followed him.

The sun must have gotten to him, it was the only explanation. Furiously he ignored the anxious Rezzonico as he surged from behind the desk in the foyer his fairly good English completely forgotten in his horror at seeing his rich guest performing this menial task.

'Register them,' Frank said woodenly in Italian. 'Tell me their room number. And shut up.'

The manager obeyed while the Duchess smilingly closed her parasol and the girls sniffed the scents of dinner like starving waifs. Frank thought grimly that they must be very upper-crust to behave so naturally. Then he led the way into the lift.

'This way, Contessa. First floor balcony rooms overlooking the riva. The very best,' he said with thinly veiled sarcasm.

The girls dissolved again and the Duchess produced another tranquil smile.

'My name is just plain Mrs Langley,' she announced. 'And thank you so much. What ever should we have done without you? I hope you are around often.'

Unaccountably Frank had a sudden memory of a time when his father had discovered some unexpected money in his trouser pocket and had bought Francisco an ice-cream. It was the same feeling. A gift, out of the blue. He felt his face grow warm.

'I'm leaving tomorrow,' he said abruptly.

'Oh dear. I am sorry. Christine – Sue – our new friend is leaving tomorrow.'

'Yes, darling. We heard.' The fair one, Christine, smiled at Frank with the same almost conspiratorial air that her sister had had. OK, so this was no real duchess, but Frank knew that English landed gentry didn't need titles. Maybe she was slightly batty? They often were, in-breeding or something.

The lift stopped and they walked along the corridor to number twenty-three. The Duchess turned to him with another of her darned baby-smiles.

'I hope your next job will be a success,' she said in a low voice and her gloved fingers pressed a coin into his hand. She was tipping him. Just like he'd been tipped forty-five years before when he'd humped bags for people like this.

Angrily he searched his mind for the kind of words she deserved and then he looked at her eyes so nearly level with his. They were shadowed beneath the brim of her hat, but just for an instant he felt he could see right through their clear greyness into the woman's soul. And he saw fear.

Mumbling something, he turned and went back along the corridor gripping the coin in the palm of his hand. This time his frown was not angry; it was puzzled.

Back in his tiny odorous room, he stared at his luggage in surprise. The fair girl was Christine and the dark, sassy one was Susan and the world – anywhere – was obviously their oyster. But Mrs Langley who was used to getting just what she wanted for herself and her daughters, who probably never even had to *think* for herself . . . she was scared. What could a woman like that be scared of?

Frank picked up the telephone and this time got hold of the manager without difficulty.

'I've changed my mind,' he said briefly. 'I'm not leaving tomorrow after all.'

'No?' Frank could almost hear the man swallow. 'And you will want the room upstairs? With the view?'

'Certainly not,' snapped Frank. 'I want to stay right here. Any problems?'

'No problem, signor. No problem at all. You are . . . all right? Your arms – the luggage was heavy.'

'I'm no chicken, Rezzonico, but I can manage a few bags,' Frank replied brusquely and clapped down the receiver to massage his aching muscles.

Then he opened his palm and stared at the coin the Duchess had given him. It was English. A ten pence piece. Worth about a nickel. He'd heard Queen Victoria was damned mean too.

Well, Venice was as good as any other place while he lived through his banishment. And the Duchess might prove interesting. Yes, he would stay a while.

CHAPTER TWO

Abigail woke early and lay for some time orientating herself. An unusual milky wavering light filled the room as if it was itself beneath water and the sounds were very unfamiliar. Normal traffic noises were completely absent so was birdsong. Smells were different too: the sharp tang of coffee was underlaid by the deep all-pervading presence of sea. She turned on to her back and closed her eyes against the shapeless bulk of wardrobe and dressing table, unwilling to admit that so much strangeness momentarily terrified her.

Twice before these moments of fear had temporarily paralysed her; the first time when she had cannoned into a passer-by outside the shop two weeks before and last night when she had tipped the porter and his dark, rather unhappy face had become a vague blur. Stephen had warned her. 'At first objects will simply lose their outline, Abbie. You'll be able to cope with that because the brain can jump that kind of hiatus fairly easily. Later there will be short periods of non-vision—'

She had laughed. 'You're avoiding the word blindness, my dear.'

'Because it has connotations of darkness. You won't be blind in that sense until Christmas. And I think you'll manage this crazy holiday without too much . . . inconvenience. But be careful, Abbie.'

'Of course I will. I wish you could understand why I am doing this, Stephen.'

'I understand only too well. You want to spend your legacy on the girls – a memorable last fling, isn't it,

Abbie? Otherwise they would insist on spending it on you. Afterwards.'

'No, it's not that.' She laughed again. 'Though that would be a shocking waste, wouldn't it? Not at all what Grandmamma had in mind when she gave me her emeralds.'

She lay now trying to recapture the absolute certainty she'd had at first that this really *was* the sort of thing Grandmamma had in mind. When Grandmamma had talked of breeding she had meant an innate acceptance of certain values; values which had held good in her day. And when she spoke of Venice, she had meant romance. So surely to bring her girls to Venice was to visit the romantic past? To show them the things that Grandmamma held most dear?

Abigail sighed and turned on her side. It had not been easy to maintain her conviction in the face of Christine's evident unease. She had had her evening out with David Blake and Abigail had known it had not been a success. Christine's remarks to Sue had been revealing.

'The play was awful – you'd have died. The main character kept forgetting her lines.'

Sue had lifted an eyebrow at her mother. 'Too bad. And David?'

'He didn't forget his lines if that's what you mean. He's easy to be with. Conversation does not flag.'

'You sound thrilled.'

'He's the same with everyone. I think I'd have preferred an embarrassed silence.' Christine's sigh had been long and gusty. 'I've got to face up to the fact I'm just company.' She shook her head ruefully at her mother. 'You were right as usual. I told him about the holiday, even hinted that it was a match-making expedition, but he said how nice, do have a good time, see you in October . . . it was awful.' She shook her shoulders impatiently. 'He's just a philanderer or whatever you said. He'll have forgotten my existence by the time we get back.'

But it was obvious she wished she was staying behind doing her best to make it impossible for David Blake to forget her existence. She might even be in love.

Abigail sat up in bed shaking herself much as her daughter had done. If Chris knew that David Blake was a philanderer or dilettante or whatever he was, then of course it was best to get right away from him. Take a holiday somewhere . . . where anything could happen. She swung her feet out of bed. She could see wardrobe and dressing table quite clearly now and the balcony beyond the floating curtains looked inviting. She was certain she had done the right thing.

Not stopping to put on her dressing gown she opened the tall Empire window and stepped outside. Below her was the sun terrace of the hotel, then the narrow canal leading out into the wider sparkling waters of the Grand Canal. Opposite were two smaller hotels and between them a glimpse of what must be the Campanile. Everything sparkled and seemed mint-fresh. She took deep breaths and waved foolishly at a long gondola gliding past with enormous dignity.

Christine's voice said from the next balcony, 'You're like a little girl at a party, Mother. Whatever must that poor gondolier think of the permissive Inglesi?'

Beyond her Sue broke into tumultuous giggles. Both girls waved madly and then stared in mock-innocence when their mother reproved them.

'Get yourselves dressed as soon as you can,' Abigail concluded. 'We have a lot to do today.' She turned back to the wonderful view to find the gondolier leaning on his pole before he turned into the Grand Canal to kiss his hand in the direction of La Paloma. With her sudden mischievous smile, Abigail kissed her hand back.

'It's going to be such fun,' she said to the girls. 'Your Great Grandmamma was quite right, darlings. Venice is definitely the place to come. Such old fashioned courtesy, such charm.'

It pleased her very much when Christine stopped laughing long enough to say, 'We're going to enjoy every minute—' in a very determined voice.

For the first time since his arrival Frank fell instantly asleep that night and woke refreshed as the first sounds of breakfast clattered along the airshaft.

He was lying on his side in exactly the same position he'd been in last night. Six inches from his eyes on the bed-table was the English ten pence piece. He grinned, remembering. Temporarily at least some of the pointlessness of his trip back to Venice was gone. OK, he was still studying zoo animals, but the Duchess and her two daughters were exotic specimens. Could be they were worth watching.

Still grinning lazily, he rolled on to his back and stared at the ceiling. He'd never been to England, never wanted to. It made him think of Venice, living on the past. The Royal Family and Shakespeare. And the Smith – Sprinter works of course. The final anachronism might well be the Smith – Sprinter works. His grin became bitter. Hadn't Smith – Sprinter been the cause of his final rift with Steve? Maybe England and all things English were bad for him.

He let his mind drift back to that fatal Board Meeting.

It had been a dark day, cloud from the Lake sitting on top of Detroit making it grimmer than it need have been. He had skipped breakfast to attend to final details of the agenda and his head throbbed dully so that his one concern was to get through the meeting, take some aspirin and lie on the day-bed in his office. And then they got hooked up on Smith – Sprinter.

The English factory near Coventry was Steve's baby. He was crazy about everything English and when he'd heard that the small custom-made car plant was going for a song he'd been filled with enthusiasm.

'Dad, don't you see – England's the place for our sort of business. Hand-built cars full of gimmicks . . . that's OK for our plant here. But "made in Great Britain" still means something. There's a ready-made market over here for their Smith – Sprinter car. It hasn't altered its basic design since 1934. If we inject some capital . . .'

Frank had allowed himself to be carried away against his better judgement. Because it was Steve. And look what it had done for him. The figures for Smith – Sprinter told their own sad story.

Frank asked the accountant to read them aloud to the Board and then looked at Steve.

Steve said without much hope, 'Can we give them another year? I understand there's a few difficulties on the shop floor which might be ironed out by a personal visit. We're in the position of being absentee landlords.'

Frank did not bother to reply in words, he merely shook his head and turned to the next item on the agenda.

One of the directors, young like Steve, said, 'Mr Chairman, I would draw your attention to the fact that a closure of the Coventry plant would mean hardship in terms of unemployment – considerable unemployment.'

Frank's head pounded. He said brusquely, 'There's always work for men who want it. Shall we get on to the next item?'

Nevertheless he emerged from the Board room feeling discouraged. OK he *was* right. The English firm was losing money steadily and when that happened you cut your losses and got out. That had always been his policy and it had always worked. But . . . Smith – Sprinter was Steve's baby.

All Steve said was, 'You look tired.' But there was no concern in his voice. It was a criticism.

Frank snapped, 'It's twenty-five years since I had a holiday. Even then it was with your mother. No damned wonder I look tired.'

Maybe it was because of the Board meeting, or the remark about Virginia . . . anyway, Steve came back with, 'Why don't you go away? Back to Venice or somewhere? Take up painting. Get off my back . . .'

Frank shut his eyes tightly. Strange that every time he tried to think things out constructively he came back to the same point. Like one of those blasted maze things. Didn't they have a famous one in England? Hampton Court or somewhere?

He swung his legs out of bed. It was still early but he'd get down to the dining room and find a secluded table with a good view for watching the zoo animals. He picked up the ten pence piece and stared at it. What a nerve the woman had. Obviously used to money, yet handing out nickels as if she was living in the Venice of forty years ago.

Quite a few heads turned in the restaurant an hour later when the English trio descended and were led to a table next to the verandah by the manager himself. He had worked out the previous evening that if Frank Morrell of Morrell's Mechanics Michigan could carry cases for these English ladies, then he, Paolo Rezzonico, could make certain they had the best table and the best service La Paloma could offer.

Abigail beamed upon him. 'Grazie,' she murmured experimentally.

He beamed back and beckoned to a waiter. Abigail looked smugly at the girls. 'What did I tell you?' she asked. 'The very best hotel, my dears. Such exquisite service.'

'*And* he understood your Italian, Mother,' Sue teased.

The waiter came forward and produced a menu. 'Grazie,' Abigail said confidently. The menu was immediately withdrawn and the waiter with raised brows made a few unintelligible remarks.

'Why did he take away the menu?' Abigail asked,

astonished. 'I said thank you very politely and he just removed it from beneath my very nose! And what's he saying now?'

Christine and Sue were quite unable to answer her, they were concentrating with all their might on restraining their giggles. Their eyes watered uncontrollably as Abigail turned to the waiter and engaged in combat.

'La Prima colazione!' she said very clearly in an execrable accent. 'Caffee! Toastato! You know – just an ordinary, everyday breakfast!' She flapped her hands helplessly and Christine was attacked by hiccoughs.

Sue suddenly noticed the man who had humped their cases last night. He was sitting eyeing them from a corner table, and, remembering how he had come to their rescue before, she raised her eyebrows in a silent call for help. It was obvious now that he was no hotel employee. Probably a guest on a shoestring budget like themselves. Oh well . . . he had realized last night that Mother was too innocent to be allowed out on her own and as he was still in the hotel . . . and terribly shy from the way his eyes avoided hers. She waved and he stood up reluctantly.

Abigail smiled right at him, her grey eyes very clear.

'Oh how very nice – it's you.' She stilled her hands. 'I really don't quite know what's happening. The waiter offered me a menu—'

'Yes, I saw.' The man straightened abruptly and spoke fluently to the waiter. Then he turned back to Abigail. 'You see, signora, in Italy when you say "thank you" to an offer it automatically means "no thank you". To accept, one says "Si, per piacere". The waiter thought you did not require the menu so he made a few suggestions himself. Among which were toast and coffee.'

The girls succumbed at last and Abigail with grave dignity poured two glasses of water and pushed them across the table.

'I'm very grateful to you, Mr – er – signor—'

'Morrell, ma-am. I'm American.'

Abigail was wide-eyed with admiration. 'But you speak Italian so well, Mr Morrell. How terribly clever of you.'

'Not really, Duchess – er – ma-am. I'm Italian-American. I emigrated from Venice when I was fifteen. This trip is kinda . . . well, I guess you'd call it a sentimental journey.'

'Oh.' Abigail tried not to look at Mr Morrell's shabby trousers. 'So you don't actually work here? I mean, I was under the impression—'

Susan said, 'Obviously not, Mother. Mr Morrell is a visitor. Just like us.' She smiled again at the shabby little American wishing she could tell him that their finery was simply Grandmamma's emeralds being put to practical use.

Christine felt the same. 'Won't you join us, Mr Morrell?' she said opening her eyes at him in the way Abigail had. 'We could use a little help with our Italian.'

Mr Morrell seemed uncertain whether to accept the invitation or not. Then with that same abruptness, he seated himself on the proffered chair and began to explain the basics of Italian pronunciation. He seemed surprised too when an extra coffee cup appeared by his elbow. Poor man, it was quite obvious to the Langleys that he was completely over-awed by their outward appearance. They worked hard to put him at his ease.

It was true Frank was in a state of surprise, even shock. But the surprise was mostly at himself. How come, he asked himself, was he sitting here at this table, sharing breakfast with this Olde English Dame, helping her out, making suggestions, allowing himself to be . . . *patronized*? Oh sure, it hadn't escaped his notice that they thought he was some hick on a package trip. The ten pence piece had been for a porter; the cup of coffee was for an impoverished traveller who might be useful because he spoke the lingo. What he ought to do was stand up, bow from the waist very stiffly and get the hell out of the place. But the Duchess was speaking.

'You might remember, Mr Morrell. There used to be select little parties with guides who knew their way around.' There was a slight crease between those fine grey eyes. 'My Grandmother told me how well arranged these outings were.'

'Oh *Mother—*' the little blonde, Christine, spoke up. 'Do we have to go on show the very first day?'

The brunette gave her a look and said hastily, 'It would be nice to find our own way around by ourselves, Mother.'

But the Duchess said firmly, 'An organized party is more practical, Sue. We shall get into difficulties with the language if we try to be too adventurous our very first day. Can you help us, Mr Morrell?'

Frank was amazed at the way the girls immediately gave in to their mother's wishes. He knew back home young people followed their own inclination in the face of much stronger opposition than this. Yet, here *he* was, still sitting here, not standing up or bowing from the waist . . .

He said, 'There are water-bus trips most every day. Organized by the management. To places of interest and so on. Is that the kind of thing you meant, ma-am?'

The Duchess said doubtfully, 'Well, yes. I suppose it was. Are those trips patronized by *nice* people?'

Even the girls seemed to realize this was the ultimate in snobbishness.

'*Mother!*' The blonde one was quite pink. 'I'm sure all the people at La Paloma are respectable, aren't they, Mr Morrell?'

Well, put like that . . . maybe the Duchess was worried some guy would make a pass. He said reassuringly, 'Most of them are. Sure. You'll be quite safe with the Paloma guests.'

*

Abigail wondered a little confusedly if 'safe' was exactly what she meant. However it was impossible to explain to this dark, compact man from the other side of the world the intricacies of presenting one's daughters without a proper season. She smiled vaguely at him instead, and was surprised to see his rather bleak face warm for just an instant. But it was only an instant. Poor man, life had obviously been grey and dull and hard for him in a foreign country so far from his native Italian sunshine. How lucky she had been with memories of two wonderful men, her full and interesting life at the shop and her beautiful daughters. The room grew misty around her and she was only half aware of the American standing up and moving away. She held on to the edge of the table.

Christine hissed, 'Really, Mother! It's not a bit of good you sitting there grinning like a Cheshire cat. Your feet are going to ache just as much as ours after a day's sight-seeing. Museums that once were palaces. Art galleries where Titian lounged around with the local beauties but where we are expected to stroll endlessly admiring everything in sight!'

Sue, all prepared to join in with her sister, glanced at Abigail and changed her mind.

'It might be rather fun, Chris. We're here for a month so there will be plenty of time to get around alone – when we know the place a bit better.'

'But it's all so obvious,' Christine protested. 'We might as well walk around with labels pinned to our clothes – "available for marriage but only titles need apply". I'm sure that Mr Morrell must have guessed what was going on.'

'Of course he didn't,' Sue said, frowning at her sister as she darted veiled glances across the table. 'And we promised to give Mother's way a chance, Chris, so we might as well get it over with. For goodness' sake forget David Blake. He'll still be waiting when we get back if he's serious.'

'Exactly,' said Christine wryly. But she smiled, surrendering because it was a small thing to do for her mother who had done all this for them anyway.

Abigail focused them at last and patted Christine's hand. 'We're going to enjoy every minute of this wonderful place, darling – remember? And we've got dear Grandmamma to thank.' She came back to the present with difficulty. 'Ah here comes that poor shy Mr Morrell. Be nice to him, girls.'

'Well, ladies. There's a tour of the Grand Canal this very morning. Assembling in the foyer now.' Mr Morrell seemed anxious they should not miss it. He gathered up Abigail's scarf and straying handkerchief.

'You really are so *kind*,' she thanked him.

Frank told himself he was thankful to see them go. If he'd even imagined someone like the Duchess then he would have considered her extinct, yet here she was at this second-class hotel, grand and mean and compelling. And Frank Morrell was not in the habit of being compelled.

Yet without the Langleys, Venice was grey again. He went to the swimming pool, ordered coffee, then cancelled it. He supposed Dino would turn up soon and they would take his painting gear down on some deserted riva. Or maybe he could hire a boat and they could go fishing.

He gave his growling hiss and stood up abruptly. He would find Rezzonico and enquire when the water bus was returning from the tour of the Grand Canal.

He walked briskly into the foyer and there – down on the steps – teetering over the edge of the water – waving – surely about to fall in – was the Duchess herself.

'Hey!' he ran forward and caught her arm. 'Hey, steady there, ma-am.' Couldn't she see she was going head-first into the drink? 'Come away from the edge a piece.'

She gurgled – he'd never heard a woman gurgle before. Virginia's laugh had been ear-splitting and often unamused.

'Do excuse me, Mr Morrell. I get carried away. Almost literally that time!' She hung on to his shirt sleeve in a proprietary way and he found himself leading her to one of the wrought-iron seats. 'I'm so pleased the girls got the last two places on that trip you see. There seemed to be several very suitable people among the party. Very suitable indeed.'

'Suitable?' He watched her hand leave his arm and hold the edge of the verandah balustrade. Her fingers were long and completely useless.

'Yes. People. Gentlemen, you know. Who will keep an eye on my daughters. In my absence.'

He wondered whether she knew what sort of an eye would be kept on those two gorgeous English girls. On the other hand he had an impression that in spite of all the laughter and teasing, Christine and Susan Langley were well able to take care of themselves. Was this the one – the Duchess herself – who needed protecting? He shook himself mentally. A woman with such sublime assurance – practically arrogance – could well look after herself.

'So you couldn't get a place on the tour?'

'I'm afraid not. It doesn't matter. The sights would be wasted on me.'

He almost smiled at her attitude. She might not have been to Venice before but she knew it all anyway.

She went on, 'I think I shall wander around the corner to St Mark's and have my coffee in the piazza. I might be able to take in one thing at a time.' She seemed to recollect herself. 'I mean, I need time to absorb the – the atmosphere.' Her voice ran out and she looked for a moment uncertain.

Frank looked away from those clear eyes and spotted Dino wandering along the riva.

He blurted, 'I think I can fix you up with a suitable guide, Duchess. A young man who is very able and informative—' after all she'd never make it alone to San

Marco without falling in the canal. Besides, if he tipped Dino well enough he would keep her out maybe most of the day. He signalled hastily and Dino joined them. 'Signor Dino Carlos. Signora Langley. The Signora would like a quiet stroll along the riva. Not too close to the water, Dino. Perhaps a rest at the café on the edge of the piazza where she will have a good view of the Campanile. You understand, boy?' He pushed a hundred lire note into Dino's hand. The dark face split into a massive grin.

'I show you my home-town, signora,' the boy said simply. 'We look at tourist views. But we also look at people, yes? Signor Morrelli not look at people when he paint. Just gondolas, church towers. You – you like people?'

The Duchess put out her hand and took his in a gesture that was at once child-like and gracious. 'I like people, Dino,' she agreed. She stood up and they walked slowly down the wide steps of the hotel to the cobbled riva where Dino paused and looked over his shoulder.

'You not come?' he said to Frank.

The Duchess did not bother to look round. She was concentrating on the steps. 'Of course he's coming,' she said in that blasted high-handed voice of hers.

Frank gripped the edge of his iron chair like a stubborn schoolboy defying his teacher. And then the Duchess glanced round for him, expecting him to be there, and there was that sudden look of bewilderment again in her eyes. Almost fear.

Frank stood up and hurried to join her.

For Abigail the morning was full of blurred and hazy colours; full of people who seemed friendly; full of a simple happiness that had its roots in the fulfilment of her wish to visit the past and show her girls the kind of romanticism that upheld their values, never lowered them. And there was something else bound up in this happiness too. A sense of security and safety that had to do with being with Dino and Mr Morrell. It was a feeling she had not experienced since Ambrose died and she gave over the responsibility of the little outing – of herself even – with confidence.

For Frank the next two hours were full of contradictions. His objective interest in an exotic zoo specimen turned into a very personal exasperation. An exasperation that made him want to wring the Duchess' neck one minute and stand between her and the harsh world the next. And an amazement too that the world seemed not to recognize Abigail Langley's sheer effrontery; in fact seemed to enjoy it and lose some of its own harshness. People kept on smiling at her and saying 'Buon giorno' and she would smile back and repeat the words delightedly.

And for Dino it was a morning of contentment. He was warmed by this new signora's smile; by Signor Morrelli's interest in her after his boredom of the last few days. He played with the pigeons, feeding them peanuts. And he wondered why Mrs Langley's eyes were so wide and clear.

They sat together at a table in an open-air café to one side of the huge area of St Mark's square. To Abigail the golden onion domes of the cathedral seemed to merge with the red of the tall Campanile and then break up into the dark shadows of the Library. And everywhere she looked were stone lions, tall columns, fluttering pennants and people.

Mr Morrell was rather like one of the lions. She could see him very clearly in the autumn sunshine. Dark – well that would be his Italian blood of course – and bigger than she had at first thought. There were powerful shoulders beneath his thin shirt. And the way his head thrust forward; not so much a lion perhaps as an English bulldog.

She smiled at the paradox.

'Tell me, Mr Morrell, why did you call me Duchess just now? I hope you are not under any misapprehension.'

He mumbled something about an American slang expression and she leaned across the table reassuringly.

'Don't apologize, Mr Morrell. It's quaint. How would you put it – cute? Do call me duchess.'

'I wasn't apologizing, ma-am—' his colour was deepening again, he was so easily embarrassed. She patted the back of his hand.

'I had a special name for my husband that sounded unusual.' She gurgled recalling the first time she had met Ambrose. 'Mr Money-man.'

'Really ma-am?' The dark eyes looked almost annoyed. 'I guess he was a kind of Universal Provider. Like most husbands.'

Abigail stared between the columns towards the canal and glinting water. 'He certainly gave me everything I ever wanted,' she said softly. Then she came back to the present. 'Are you married, Mr Morrell?'

'Not now. I had a wife. And she certainly took all she wanted.'

Abigail's face stretched with sympathy. 'She died?'

'Divorced,' Mr Morrell said briefly.

Abigail realized she had intruded, and in an effort to relax this stiff, unhappy man, she confided in him again. 'My husband died fifteen years ago, so it's easier for me.' She tried to imagine Ambrose leaving her for another woman. It was a chilling thought. She added gratefully, 'He gave me everything you see. I can't ever lose what he gave me.'

Mr Morrell looked away from her. He spoke tightly. 'I guess Virginia – my wife – doesn't do too badly either. In alimony.'

Abigail was shocked and then deeply compassionate. Mr Morrell had been unbearably hurt during his lifetime. How lucky, how very lucky she had been.

She said impulsively, 'I wish you weren't leaving today,

Mr Morrell. I feel I . . . that is, we . . . the girls and I . . . could help you.'

His colour heightened again and he pushed his chair back suddenly so that the metal legs scraped on the pavement.

'I don't need your charity, Mrs Langley—' he was spluttering and Abigail reached across the table again and put her hand over his, restraining him from standing up and rushing off.

'I didn't mean *money*, Mr Morrell!' she said in a low voice. 'I haven't much money at all and in any case I wouldn't dream . . . Please forgive me for giving you the wrong impression. I merely thought we could cheer you up.'

Even to her own ears this sounded inadequate. To be divorced, to save up for this sentimental return to his old home, to be so lonely and embittered – all this called for more than cheering up. Yet the trite words seemed to work. She felt his hands relax beneath hers and a slight smile appear on the thin mouth.

'You haven't much money, Duchess?' he said using the nickname with curious deliberation.

She smiled back delighted she had not hurt him irretrievably.

'Well, obviously I have enough to come here,' she admitted. Her smile became roguish as she considered telling him about the emeralds.

Then he said, 'Obviously. And to keep up a certain standard of course. Clothes and luggage and . . . tips.'

For a moment she thought he was being sarcastic. Then she remembered last night when she had thought he was the hotel porter off duty. She laughed, realizing he was teasing her.

'Mr Morrell, I confess to you I haven't tipped anyone for years!'

He nodded and she sensed they were in complete agreement. 'No, I could tell that, Duchess,' he said.

★

Frank stood up at last, his exasperation fermenting into sheer incredulity that anyone like the Duchess could exist in the twentieth century. Not much money indeed. When her husband, poor devil, had left her everything he had. When she was too mean to tip – and when she did she splashed out with a nickel.

Yet here she was charming Dino all over again with those eyes of hers, promising they'd come to San Marco another day and find that same pigeon and feed him more peanuts. He looked at her as she crouched with the boy stroking the silver-blue plumage.

'Let's give him a name, Dino,' she was saying. 'So that we can call him next time we come.'

Dino's face was alive with enthusiasm.

'Garibaldi!' he said. 'The saviour of Italy!'

The Duchess nodded gravely at the pigeon. 'How do you do, Garibaldi,' she said formally. 'I'm pleased to make your acquaintance.'

Frank snorted impatiently. Anyone could bewitch a child with such nonsense. He marched to the edge of the square, glad he was adult and immune. But then he waited for her to catch him up.

'Good view of San Giorgio this side,' he grunted as she came across clutching Dino's hand. That was another thing – OK on the riva it stopped her teetering off into the drink – but here? Just another affectation to keep clutching the kid's hand.

She paused and put her free hand to her hat brim. 'Yes.' She sounded hesitant. 'It's another church is it?'

Dino laughed. 'Si, signora! A church.'

'The water glints so. I can't quite make it out.' She turned abruptly from the magnificent spectacle. 'There goes Garibaldi, Dino! See?' Thousands of pigeons had risen from the piazza at the sudden arrival of a military band. Dino waved foolishly, laughing with her. Then they began to march in time to the drum-beat. Frank snorted and followed irritably.

He led her a long way back to La Paloma indulging this wish of his to show off his Venice. However, she showed little interest in the magnificent buildings and vistas yet she slowed down to watch a couple of women gossiping in a dark archway.

'What are they doing?' she asked. 'Are they housewives? Where would they buy vegetables and meat?'

He answered briefly surprised at the mundane enquiry.

Then they passed a building that had been a palazzo and was now a popular casino and club. Even at midday the verandah was thronged with people. The Duchess halted and stared across the canal.

'That looks like a party,' she said wistfully. 'One of those house parties my grandmother spoke of.'

He said brutally, 'It's a casino, ma-am. A kind of everlasting party I guess. Not long opened. Everyone goes there.'

She looked at him then back to the verandah. 'Everyone, Mr Morrell? You mean, it's the thing to do?'

'Sure. If you've got money to throw away.'

She was suddenly brisk. 'Then I must bring the girls. Tonight. Tonight we'll go to the casino!' She smiled at him brilliantly. 'Thank you, Mr Morrell. You have done us another service before you leave.'

For a moment he was tempted to tell her he wasn't leaving. Tempted to offer to take her and the girls to the casino that evening. Then he stopped himself. A woman who never gave tips yet who grasped eagerly at a chance to 'throw away' her money at the gaming tables deserved to do it alone.

He said dryly, 'Any time, Duchess.'

*

By the time Abigail shepherded her daughters into the baccarat room of the casino that evening, her innocent aplomb was somewhat diluted. The subdued hush through the carpeted rooms seemed more suited to a cathedral than a place of entertainment and in the dedicated concentration of the players she saw no hope of any suitable introductions. She also had a suspicion that three ladies alone in this place gave a wrong impression.

Christine, sensing her mother's confusion, took over.

'Come on, darling. Here's a chair. We'll stand behind you. Now those discs we bought – yes, they're chips. You can stake them on any number up to nine.'

Abigail protested. 'Chris, how do you know all this? I'm sure we've never played this game at home.'

Christine said unguardedly, 'David took me to a place in town after the theatre and we played baccarat.' She leaned hastily forward and picked up her mother's scarf. Sue was, as usual, convulsed with more or less silent laughter and was no help at all. But Abigail was already engrossed in the game.

'He's giving me no cards, Chris. I've put the chip things down. Why don't I get any cards?'

'Only the players up there receive cards, darling,' Chris whispered desperately against the hush of concentration.

A young Italian on Abigail's left turned to her. His eyes danced with amusement, then, as he saw the three women with their heads close together, they widened with sudden admiration.

'Scusi, signora. We have put our money on those players. You understand? They run for us, like racehorses. But we stay still.'

Abigail was charmed. 'How well you put it. Of course, I see now. Oh, a king. That's good, isn't it? A court card.'

'Too good, signora. Nothing over nine. We go down.' The young Italian made his mouth into an inverted U and the Langleys, all laughed sympathetically. Immediately several people joined in the informal lesson.

'You mean—' Abigail looked round. 'You mean, the name baccarat means . . . nothing? Literally nothing?'

'Exactly madame,' a plump French lady spread her hands. 'Anything over numero nine . . . baccarat!'

The young Italian said to Sue, 'Permit me to introduce myself, signorina. My name is Vittorio Pucci. I am from the mainland where I work in my vineyard.'

'Oh . . . how nice.' Sue felt her face grow unusually warm and her giggles were halted on a breathless crescendo. 'We're the Langleys. My mother . . . my sister Christine. I – I'm Sue.'

Abigail and Christine smiled and leaned over Sue to shake hands. Signor Pucci took each hand and lifted it to his lips.

'Sue.' He repeated the name wonderingly. Then he said carefully, 'Meesis Langley. Chris-steen. This is so pleasant.'

The game had stopped and people were looking on with amusement. Sue said, 'Thank you for your help, Signor Pucci. You see we really are innocents abroad.'

He smiled into her eyes. 'You have made a difference to the baccarat table, that is certain. You will play again, Meesis Langley?'

Abigail, suddenly in her element, shot Christine a look that said 'You see?' and shook her head. 'I'd like a game that is rather more positive,' she announced to the obvious relief of the banker. 'Can you suggest something, Signor Pucci?'

He rose immediately and offered his arm. 'Roulette perhaps? There is a fascination in the movement and it can be exciting.'

'Yes. I do know about roulette.' Abigail allowed herself to be escorted very slowly through the rooms. 'You are visiting Venice for long, signor?'

'A few days only. I have business to attend to in connection with the sale of my grapes and as I know no-one in the city I am delighted to make your acquaintance.' He looked around and met Sue's bright brown gaze. She dimpled and he smiled warmly. He was tall for an Italian with short crisp hair and good square hands. And a sense of humour. Sue decided suddenly that if ever she became serious about a man he would have to have a sense of humour like hers. Perhaps it was more a sense of fun. She didn't know. But Vittorio Pucci had it anyway.

Mother was still pumping him gently.

'We don't quite know what to look for on our sightseeing trips of course,' she said. 'Perhaps you could recommend somewhere really special.'

'I am sorry, signora, that is not possible. I do not know Venice at all. I inherited my vineyard at the beginning of this year only and there has been a great deal to do. This is the first time I have ever been to Venice.'

Abigail beamed on him. 'A family inheritance. We too are here because of an inheritance. How interesting.' She moved gently on and somehow when they arrived at the roulette wheel she was with Christine and Sue had taken her place next to Signor Pucci.

Christine said, 'Mother – don't get too hopeful. It's just our second night in Venice. And maybe Sue hates him.'

Abigail nodded tranquilly. 'Perhaps. I don't think so, but perhaps. However, he seems a nice enough young man and if he is lonely—'

'What about if he is also penniless?'

'He could hardly own a vineyard and be penniless, dear. But if he is hard-up, well, there are other things that matter.'

'I thought you said—' Christine tightened her lips in mock exasperation. 'Mother. You're just an old romantic at heart.'

'That boy has background and breeding, Chris.' Abigail protested. 'And family feeling. He – he's *nice*,' she finished inadequately flapping her hands and knocking someone's handbag.

There was a flurry of apologies and then Chris said in a low voice, 'He's winning anyway.'

Abigail nodded, satisfied. 'He must be well-off then,' she said comfortably. 'I've noticed that it's only the wealthy who win at cards.'

'It's not cards. And anyway he's losing now,' Christine reported.

'Lucky in love then,' Abigail remarked.

'Mother. There are times when I could kill you!'

Sue said, 'Are you a regular gambler, signor?'

He laughed. 'Certainly not, signorina. This is a small . . . how do you call it?'

'Flutter?' Sue supplied, dimpling.

'Quite so. Flutter. I am here on business and I do not know where to spend an evening. So I put aside a little money and when that goes – so does Vittorio Pucci!'

Sue nodded. It was the kind of thing she would do herself and somehow bridged the enormous gap between a stage manager and a vineyard owner.

He was saying urgently, 'Signorina Sue. May I see you again? Will your mother object? I am a farmer and you are aristocracy, yes?'

Sue laughed. 'No. Oh no. That was not what Mother meant when she talked of an inheritance. We're very ordinary but my Great Grandmother left us some money and we came on holiday to – to be together!'

His smile was totally relieved. 'I am glad. It makes it easier to . . . be friends. We can be friends?'

Sue found herself blushing again, a thing she rarely did. 'I think so. My mother and sister—'

'Them also. Of course.' He stared down at her earnestly.

'Signorina, this is not the pick up. I know Italian men have a bad reputation . . . I would like the company of all of you.'

Sue said, 'Oh.'

'And especially of you.'

Sue lowered her eyes again knowing full well that her dark lashes made a perfect crescent on her cheek. 'Oh,' she said.

Abigail rejoined them as soon as they moved from the table.

'It is late,' she said. 'And we arrived only yesterday.'

Signor Pucci looked desperate. 'Meesis Langley. Please. You will permit me to share a bottle of vino with you? On the terrace perhaps?' He looked young and charming and Sue swept her eyes appealingly upward in her mother's direction. Abigail agreed graciously.

'You are after all, an expert in wine,' she said.

They found a table on the verandah and managed to catch a harassed waiter. Abigail sat back and recalled her morning with Mr Morrell. Yes, he had been helpful. And right. Everyone came here. She should have asked him to come; after all it was his last evening and last evenings could be melancholy. Besides it would have been nice if he were here. He would know if this charming young Italian was . . . suitable. And he would provide that rock-like security she had felt this morning.

Not that Signor Pucci needed help socially. It was as if he'd known them all for years. He talked a lot and gesticulated and when the wine arrived with a plate of wafery biscuits, he pronounced it excellent. Abigail watched and listened carefully and was glad that he made no attempt to detach Sue from her family or in fact to pay her any special attention at all. He was as frank and open as Sue herself and laughed as much too. His manner towards Christine was impeccable, yet there was no doubt in Abigail's mind that it was to Sue he was attracted.

Ah well. She must wait and see. It really was amazing how it was working out – and they'd only just arrived. And if – just if – anything came of this chance meeting, how wonderful it would be for Sue to live in this wonderful sunshine far away from English hospitals. That was one thing she could not bear. To be a constant nagging responsibility on her dear girls.

Vittorio was begging them to pay him a visit before they left Italy. He would show them his vineyard, which had belonged to his uncle and before that to his grandfather and was in much need of modernization but at least still belonged to the family and had not been taken over by one of the big combines.

Abigail said suddenly, 'My dears, talk it over among yourselves for a while. It sounds interesting and I am agreeable to whatever you decide. I am going to stroll down to the water for a few moments.'

Sue said, 'Mother, wait. We'll come with you.'

But Christine shook her head. 'Let her go,' she said softly. 'She wants to be on her own. To talk to Father.'

Sue explained to Vittorio. 'Mother is very happy tonight. And when she's happy she needs to be alone for a while. To – to be sort of *grateful*.'

And Vittorio Pucci from a foreign country understood instantly.

'I too feel like this. I stand on my terrace sometimes, signorinas, and I breathe very windily' – the girls laughed – 'and I give thanks . . .'

Back at La Paloma, Frank was suffering from a gloom that made yesterday's greyness seem bright by comparison. The Duchess had spent the afternoon in her room and when the girls returned from their tour of the Grand Canal they had joined her. At dinner time there had been an earnest discussion about the evening's plans. Frank, reduced to eavesdropping across intervening cutlery-clatter, gathered that Susan and Christine were pleasantly surprised by the Casino suggestion and that they were warning the Duchess against organized sight-seeing in general.

After the meal they came across to his table and thanked him for taking their mother to San Marco and asked him to join them for coffee and the Casino trip.

'Thank you, no.' Frank said shortly, remembering the morning's exasperation. 'And I can't afford to gamble.' What he meant was that to play at gambling did not interest him. Part of his job was to gamble with vast sums, with employment figures. Now . . . that was something else.

'Neither can we,' Sue dimpled. 'But Mother is hoping we might meet someone interesting there.'

The girls were as bad as the Duchess. And she – she wanted to meet someone interesting did she? After a boring morning with a shabby little Italian – American.

'I wish you luck,' he said dryly.

Now all that remained for him to do was to go to his room which would smell of tonight's scampi mixed with washing-up liquid, and go to sleep. Except that he wouldn't sleep.

Maybe a walk would help.

Emitting his growling grunt, he levered himself out of the lounge chair, caught up his jacket and ambled through the foyer and out on to the riva. Nobody asked him where he was going or called goodbye. He hadn't noticed that kind of thing before. Now, after the chatter and laughter that surrounded the Duchess, it suddenly seemed odd. The Langleys had arrived just yesterday and already everyone smiled at them and asked them if they were enjoying themselves. He had been here two weeks and the only people who spoke to him were Rezzonico and Dino. And he paid them.

He put his hand in his pocket and his fingers closed

over the ten pence piece. Unwillingly he smiled. OK, the Duchess was a condescending snob but at least the boot was on the other foot – she paid *him*!

He walked aimlessly for fifteen minutes and was furious with himself when he found he was nearing the casino. He turned at the next bridge and cut along the riva behind the old palazzo. It was quiet here. Steps led down from the gaming rooms but there was no verandah and no strolling couples. He glanced grimly at the tall lighted windows and then halted suddenly. A single figure was silhouetted against the splash of light. A tall graceful figure, in a sea-green gown that looked as though it had been designed in Paris.

He lifted his hand in a curt salute, exasperated all over again simply by the Duchess' unconscious grace. She was staring right down at him and he waited for the usual warm smile, fighting down a small spark of pleasure that his feet had after all led him this way. He waved again. She continued to stare; no smile, no answering wave.

Furiously he forced himself forward. Nobody had ignored Frank Morrell like that for thirty years. And nobody would have the chance to do so again. He'd pack and leave tonight. Immediately. The blood pounded in his head.

Then it happened.

He heard her say in a surprised voice, 'Why, isn't it Mr Morrell?' and then there was a small cry. He turned. Her arms were stretched wide and in front of her as if she were feeling for something that was not there. Her legs were trailing in the green dress. She was falling.

Somehow he reached her before she hit the cobbled riva. She was in his arms and her eyes, wide and frightened, were six inches from his.

He knew then that he hadn't imagined a thing about the Duchess. Somewhere beneath the poise, the unconscious condescension, there was a woman who was fighting a battle. Who needed help.

CHAPTER THREE

It was a momentary impression, then the usual smile relaxed her face.

'Oh dear.' She put her hands on his shoulders and helped herself to her feet. He was still gently clasping her waist. 'I do assure you, Mr Morrell, I haven't been over-indulging.' She gave one of her laughs that suddenly reminded Frank of wind-chimes. 'I do apologize. I gave myself such a fright. And you – did I hurt you?'

'Of course not, Duchess.' Frank wondered why he was trembling and dropped his hands to his side. 'You're all right? Nothing strained or broken?'

She seemed to mentally check up on herself. The sea-green gown had a sort of scarf arrangement and she adjusted that somehow.

'I'm in one piece thank you, Mr Morrell.' She shook her head ruefully. 'Yet how can I thank you? If it hadn't been for you—'

'Thank God I was around—' he thought how nearly he hadn't been there and shuddered. 'Thank *God* I was around, Duchess.' His voice was deep with sincerity and she patted his arm.

'You are a gentleman, Mr Morrell,' she said and there was no laughter in her voice either.

Frank felt himself getting very warm and was glad when the blonde daughter – Christine – came down the steps.

'Oh. There you are, Mother. We were getting worried – you were gone such ages.' She noticed Frank's red face and glanced sharply at her mother. 'Are you all right?'

There was a short silence. Frank said, 'I happened to be passing by and—' he felt a sudden pressure on his arm and glanced at the Duchess. There was a mute appeal in her eyes. What the hell was the matter with him that he kept reading messages that no-one else seemed to see in those big grey pools of hers? He swallowed what he had been going to say. 'Your mother was watching the water and we . . . got talking.'

'Mr Morrell and I have had a lovely chat,' the Duchess agreed comfortably as if they'd been sharing an English cup of tea in the darkness. But Christine found nothing odd in that. Of course she'd been living with her mother all her life, Frank thought grimly.

'Well, we're missing you, darling.' She took her mother's free arm. 'Just come and say hello and goodbye to Signor Pucci before we go back to the hotel. You look a bit tired and it's been a long day.'

She started back up the steps and the Duchess allowed herself to be led. Frank found he had to follow. The Duchess' prompting hand on his arm had not been removed. He stared at the massed chestnut hair and the long neck accentuated by its encircling chiffon scarf. She was nearly the same height as he was, yet her racehorse slenderness seemed to claim his protection. If Christine thought it was time she rested then – somehow – it was up to him to make sure she got back safely to the hotel and did just that. Unexpectedly he had been enjoined as the Duchess' ally. Well . . . he had nothing better to do had he?

Abigail was glad Mr Morrell stayed at her side for the rest of the evening. It was ridiculous to be put out by that little fall and of course it was absolutely nothing to do with her eyes. It was dark and the lights wavering in the water had dazzled her so that she completely forgot she was standing at the top of the steps. It could happen to anybody. Yet, probably because Mr Morrell knew Venice so well and was just as hard-up as the Langleys, it was comforting to have him near. And it was almost as if he'd been able to read her thoughts just now. Strange. She'd been standing there thinking of Ambrose, grateful for his eternal understanding which made it unnecessary to explain her motives and along had come Mr Morrell who also seemed to understand without the complication of words.

He was introduced to Signor Pucci whose gay enthusiasm was unfailing. He had been trying to explain to Sue with much laughter the difficulties which beset a small green grape from its birth to its final end in the giant vats of the wine makers.

'You are first of all from Italy, signor?' he greeted Mr Morrell standing up ceremoniously at Abigail's approach. 'Then please to tell this young lady I am not making up the dangers of the vines. The spider mites—' he played his fingers dramatically in Sue's direction and she succumbed to her inevitable laughter. 'The black measles—' he clasped his hands around his own throat. 'The powdery mildew—'

Mr Morrell nodded, his rather stern face relaxing at Sue's obvious enjoyment of such drama.

'Sure. Vines are delicate plants, Miss Langley. They are subject to many diseases.'

Signor Pucci spread those expressive hands before Sue in a gesture Abigail found curiously touching. It reminded her of a mannerism Denver had had.

'You see, signorina? I do not – what is the word? I do not make the exaggeration.'

Sue shook her head. 'I did not think for one moment you would do so. But none of us realized the – the *dangers* those poor little grapes go through before they become – this!' She lifted her glass and for some reason they all drank as if to the health of Signor Pucci's vineyard.

He turned again to Mr Morrell. 'I talk too much. But you will understand, signor. The vineyard belonged to my grandfather. Then my uncle. And when he died without son or daughter, it comes at last to me. That is why I am full of pride. You will excuse me.'

Abigail smiled approvingly. 'I think it's marvellous. Many young men in your position would be casual. Would take it for granted perhaps.'

Sue was suddenly serious. 'You are rather like our mother, signor. She appreciates every last little thing about her life. That's not pride.'

Christine expanded. 'In our country we call it "counting your blessings".' She grinned at her mother. 'The times we've heard that little phrase!'

Abigail met Mr Morrell's dark eyes. They were puzzled. 'Perhaps this is a saying you do not have in America, Mr Morrell?'

'Sure. We have it.' His thin mouth half smiled. 'It's generally used when you're down and out. I wouldn't have thought you had much opportunity to say it, Duchess.'

Abigail heard the reproach in his voice and shook her head immediately. 'You're quite right, Mr Morrell. I've never been down and out in my life. I've got everything—' she let her gaze rest for a moment on Christine's blonde head and then Sue's laughing face as it turned towards their new friend. Then she turned back to Mr Morrell. 'But I wouldn't want to take it for granted all the same. Like Signor Pucci. So I . . . count my blessings!'

She laughed gently and after a moment when he looked almost irritated he managed one of his rare smiles. He really was a strange man. Difficult, inarticulate, yet there was something about him. Abigail sensed understanding much as a water diviner senses the presence of water. Very deep down and maybe dammed back for a long time.

The girls were gathering bags and stoles ready to return

to La Paloma and Signor Pucci was reminding them that they were to visit his vineyard before their holiday was over.

Abigail smiled. 'We will see, signor. Meanwhile, if you are not engaged tomorrow would you care to explore Venice with us? We will need an interpreter if Mr Morrell is leaving us.'

The young man looked like the boy of this morning – Dino Carlos. One huge smile.

'I am enchanted, signora. May I come to your hotel in the morning?'

'Not before eleven,' Abigail said firmly.

Mr Morrell was clearing his throat and staring at her oddly.

'As a matter of fact . . . I've kinda decided to hang on here for a spell,' he said in his abrupt way.

Abigail was delighted. 'That *is* nice,' she said dropping her chiffon scarf. 'You'll be able to come with us tomorrow. Mr Morrell was born here,' she explained to Signor Pucci. 'And he is so interesting.'

Mr Morrell was making a deprecating grunting noise. Signor Pucci turned to him. 'In that case, signor, you must accompany the ladies to the mainland to see the Pucci vineyard. Please. I insist.'

'Of course,' chorused the girls. Mr Morrell's colour deepened to near-puce but luckily the lanterns on the terrace did not reveal his tightening jaw muscles so everyone thought he was merely shy.

So there were five of them in a gondola the next day on their way to San Maggiore. And again the following day at the lido beach. And there, in the warm shallow sea, under the vigilant eyes of Abigail, Frank and Christine, Sue was partially alone with Vittorio.

They swam slowly and lazily and very decorously towards

a diving raft moored some way out. Whenever their eyes met they smiled and occasionally from sheer high spirits Vittorio would dive and surface like a dolphin. Sue did not dare. She was an excellent swimmer but found that just the thought of this Italian man made her breathless.

They had the raft to themselves. It was the first time they had been alone since they met. They lay prone like seals, their heads turned on outstretched arms so they could look at each other.

Vittorio said, 'Could it go on like this, Sue? The – the happiness?' He saw her confusion. 'I'm sorry. I should not speak so. But when I inherited the vines I began to be happy – underneath all the time I was laughing. And when we met – in the Casino – so were you. It is good to be with someone who can share the happiness and who can make it more.'

'Like two facing mirrors. Reflecting ad infinitum,' Sue murmured.

He nodded. 'That is what is happening is it not? That is why I ask you if it can continue. Is it because you are on holiday?'

She said in a low voice, 'I don't know, Vittorio. How can I answer that?'

He asked, 'Are you always gay, little Sue? At home in this acting company you speak of – are you gay then?'

Sue nodded. 'Somehow Chris and I have always got something to laugh about. But . . .' she stared at him and decided to be honest. 'But not like this.'

'Exactly. I too have been happy because of the vineyard – it means so much to me to leave Milano and come here. But until now I did not know what happiness means.'

Sue rolled on to her back. 'Let's go back, Vittorio – don't say any more. Let's go back.'

'You're frightened.' She did not answer and he sighed. 'I too am frightened, Sue. Because I am afraid that after the holiday the happiness we once had will be gone.'

She sat up and clasped her knees trying to imagine the suburb back home and the dark theatre. She shivered.

His voice was persuasive. 'If we knew we would see each other again, it would be different naturally.' There was a pause and he added diffidently, 'I think I am in love with you, Sue Langley.'

Immediately she turned and her eyes were full of laughter again. 'Well, that's all right then isn't it? I thought at least you were trying to tell me you had a wife and six children.' A tiny pause. 'You haven't, have you, Vittorio?'

He pretended to be outraged, laughing with her. 'I have no-one – I have already told you that. No-one.'

'Then there is no need to be frightened.' She stood up preparing to dive. 'I can come to Venice next year for my holiday!' She surfaced a few yards away and he stood up, watching her.

'Do you think you could fall in love with me?' he called.

She glanced over her shoulder at the distant shore. 'It is too soon. I have been strictly brought up—' Her grin was like a cheeky boy's. 'But I have told you – I have never felt like this before.' She took a deep breath and met him below the surface of the water. Their lips met briefly. 'I'm happy!' she yodelled emerging with upstretched arms. They began to swim back again.

'I am glad you are not aristocracy,' he told her.

She said nothing. It pleased Mother that he owned his own property but somehow it made the whole thing so . . . arranged. She almost wished he worked in the hotel kitchens.

Frank hardly knew where the next few days went to. When he wasn't actually squiring the Langley women and the Pucci boy around Venice rediscovering his old home through their eyes, he was searching the dark lace shops with the Duchess for a shawl for Dino's new bambino or chasing pigeons in the piazza at San Marco trying to find Garibaldi.

At times he thought he would explode with sheer irritation. When he recalled how the Duchess 'counted her blessings' and never 'took anything for granted' yet chose the cheapest trips she could find and insisted that she preferred walking everywhere . . . it made him sick. Yet each time he was on the point of telling her exactly what he thought of her, she would turn great grey eyes on him and smile gently and somehow he was buying peanuts for Garibaldi and translating for her when she struck up one of her conversations with the local lace-makers.

Then Pucci went back to wherever his vineyard was and little Sue curtailed her outings so that she could get back to La Paloma to receive his twice-daily telephone calls. Christine went with her and swam in the hotel pool. So it happened that Frank and the Duchess looked around a tiny Byzantine church by themselves one late afternoon during the second week of the Langleys' holiday. The Duchess wore her lime-green suit and used her parasol as a walking stick. Maybe it was the shadows but Frank thought she looked her years. Without considering the matter he offered his arm and she took it gratefully.

'I'm not very keen, are you?' she whispered. 'I mean I know they were Christians but there's a sort of barbaric feeling about the place.'

'Christians were the worst kind of barbarians,' Frank whispered back. 'Your crusaders committed terrible crimes in the name of the Cross.' He paused then added, 'It's the same today. So-called good people are the ones who trot around doing the most damage.'

She glanced around at him fearfully. 'D'you mean Vittorio?' she murmured. 'He's certainly dented Sue's feelings – but I'm sure he's sincere enough, don't you?'

He hadn't been thinking of Pucci. 'Sure. But they hardly know one another. These holiday romances don't mean much.'

'No, you're right. But it's not like that for Sue. I can tell. And he wants us to go over to the mainland and visit him next week. You will come, won't you? You'll be able to tell whether he's serious.' Her eyes flashed at him again. 'Maybe he's just a rich playboy type trifling with a poor girl's affections?'

He almost threw up. Instead he snorted a grunt. 'More likely to be the other way round, Duchess,' he said, heavily sarcastic.

But she didn't catch on. Just heaved a sigh of relief. 'So long as you think he feels . . . something. We'll be able to sum up the situation a little better when we go over there.'

Well that was something he could spare himself, anyway. He guided her past a smelly oil lamp glowing ruby-red in the gloom.

'I'm not certain of my plans next week, ma-am.' They emerged into the daylight. The late afternoon sun was reflected in the dark waters of the narrow canal beneath them and the Duchess put up a hand to shade her eyes. 'You'll manage OK if I can't make it.'

Her hand tightened on his arm. 'Oh dear. I do hope you can come, Mr Morrell. I need moral support. And – as you know Sue and Christine are apt to be flippant on occasion.'

'Self-defence, I guess,' he commented dryly and immediately wondered whether he had gone too far.

She turned and gave him her tranquil smile. 'How clear-sighted you are, Mr Morrell. So many people might imagine them to be superficial girls. You have a deep understanding of human nature.'

Frank swallowed. He ought to be able to feel scorn at the

woman's obtuseness. But he couldn't. Once again she had turned his wrath aside and he was unable flatly to refuse the invitation to Pucci's vineyard as he had intended. He grunted again and said something about seeing how things went. And as he handed the Duchess into a cruising gondola, he wondered what Steve would say if he could have heard him. Frank Morrell had made mistakes maybe; but he had never prevaricated in his life before.

Nevertheless he tried to tear himself away; to hug to himself the isolation which had been his before they came. He was becoming the Langleys' dogsbody which was too high a price to pay for not feeling lonely. Even . . . for enjoying himself.

The next two days he caught Dino early, loaded him up with easel and camp stool and took them both off to the small square where the moored gondola nearly drove him crazy with its perpetual movement. Dino fished with string and a pin and obvious boredom. At midday he took Frank's money and bought them both cheese and fruit and a revolting drink which reminded Frank of sarsparilla. At regular intervals he said, 'Will Signora Langley need me today, signor?' To which Frank merely grunted.

The following day Pucci mysteriously reappeared after breakfast and not noticing Frank behind his palm, hung about on the sun terrace until the Langleys appeared. They were dressed for a beach picnic and greeted their visitor with delight. It was obviously prearranged and Frank felt ridiculously hurt that he hadn't been included. The Duchess peered short-sightedly around the restaurant before she joined the others at the waiting motoscafi but she probably wasn't looking for him anyway. She didn't need him; she had an interpreter in her daughter's admirer.

He went to fetch his blasted painting stuff and Rezzonico waylaid him in the foyer.

'Ah. Signor Morrelli. The ladies are getting anxious about

you. For two days they do not see you and ask me whether you are ill. I tell them you prefer to be by yourself when you paint.'

'Good man, Rezzonico,' Frank said, loathing the man. 'I see Signor Pucci is back.' He hated himself for fishing for information and did it all the same.

'For one day only, signor. Tonight they dine together here and then he returns.' The manager smiled conspiratorially. 'Which wine would you like with the scampi?'

Frank's loathing was compounded by this assumption that he was automatically included in the dinner party.

'I'm dining out. Sorry,' he snapped. It was going to be difficult to avoid the Langleys altogether, but somehow he would do it. Of course the obvious solution would be to leave Venice. The mystery surrounding the Duchess – which he had probably cooked up anyway for his own diversion – was not worth any more painting trips. If he didn't throw himself into a canal Dino doubtless would.

He stayed out late that night trying not to imagine the laughter and incessant chatter which would surround the Langleys at La Paloma. Even so the thought of his small smelly room was unattractive and he ordered a drink to be sent out to the terrace. He felt jaded and tired and the scented twilight of the terrace suited his mood.

He was half way through his vino when Christine came through the foyer doors and smiled her relief at seeing him.

'Mr Morrell. At last. We looked everywhere for you. Why didn't you come to dinner?'

He looked up at her. She didn't sit down and there was something a little lost about her. He felt a fellow feeling and stood up belatedly to offer her a chair. Even so his voice was stiff.

'I guess I didn't get my invitation, Miss Langley.'

'Oh – but you were on one of your painting trips with

Dino. We left a message with Signor Rezzonico to ask you to come and choose the wine.' She sat down gratefully while he mentally cursed himself and Rezzonico. 'And please call me Christine. I feel you must know us so well.' She looked at him closely. 'Is that it, Mr Morrell? The reason you've kept away from us this week – you've had enough of the Langleys?'

Of course he had to deny that emphatically and explain that he had misunderstood the manager's message.

She shook her head. 'It's not just tonight. You've been avoiding us, Mr Morrell. Mother's very upset.'

He almost said sarcastically – well, we can't have that. Then he decided against it because all the Langleys seemed to be impervious to sarcasm. Instead he tried the truth. 'She – your mother – is from a different world, Christine. I found I couldn't compete.'

'You mean money?' The girl actually laughed. 'Please don't worry or feel embarrassed. We're not really different from you in that way at all. I'm so glad it's only that – we wondered if it might be. Look – you will come with us to visit Vittorio's vineyard won't you? It won't be an expensive trip I promise.'

This was turning out to be like a conversation with the Duchess herself. He refused to commit himself and enquired instead how Vittorio had been.

Christine did not pretend to misunderstand. 'Just the same. Our trip was all fixed by phone but he had to come over to see her all the same.' She smiled almost ruefully. 'They are in love, Mr Morrell. Mother realizes it too.'

Frank nodded. 'Does she accept it?'

'I don't know. She's waiting to see what it's like at his home. Apparently he lives entirely alone at the moment. He's only just inherited the property and there's a lot of sorting out to be done.' She laughed. 'But you know Mother, she's incurably romantic and seeing them together today made her very happy. This is what she wanted – for her two daughters to meet rich, eligible young men. She has gone to bed early to dream about it.' Suddenly she sounded a little lost.

'I see.' He said in a gentle voice he hadn't used for years. 'And what about you, Christine? Have you met a rich, eligible young man in Venice?'

She glanced at him and then away. 'I don't think there's much chance of that, Mr Morrell. I wouldn't even notice a rich, eligible young man if he swept me off in a – a gondola!' She laughed again.

Frank was curious. He was always feeling curious about the darned Langley women and it generally ended up in him carrying their luggage or feeding their favourite pigeons.

Almost unwillingly he said, 'D'you want to tell me what you mean?'

She gave him that quick bird-like glance again and her fair skin coloured slightly. 'I suppose I do.' She tried for another laugh and failed dismally. 'You're a good listener, aren't you, Mr Morrell?'

Frank grunted. Nobody had told him that before. In fact Steve had implied just the opposite.

Christine's blonde hair fell forward like a bell, hiding her face. She spoke slowly. 'I'm in love too you see. Someone called David Blake who works with me. But I don't know how he feels about me. I've been out with him a couple of times but that doesn't mean a thing. He's taken most of the girls out at some time or other. He's got a reputation for being a bit of a wolf but he's not. He's sort of – naturally gregarious. He likes company and he's good-looking and – I think the girls exaggerate. They wish he *was* a wolf!' She swept her hair back and stared at Frank with fierce blue eyes. 'I'm one more girl to him and I came away to forget him and I can't. I love him.' Her mouth was firmly defiant. 'I suppose you think I'm a fool!'

Frank gave it proper thought. He wanted to smile at the girl, humour her, tell her it happened to everyone. But she deserved more than that because of her honesty which took no account of pride. For a fleeting instant he remembered the last time Virginia had informed him shrilly that she was in love with someone. He'd thought *she* was a fool.

He said slowly, 'I think you're brave, honey. You've got guts. You've faced a lot of unpleasant facts. Probably the worst one is knowing you've got no control over your own emotions . . .' Maybe poor Virginia had a few guts too come to think of it. He grunted. 'If it's any help, I think you did the right thing to take a holiday. Get right away from this playboy character.'

She relaxed suddenly and managed a quivery smile. 'Thank you. Anyway that's my sad story. And that's why Mother is going to be disappointed in me at the end of our four weeks.' She tucked her hair behind her ears and tried to sound business-like. 'I feel much better, Mr Morrell, thank you for being so understanding. I think watching Sue and Vittorio these past days has made me jealous.'

Frank shook his head decisively. 'Not jealous, honey. You don't begrudge your sister a fraction of her happiness. I guess – when you see other people being happy it makes you feel kinda lonely.'

She said softly, 'That's it exactly. You've felt this too?'

Frank gave this some more serious thought. Had he felt lonely all these years and only just realized it when he returned to Venice? He said simply, 'I don't know, Christine. I just don't know.'

Christine went on in the same reflective tone. 'I don't think Mother feels that. Left out or lonely. She probably never even asks herself questions like that. But I often wonder what she will do when Sue and I leave home.'

'She'll still have everything else your father left her,' Frank couldn't resist saying.

The girl smiled at him as if he'd made a joke. 'You mean the forty-roomed mansion in Belgravia and the Rolls?'

Frank was nonplussed. 'Sure – if that's what it was.'

Christine's blue eyes opened almost as wide as her Mother's.

'You're serious, aren't you, Mr Morrell?' She shook her head ruefully. 'I don't know what you thought but when father died we were so hard up that his partner's wife offered to adopt Sue and me. Mother was – as she puts it – an untrained dressmaker and she brought us up on what she earned. I wondered what you meant when you called David Blake a playboy. He is a trainee manager at the big department store where I'm a secretary. Sue is Assistant Stage Manager for our local rep. company. To use one of your phrases, Mr Morrell – we haven't a bean!'

Frank felt as if he were in a very fast lift going down.

'But – your clothes. This holiday – I don't get it.'

Christine leaned back in her chair, laughing. 'I told you. Mother is a dressmaker. Sometimes she is left with quite a bit of cloth – cancelled orders and so on. Good quality cloth.' She sobered. 'Mr Morrell, if she'd gone to Art College she might well have been a famous dress designer. She has a terrific eye for line and style.' She sighed. 'As it is – she was trained to be . . . well, useless. Except that she's never been useless in her life. Oh, don't get me wrong – we're not on the bread-line by any means. But you have no need to worry about keeping up with us financially, I expect you have more money than we have.'

Frank swallowed something. 'And . . . the holiday?' he prompted.

'Ah. The holiday. Thereby hangs a tale.' Christine leaned forward and began to talk. It sounded a tall story. There was a great grandmother who had known the Prince of Wales and who had left them some emeralds. The emeralds weren't even kept in a bank; they were just in an inlaid jewel box on the dressing table in Mother's bedroom. The girls were allowed to look at them on rainy Sundays or when they were recovering from toothache and 'flu. They could only be sold when a real emergency cropped up. And it seemed like they'd cropped up at regular intervals in Abigail Langley's life. Even allowing for her daughter's romanticism, the Duchess must have had a tough life. Yet the emeralds had stayed put until four weeks ago . . . Frank glued his cynical brown eyes to the young face opposite him and told himself it was a piece of fantastic nonsense. Yet he knew he believed every word of it.

She stopped talking at last. 'You see, Mr Morrell? We're rather like you – using our life savings on this trip. And in a way ours is a kind of pilgrimage too. You're revisiting your personal past, we're revisiting Great Grandmother's.' She grinned ruefully. 'A final fling.'

Frank nodded slowly as if under hypnosis. Then he said, 'I don't quite get it even now. Not all of it. Why now? Why did she sell the emeralds now – what was the crisis?'

Christine lifted her shoulders. 'She sees more than we realize. Perhaps she saw that Sue was frustrated with the rep. company. Perhaps she knew I was getting too serious over David. I don't know. But we trust her completely, Sue and I. We tease her – you've noticed of course. But she has this instinct for . . . for happiness.' She picked up her bag. 'Look, I must go. But please say you'll come to the vineyard with us. Vittorio will be phoning but we hope to go in two or three days.'

Frank knew that nothing would keep him away now. Christine had given him a lot of answers but not all of them. He was back to square one, intrigued by a problem. The problem of the Duchess.

He got up and walked Christine to the lifts.

'Thanks for telling me about your background,' he said in his abrupt way. 'It's answered a lot of questions for me.

I admit that when I believed you were all stinking rich it was kinda irritating to see some of the economies you made.'

'Oh—' Christine looked slightly nonplussed. 'Well – actually, Mr Morrell, that was for your sake too. Mother didn't want to embarrass you.'

For a moment Frank had forgotten his role. He stared at the girl and then laughed. 'That was good of her,' he said. 'But seriously, honey, she did mislead me. Telling me your father left her everything—'

Christine laughed too as she stepped into the empty lift. 'She didn't mean to mislead you of course.' She stopped laughing and for a moment looked near to tears. 'You see, she just meant Sue and me. That was all.' She shrugged helplessly, apologetically and then the lift doors closed on her. Frank stared at them for a moment or two and then turned for his room at the back of the hotel. He had a lot to think about.

'What I would like,' said Abigail as she wandered slowly along one of the narrow calles leading to the Piazzetta, 'Is a Venetian glass figurine to take home. I have an old friend – Ambrose's doctor actually – who would so appreciate . . .'

Dino said eagerly, 'After we have had tea and I have given Garibaldi his peanuts, we could walk back along the Merceria. There are glass shops there, signora—'

'Who charge the earth,' commented Mr Morrell grimly. 'I think Signora Langley would be happier with the Rialto street market, Dino.'

'Certainly, signor,' Dino agreed. 'But first the English cup of tea?'

'Half an hour ago we had your revolting sarsparilla while we waited for the blackamoors on the clock tower to do their stuff. Now you want tea. It's just an excuse to play with that wretched bird.'

Abigail laughed happily. She had been relieved this morning when Christine explained the position with Mr Morrell. It seemed to her she must have unwittingly offended the American – he could be almost neurotically touchy at times. Whatever Chris had said it must have smoothed everything out. He had come over during breakfast and suggested that she might like a shopping expedition that afternoon. It had been a golden excuse to get out of seeing the Doge's Palace with the girls; she was terrified of falling down the sixteenth century wells in the courtyard and her feet ached at the thought of the Giant's Staircase. They had merely looked their disgust at her swift acceptance of Mr Morrell's invitation; they knew how worried she had been about his complete absence over the previous three days.

'I would like to sit down actually, Mr Morrell,' she said now. 'Sightseeing is so very tiring.'

'In that case we will take a gondola to the Rialto.' He found a table beneath one of the empty loggias on the Square and pulled out a chair. It seemed he couldn't do enough for her.

'Certainly not, they are much too expensive. Sue says there is a water bus which leaves from somewhere around here.'

'The vaporetti?' He hesitated fractionally and she wondered whether she had done wrong to mention expense. Christine herself had been puzzled by his attitude over money. Then he said quickly, 'Yes of course. Certainly. We'll take the vaporetti.'

She watched him as he ordered tea. It was strange that at first she had thought him small; his dark bulk against the sunlight filling the Piazza was all she could see. But it wasn't only that. She wondered fleetingly whether a person appeared to increase in physical size as they became more important to one personally.

He smiled at her. 'Dino's found Garibaldi.' She looked

around but could not distinguish the small familiar figure. 'Funny. Pigeons are about the only birds in Venice and they figured a lot in my boyhood. I can't remember singling one out though.'

She sensed his nostalgia and responded quickly. 'It's strange how things turn out isn't it, Mr Morrell? When you were Dino's age you couldn't have believed that one day you'd come back to your old home as an American.'

He went on smiling so she was on safe ground. 'And you, Duchess? What were your prospects at Dino's age?'

She said frankly, 'Fairly golden actually. And completely predictable. I knew that I would be presented. That I would have a season. And that I would marry well.' She laughed without regret. 'I might have been a little frightened if I had been able to see ahead. My life was to be so completely *un*predictable.'

He said curiously, 'Forgive me, Duchess, but why didn't you marry money?'

She hesitated. Not even the girls knew about Denver. It had all been so transitory and almost run-of-the-mill for those days. But Mr Morrell was different. At the end of next week she would never see him again. She began to tell him. Dino brought his pigeon to the table and they fed him one of their biscuits and still she went on talking. Her voice was soft and reminiscent and very happy. The pigeon fluttered away and Dino went after him.

'I sometimes think that love compounds itself,' she said watching Dino's antics smilingly. 'My love for Denver made it possible to get through the war and to nurse darling Mamma. It made me the kind of person that Ambrose could love. And his love at last made me love him. And then I could pass it all on to the girls.'

Mr Morrell made a sound half grunt half snort. She wondered whether she had embarrassed him. 'And does it end there?' he asked. 'With the girls?'

'Oh no. It . . . it irradiates . . .' She shook her head laughing again. 'It's too difficult for me, Mr Morrell. I am ignorant – my education consisted of accomplishments, not learning. The girls call my bits of philosophy home-spun. But they make life sparkle.'

'Yes. Yes, I can see that, Duchess.' He made that odd sound again. 'Thanks for opening out like that, ma-am. I appreciate your confidence.'

'I find you easy to talk to, Mr Morrell.'

Later as they strolled back to the Riva degli Schiavoni to pick up the water bus they spoke very little. Mr Morrell glanced at her occasionally as if waiting for her to speak and she wondered whether he wanted her to mention his talk with Christine last night. However as that would doubtless mean an oblique reference to his own lack of worldly success, she decided against it. They were crowded in the vaporetti; people who had arrived by launch from Jessolo for a day's sightseeing jostled and laughed and Abigail found it easy to laugh with them in spite of the language barrier. As so often happened she found herself surrounded by charming people all pointing out famous landmarks which she was unable to see. Dino translated vociferously, jumping up and down with excitement; Mr Morrell grunted a few words in her ear occasionally; she felt the same bewildered sense of euphoria she had felt in the Casino the night they had met Vittorio. When they alighted at the Rialto landing stage the colours and lights were merging into a whirling whole. She hung on to Mr Morrell's arm and smiled brilliantly and measured her steps to his.

'Are you OK, Duchess?' His nasal voice was her bridge with reality. She nodded vigorously. 'It's kinda narrow here . . . all these shops . . .'

'Sue must come here,' Abigail said, turning her head from side to side. 'She's always quoting Shakespeare at us and she'll be able to imagine Shylock doing his bargaining.'

She wondered where Dino had got to. 'Is there anywhere selling glass, Mr Morrell?'

'The other side, Duchess. The street market. They usually have figurines for sale there with a very slight flaw in them – not discernible unless you're an expert.'

She recognized his tact. 'Thank you. Thank you, Mr Morrell. I dare say they are less expensive than in the Merceria?'

'Half the price.'

Apparently they had reached the market because he slowed his walk to a gentle stroll and after a while said, 'Well? What do you think?'

She swallowed. The colours had dimmed to grey shot now and then with an odd blue light. She said, 'Would you choose? I don't quite know what a man would like. He likes horses and children.'

There was a pause. She did not dare to let go his arm and she could tell he was having difficulty in picking up a figurine with one hand.

'How about this? Not quite a horse but the nearest to it.'

She laughed, wondering which animal was nearest to a horse. 'That will do beautifully, Mr Morrell. Thank you very much. Let me find you some money.'

She needed both hands and even so fumbled hopelessly with her handbag. She could hear Mr Morrell bargaining with the vendor and then Dino's high voice near at hand calling something.

Mr Morrell said, 'Just a minute, Duchess—' and she knew he had gone. She stood very still and after a while closed her bag. The murky grey light, pressing against her eyes, darkened. She tried to control her beating heart. Stephen had said there would be no real blindness until Christmas, so this was merely nerves. She was imagining the pressure too. And the drumming of human voices against her head like hailstones.

Someone cannoned into her and she was reminded of the sharp-voiced young woman outside the shop the day she was going to meet Stephen. A softer voice spoke, in Italian; she smiled automatically and turned towards it. There was a pause then it spoke again and a hand on hers led her forward. The hand became more imperative and was now tugging at her handbag. Frantically she clung on, moving faster so that it could not leave her wrist. Someone twisted her arm backwards and she was suddenly angry.

'Let me go – this minute! D'you hear me!' She wrenched herself free and her vision miraculously cleared just as Mr Morrell arrived by her side. He spoke furiously to a shabby young woman in black.

'Are you all right, Duchess?' He held the girl's wrists easily in one of his hands. 'Nothing stolen?'

'I'm fine. Really, Mr Morrell – fine.' Her voice was breathless with relief. The impact of being able to see again was so startling and wonderful she wanted to laugh. 'Please – let the girl go. She imagined – she imagined I was more helpless than I am.'

'Helpless?' he grinned at her above the girl's dark head. 'She doesn't know you, Duchess!' He looked fiercely down. 'Does that make it any better though?' He spoke angrily again in Italian and the girl cringed. People crowded round offering advice.

'Mr Morrell, she isn't strong enough. There was someone else – she is just the scapegoat. Please let her go.' The girl had lent her the anger which had cleared her eyes and she couldn't bear to see her arrested.

Mr Morrell shook his head despairingly. 'OK, Duchess. If you're sure no harm was done.' He released the girl and she disappeared in the crowd like a frightened puppy.

Abigail dusted her arms off automatically then looked around her and smiled at the faces peering curiously from the stalls.

'It's marvellous here, Mr Morrell. So much colour and life – look at all the boats! Oh and those fish! I don't know when I've enjoyed myself so much.'

Her audience might not have understood her words but they got the meaning and grinned back, relaxing. Mr Morrell raised his eyebrows.

'You have a funny way of enjoying yourself, Duchess.'

A stall holder came forward and spoke in hesitant English.

'Your glass, signora. You left it just now.'

He placed in her hands a ruby red figurine of a unicorn. She took it almost reverently and turned it to catch the sunlight. It's single horn glinted aggressively. Obscurely it made her think of Mr Morrell.

'It's beautiful,' she breathed. 'So much more romantic than a horse.'

He grunted as if irritated, then unwillingly he gave his upside down grin. They turned and walked up the steps of the Rialto again to where Dino was still stalking the pigeon he was convinced was Garibaldi. Abigail held Mr Morrell's arm though she no longer needed it.

CHAPTER FOUR

The small local train calling at all stations between Venice and Verona was crowded the following Friday. Abigail and Christine shared a seat. Frank and Sue sat opposite them. Across the aisle was a family who – they informed Abigail through Frank – were visiting relatives and had presents of Venetian glass in the large cartons which surrounded them. Every time someone walked down the train they played a kind of musical chairs with the cartons and there was much commotion. Sue punctuated their conversation with her own chatter. Abigail was used to her younger daughter's vivacity but she recognized her staccato outbursts now as nerves. For one thing she hadn't seen Vittorio for three whole days so naturally the sun was shining very brightly today. For another she was prepared to be overawed by the grandiloquence of old Italy. Abigail fended off the Italian family long enough to say sympathetically, 'Fine feathers don't mean a thing, darling. Vittorio is nice – that's all we need to know.'

'Of course. You're right I know. I just wish he was *working* somewhere. Of course he will have to manage the place, obviously. But you know what I mean. *Working*.'

'Most Italian vine-growers work manually,' said Mr Morrell. 'Unless they are managers put in by the big companies.'

'In any case, darling, there's a terrific lot to being a proper organizer. It's by no means easy.' Abigail thought of Denver and how she would have helped him run his estate. She had remembered Denver a great deal lately as she watched Sue's precipitous rush into love. It was all happening just as dear Grandmamma had said it happened in Venice. 'Something to do with the air, dear child,' she'd said all those years ago. 'It's full of romance. Lord Byron . . . Mr Browning . . .' Yes, Grandmamma was right.

Sue was talking to Mr Morrell now, still about Vittorio. Strange how easily they could all talk to Mr Morrell.

'It's quite a small vineyard as they go—' she was wearing a tan coloured dress that gave her brown eyes tawny lights. 'Vittorio would like to expand. That was why he came to visit Venice two weeks ago – to see his bank manager about an overdraft as well as seeing the firm who buy his grapes.'

Mr Morrell nodded, obviously understanding the whole set-up. After their trip to the Rialto market on Monday Abigail had felt an implicit faith in his local know-how and she leaned forward to enquire more about Vittorio's present situation. Unfortunately the small girl across the aisle chose that moment to be sick and as Abigail was the only one with tissues she found herself spending the next ten minutes cleaning the child up and comforting her with meaningless words of English. And then the train jolted to a halt and a voice was yelling 'Giacciona' and they had arrived.

Somehow they tore themselves away from their new-found friends and tumbled out on to a gravelled platform. Abigail was almost certain she saw Mr Morrell press some money into the small girl's hand but her sight was so unreliable now and poor Mr Morrell couldn't afford to be generous. He had obviously thought her extravagant when she chose a shawl for Dino's new bambino last week and had made a point of taking her to the street market for her glass figurine. However, the child certainly looked more cheerful and waved from the train window as if they were the relatives she was visiting.

Abigail settled her skirt and rearranged her hat to sit on

her chignon. She was wearing the green linen suit again and with its narrow skirt and the saucer-shaped hat she knew it gave her an Edwardian look that might not be exactly up-to-the-minute but suited her personality well. Besides the wide hat shaded her eyes so beautifully.

She could hear a raucous honking somewhere near at hand and after a fractional pause in which she detected – what? Surprise? Mr Morrell's familiar square hand arrived beneath her elbow and his voice, reassuring, said in her ear, 'Best foot forward, Duchess.'

The next moment she realized why the surprise and the following reassurance. Vittorio's welcoming face was smiling at them and it was his hand that was honking the horn. But he was not driving the sort of conveyance Abigail had expected of a vineyard owner. He was now waving – and calling – from one of the most battered pick-up trucks Abigail had ever seen in all her life.

'I cannot switch off the engine!' he cried gaily as they came up. 'Scusi Signora – Sue – Christine – Signor Morrell. She will not start again once she is off!'

There was much laughter. Sue said, 'You first, Mother – we'll squash in behind. Oh, Vittorio, we've had a marvellous journey. Everyone was so friendly and the weather is so marvellous—'

Christine said a little doubtfully, 'Hello, Vittorio. Yes, I'm fine thanks. Mother . . .'

Abigail told herself firmly that the truck didn't mean a thing. 'Yes, I'm comfortable, thank you. We're ready when you are, Vittorio.' Mr Morrell's hand still cupped her elbow and its gentle pressure was more reassurance. It was strange how their positions had reversed. After all when they had first met and she had made that stupid mistake about his occupation, she had spent a long time trying to reassure *him* and put him at his ease. Now he was stronger, in control of most things except his chronic shyness. When he could forget that he was so much more alive; his eyes seemed to look out instead of inside himself all the time. And he wasn't so shabby either. As an expert on textiles Abigail recognized that his sports coat and trousers were cut from a very good cloth. She supposed he had included a few good outfits in his expenses just as she had.

They were out of Giacciona now and speeding between flat fields. Vittorio shouted happily above the noise of the chugging engine. 'Rice! Soon the Po will flood these fields, the road will be a causeway.'

'I pictured hills and terraces covered in vines,' said Abigail as if to herself. She tried to imagine Sue in this rather depressing landscape. A little wriggle of fear fluttered her heart.

Mr Morrell's hand closed on her elbow. 'Here are the hills, Duchess. Can't you see? That kinda mist hanging over them are the vines. My father called it a grape-haze.'

Abigail narrowed her eyes in an effort to focus. 'Grape-haze,' she murmured. It sounded a soft and comforting word for what she saw so often now. 'Your father was a poet, Mr Morrell.'

Unexpectedly the American laughed. Then he said in a tone of surprise, 'All Italians are poets I guess, Duchess.'

The gentle slopes of the Venito hills appeared and the truck began to pant and labour. Vittorio called, 'Not much farther!'

Sue carolled back, 'It's marvellous, Vittorio! The air is so clear and the views back there—' She gestured widely nearly sweeping her mother's hat away.

Of course she was prejudiced Abigail thought. But Christine echoed more matter-of-factly, 'It certainly is panoramic.' She glanced sideways under her mother's hat brim. 'Not as I imagined but better if anything.' She paused and then added significantly, 'More personal. Vittorio's very own place.'

It certainly wasn't as Abigail had imagined. The truck bumped along a track that would be deep mud at the first rainfall, and into a yard littered with crates and boxes. The house sitting on one side of the yard was unattractive, its pink stucco in need of rejuvenation. There was a peeling door in the middle of it and four windows, two up and two down. Like a child's drawing. The lower windows sported flower boxes which were a tangle of geraniums and nasturtiums.

By the time Abigail emerged from the cab, Sue and Christine were already circling the yard like eager puppies. Sue ran to her mother and clasped her arm cajolingly.

'Darling, isn't Vittorio lucky? To be his own boss in a climate like this! Breathe the air – doesn't it make you feel wonderful? Hasn't this whole place got the most wonderful potential! Mother – don't you think that dear little house, for instance, has potential?'

Abigail forced a smile and nodded. 'It certainly has, Sue.' She gazed around her, searching for something else to say. 'Am I missing the – the presses? You know where they tread the grapes.'

Apparently she had said something funny. The girls spluttered and Vittorio smiled at her warmly.

'I grow grapes only, signora,' he explained. 'They are collected by the factory. But there is a small press in the house. My grandfather always had a few bottles of his own wine to offer. Unfortunately since his death, my uncle has let such traditions finish. But I hope one day that the Pucci vineyard will welcome travellers as in the old days.'

It sounded very nice. A laudable ambition. Abigail could imagine it very well. But oh dear, the work that was needed before it could come about! And Sue, still living in jeans and smocks as she had done at the rep. theatre, still with her sleeves rolled up, still the odd-job woman. It was a far cry from Grandmamma's prophesies.

Everyone began to move into the house. It was dark and Vittorio called something as he led the way.

Mr Morrell said into her ear, 'He is warning us that the tiles are uneven. May I take your arm?'

'Oh please . . .' she felt a little better holding the now-familiar sleeve. They were in a passage-way like a tunnel and smelling distinctly damp. Then a door opened and Mr Morrell shepherded her through a kitchen that was glorious in its chaos and lacking every modern convenience except a sink and a gas stove.

Cries of delight echoed back from the front of the house.

'Mother, come and see this . . . oh look . . .'

Mr Morrell went first through another door and immediately said out of the side of his mouth, 'This is more like it, Duchess.'

Except that the room was bathed in the golden autumn sunshine she couldn't see a thing. The girls took her from Mr Morrell and she sensed she was being led on to a wide verandah.

'The house is built to face the south – like the vineyards,' Vittorio was saying. 'This also enables us to watch over our crops.'

Christine said in a low voice, 'Mother, this really is lovely. Even Great Grandmamma couldn't have envisaged such splendour as this.'

So there must be a view. Abigail smiled widely fearing that darling Sue might be more disillusioned than she was herself.

'She certainly couldn't,' she said injecting some animation into her voice. Again she searched for something particular to say. 'My goodness, look at those grapes.'

Once more there were hoots of laughter.

Mr Morrell came to her rescue. 'The grapes are over, ma-am. I guess the grape-haze had you fooled. It's kinda like a mirage.'

'That must be it.' Abigail turned away from the misty blue vista and blinked determinedly. Immediately a round table came into focus, beautifully laid with a cold lunch. 'Oh, Vittorio – how very kind. Did you do this?'

His dark face was alight with pleasure at their pleasure. He spread his broad capable hands. 'With these, signora.' He looked at them all proudly. 'I know I boast always. But I do everything here.'

Abigail felt a rush of warmth into her heart, especially as she saw Sue's face clearly just then and it was melting with tenderness. Over the past two weeks she had grown fond of this boy and looking back he had never once sailed under false colours. Her wrong impression had been entirely her own stupid mistake. Now, she admired him for his hard work and for this final touch. No wonder the kitchen had looked derelict, he must have ransacked it to prepare this spread for his guests. Even so, the thought of Sue coping in that kitchen was disheartening and she looked away from her daughter's open face and tried to tell herself that Vittorio was just a very good holiday friend.

She let herself be led to the table and settled in a high-backed mahogany chair that must weigh a ton. With one or two gentle questions and her usual listening smile, she encouraged Vittorio to talk about his home. He did so with all the optimistic insouciance they had come to expect of him.

'You understand—' His dark eyes found Sue's. 'I worked in a car factory in Milano – that was to be my life. And then the lawyers told me I now owned this place and the factory was offering me a good price for it.' He laughed. 'Can you guess what I told them?'

Sue nodded, her eyes alight with his enthusiasm.

'When I stood on this terrace I said to the lawyer who arranged everything – I will never give it up. I would rather starve here than grow rich in a Milano suburb!'

Everyone clapped at this oratory. Even Abigail, although her heart chilled at the thought of Sue starving in any kind of beautiful independence.

Vittorio laughed and continued unabashed. 'So I read all the books and I talked to everyone around here and I watched the small green flowers grow – I dusted them with sulphur – I picked the grapes. And then I came to Venice to see the firm who bought them and to get the money from the bank. The overdraft.'

Sue nodded and Christine said, 'You're going to expand quite soon then, Vittorio?'

He laughed still more. 'Not yet, Christine. But with their help and a good crop next year I will only be ten million lira in debt!' He looked around at them, grinning broadly. 'That is not bad, eh?'

Even Sue was silent at this and Abigail was horrified. Frantically she did some inaccurate conversions in her head. Wasn't that in the region of twelve thousand pounds? It was incredible. Awful.

Mr Morrell's voice dropped into the silence.

'The night we met you spoke of pests. You dealt with the mildew with sulphur. What about the spider mites and black measles?'

'Ah—' Vittorio turned to him with renewed energy. 'This is why I needed the cash. Wine growers can buy a service, a crop-spray from an aeroplane. You have heard of it?'

Mr Morrell nodded curtly. 'You will need fertilizer too of course. Your uncle let the ground go besides running up this debt.'

'This also. I have it all written down if you are interested.'

'The bank manager loaned the cash on the evidence you gave him?'

Vittorio nodded. 'He was courteous. Kind. I went several times to discuss my – my expenditure. He suggested I increased the loan to cover the fertilizer.'

'So. He thinks you are a good investment.' Mr Morrell turned back to Abigail. 'And bank managers are not easily fooled.'

She tried to smile at him, realizing that these short pointed questions had been for her benefit. But in the meantime, while the 'good investment' was maturing, there would be years of sheer grind.

It didn't seem to worry Vittorio, he was smiling and pouring more wine.

'How could he doubt that?' he asked no-one in particular with frightening confidence. 'The Pucci vineyard is the best investment I have ever seen.' He paused with the bottle at an angle over Mr Morrell's glass. 'You know, signor, for a tourist, you understand a great deal of the business, eh?'

Mr Morrell shook his head at the wine. 'I am a great deal older than you, Vittorio,' was all he said.

After lunch it was proposed that they look at the vines. Abigail begged to be excused, pleading tiredness. Vittorio fetched her a footstool and a glass of iced water. He couldn't have been kinder. He was a sweet boy – she told herself this very sternly a great many times.

She sat quietly, composing herself and 'counting her blessings'. The far Adriatic appeared for a moment out of Mr Morrell's grape-haze and then receded again. She had of course been unable to focus long-distance objects for some time now but she did wish that things would stay still. She closed her eyes and the curious molecular disruption eased considerably. Forcing a smile at the panic which had gripped her she opened her eyes again. The terrace, the luncheon table, the heavy Victorian furniture . . . everything . . . was merging into that grape-blue mist. Her heart beating violently she waited for the darkness. Gradually it came.

Frank followed the others through the door without much enthusiasm. He had seen run-down vineyards before and his feet ached at the thought. Besides he had more than a suspicion that the Duchess was going to sit alone and brood in spite of the fact that he had tried to show her the Pucci place might well be a good thing.

He tapped Christine on the shoulder.

'I'm going back to the house,' he said briefly. 'I'm too old for sightseeing.'

She looked uncertain. 'D'you think I should come? I'm worried about Mother but I don't want it to be obvious. We mustn't hurt Vittorio.'

'No. Stick with the others. Sue's got some adjusting to do as well as your mother and she could probably use your moral support. I'll sit with the Duchess if you think it would help.'

Her face lit up. 'I wish you would. Your sound common-sense is just what she needs.' Her smile became rueful. 'You'll soon be expert at comforting the Langley women won't you?'

He reached for his old armour of cynicism. 'It'll be a pleasure, honey.' But it didn't come off and he was glad it didn't.

He stood still and watched them all disappear down the hill. Then he turned and went softly back into the house, through the kitchen and into the room behind the terrace. It really was something. He stood just inside the door taking in again its generous proportions, the open fireplace, the wall-length windows that led outside – and led the outside indoors. The old-fashioned flock paper and heavy mahogany furniture somehow suited the Langley girls so much. It seemed a room made for Sue's vitality – surely her mother could see that? The whole place was crying out for Sue's gaiety and energy and abundant love. Of course it might still come to nothing . . . maybe she'd chicken out after today. He shook his head irritably. Of course she wouldn't chicken out, not one of the Duchess' girls. She'd enjoy working on this place, she wasn't meant to sit around tea-tables and yell at servants. And the Duchess could come visiting and sit here doing her needlework or what ever she did and . . . he stopped his thoughts and held his breath as a sound caught his ear. Beyond the wide window, on the verandah, the Duchess was crying.

For a moment he was paralysed; not with embarrassment but with sheer surprise and then anxiety. And then he was across the room, through the tall French doors, kneeling by her side offering his handkerchief like any corny hero in any corny film.

'Here,' he said roughly.

She hiccoughed and snuffled a bit into the square of linen his secretary had got him from Detroit, and then lifted her head and gave him a watery smile.

'I'm sorry, Mr Morrell. I thought you had gone with the others.'

'I was tired too,' he said shortly. 'I'm not as young as I was.'

'No.' She shook her head. 'That's my trouble, Mr Morrell. I'm old and foolish.'

He said vigorously, surprising himself, 'You're neither. You could never be old, Duchess. And is it foolish to want a little luxury for your daughter?'

She sighed. 'So you know? Is it so obvious?'

'Well, the girls guess how you feel of course.'

'And you.'

'And me. I'm a parent too.'

'Yes.' Her grey eyes stared into his. 'You are very understanding, Mr Morrell.'

'I understand that you are worried. But needlessly. She would prefer it this way herself. She'd be bored with nothing to challenge her. And I meant what I said during lunch. In five years' time this place will pay.'

'Yes. I believe you. Thank you.' There was a pause then

she drew in her breath and went on, 'I have to tell you something, Mr Morrell. It is a responsibility to be the recipient of a confidence – and this must be a confidence. Can you . . . bear it?'

Frank almost held his breath. Here it was, coming now. The mystery that for him had hovered like a question-mark above the exasperating Mrs Langley was about to be revealed.

He said, 'I think so. It can't be too awful – you couldn't commit a murder if you tried, Duchess.'

She didn't laugh, she hardly seemed to hear what he said. There was another pause and then she whispered, 'Mr Morrell, will you please hold me for a moment?'

Frank stared. Her gaze did not falter. It was as if she didn't see him. Gently, tentatively, he put his arms around her.

'Don't say anything. Don't look at me. I can tell you this because we are alike in many ways. We are both no longer young. We are both poor. We have both staked everything on this trip to Venice. Yet we are ships that pass in the night. After this holiday we shall never see each other again. Can you understand?'

Her voice was a whisper beneath his chin. He held her tighter feeling the tremor in her shoulder.

'I understand.'

'Mr Morrell, I have a progressive complaint of the eyes. I can see very little in the distance and occasionally things right in front of me merge into a kind of greyness. I am going blind, Mr Morrell.'

He held her as if he could never let her go; no longer supporting her but clinging to her desperately while his mind spun and various facts clicked into place. Her lack of interest in sight-seeing but her terrific interest in people. The time she had almost fallen into the canal and then that special night at the Casino when she had walked blindly off the top of the steps and into his arms. The whole episode of the Rialto when she had peered and smiled and never once let go of his arm.

Now he knew why she had cashed in on the emeralds when she did. Now he knew her secret. The small feeling of triumph that had flowered when she announced her confidence shrivelled and died. For the first time in nearly forty years, Frank Morrell's dark calculating eyes filled with tears.

CHAPTER FIVE

The Duchess' voice was steady again when she spoke.

'Mr Morrell, I must stress again, this is for your ears alone. Christine and Sue . . . they must have no inkling of what I have just told you.'

Frank did not relax his arms; he could not bear her to see his tears. 'They will have to know soon enough,' he agreed throatily, for once not questioning the Duchess' motives.

She sighed. 'Exactly. I knew you would understand.' She pushed gently against his shirt front releasing herself. Her face was the one he recognized again, unshadowed, slightly smiling as if in anticipation. 'That's better. It's easing now. I can see your outline. Forgive me for breaking down like that, Mr Morrell. It's the suddenness – the pressure. I shall get used to it of course.'

He cleared his throat. 'There must be something that can be done, Duchess. Surely an operation—'

'No. Put all thoughts like that out of your head please, Mr Morrell. They are a waste of time and energy. That is where you can help me – with your energy.'

'Anything. You know that.'

'You have already been so kind I felt you deserved an explanation. But I think I shall need even more of your time and energy over the next two weeks and if you are really intending to stay in Venice . . .?'

Nothing could have moved Frank from Venice now. He nodded brusquely. 'I'll be around, Duchess.'

She said nothing more and he crouched there for a moment longing to pester her with fruitless questions about the actual condition of her eyes. But he knew that the subject was closed. She had explained herself and asked for further help and that was that.

With the same tentative diffidence with which he had taken her in his arms he reached up and replaced her hat. It was a tender, intimate gesture and the small action made his hands tremble. The Duchess looked past him tactfully as she smiled her thanks.

'Your grape-haze is very beautiful, Mr Morrell,' she murmured.

He glanced over his shoulder. The view of vines and distant sea was crystal clear and there was no sign of a mist.

'It sure is, Duchess,' he agreed huskily.

Frank was quiet on the trip back to Venice. For one thing he wanted to be at the ready in case the Duchess needed any of the help she'd asked for. For another he was silent with wonder at the change in himself. He felt physically soft like a jelly and was certain if he prodded his stomach it would float amorphously like a miniature water bed. He knew that somewhere inside himself the impatience which had always been ready to rise to the surface when he was with the Langleys had melted for good. The process had started when Christine confessed their true financial state and spun him that amazing yarn about the family emeralds. It had ended this afternoon when he had literally wept in the Duchess' arms like a little kid. He was now her ally. He had pledged himself to protect her, even against her own daughters. Frank had done some deals in his time, but nothing quite so two-faced as this one.

Sue and Christine did most of the talking. Almost as if they'd rehearsed it beforehand.

'What did Vittorio say about the grapes?' Christine asked, tucking her arm into the Duchess' to secure her attention.

'They're a special kind. With a high glucose content which makes very good sweet wine.' Sue looked knowledgeable. 'That's unusual in this area. So it makes the Pucci vineyard sort of special.'

'And even without the crop spray and fertilizer, he had a very good yield this year, didn't he?'

'Well, as Mr Morrell said at lunch, the bank manager must have been impressed mustn't he? So after the spray and the fertilizer he should do wonders next year. Don't you think so, Mother?'

The Duchess, whose head had been turning from one to another like a Wimbledon spectator, suddenly put her spare arm around her younger daughter and hugged her. 'Darling, you don't have to convince me of anything. I know just how you are feeling now. I hope – just for an instant this morning – you didn't feel let down?'

Sue said swiftly, 'Vittorio never exaggerated – not once—'

Christine backed her up. 'You must admit, Mother, *we* gave him all the trimmings—'

The Duchess nodded. 'We did indeed. But as we believed in them – I repeat, Sue – do you mind?'

'Of course not. I prefer it that way. If you remember I said to you I'd prefer him to be an ordinary working man.'

'You did. So that's all right then. Well . . . we must wait and see.'

Sue pleated the skirt of her tan silk dress. 'Yes. There are only two more weeks of our holiday. Not quite that. And he's so busy.'

'Maybe we could come here again next year, Mother?' Christine tugged at the lime-green sleeve like a child asking for ice-cream. 'If we all saved like mad and made it a package trip?'

But the Duchess glanced at Frank and said doubtfully again, 'We must wait and see.'

There was a small silence. Sue had recognized her

Mother's natural disappointment yet had not reckoned on such caution.

'If he – if he comes to Venice again, you won't mind me seeing him though will you, darling?'

'Of course not, Sue. But be careful. You could be hurt. Vittorio has a lot on his mind besides you. You've only known him for two weeks and there's plenty of time really . . .' Her voice faded as if she would like to take that back. Then she went on briskly, 'When *is* he coming over next?'

Sue laughed again. 'In two days' time,' she confessed.

Amid the general laughter Christine noticed Frank's silence.

'You weren't just being polite were you, Mr Morrell? You thought the vineyard was a good proposition?'

Frank glanced under the brim of the saucer hat he had so recently put on.

'I sure did,' he said decisively. 'In five years maybe—' he caught a gleam of worry in the grey eyes opposite him. 'Sooner than that if he could persuade someone to invest a little money in mechanization.'

Christine looked doubtful but Sue clapped her hands. 'Hey, that's an idea. When we get home I'll have to cultivate all my rich friends—'

She laughed joyously. Frank tried to signal to the Duchess that Sue couldn't care less whether the vineyard was an instant success or not. But they had arrived at the station and he went ahead to secure a motoscafi for the trip to La Paloma. When he returned, the girls were exclaiming at the evening silhouette of a gondolier piloting his craft under a bridge. The Duchess was smiling vaguely.

He took her arm and pointed upwards. 'I kinda like the skyline. The way the roofs gleam—'

She picked up her cue neatly. 'It's all those copper domes. They do take the eye, don't they?' She let herself be led to their boat and the smile she turned on Frank was one of pure gratitude.

They spent a day exploring the medieval city of Padua. The girls exclaimed over the Giotto frescoes and Galileo's chair. Frank enjoyed the University. Abigail could have spent the whole day in the botanical gardens. Vittorio phoned them when they got back to say he was seeing his bank manager the next day and was it permitted to take Sue out afterwards? Just Sue.

Abigail smiled at her daughter fidgeting by her side for her turn at the telephone.

'It is permitted, Vittorio. But you will be back here for dinner?'

'Thank you, signora. Of course, signora. And I will take such care of Sue I promise, signora.'

'Good. Well, here she is. And we will see you tomorrow evening.' She covered the mouthpiece. 'He thinks I am surprised by the sudden appointment with his bank manager. Do tell him he doesn't need such excuses.'

But Sue raised her eyebrows. 'Doesn't sound like him.' She listened attentively to the phone and lifted her head. 'It's true, Mother. He has got to see his bank manager – special request.'

Abigail made an apologetic face and went back to the interminable job of fixing her chignon. Maybe she would have her hair cut when she got back home. If she wasn't able to arrange it herself it might be better . . .

Christine Langley dressed for dinner without much interest. Right from the start she had found this holiday harder to swallow than had Sue, and now, with nearly three weeks of it gone and no letter from home, she knew it had been a mistake for her.

She stared at her mirrored reflection. She was wearing a dress her mother had made for her in a tangerine silk.

It deepened her golden tan and brought out honey tints in her fair hair making her a much more vivid person than the slim fair girl who was normally rather in the background of the Langley trio. She sighed. Maybe if David could see her now he might be able to single her out from all the other girls at Tillingham's.

She turned impatiently from the mirror. If David had felt a fraction of the feeling she felt for him, he'd have written. Or told her before she went that he would miss her. No, Mother was right. He was definitely what she would describe as a philanderer.

Christine smiled unwillingly at the thought. What a character Mother was. How marvellous at her age to be able to make this crazy gesture, selling her legacy to give her girls a chance to see what remained of her old romantic world. It probably was the sort of emergency Great Grandmamma had in mind too; perhaps they were all a little crazy before they lost their money. In the good old days. Not that Mother had seen much of it, what with the war and losing Daddy after such a short marriage. Yet, how exciting she always made everything seem. Christine remembered dressing-up parties with outrageous costumes made by her mother for all her friends out of scraps of left-over materials. Firework nights when the fireworks had consisted of a few packets of sparklers but where the bonfire had been enormous, the Guy a work of art, and there had been hot jacket potatoes in the embers. And now, this holiday, a prime example of her mother's belief in enjoyment. She couldn't even hold back from Sue's romance although it was a far cry from her hopes and aspirations. Yes, her gentle smile of anticipation was a sort of trade-mark and it was resoundingly echoed by Sue's vivacious enthusiasm and by Christine's own quieter brand of happiness.

Her smile deepened as she picked up her bag and made for the door. For some reason she was thinking of Mr

Morrell now: poor Mr Morrell, dragged under the Langley wing so unwillingly at first and now providing a strong arm for them all to lean on. Did her mother realize that in launching her girls, she had acquired an admirer for herself?

She tapped on her mother's door and Sue's face appeared.

'Just helping Mother with her hair, Chris. She can't seem to find a thing tonight and we were delayed because Vittorio rang through.'

'OK?' asked Christine.

'OK. He's picking me up tomorrow morning. You – you don't mind if we disappear for the day, do you?'

'Of course not.' Christine knew that Sue was hoping very much Vittorio would mention marriage tomorrow. 'Look – I'll go on downstairs and get a table next to the terrace. Don't be long.'

She walked slowly to the lifts. It was ridiculous to feel left out yet, momentarily, she did. Tomorrow Vittorio was taking Sue off for the day and Mother would probably rest and then Mr Morrell would suggest a walk to the Piazza for tea and . . . and . . . darn it all, she was almost playing gooseberry!

She shook herself with another smile as the lift doors opened on to the brightly lit foyer. And then the smile died and her eyes slowly widened and became very blue indeed.

The man who was signing the hotel register looked up and was still too. Signor Rezzonico pointed helpfully to the calendar on the desk but the young man ignored him and put the pen down on the open page.

'Chris . . .' he took a few steps towards the lift. 'Chris – I hope you don't mind. I had some leave to come. In fact Old Man Tillingham himself asked me to take it before October. And I wanted to look up some of the baroque-style . . . baroque is the in-thing for antiques now . . .' His voice trailed away.

Christine breathed, 'David Blake,' as if trying to convince

herself it really was the man from Tillingham's Department Store who was friendly with everyone but would never go out of his way to single out one special girl. She went on staring. 'Baroque?' she queried. 'In Venice?'

'Well, of course Rome is the obvious choice. But Tillingham's antiques aren't obvious. And – and I remembered you'd said La Paloma was a very good hotel. So I phoned and they'd got a room and – well – here I am.'

Christine began to smile. 'Yes. Here you are.' The antiques at Tillingham's weren't the only things which weren't obvious. Devious might be a good word for David Blake. And it made her very happy.

He came across at last and took her hand. 'Chris, say you don't mind. I realize it's an awful cheek, turning up like this. Of course you don't have to see me if you don't want to.'

She let her hand stay in his. 'Venice is very cosmopolitan. I think it can contain the two of us.'

'I haven't had a holiday for two or three years and when you told me about yours . . . it sounded so *romantic*—'

She couldn't resist a giggle. 'Yes. That's the right word. Romantic.'

He dropped her hand. 'I see. I was rather afraid . . . do you mind me turning up like this then?'

'No.' She wished she didn't want to laugh and jump around like she had at one of Mother's old firework parties. 'No, I don't mind at all. In fact—' her grin was getting out of control. 'I'm glad.'

There was a pause then he laughed with relief. 'I know I'm making an idiot of myself, Chris – you can imagine what the rest of the staff said when I told them I was coming here.'

'You told them? I mean, they know you've come to to—'

'Well they didn't believe the baroque bit any more than you did. Of course they knew I'd come to see you.'

It was practically a declaration of intent. She found she was holding his hand again and they were both laughing.

Rezzonico joined them also smiling. 'You know the Signorina Langley? You are one of their party?'

'Mr Blake is a friend from home, signor. This is Signor Rezzonico, David. The manager of the hotel. He has been very kind to us.'

'It is easy to be kind to such charming ladies,' Rezzonico said formally. 'Will you be joining them for dinner, signor?'

David raised his eyebrows at Christine. She removed her hand from his and glanced over her shoulder at the lift.

'David, would you mind very much if I introduced you to Mother tomorrow evening? You see, my sister will have a guest then and – and it might be better. Easier.'

He looked rebuffed and though her heart melted for him it also skipped joyously at this further evidence of . . . attraction. She was superstitious about using the word love.

'No, of course I don't mind,' he said insincerely. 'I'll eat in my room actually—'

'We could walk afterwards. St Mark's is marvellous by moonlight.'

He smiled again. 'We'll walk. Please.'

'Nine o'clock. On the steps of the hotel.' Christine jumped at the sound of the lift doors but it was not Abigail or Sue. She smiled at the bewildered Rezzonico. 'Make sure Signor Blake has a very good dinner, won't you?'

There were still a lot of people in the Piazza. Christine and David strolled along the loggias and took their stance in the middle of the square to view the five basilicas.

'This is the heart of Venice,' Christine announced.

David said, 'Yes. Chris, don't you want me to meet your mother?'

'Of course I want you to meet her. The copper horses came from Constantinople you know.'

'Interesting. You're hiding something from me. There's a man around isn't there? Someone you've met here. With money. Or a title, blast him.'

'There is no-one in the least like that. Though it is strange you should mention it. Perhaps my mother and you have the same idea about Venetians.' She looked up at him with dancing eyes. The line of his jaw was very pronounced from this angle and though normally he was rather sandy in colouring the moonlight gave him a blond, Viking look. She said breathlessly, 'You're not paying attention. That is the Library and that bit joined on to the cathedral is the Doge's palace and—'

'Chris. I love you,' he said.

The heady effervescing joy which had been hers since she saw him in the foyer this evening steadied into a tranquil happiness sitting on a broad base of assurance and self-confidence.

'Thank goodness,' she said. 'If you hadn't I'd have been wrong about the most important thing in my life. And if I was wrong about that who knows how many other wrong ideas I might have?'

He stared down at her. His eyes were as blue as hers.

'Does that mean—? Chris, it can't mean . . . you're so beautiful and friendly with everyone around the place. Why should you have looked twice at me?'

'Be honest. You must have known I've looked twice otherwise you wouldn't have come out here.'

'I don't know. I'm not going to argue. Oh, Chris.'

'Oh, David.'

They walked quietly in the deep shadows of the Library. In the midst of her exultation Christine wondered fleetingly how her mother would take this new suitor. Another ordinary working man. Of course it would be all right. She would understand eventually because she would see that they were really in love but at first . . . what had she called David? Not a gigolo . . .

She said, 'David, I'm afraid I've given my mother the wrong impression about you. And in any case she is just a little anxious about Sue and her romance with an Italian wine-grower—'

'You see? What did I tell you? Rich Italians all over the place and your sister is younger than you!'

'Do shut up and listen. Sue and Vittorio are going out tomorrow so I'll have plenty of time to talk to her.'

'Chris – I've only got a week. Surely I can see you tomorrow. I thought we might have the day on a beach somewhere. Just the two of us.'

She smiled to herself; she had never been able to imagine David Blake – ardent.

'It would be marvellous.' She hesitated. 'All right. She'll probably take a walk with Mr Morrell in the afternoon and be back for tea at four-thirty. I can talk to her then.'

'Oh, Chris.'

'Oh, David.'

As Abigail watched Sue get ready to meet Vittorio the next morning, she felt again a rush of gratitude towards Mr Morrell. It was a familiar feeling lately. Since the trip to the vineyard he had been tact itself, never referring again to her confidence in him, yet always at hand to guide her feet and prompt her sight-seeing. Life had once again become pleasant and easy and she did not regret her momentary breakdown.

Sue was teasing her now. 'I suppose your gentleman-friend will be taking you out again today, darling? I mean, with me out of the way and Chris swimming at the lido beach all afternoon, I assume—'

Abigail interrupted with unusual sharpness. 'Sue, please

don't talk like that about Mr Morrell. He's a gentleman.'

Sue glanced at her mother in the mirror with some surprise. 'Of course he is, Mother. Otherwise Chris and I wouldn't leave you alone with him.'

'As a matter of fact, he did suggest a stroll around the Piazza this afternoon. He has some business to attend to this morning.'

Sue continued to look surprised. 'Business? I didn't know he had any business interests here. In fact he doesn't seem to have any interests at all in Venice. And as he was born here that makes him rather sad, don't you think?'

'He hasn't had a happy life. And he has stayed here for longer than he intended – d'you remember he was leaving the day we arrived? I am wondering whether he is in financial difficulties because of me . . . us. Could he be trying to borrow some money, I wonder?'

Sue went to the window and peered out searching the passing boats for a familiar figure.

'Well, don't ask him for goodness' sake, darling. He's very touchy about his personal life.'

Abigail frowned. 'I know. I just wish there was something we could do.'

'It's not your responsibility—'

'I'm afraid that's it. I *do* feel responsible, Sue. Perhaps you could ask Vittorio's advice, dear? After all Mr Morrell was an Italian originally and—'

Sue turned from the window flushed and happy. 'He's coming,' she said. 'Vittorio. He's just arrived.' She whirled across the room and pecked at her mother's forehead. 'Now you're sure you'll be all right on your own? Shall I bring Vittorio back here for lunch and we could swim in the hotel pool afterwards—'

'I'm looking forward to a day of absolute peace!' Abigail replied tartly. 'Go away. And give my love to Vittorio!'

'Mother, you're marvellous. And you really are improving.'

She swooped on a pair of tights and a chiffon scarf discarded on a chair. 'You're not tidying up after me any more!'

She was gone and Abigail stared around the room wondering whether there were any more muddles she simply could not see. It was as well there were only another ten days of the holiday left. If only Chris could meet someone kind and interesting and loving the whole thing would have been so worthwhile.

The bank manager was smaller than Frank but with the same astute Venetian look to him. His name was Umberto. He stood up and leaned across his massive mahogany desk holding out a welcoming hand.

'I have heard of your firm, Signor Morrelli, naturally. No, it is not necessary to produce your passport.'

'You've made enquiries since I phoned,' Frank deduced. 'You don't have to apologize, I am glad you did so. Shows you're a business man.'

Umberto spread his hands. 'Your proposal was unexpected to say the least, signor. An investment of such a size in so small a vineyard is not suggested every day.'

'Good job too.' Frank took the chair indicated and crossed his legs. 'I have a special interest in the Pucci vines, Umberto, and I want that property to be developed without delay.'

'That will please my client, signor.' The bank manager produced a closely written sheet of paper. 'I have a document drawn up. If you would like to read it . . . I have asked Signor Pucci to call today to see it also.'

'You don't let the grass grow under your feet,' Frank commented dryly skimming expertly down the investment agreement.

The small man gave a tight smile. 'He was in any case coming to Venice today to visit some friends. It was a good opportunity.'

'Sure.' Frank tried not to grin back. He was feeling good. At the helm again, wheeling and dealing. In a way he never had before; was it possible that happiness could be a currency? 'You must have faith in Pucci yourself, signor. I notice you're not advising me to hang on to my money.'

Umberto spread expressive hands again. 'Signor Morrelli, the vineyard is a good one. The young man is a hard worker. In five or six years he would in any case be in a position to raise another loan with this bank and mechanize on his own. So he is a good investment. On the other hand, you will not make an overnight fortune. You understand that, of course. You have gone into the whole thing very carefully.'

'Not really. But I've got money to spare. And I've also got a very good reason for not wanting him to wait five or six years.'

'Then that is *his* good fortune,' Umberto smiled as he took back the agreement. 'He will not know how to thank you, signor.'

'Ah.' Frank shook his head curtly. 'That's what he mustn't do, Umberto. He would be embarrassed. The money would no longer be a business investment but a temporary gift from a new friend. I do not wish young Pucci to know about me. I must be one of your faceless investors.'

Umberto smiled again. 'You are most understanding, signor. Vittorio Pucci has pride. It is one thing to accept unknown help, quite another as you say, to be given the personal "helping hand". However, signor—' he placed a Venetian glass paper weight on the agreement. 'You do not think he will guess? He cannot know many men who are in a position to invest money in his vineyard.'

Frank looked levelly at the other man. 'Vittorio Pucci has no idea of my true identity, Umberto. I'm just Frank Morrell, ex-patriate. OK?'

The bank manager raised curious brows for an instant and then lifted his shoulders slightly. 'Certainly, signor. And now, may I offer you coffee?'

Before Frank could answer, the intercom on the big desk buzzed and Umberto flicked a switch. He spoke rapidly and then looked up at Frank.

Frank nodded. 'I heard. It's Pucci now. Is there somewhere I can wait? Then I can sign and be done with it.'

Umberto opened a door behind the desk and ushered Frank into a small room. 'I will have some coffee sent into you, signor.'

Frank gave his curt nod again. The door was too thick for him to hear Vittorio's entrance or any of the subsequent conversation. But as the minutes ticked by his mouth curved involuntarily. Maybe the boy had Sue with him and it was easy to imagine her excitement when she learned of the unknown investor. Yes, he admitted it made him feel good. And what was that Umberto had said? Something about understanding Vittorio's pride. Suddenly Frank gave one of his half-grunts. Steve had pride too. Maybe, just maybe, he hadn't understood that as he should have done.

Sue said, 'Tell me again. Slowly. And all in English – I know *il direttore* is Signor Umberto and *il danaro* is money but *credito*—'

Vittorio said, 'Forgive me, Sue – I am excited. This means . . . so much to us, carissima. I wanted to ask you today to wait for me. Until I could make the house fit for you—'

Sue tried to catch her breath. 'You mean—?'

'I mean now we do not have to wait. Oh Sue – my happiness – we can get married in just a few short weeks!'

'You – you're asking me to marry you, Vittorio?'

'But of course. You have seen my home and you do not disapprove. It has all been done most proper and correct.'

He stopped and whirled her round to face him. Shops were closing for the long mid-day break and last-minute customers stopped to stare. 'Sue. You *will* marry me won't you?'

'Oh, Vittorio.' Tears stood in her eyes. 'Darling. We've known each other such a short time—'

'And we knew the moment we met. In the Casino. Did we not?'

'I wasn't going to argue. I have been completely and absolutely certain. But you. It is different for you. You are just beginning a new life. A dream—'

'You are my dream, *cara mia*. You make everything come true for me. And now . . . now . . .' He began to tell her again. She questioned him and he went through it a third time. And then they walked quietly through the now-deserted calles, looking at each other now and then with enormous eyes, almost frightened to believe in this terrific stroke of luck.

Sue said hesitantly at last, 'You're sure there's no snag? I mean you haven't signed anything that's written in very small print?'

'I read it very carefully. And Signor Umberto is completely honest. I think he is my friend.' He took her hand. 'Let us be happy about it, Sue. Let us talk about getting married. I will come to your country, yes? Everything must be done according to custom and to make your mamma happy also—'

'I want to rush and tell her but it's too soon. I haven't taken it in myself yet. Oh, Vittorio—'

'Yes, my little Inglesi?'

'I am so *hungry*!'

After the agreement had been duly signed, Frank took Umberto to lunch. The bank manager was surprisingly easy to talk to and though Frank told himself at first that his money was oiling the wheels as usual, he did not believe it for long. Umberto seemed personally delighted about the transaction and confirmed that Vittorio had been amazed and deeply grateful to his unknown investor.

'There is a trend in young Italians to work for themselves,' he commented. 'It is an optimistic streak in them of which I approve.'

Frank said, 'It happens in America too.' He was thinking of Steve again and the way he had himself blocked his son's path to independence.

'It is doubtless world-wide,' agreed Umberto. 'Our young people are often maligned, signor, but for what? Their originality? Their drive?' He smiled as if he and Frank were old buddies. 'Perhaps we are in the midst of a new renaissance and we do not know it.'

Frank's thoughts slid naturally to the Smith-Sprinter works. For the first time he hoped whole-heartedly that Steve was managing Morrell's Mechanics on his own. Even that he had somehow managed to pull his English chestnuts out of the fire. The young should be encouraged and helped; like the Duchess encouraged and helped her girls.

At two-thirty he arrived at the steps of La Paloma just in time to see Christine being handed into a gondola by a tall fair young man in an English sweater and slacks. There was no sign of the Duchess and of course Sue was off with Vittorio somewhere.

Frank stopped, feeling an unwonted sense of responsibility towards the unchaperoned girl.

'Hi there!' he made up his mind and walked back down the steps on to the riva. Chris looked over her shoulder and immediately turned towards him with a smile. 'Your mother not going with you?' he asked without finesse.

Christine's smile grew mischievous. 'I think she is waiting for you, Mr Morrell. A gentle walk to San Marco wasn't it?'

Frank gave his inverted smile, recognizing when the tables were being turned on him. He grunted an affirmative.

Christine went on, 'We've been swimming all morning at the lido.' Her blue eyes were suddenly vulnerable as she looked at Frank. 'Mr Morrell – this is David Blake. The playboy I was telling you about the other night. He had a holiday too, so he came over here to see me.' There was unconscious pride in her voice.

Frank looked at the young man by her side. He was how Frank imagined most Britishers to be; tall and fair and very casual, almost chilly. Then a broad smile split his expressionless face and he looked as happy as Christine.

'Playboy? I don't get it – what have you been saying, Chris?' He took Frank's hand in a grip that surprised Frank who had expected what he called a 'damp fish' shake. 'I'm no playboy, sir. I work for my living.' He pumped away heartily. 'Chris has told me about you and what a sport you've been and I want to thank you.'

Frank found himself grinning back. 'And she's told me about you too, young fella. Kinda inaccurately I guess.'

Christine said demurely, 'I may have misled Mr Morrell unintentionally . . .'

Frank said sincerely, 'I'm pleased to make your acquaintance, David Blake. You've come a long way but—' he waved his hand to indicate the gleaming water and intense blue sky and Chris silhouetted so gorgeously against them. 'I think you'll find it worth it.'

They all laughed as if he'd said something wonderfully witty, and then Frank added, 'Say, how does your mother feel about David's long trip?'

'She – she doesn't know. Yet.' Christine almost fidgeted. 'Actually I intended to talk to her earlier but she was lying down. Then we came back for lunch and she was having it in her room and I couldn't very well take David in, could I?' She looked pleadingly at Frank. 'I was rather hoping you could help. I mean, if you're going to be with her all afternoon . . .'

David said, 'Am I so frightening, love? Or is it your mother?'

Frank said firmly, 'Mrs Langley is tops. What's OK with her girls, is OK with her. She needs to know it's OK, that's all.'

Christine said, 'She's a bit anxious about Sue and Vittorio – I've explained about that. It's just the suddenness of your arrival.'

'Anything you say goes, Chris. It's just that—' Blake shrugged wide shoulders. 'I should have thought keeping my presence here a secret would make it worse.' He wrinkled his face distastefully. 'Under-hand.'

Frank was glad he felt like that. Showed he was honest anyway.

He said, 'Look. If I see a chance this afternoon I'll try to pave the way. But at least by this evening the Duchess won't have to worry about Sue and Vittorio any more.'

Christine looked surprised. 'Why? Have you seen them?' She clasped her hands. 'Has he asked her to marry him?'

'Probably.' Frank cursed himself for a slow-witted idiot. 'Tell you what. Bring David in to dinner tonight. Let's have a party. Your mother can't resist happiness.'

Christine said, 'Oh, Mr Morrell, you know her already so very well. I was thinking that only last night' . . . She turned towards her young man and for a nickel Frank guessed she would have burst into tears . . . 'and then you were standing in the foyer.'

Blake encircled her with his long arm. Frank knew when he was no longer needed. But still he waited there and waved the two of them goodbye just as the Duchess would have done. He was getting sentimental and sloppy. But it made him feel really great.

He rang the Duchess from the desk.

'I'm back,' he said without preamble. 'Would you like a walk to the Piazza? Or tea on the terrace?'

Her voice, always warm, was surely a little warmer than usual?

'Ah, Mr Morrell. How nice. You have completed your business satisfactorily?'

'Most satisfactorily, Duchess.'

'I *am* glad. And I'd enjoy a stroll if you're feeling up to it after your long morning.'

'I feel great,' he told her honestly. 'I'm in the foyer.'

'Er . . . Mr Morrell . . .' she sounded suddenly diffident.

'Yes? Go ahead, Duchess.'

'I wonder – could you possibly come up and give me a little help? I seem to have mislaid my bag and I usually wear a blue necklace with this dress which has also disappeared.'

He swallowed the lump which seemed to stick in his throat often these days and grunted acquiescence.

'I'm on my way.'

He took the stairs two at a time because he couldn't wait for the lift. She was waiting for him, her door open, her smile as serene as usual. She was dressed in a blue dress of some light material covered in daisies. Her hat was slightly askew. The room was meticulous.

'I've tried to put everything away where I shall know where to put my hand on it,' she excused herself, laughing. 'And now of course I've forgotten which drawer my bag and jewel box—'

Frank grunted and swallowed again. Her bag, a straw one to match the hat, was looped on the back of a chair. What seemed to be a jewel box was right beside it.

'Here we are,' he said heartily. 'Perhaps you will allow me to choose a necklace and fasten it for you?' He picked out a double row of beads which matched the frock the Duchess was wearing and handed them to her. She laughed again and turned her back to him, handing the ends of the necklace back and lowering her head in a curiously submissive gesture that made his hands shake. He tried not to eye the nape of her neck and the curling tendrils of hair. In the same unnatural voice he began to tell her about the Venetian ladies of old and their propensity for taking a completely innocent 'lover' to pay court to them while their husbands were about their businesses. Realizing where that was leading him, he stopped suddenly. She was still laughing as she turned to face him again, adjusting the beads over the neck of her dress.

'I heard a story too . . . it seems that the scent of countless decaying sea-animals hereabouts acts as a sort of romantic stimulus . . . what a prosaic explanation for the feeling of exhilaration one gets in Venice.'

Frank nodded and looped her bag over her arm. 'There's a chemical reason for all our emotions of course, Duchess.'

Her laughter died. 'You're thinking of Sue and Vittorio. You're warning me that theirs is simply a holiday infatuation—'

'I wasn't thinking of Sue and Vittorio at all.' He reached gentle hands to her head. 'Excuse me, Duchess, your hat is a little . . .' he adjusted the straw saucer with infinite care. Already – and this was only the second time he'd done it – he knew the exact angle at which it sat on the bulky chignon. His eyes were on a level with hers and he knew suddenly that she could see him very well. She was registering Frank Morrell. He swallowed. 'That's fine. Just fine,' he said lamely dropping his hands like a naughty schoolboy.

Her own voice was faltering when she began to speak. 'Mr Morrell . . . I wish to mention something rather personal and I don't wish to offend you in the slightest.' He wondered what in God's name was coming now. 'Your visit to the bank this morning. Forgive me for intruding. Did you have to borrow money to stay on in Venice?'

He saw her drift immediately and could have laughed at

her wrong-headedness. He had dreaded telling her his true financial position, but surely this was the moment. Her grey eyes were huge with concern and a kind of guilt. At least he could reassure her that he was well-oiled enough to hang on here until the end of her holiday.

He put his hand on her arm. 'I didn't borrow any money, ma-am. I promise you that. I can well afford this holiday and if I'd left here at any time it would have only been to continue it elsewhere.' He looked straight at her to convince her of the truth of his words and then for some reason he couldn't look away. He knew he'd got to tell her the whole truth before it became some sort of subterfuge. 'Listen, Duchess – I have to tell you something—' he began hoarsely.

But abruptly she moved away. 'That's fine, Mr Morrell. I am so relieved about that.'

He caught her arm before she stumbled into the bed, knowing he had frightened her and unable to think how or why.

'This way, Duchess,' he said gently, guiding her to the door. He opened it wide. 'You're quite safe with me.' Even to his own ears that sounded ambiguous.

Her smile trembled a little. 'I'm sure I am, Mr Morrell.'

Abigail wondered what on earth was the matter with her. She was suddenly acting like a self-conscious schoolgirl and doubtless embarrassing poor Mr Morrell. She tried to control the slight shake in her arm as he cupped it in his now familiar hand and guided her into the lift. It was probably her failing sight but when she had her moments of clear vision as she had just now, it was just a little startling. And his brown eyes had been so clear, so unguarded and so extremely close to her own.

She tried to walk a little ahead of him down the hotel steps, but she couldn't quite remember how wide the riva really was, so she had to pause and then the business-like way he got between her and the water and took her arm again was momentarily reassuring.

'I'm afraid I'm on pins today,' she excused herself as they fell easily into their strolling step. 'Sue was like an excited child when Vittorio called for her this morning. If he doesn't propose I'm afraid it will break her heart.'

'And if he does? How will you feel about it then, Duchess?'

'Happy. How could I be otherwise in the face of their complete certainty?' She sighed. 'Of course they'll have to wait. He won't be able to afford to come to England to go through a marriage ceremony just yet. Which, in the circumstances, is a pity.'

He did not pretend to misunderstand her. That was what she liked about him. He had accepted her imminent handicap just as she had and made no attempt to discuss it endlessly and fruitlessly.

He said conventionally, 'Maybe they won't have to wait too long after all, Duchess.'

She accepted his courtesy-comfort. 'Maybe not. And in any case they're young.' She smiled ruefully. 'But, oh dear, Mr Morrell, that kitchen—'

He laughed sympathetically. 'It sure didn't have much in the way of mod cons. But she'll have fun getting it the way she wants it.'

'I know you're right. I'm like a dog worrying a bone. You think he *will* propose? You don't think his lack of money might inhibit him?'

'I'm certain when they come in tonight they will be engaged.'

Again it was just polite comfort but it encouraged Abigail nevertheless. She glanced at him delighted to see him smiling; he honestly wasn't bored by her maternal worries.

'You're in good spirits, Mr Morrell,' she congratulated him.

'I am.' He paused a moment and stared across the glinting water at a view she could not see. 'In an odd way – in spite of what you told me about your eyes, Duchess – I'm happy. I'm sorry if that sounds brutal – I can't explain it.'

She said judiciously, 'I think you're just beginning to realize you're back home, Mr Morrell. It's as simple as that.'

He turned his brown eyes on her. They were as clear as milkless tea. 'You're right, Duchess. I've come home.'

Abigail wondered whether she was imagining a depth of meaning behind his words that wasn't really there. She was very conscious of his arm entwined in hers, of the solidity of him planted between herself and the water. Her hands were beginning to tremble again and the golden autumnal sun was too warm on her face in spite of the shade of the straw hat.

'Shall we sit down and order some tea?' she asked faintly.

He smiled right at her. 'Just around the corner, Duchess,' he said. And again she wondered at his real meaning.

He took his tea in the American way, with no milk and a squeeze of lemon. She watched him while he described the scene around them for her benefit, and she wondered what kind of woman his wife had been to turn this warm man into the guarded, withdrawn person he had been three weeks ago.

She said abruptly, following her own train of thought, 'I wish you could feel some kind of friendship towards your wife, Mr Morrell.'

He stopped in midstream and stared at her in astonishment but without anger.

'What brought Virginia up, for Pete's sake?'

'It doesn't do us good – any of us – to dislike our fellow beings. You are rested now. A different person from the one who sat here not long ago. I understand your bitterness, Mr Morrell. But I don't want to think of you going back to America and feeling it again. I couldn't *bear* that.'

He was silent for a long while. Then he said slowly, 'You really want me to be nice to Ginny? She's thinking of marrying again. He'll be her third husband since me. Younger than her.'

'She's just looking for happiness. We all do it.' Abigail smiled. 'If you help her – encourage her – you'll be happy too.'

He laughed. Not his usual curt bark. A gentle laugh. 'It sounds a bit too easy, Duchess. But OK. I'll wire her congratulations when I get back.' He paused then went on as if the subject had not been changed. 'And when you get back. What happens to you?'

She did not prevaricate. 'My doctor is a friend. He will find a nursing home. Or something similar.' His hand was covering hers and she stayed very still, willing herself not to shake. 'I am not frightened, Mr Morrell. You mustn't worry about me when you get home. I have so much happiness—'

'Isn't there anything that can be done? Really?' he interrupted her roughly.

'Stephen mentioned an operation that has been performed in America. So perhaps, in a few years' time . . .'

She realized that his hand was gripping hers hard. 'Abigail.' His voice was as deep as an organ note as he used her name for the first time. 'Abigail, I have something to tell you.'

Somehow she pulled her hand away, panic fluttering in her throat. What on earth had she done? By asking for this man's help and protection she had forced him into this unnatural intimacy where he thought . . . he imagined . . . be it for reasons of Venetian traditions or simply the chemical reaction set up by dead fish . . . that he had to go further. She recalled the occasions this afternoon when she had felt decidedly peculiar. Almost as if the years had dropped away and she were in love again! And he must have felt the same.

She almost laughed it was so ridiculous. Yet his brown eyes were filling her whole world once more and she felt almost faint. She had to stop him. They were both practically elderly. And in any case he was in no position to take on another . . . anything.

'Mr Morrell,' she said breathlessly. 'Please remember – ships that pass in the night.'

He shook his head, actually grinning. 'My dear, I haven't forgotten the rules. But we could make new ones. You see, Abigail, I want to be honest with you. Just listen for five minutes. Will you do that?'

She stared at him for a long moment, then nodded mutely. Unbidden, a spurt of excitement bubbled somewhere in the region of her diaphragm. Was it possible – just possible – that it could happen again?

CHAPTER SIX

Frank felt like Santa Claus. He didn't know where to begin – which surprise gift to come up with first. He'd wanted to tell her back at the hotel but she'd stopped him; a couple of times she'd stopped him. But not now. Her beautiful smiling mouth was slightly open and her eyes, her wonderful grey eyes . . .

He blurted, 'Abigail – Duchess. I'm Frank Morrell. Head of Morrell Mechanics in Michigan.' He stopped himself, laughing. 'You won't have heard of me of course but I'm well heeled. Well off. I know a guy back home – he's director of a medical research centre – I gave him a donation a while back. Tax relief of course but no skin off his nose – and I think he's the one your doctor told you about. Anyway he'll know someone who can fix up your eyes. You can come back with me next week, Duchess, and I'll make a few phone calls and . . . say, is anything the matter?' She had a still, immobile look; the smile was still there but it was frozen.

She seemed to swallow, then she said breathlessly, 'I don't understand. You're . . . well off? But – your room at the hotel – and you told me you were like us – on a pilgrimage—'

'I was – in a way. And when I likened our circumstances I thought you were landed gentry!' he laughed again trying to convince her. '*You* said I was hard up if you remember, Duchess.'

'But – but you didn't contradict me.'

'It suited my book to have people think I was practically

down and out. You don't know what it's like to have folks crawling round you for the odd hand-out' – she sat up straight and he hurried on – 'that was why your friendship meant so much, don't you see, Duchess?'

She said in the same breathless voice, 'I can't believe that you would be so deceptive, Mr Morrell—'

He was conscious that this time his laugh sounded hearty. He cut it off and reached across the table for her hand. She withdrew it.

He said urgently, 'Listen, Duchess, OK so it takes some getting used to. But otherwise there was no deception. I came to Venice tired, bitter if you like – you know why. I liked the power of being a businessman, manipulating . . . events. When that was gone and all I had was the money I felt sickened. But now I discover that money is useful.'

He grinned at her encouragingly but she didn't smile back.

'It has a power all of its own, is that what you mean, Mr Morrell?' she whispered.

'Sure. Yeah, I guess I do. It can give you back your eyes.'

'Your money.'

'You needn't look like that, Duchess. There's plenty. I can buy you a hospital all to yourself – I can buy you . . .'

'New eyes, Mr Morrell?'

He had never seen her face so full of pain. Even overlooking the Pucci vines she hadn't looked like this.

He said in a low voice, 'All right. No-one can do that my dear. But we can try. Just come back with me next week – tomorrow—'

'You know it is out of the question, Mr Morrell.' She was gathering up her bag and gloves. 'I couldn't possibly accept such generosity—'

'Listen, Abigail. I told you we could make new rules. I've already started to make them. You wondered why I went to the bank this morning. It was to arrange a loan to

Vittorio. That's why I am practically certain he will have proposed to Sue.' He smiled as she relapsed into her seat. 'You see? I can change everything, Duchess – just trust me.'

'You . . . what? You arranged a loan to Vittorio? What do you mean, Mr Morrell – explain, if you please.' She sounded different now, sort of haughty and he felt the prickle of irritation he had felt when he knew her first.

'Nothing to explain,' he replied sharply. 'I know you'd like Sue to be settled quickly. It's obvious if they have to wait it'll be for a long time. So I telephoned the Bank Manager and asked whether Pucci would accept a loan for modernization purposes as I have an American market interested in the sweet stuff he can produce. That's true,' he added defensively. 'It's a lady's wine and Virginia has shares in a company . . .' his voice trailed away as he met her eyes. She was angry. He concluded aggressively, 'Dammit. You wanted me to contact Ginny again—'

She said in a high voice that shook a little, 'How dare you, Mr Morrell! What gives you the right to interfere in my affairs in this high-handed manner?'

She seemed to wait for an answer to this rhetorical question so he snapped, 'The money's sitting there doing nothing! It's an investment goddam it, not an act of charity!'

'So – again – money is your justification? For going behind my back and manipulating my daughter's affairs—'

He tried to sound reasonable, 'Duchess, I couldn't *do* it without money.'

She stared at him for a moment and then seemed to slump in her chair. Her eyes were unfocused and he knew she could barely see him.

'Exactly,' she said quietly. 'Without money, it couldn't be done. I am glad that the help you gave me was without money, Mr Morrell. I thank you for it. It was, of course, beyond price.' She coughed discreetly and concentrated on pulling on a glove. 'Perhaps we should go now. Christine will be back from her swimming expedition.'

He recalled his promise to Christine guiltily. Somehow he felt he was fighting for survival but for the moment his own exasperation supported him. Almost brutally he pulled her up and took her arm.

'You can't see, can you? Not even a grape-haze! This is how it's going to be, Abigail. All the time. And you're too stubborn – too proud – to take my money—'

She interrupted him coldly, 'Kindly take me to the gondola, Mr Morrell, and then leave me. There is nothing more to be said.'

He snorted furiously. 'All right. No more on that subject. But I haven't quite finished.' They began to walk and it was infuriating how easily, how comfortably, they did so. 'You might not like this either but it's nothing to do with me. Christine talked to me the other night – told me about this guy David Blake from back home.' He felt her arm stiffen in his. 'OK, none of my business. But whether it's my business or not – she loves him. Really loves him. And he's here in Venice. He turned up last night.'

She stopped. Beneath the brim of her hat her face lost its frozen look. She said, 'D'you mean he came all the way over here – just to see Christine? Are they together now?'

'Yes. At the lido. She wanted me to tell you—'

'Oh, Mr Morrell,' she turned to him with her old confiding smile. 'I hoped so much that Christine—! He must love her so much! Now, surely you can understand? Now, everything will be all right. I'll explain to Sue about the money and they'll manage somehow and it will all work out just as Grandmamma said.' She actually managed a small laugh. 'Perhaps not quite as she envisaged. Better in a way because neither of them can have any doubts. Christine's young man couldn't wait until she came home and Sue really fell in love with Vittorio when she discovered he was a working farmer. D'you see now, Mr Morrell, how money might *spoil* a – a relationship?'

He stared at her. 'No, I'm afraid I'm not with you there, Duchess. You can't possibly mean you intend to tell Sue about the loan?'

'Of course. It's not fair to let her go on thinking someone wants to invest in the vineyard—'

He lost his temper. 'But that is exactly what someone wishes to do! But someone knows that to make the whole thing public will spoil it for those kids. This way they not only have the money they have the belief of someone in their capabilities!' He felt himself lost among impersonal pronouns. 'Dammit, Duchess. It's none of your business! I loaned that money to Vittorio and as far as I know he's not even engaged to your daughter yet!'

'We both know why you loaned him the money, Mr Morrell.' She was withdrawing again; quietly inexorably she was putting up the barriers. 'If I wasn't going blind you wouldn't dream of making any investments in Italy at all. You would still maintain your incognito. The rules we originally made would still hold good. My . . . disability . . . cannot justify breaking those rules.'

He gripped her arm hard knowing he was probably hurting her and feeling glad about it. 'You're stiff-necked,' he said angrily. 'And pig-headed!' She made no response and in spite of having her arm he knew she was miles away. 'I was right about you in the first place,' he concluded coldly. 'You're patronizing. Now you can't patronize me any longer you don't want to know! OK. That's OK by me. But if you tell Sue – if you so much as bat an eyelid when she breaks the news tonight, I – I'll murder you!'

He handed her into the waiting gondola and for a moment their eyes met. He felt again the sense of sharing a secret with her and then she turned away and settled herself ostentatiously. He was back to his first days in Venice. Alone and frustrated.

Paolo Rezzonico waited in the shadows at one end of the terrace that evening, ready to spring his surprise which was a magnum of champagne nestling in the ice bucket in front of him. He smiled as he watched the party in progress at the special table he had laid on Mr Morrell's instructions. He had worked in many hotels, looked after many people, but he had never met a family that charmed him as the Langleys did. Signora Langley with her hair the colour of Corsican chestnuts before they became marrons glacés, her intense pleasure in every small thing, her white, fluttering hands that were by no means incapable. She was, as Signor Morrelli said, a Duchess. Her two daughters at once echoed and emphasized the elusive quality of quiet joy which she emanated. The dark one chattered and laughed like sunlight on the water; the fair one glimmered more mysteriously . . . moonlight under the Rialto.

Rezzonico smiled. He was becoming poetic. And why not? Signorina Chris was calmly, beautifully happy with her young man from England. And Signorina Sue was about to announce her engagement and was chattering about an unknown benefactor who had made it all possible. Not much escaped Rezzonico and he could guess who the unknown benefactor was. He glanced at Signor Morrelli and was puzzled to see him staring grimly at Signora Langley. He was piling the petits fours on top of each other and he paused, holding an almond button between thumb and forefinger and waiting.

She said, 'That is marvellous, Vittorio. And you have no idea—?'

'None whatsoever, Mrs Langley,' he said, grinning hugely. 'But it means that Sue and I . . . we do not have to wait. You will not mind a very quick wedding, Mrs Langley? At Christmas perhaps?'

There was a tiny pause. Rezzonico noticed the almond button disintegrating between Signor Morrelli's fingers.

Then Signora Langley said, 'There's nothing I'd like better, Vittorio. And if you could come to England—'

'But of course. That is what we want and now – it is possible!' He laughed as he carried the little signorina's fingers to his lips. 'It is like a miracle is it not?'

Signora Langley bent her head for a moment. 'A miracle indeed,' she agreed.

It seemed an opportune moment. Rezzonico wheeled the ice bucket across the terrace. Everyone applauded. Signora Langley said suddenly, 'Mr Morrell – you shouldn't—' and he replied just as quickly, 'I can assure you it's nothing of my doing, Duchess.'

It was Rezzonico's cue. He said, flourishing a napkin, 'It is, as you say, on the house. For my favourite guests!'

They pulled up a chair for him and he sat down between Signora Langley and Signor Morrelli. He smiled as the petits fours toppled on to the table. This was how it must have been in the days of the English Poet, Mr Browning.

It was only a few days later when Abigail knew she would have to tell the girls about her eyes. Without Mr Morrell's help – and somehow she could no longer accept Mr Morrell's help – her day to day living was becoming very difficult. She had pleaded tiredness as much as she could without arousing suspicion. And she could sense David Blake's puzzlement. She did not wish him to think that she was avoiding him. So she corralled the two of them into her room before David squired them to the theatre. She announced that she had something to tell them and they settled meekly into the gilded chairs by the window from where, just over three weeks ago, they had waved to the gondolier.

It might have been a repeat of the evening back home in the parlour when she had first expounded her Venetian plan. She paced slowly between her bed and the door, her hands slightly in front of her. As then she began, apparently irrelevantly, a long time ago when Grandmamma had first been noticed by the Old Prince, and, as then, the girls tried not to fidget while she came to the point.

'I often wondered what she meant when she used the word "emergency".' Abigail paused in her perambulations and a small reminiscent smile curved her mouth. 'After all there was the time at the end of the war when we had no coal and poor Papa had influenza.' She shook her head. 'Then he was allocated a bed in that nice hospital at Eastbourne. So the emeralds stayed in my jewel case.' She touched the door with her finger-tips and turned. 'Obviously I could have sold them a dozen times over when your dear father died. Yet . . . something held me back.' She came to the bed again and faced the girls. 'Then I went to Stephen. Stephen Crawford. And he decided to send me for some tests. It was about then that I first began to feel the time had come.'

The girls stopped twisting their hands. They stared at their mother; she had their complete attention.

'He telephoned me at the shop and wanted me to go to the surgery. I asked him if we could meet outside somewhere and he said it wasn't usual but the park was an easy walk for us both. Of course I guessed right then. But I went to the park anyway because I could go on planning all the time and the flowers were at their best. Besides there was a taxi rank right outside the gates.' Abigail smiled with a return of the sudden excitement she had felt that August day. 'The time really had come, my darlings. I got a taxi and went straight home, asked him to wait, collected the jewels and went to Emerson's. The old man is still alive and I knew he would be absolutely fair with me.'

She stopped speaking. Sue had pushed herself back against her chair and her wrists and knuckles were white with strain; she looked as if she were in the grip of a ghastly nightmare. Christine glanced desperately at her and then leaned forward.

'Mother. Please tell us. You have some dreadful illness. That's it, isn't it?'

Abigail squeezed her eyes shut and then opened them and saw her daughters properly. She knelt before them and took their hands, shaking her head reprovingly at herself.

'Darlings, how could I be so selfish? Of course I'm not going to die! Is that what you thought? I'm as strong as ever – I promise you—'

Both girls gathered her up and for a moment they stood silently, a tightly knit triangle. Then, relaxing a little, they moved to the bed and sat down still holding each other.

Sue tried to laugh. 'What was it then? The emergency?'

Abigail used her most matter-of-fact voice. 'It was simply a defect of vision. Something that comes with old age – yes, you can protest but I am getting *old*, my dears. And I thought if I couldn't keep an eye on you much longer, it was about time there was someone else.' She felt them both tremble against her and put her arms around them and held them – one against each shoulder as she had when they were tiny girls. She was as steady as a rock. 'You see, darlings,' she said softly. 'It suddenly occurred to me. I've never been alone or lonely. First of all there was Papa, then your dear father. Then you two girls. And that's how I want it to be for you.'

Sue said in a high voice, 'You mean . . . you mean . . .'

Abigail interrupted firmly. 'Now darling. There's a lot of unnecessary melodrama attached to the word you're thinking of. Try not to use it—'

'Mother, I'm not with the rep. company now! When you say "defective vision" you mean—'

Christine finished for her in a curiously dry voice. 'You mean you're going blind. Don't you, Mother? You've already had periods of blindness. That's why Mr Morrell has been helping you. You told him so that you could get away with not telling us. You put on a show for our sakes. Haven't you?'

Abigail said quietly, 'I have done what I thought best, Chris. I would do it again. Some people might think I had wasted my legacy. I would not agree. When you have had time to think it over I'm sure you'll see it as I do.' She drew away slightly to look from one to the other. 'We have had such a happy time here together, girls, haven't we? It is a time we will never forget.'

There was another silence. Christine looked over her mother's head and met Sue's brown eyes. Slowly she picked up Abigail's hand and pressed it against her face.

'How could we forget?' she whispered.

Again they were still.

At last Sue said, 'Now will you let us take care of you for a change please, darling?' Her voice wobbled ominously but she kept her tone brisk and cheerful. 'We'll change our reservations for tomorrow and see Stephen immediately we get back. I think another opinion—'

Amazingly Abigail began to laugh. 'Darling, we will do no such thing. Have you forgotten Vittorio is coming on Friday to say goodbye? And David must have his full week. It is for David's sake I am telling you all this.' She patted them both affectionately. 'There is nothing Stephen or any other doctor can do, my dears. Try to accept that. It will distress me unutterably if you insist on me going from specialist to specialist. You both know that Stephen has explored every avenue, he is our friend. You can help me by forgetting this – don't follow me around or worry when I rest. We've got another two days here and we can enjoy them.' She smiled. 'Can't we?'

Blue eyes and brown looked at her wide-eyed for a moment.

Then Christine said, 'Of course we can, Mother. Can't we, Sue?'

And Sue echoed tremulously, 'I'd like to see anyone stop us.'

Frank was angry. He seethed and burned with an anger and resentment he had not known for years – perhaps had never known. He told himself he loathed Abigail and all she stood for, yet there was part of him that – doubtless from sheer force of habit – worried over her and wondered how she was fixing her hair and her hat and whether she'd fall in the goddam water that day. Then there was his pride to contend with. He freely admitted that had taken a helluva knock but he was also damned if he was going to let Abigail or the girls or their boyfriends see it. To ignore Abigail yet put up a pretence that everything was just the same, was a difficult, irritating, yet all-consuming job. He resumed his painting trips with Dino and joined the Langleys for dinner and told himself he was enjoying embarrassing the Duchess by his presence.

And then, halfway through the week, it became obvious that their secret was a secret no longer. The others knew about the Duchess' imminent blindness. Their gaiety did not lessen, rather it increased. David Blake suddenly stopped squiring Christine so assiduously and walked with the Duchess as if he were treading glass. Frank tried to summon up a cynical pleasure. So . . . she hadn't been able to manage without him, she'd had to tell the girls and Blake. And none of them could cope with the situation as he had. They couldn't accept it and make it unobtrusive. She was probably missing him.

He had convinced himself of this when Sue appeared

along the riva one morning as he was setting up his easel in line with the Rialto. She was wearing the slacks in which she had arrived and her dark hair was brushed forward somehow so that she reminded him of a young boy. She greeted Dino easily and then stood fidgeting by Frank's stool obviously with something important on her mind.

He ignored her while he mixed a gaudy blue and started splodging in a sky. Then he said, 'You want to ask me something? Tell me something?' He grinned up at her. 'I know. Dino's already done that one. I'm no artist.'

She did not smile. 'We wanted to thank you, Mr Morrell.' She glanced at Dino as he chased a possible Garibaldi. 'I don't know how to say it without sounding ingratiating . . . if that's the word.'

He felt a surge of hope. Had he won? After all, had she broken down? 'Your mother has changed her mind? She'll let me help?'

Sue looked surprised. 'How do you mean? You do help. All the time. What more could you do?'

He squirted some cobalt on to his palette viciously. 'Nothing. What do you want to thank me for, little girl?'

'Well. Helping Mother. Of course. She couldn't have managed without you and she didn't want to tell us until the holiday was nearly over. You know how she is.'

'Yes. I know.'

'But – but you see . . . when she told us about her eyes and you being so marvellous and everything . . . she mentioned that we need not worry about you any more. That you were . . . sort of . . . rich.'

'That is so,' he said woodenly, concentrating on the worm of cobalt trailing across the palette.

'Yes. Well. Perhaps I'm wrong about this, Mr Morrell. But it occurred to Vittorio and me . . .' she hesitated for a moment, then as Dino turned back she finished with a rush, 'It occurred to us that perhaps you were the person who had invested in the vineyard.'

'Me?' Frank heard himself laughing. 'What in heaven's name would I do with a slice of vineyard, young Sue?' He turned his head and yelled at Dino, 'Where's the Prussian blue, boy? This sky's all colours of the rainbow!'

She waited quietly while he engineered more commotion, then she said, 'If it was, we'd like you to know how grateful, how very grateful—'

He interrupted desperately. 'I guess your "unknown benefactor" – as you call him – is a man who knows a good thing when he sees one. In which case he ought to be thanking you.' He watched Dino sorting the tubes of paint and knew desolately that there was only one thing to do. He couldn't win here, they were too strong for him with their tight, loyal little family circle. 'Actually I'm glad you happened along, honey. I have to leave tonight. Unexpectedly. So in case I don't run into you at dinner, say goodbye for me, huh?'

'You're leaving tonight?' Sue and Dino spoke together like a perfectly rehearsed chorus. They wore identical looks of dismay.

'You can go to school tomorrow, young man,' Frank said sternly to the one. And to the other, 'You're leaving yourself on Friday. Had you forgotten?' He stared at her trying to imprint her image on his mind. 'Look after that mother of yours, OK? Arrange the wedding while she can still see it. And wish Chris and David all the best from me.'

He turned to his easel dismissingly and gave his ear to Dino's wails. He felt Sue's hand on his shoulder and did not turn round. Then it was gone.

'Come on,' he said to Dino. 'We've done all we can do to the Rialto. Let's go buy a present for your bambino. Maybe one for you too. Then you can help me pack and that should be that.'

He couldn't help feeling cheered by Dino's excitement. Slowly his hand closed over the English ten pence piece in his pocket. Sure . . . she had her own kind around her now. She didn't need him after all. He was an outsider again.

CHAPTER SEVEN

It was no better when he reached home. He hadn't phoned Steve so no-one would be expecting him. He'd be like Ossie White who turned up at the office after he'd retired because there was nothing else for him to do. Ossie was lucky. He'd died a couple of months after retirement.

He stared out of the cab as he drove to the factory from the airport. Already it was Fall back here and the Venetian summer seemed a long way off. There were Halloween masks in the shop windows and the strings of kids waiting for school buses wore bright scarves and mitts. He grinned wryly. He'd never noticed things like that before . . . before Abigail.

He remembered to thank the driver too before he hurried through the plate-glass doors of the executive block and took the elevator to his office. Everything looked the same. More than that, it sounded the same. The low hum that came from the factory in spite of the sound-proofing always seemed to Frank to be synonymous with efficiency. So . . . Steve had kept going that indefinable rhythm of Morrell's without the Old Man. Frank grunted. It was what he'd wanted wasn't it?

He opened the door of his office and stopped on the threshold suddenly unsure of his whereabouts. Steve sat at his desk, perfectly at home, one hand propping his dark head, the other holding a telephone to his ear. It was natural that during his father's absence he should use this office, but Frank felt the ground shift under his feet. He'd thought to go to earth here like some animal; ease himself slowly into some particular project so that there'd be no question of taking over from Steve. No possible . . . confrontation.

Steve looked at the open door and rose as far as the telephone cable would let him, astonishment and something else written large on his face. Apprehension?

'Dad! By all that's holy—! Why didn't you let me know—' he went on in a series of short explosions then spoke into the receiver, 'Hang on, Maxwell. Dad. Sales on this line. D'you want to talk to them?'

Frank felt weary. He shook his head. 'Carry on, son,' he said. 'I'll take the witness stand.' It was a joke from way back and established that he did not intend to do any usurping. Nevertheless as he sat down gingerly in the visitor's chair he felt a stranger in his own domain. Maybe the Venetian holiday was simply going to prove there was no place for him. Anywhere.

Steve flicked a switch. 'No more calls please, Miss Parker. Black coffee and hamburgers as soon as you like.' He looked up. 'Could you manage a steak, Dad?'

Frank shook his head again grateful that Steve had thought of breakfast. That would give them something to do for, say, half an hour. Then what?

Steve leaned forward and clapped him on the shoulder and then sat back asking him the usual questions about his flight, the weather, if the old country had changed much in forty years. Frank answered automatically. Miss Parker came in with a tray and there was silence.

'Well . . . say . . .' Steve looked at a loss. 'You heard, I guess?'

'Heard?' Frank drank some wonderful American coffee and wondered what Abigail was doing now.

'About Smith – Sprinter. I told them to clam up – not to get in touch with you. I would have gone through with the closure, Dad, just as you wanted. But some eager guy phoned, huh? Don't get me wrong – I'm glad to see you. But I could have dealt with it.'

Frank forced himself to concentrate. 'I can see that, Steve. You're doing wonders – *have* done wonders.' He cleared his throat knowing he was shutting the door on himself. 'I should have let you take over before this.'

Steve grinned, surprised. 'Say, Dad. Thanks. But . . . you're here.'

'I wanted to come home. That's all. Nobody's phoned or cabled a word about Smith – Sprinter. That's your baby anyway.'

There was another silence and a kind of easement began between the two men. They finished their coffee.

Steve said hesitantly, 'Matter of fact, I could do with your advice about Sprinters. It wasn't quite so straightforward as it seemed.'

'Go ahead. I'm listening.'

'Well.' Steve got up and began to pace the office. 'We wrote to the guy we put in as manager. Told him we wanted out and to sound out possible buyers. He put us in touch with British European and then got out fast. We started negotiations direct with B and E. Then we get a letter signed by all the employees at Sprinters – twenty-four signatures – saying they want to take over the firm themselves.'

'Ha!' Frank snorted a laugh. It didn't strike him as ridiculous. Rather as gallant. Somehow . . . somehow like Abigail. Keeping the flag flying.

Steve misunderstood. 'Damned silly I know. Our money would be tied up for months – we'd probably never see it again. Messy.' He paused by the desk and pulled a letter from a folder. 'I told them so, of course. We had this back. Same twenty-four signatures. Telling us we're being unreasonable, demanding a personal interview with me. Pointing out there will be a certain number of redundancies if B and E take over and threatening us with bad publicity. Pathetic, isn't it?'

Frank read and nodded. 'Pathetic,' he agreed. But with a kind of admiration. He looked up. 'It wouldn't be the first time that workers have taken over their own firm. Now and then it works.'

'Sure. But they need a guiding hand. Look at that letter—'

'Maybe they know someone.' He read the letter again. It was, after all, something he could do. 'Let me look at the production and sales figures again, Steve. No, I won't stay here. I'll take them back to the apartment. If you could call round tonight we could talk again. See if it's a viable proposition.' He stood up with some of his old energy. Some of the helpless frustration he'd felt over the last week dropped away and he paused, gnawing his lip. 'Say, Steve. D'you remember that contribution the firm made a few years back to the Carmel Medical Foundation?'

Steve looked puzzled but nodded.

'Can you remember the name of that medic who was researching eye deterioration? Crazy name. Tall, thin—'

'Shepherd. Lancelot Shepherd. He's a leading authority as a matter of fact.' Steve looked sharply concerned. 'Is something the matter with your eyes, Dad? Is that why you've come home?'

It was an unexpected comfort to have Steve anxious over him. Frank smiled. 'No, son. It's someone I met in Venice. A woman.'

He slept most of the day and woke at five, showered, wrapped himself in his bathrobe and got down to the Smith – Sprinter figures.

At nine o'clock his personal call came through from Doctor Shepherd.

'Morrell? Frank Morrell?' The voice sounded cautious. 'I remember meeting you at the opening of the new lab don't I? Morrell's Mechanics.' The voice became warmer remembering the donation. 'What can I do for you, Frank?'

'Something in your line.' Frank tightened his grip on the receiver realizing the enormity of his request. 'I need your help.'

'Ah.' The voice was professional now; on safe ground. 'A physical?'

'No. Not quite so simple. It's a friend of mine. Eye trouble. A detached retina among other things.'

Interest quickened imperceptibly along the humming line.

'Optical surgery. My line all right. Send him along, Frank. I'll be glad to have a look at him and consult with his own doctor.'

'I told you it wasn't simple.' Frank swallowed. 'It's a woman for one thing. Not young. My age probably. And she refuses help.' He cleared his throat. 'Sorry, Doc. We have to work out a way of doing this without her knowing I'm back of it.'

There was a pause. Shepherd said at last, 'I can work through her own doctor if she's seeing him regularly. Look at her notes. Then the suggestion could come from him – he might be able to talk her into it. Do you know the name of her doctor?'

'Crawford. Doctor Stephen Crawford.' Frank counted three and added quickly, 'She lives in England. Near London. And she won't come to the States so . . .' his voice became strong. 'Look, Doctor, I'll double my last donation – anything. Only have a look at her – see what you can do. She's going blind and just accepting the fact – it's incredible—'

'Hold on, Frank.' Shepherd's voice was definitely warm. 'I don't need any bribes to take a vacation in England. Though of course the Foundation's research programme can always do with funds.' He coughed and went on hurriedly, 'Suppose I fix up a lecture at the Optic Research Institute in London early next month? Could you be in touch with Doctor Crawford by then?'

It all became suddenly and beautifully clear to Frank. 'Sure. I'll go see him . . . Lance.'

Steve arrived a little later pushing before him a trolley of food.

'Did you eat dinner? I thought not. Neither did I. There's steak here and some ripe cheese and coffee is on the way.'

'Great.' For the first time in days Frank felt hungry. He pushed the Sprinter file to one side. 'Steve, maybe I haven't told you this lately. You are a good boy.'

Steve actually flushed as he passed a plate and napkin. Then he said with difficulty, 'Dad. I just want to say . . . I'm sorry the way I spoke to you after the Board meeting that day. I was irritable and depressed about the Sprinter business but that was no excuse to take it out on you.'

'I'm glad you did, Steve. It was true, every word. I didn't think Morrell's could run without the Old Man. I didn't think you'd be able to cope alone.' He looked up from his food and grinned. 'I wanted to be proved wrong, but I was so used to being right that I wanted it that way as well.' He laughed shortly. 'I was a crazy mixed-up old man, Steve.'

Steve said tentatively, 'And something happened. This woman you met – she helped sort things out?'

Frank hadn't thought of it quite like that. He'd offered to help Abigail and been turned down. He hadn't considered she had helped him.

He nodded slowly. 'Yes. I guess that's it, Steve. She gave me a new set of priorities.' He stared at his son. 'They must be the right ones too, Steve. You and I have never talked like this before.'

'Maybe we lacked opportunity, Dad,' Steve began defensively.

'No. We had opportunities. Plenty of them. But we were too busy worrying about our own positions. I was concerned for the firm – who was big enough to be boss. You wanted to assert what you'd learned in business college.' He sighed. 'The Duchess showed me that people are what matter. What makes them happy or sad. When you thought I was ill this morning you stopped being the big executive. When I accepted that you had always been capable of running Morrell's I became a proper father.' He grinned again. 'That's why we can talk, Steve. We're talking like father and son, not like two VIPs jockeying for position.'

Steve grinned back. 'Hey. She was quite a woman. And a Duchess?'

Frank grunted. 'Not quite. That was my name for her. She's Abigail Langley. Mrs Abigail Langley.' He sat back. 'She's a widow in her fifties – looks like Royalty – two lovely daughters, both head over heels in love with nice guys. She's happy about that. Everything has worked out nicely for her except one thing.'

'She's ill. You want Doc Shepherd to look at her.'

'She's going blind, Steve. Losing her sight. She had periods of blindness while she was in Venice but she wouldn't admit it to anyone but me.' He grunted again. 'I was privileged because she thought I was poor.' He stood up and went to the wide window overlooking the city. 'When she found out I could pay for an operation she dropped me as fast as she knew how. And boy, was that fast!'

Steve said blankly, 'I don't get it. Was she scared of surgery? And if so why have you been in touch with Shepherd?'

Frank turned and looked at his son. A few hours ago

he could have told no-one of how he had been turned down flat. Now it was different. He began to talk about Abigail . . .

Stephen Crawford, watching the two unhappy and frustrated girls sitting opposite him in his surgery, thought how proud his old friend Ambrose Langley would be of his daughters right now. They had been arguing with him fruitlessly, refusing to accept the inevitable, hinting very delicately that he was past it and should have consulted another opinion.

'My dears, I left no stone unturned, I promise you. Not in this country anyway. There has been an operation performed in America and I told your mother of it but she refused to consider it.'

Sue said in agony, 'She could have used the money from the emeralds to go there—'

'She wouldn't have done that.' Christine covered her sister's hand with her own. 'You know she wanted to take us to Venice for many reasons.'

Stephen put his finger-tips together carefully. 'As a matter of fact, Christine, I have been approached by a Doctor Shepherd from the Carmel Foundation in Michigan. You probably do not know, but part of their research programme is into eye deterioration. This man – Doctor Shepherd – is anxious to see your mother's notes and discuss her case with the consultant and myself.'

Sue and Christine could contain themselves no longer.

'You mean there's some hope?' Sue had pulled Christine up with her. 'Why didn't you tell us this immediately? When can he see her – have you made an appointment?'

Christine breathed, 'Stephen, how can we thank you?'

'Don't. Not at the moment.' Stephen straightened his hands warningly. 'Look girls, perhaps I should not have mentioned this. Not yet anyway. The letter I have received was very guarded, naturally so. No doctor dare commit himself on a case he hasn't even seen. But he is a specialist in his field and he wants to see your mother. Further than that we must not allow ourselves to go.'

Gradually the sisters subsided, but their eyes remained wide and expectant with hope and questions. It was Sue who came up with the only one Stephen might be able to answer.

'How did Doctor . . . Shepherd . . . hear about Mother?' She glanced at Christine. 'Mr Morrell came from Michigan, didn't he? D'you think he could be behind this?'

Stephen said blandly, 'Your mother mentioned an American who helped her a great deal while she was on holiday. Surely he would have discussed anything like this – has she said anything?'

'No.' Christine looked back at her sister. 'They didn't even say goodbye. You don't suppose they quarrelled about this, do you?'

Again Stephen intervened. 'It's hardly likely. And it would take more than money to move Doctor Shepherd. No, I believe he's lecturing at the Optical Institute and I daresay the consultant mentioned this case.' He put his finger-tips together once more with great care. 'However, it might be better not to mention where Doctor Shepherd comes from. In fact leave Mr Morrell's name right out of it.'

Christine nodded. 'We will.' She got up to leave and added doubtfully to Sue, 'But she'll know all the same.'

Stephen closed the door after them. It all seemed very underhand and unnecessary to him but the small dynamic American had assured him that the only people who could persuade Abigail to undergo this examination were the girls.

In the darkened room Abigail stared into the piercing needle of light. Beyond, she could just make out the outline of the surgeon's face and the gentle touch of his hands. Standing calmly by her side Stephen Crawford gave the situation a lifeline of reality.

The surgeon said conversationally, 'Detached retinas are funny things, Mrs Langley. Sometimes you can nail 'em down, sometimes you can't. The opacity of the corneal cells requires first of all a graft. It can be done – whether it will work is another thing.'

Stephen's voice came tranquilly from her right side. 'We have nothing to lose have we, Abbie?'

She made a vain effort to stop the landslide which had begun when Christine and Sue burst in with their news a week ago.

'It must be an expensive business, Stephen, and as you know—'

'As *you* know, my dear, the Foundation for which Doctor Shepherd works looks on this as very valuable research in the field. In other words, Abbie, there are not many patients who are willing to submit to experimental surgery.'

Doctor Shepherd had moved away. He said mildly, 'It's not quite so hit and miss as you make it sound, Crawford. It has been done before – and successfully.'

'Also unsuccessfully,' Stephen said dryly.

'In the final analysis it is always the patient's own resistance which is the deciding factor of course. This is so in all operations.'

Abigail said quickly, 'Of course. I absolutely understand the position, Doctor. I have complete faith in your ability and in the chance of a cure which you are offering. But . . .' she hesitated, unable to voice her real reluctance. Perhaps it was outrageous of her to suspect Mr Morrell.

The curtains were twitched aside and Abigail felt the world returning. Stephen rubbed his hands with unusual briskness.

'Then that seems to be that, Abbie. Doctor Shepherd

would like you to go into the Clinic as soon as possible of course so—'

'Tomorrow would be as good a time as any,' murmured the surgeon already washing his hands at the basin.

'Tomorrow?' She felt a flutter of panic. 'I'll have to see if Sue can look after the shop. And there's Mrs Jenner's fitting on Thursday. I don't know whether . . .'

'Tomorrow will be fine. I've talked to Sue and Christine and they can cope with anything that comes along. In fact they would like to – they feel so helpless, Abbie. I'll come for you myself, it's my day off. We can talk going up in the car. No good to have too much thinking time.'

Abigail looked vaguely around the familiar surgery. She wasn't sure what she wanted any more. Both girls had made it plain to her that they were not going to be happy to get married and leave her in a residential home. And she refused to consider the alternative – living with them in turn. So this offer seemed nothing short of miraculous. Except that Abigail remembered all too clearly where the last family miracle had come from.

They gave her no food that first day and the following morning she had a tablet and let them help her into a theatre gown and scrape her mass of hair into a cap. Then there was an injection. She lay limp and supine, her personality retreating from her physical body. Vaguely she was aware of Doctor Shepherd's face smiling into hers.

'I like to see my patients before I scrub up,' he told her briskly. 'Physically we shall be very close during the next hour. We must be mentally in tune as well.'

She liked that and smiled at him. Her tongue seemed large in her mouth but she managed to whisper, 'Thank you, doctor. I just wish . . . I just wish . . .'

He was alert, bending over her, taking her hand reassuringly in both of his. 'What do you wish, Mrs Langley?

Please let there be no reservations now. It is important that you co-operate fully.'

'I wish this . . . this . . . wasn't just an act of charity.'

He said smoothly, 'Doctor Crawford explained to you that the Foundation frequently finance—'

She murmured, 'I know about Mr Morrell.'

There was a moment of stillness. Abigail could see the face so close to her own making its decision. Then the doctor said slowly, 'I am glad.' His eyes crinkled into a smile. 'I hate deception.'

She could feel herself slipping backwards. 'It isn't right,' she breathed urgently. 'Charity . . . charity is so cold without love . . .'

The doctor's face came closer. His eyes were suddenly full of understanding. His grasp on her hand seemed to be holding her up as if she were floating in warm water.

'I see. I understand now. Listen, Abigail. Can you hear me?' She lowered her eyelids and with an effort of will lifted them again. 'Good. Some people have to learn to love. They can learn through charity. But if their charity is refused, the learning stops.' She heard him take a deep breath as if this were a moment of crisis. 'Are you prepared to block Frank Morrell's ability to love?'

She looked at him. In that moment she knew he would not lie to her, not even for the sake of the operation. She saw her own life spreading behind her like the wake of a ship, flowing with love. Love that had never been dammed back in spite of death and poverty. Until now.

Very gradually her hold on the doctor's hand slackened and she found she could float on her own. She closed her eyes and without effort her mouth curved in a smile. The last obstacle had gone.

Lancelot Shepherd who had been named for a chivalrous knight, straightened his back still staring at the nun-like face on the bed. Her skin reminded him of dried rose petals, and the crow's feet which extended her eyes as she slept were indelible signs of age. Yet he knew with a kind of excitement that the knack of falling in love never died with time. And it was always beautiful.

Frank let Steve help him out of the hearse-like limousine which was the only chauffeur-driven car they seemed to hire out in England. The Smith – Sprinter factory looked like nothing he had expected, a red-brick building among other red-brick buildings, all apparently separate concerns. No gates leading to parking lots, just a door with a brass plate inscribed 'Smith – Sprinter Cars'. They left the chauffeur to drive the hearse some place and knocked on the door. Steve grinned and said, 'Great, eh Dad? Hasn't changed since old Ned Smith came here at the turn of the century.' Frank grunted. He had spent the last three weeks doing a strenuous sight-seeing tour of London and Coventry besides pressuring Stephen Crawford and liaising with Lance Shepherd. He was tired and strangely confused. Nobody could honestly like a place where it rained all the time and service and comfort were foreign words; but maybe you didn't have to like a place to fall for it.

The door was opened by a middle-aged woman who ushered them down a passage nervously.

'I just type and make tea,' she said as if she needed an excuse. 'The men are waiting for you in the canteen. We didn't realize you would both be coming.'

It had been Frank's idea. He had been determined not to tread on Steve's toes, not to jeopardize their new relationship in any way. Now he saw that the two of them might comprise a threat.

He said easily, 'I had other business here anyway. And it seemed like a good idea.' He kept smiling at the typist-tea-maker until at last she smiled back.

'In here.' She opened a door into a large room smelling of heavy oil and steamy food. The room was lit by a skylight on which the incessant English rain pattered relentlessly. Along the centre a dozen or more men were ranged around a trestle table. They wore the grim look of a committee.

The typist said breathlessly, 'Mr Morrell. And . . . Mr Morrell. That is, Mr Frank Morrell and his son, Mr Steven Morrell.'

The men looked up, surprised at first and then grimmer than ever. Frank could feel their antagonism like a solid wall across the canteen. At one time it would have brought out his own stubborn aggression. Now he wanted to gain their confidence.

On the counter a row of empty mugs announced that the men had just had something to drink. Frank's stomach craved good coffee but he said briskly, 'Can we have some tea? And sandwiches maybe. Your motorways are very good but we didn't stop on the way.' He sensed Steve's surprise and clapped him on the shoulder purposely misunderstanding. 'I got used to tea when I was on holiday. It has a very settling effect.'

A short man at the top of the table, obviously the speaker for the group, rose uncertainly.

'The canteen staff, well, we sent them off. So's we could be private-like. We thought you'd rather have it that way.' There were one or two assenting sounds from the others and a few hostile glances to go with them.

The typist said, '*I'll* make some tea.' She bustled behind the counter, an unexpected ally for the Morrells. 'I quite agree there's nothing like a nice cup of tea.' She found clean mugs and lifted the heavy enamel teapot. 'Mr Simmonds – Albert Simmonds that is – is our Works Manager.' She glanced from Frank to Steve and then back to Frank. 'Of course the man you put in charge left when your letter arrived.'

'*My* letter,' corrected Steve. '*My* father was on vacation during the negotiations with British European.'

'He's just come along to make the final chop has he?' said Albert Simmonds belligerently. 'Thought it'd be more final from the head man himself.'

Steve turned defensively but Frank said, 'You could put it like that. Or you could look on me as an arbitrator. My son is busy running the American side of the business. I'm semi-retired.' He felt the temperature thaw slightly as he took his time over his tea. Then he let his gaze wander over the roof and down the unpainted walls. 'You don't seem to have done too well for yourselves in the way of off-duty accommodation.'

If he hoped to bring out any dissension among the men with this provocative remark he was disappointed. A general babble of resentment was eventually controlled and voiced by Bert Simmonds.

'We been too busy turning out Sprinters to worry about the canteen,' he snapped. 'And that isn't easy when the bosses are thousands of miles away and don't know anything about local shortages and put us in a manager who spends more time playing golf than—'

Frank held up his hand in a gesture of peace. 'OK, OK, Mr Simmonds. You've told me what I wanted to know. The fact that Sprinters are losing money has nothing to do with the workers. Is that what you are saying?'

'Would we want to take over the business ourselves if that was so?' Simmonds glanced around the table, rounding up agreeing murmurs. 'Sprinters are never going to make a lot of money.' He looked Frank in the eye. 'But it will pay our wages and keep turning out cars. That's what we want. We don't want to mass produce cars like the B.E. people do.'

Frank smiled and drew up a chair to the trestle table. The aggression was in the open now and consisted of a long-smouldering resentment which seemed to have a basis in hard fact. He recalled the financial figures. Could they be accounted for by lack of guidance – by sheer lack of interest?

Steve said, 'We never thought we'd make a fortune out of you. It was a prestige thing mostly. But you must realize we cannot totally subsidize you –'

'We don't want any more subsidies.' A voice said angrily. 'We're not asking you to keep the company. We want independence.'

Bert Simmonds added, 'We need a holding-off period. We can't buy you out immediately, of course, but if we could have time.'

Steve used his father's words unconsciously, 'Time is money, Mr Simmonds.'

The resentment flared again. 'Money isn't everything! If you sell us to British European the Sprinter will never be the same. You're in the car business so you should know that. How would you like it if Morrell's got swallowed up by one of the Detroit concerns?'

Steve was silent and Frank said quietly, 'We wouldn't.' He looked round at the tense faces surrounding him and sipped his tea until the atmosphere simmered down again. Then he went on slowly, 'We like the idea of you running your own firm. But we don't see much chance of success. Sorry.'

There was a startled moment while the men accepted they had Frank on their side, then protests broke out at his pessimism. However, the protest was not universal and Frank noticed that Simmonds said not a word.

He cleared his throat. 'I have a proposal to make. It's news to my son too.' He glanced almost warningly at Steve. 'It's this. You need an outsider. A business manager. No, OK – not like the guy we gave you last time. Someone who knows the car trade inside out and will be willing to step down when you're on your feet.' He looked round challengingly. 'I could do that job. I could stay during the holding-off period anyway. And I wouldn't need pay either.' He put his mug on the table. 'I'm no philanthropist, mind you. This is a way of making sure we get something out of this whole business. I shall be safeguarding Morrell's investment if you like, and when you've made enough to buy us out . . . I'll go.' He stared at Simmonds defiantly. 'I won't take away one inch of the Sprinter character and I'm a damned good businessman. Take it or leave it.'

He could feel Steve stiffen by his side. The silence was electric. Simmonds stared and then looked round the table. One or two of the men cleared their throats. No-one seemed to be breathing.

At last Simmonds said portentously, 'We should have to have discussions on that suggestion of course but—'

'We haven't got a lot of choice really have we?' someone said with a grin in his voice. 'What happens if it won't work?'

Frank said, 'It'll work. But you haven't got much to lose have you?'

Simmonds said, 'We'd have to have a manager, that's for sure. And I'm going to have my hands full with production . . . it's more than generous of you, Mr Morrell.'

'Nothing of the sort,' Frank snapped. 'I've told you, we don't want to see our money wasted.'

The atmosphere suddenly relaxed. The typist walked round the counter with an enamel tray of tea. Frank risked a look at Steve and realized with a shock that his son was having difficulty in holding back his laughter. To cover him he delved in his brief case and spread out half a dozen copies of his own notes on the Sprinter figures over the past year.

'I'd like you to take a look at these, gentlemen, and give me your comments. You'll see your production costs are up, selling figures down. I want to hear reasons, not blame. Those of you who worked for Ned Smith must have made comparisons between past profits and present-day losses and I want to hear your conclusions.'

'Another cup of tea, Mr Morrell?' murmured a voice behind him.

He smiled upwards. 'That would be kind of nice, Miss – er – Mrs—'

'Miss Elizabeth Parker. Everyone calls me Betty.'

'Thanks a lot, Betty,' Frank said.

Driving back through a grey damp afternoon, Steve ribbed him in a way he'd never done before. It seemed to finalize the relationship of the two men; father and son; companions. Frank grinned quietly, snorted now and then and enjoyed it.

'When you had the cheek to put it over as a hard business deal – safeguarding our assets! And all the time you wanted to do them a favour – you wanted them to succeed!'

Frank stuck to his guns. 'I'm no do-gooder, Steve, and you know it. If they were going down the drain I'm damned if I'd go with them. I've looked at the facts and figures until I can recite them aloud and I believe they can do it. Besides . . .' he looked sheepish. 'I'd like to be in England over the next few months.'

'Sure, Dad. And you want to keep out of my hair back home too, don't you?' Steve hit his shoulder. 'You don't have to prove anything to me, Dad. And thank God I don't have to prove anything to you any more. OK?'

Frank made a sound, half-grunt, half-snort. 'OK,' he said.

Steve went on tentatively, 'So . . . if there are no more battles . . . with anyone . . . why don't you give Lancelot Shepherd a ring and then go and see your Duchess?'

Frank stared out of the window at the outskirts of London. When had he realized that he loved Abigail? Had it come to him gradually over the last few weeks as he carefully engineered a clear path for her operation? He didn't know. He had certainly fallen in love some time during those magical crazy three weeks in Venice and had known fully the misery of rejection during the fourth week. But he'd been stupid, too self-centred to recognize it. He wondered fleetingly whether he could have done something about it if he had recognized it in time. One thing was certain, he could do nothing now. To visit Abigail would be as good as demanding payment . . . he might be from a different world, but he saw that OK.

As if reading his thoughts, Steve said softly, 'She must love you, Dad. She wouldn't have accepted any of it – Lance or her daughters couldn't have pushed her into a thing – if she hadn't loved you.'

Frank said, 'She didn't know it was from me, Steve. I made damned sure my tracks were covered.'

'You told me she was intelligent. And . . . intuitive?'

'So she was.'

'Then she knew. Stop fooling yourself, Dad. Put yourself in her position. Of course she knew.' Steve gave a fair imitation of his father's impatient snort. 'For God's sake go and see her, Dad. Just *see* her. What the hell's the good of getting yourself a job in England if you can't see her now and then?'

Frank looked at the speeding suburbs again. OK, so why had he landed himself in Coventry for the next six months if it wasn't to see Abigail?

'Hells bells,' he said violently. 'I'll see her tonight – and if she doesn't like it she can . . . go jump in a lake somewhere!'

Steve's laughter somehow reminded him of Christine and Sue when their mother said something perfectly reasonable.

In spite of himself his voice shook when he got through to Shepherd's hotel.

'I haven't wanted to make a nuisance of myself but naturally I'm anxious to know . . .'

Shepherd sounded soothing. 'Mrs Langley underwent the operation several days ago and the bandages came off on Monday. It's early to be over-optimistic but she has complete vision.'

'No periods of blindness at all?'

'Not so far. I shall be examining her again in a few days' time but I am fairly confident that she will continue to improve.'

Frank said bluntly, 'Lance, I'm going to see her.'

If he expected opposition he was wrong. 'A good idea,' the professional voice said. 'There's nothing like a visit from an old friend.'

It was late but he found a florist's open and bought some late roses. Holding them like a shield in front of him he took a taxi to the Clinic and hurried into the foyer. Christine and Sue recognized him instantly in spite of the barrier.

'Mr Morrell!'

It was Sue. And there was no hesitation in the greeting; he could have sworn she was delighted to see him.

Christine was close behind her, smiling her pleasure. 'We wondered when you'd come. How can we ever thank you?'

Frank heard himself stammer, 'You know? How did you know? Does . . . does *she* know?'

Sue gurgled a laugh very like her mother's. 'How could we know? After helping Vittorio so quietly we knew it was like you to be self-effacing.'

'Mother couldn't have accepted it any other way, Mr Morrell,' Christine said swiftly. 'It was wonderful and tactful and—'

Frank interrupted. 'How is she? Will she mind me coming? What will she say?'

Sue was laughing openly. 'She is fine. And we don't know whether she'll mind or what she'll say. You'll find out though, won't you?'

Christine added, 'She tells us that each day it is as if another muslin veil is pulled from her eyes. Maybe . . . maybe she is seeing everything more clearly now, Frank.'

Frank swallowed knowing that he had already been accepted into the family. 'Maybe. And thanks . . .' he took a step then turned back. 'How are those young men of yours?'

Both girls spoke at once. 'Wonderful!'

The ward sister showed him to a side room and he knocked before his courage could desert him.

'Come in!' It was Abigail's voice, low and clear with that elusive quality of excitement that had so intrigued him in Venice.

He opened the door. She was sitting in a chair by the window, her back towards him. It was already dark but the curtains were wide on a view of street lights and stars. Her chestnut hair was spread on her shoulders and for the first time he could see shadows of grey there. It made her vulnerable, as her blindness had done in Venice, and Frank felt tears in his throat.

He cleared it and said hoarsely, 'Abigail.'

She turned, surprised but not shocked at hearing her name. Then before she could control her face, a smile of pure welcome lit her huge grey eyes. She said nothing. Just looked back at him. In that long moment their love was accepted. It was there between them, an inescapable fact.

He said again, 'Abigail.' The name was wonderfully familiar to him. He smiled slightly. 'I'm so glad . . . so happy . . . about your eyes. You can see properly, can't you?'

She nodded slowly. Then she stood up and came towards him to take the flowers from his outstretched hands. She bent her head and her hair fell forward among the petals.

'Can you see too, Frank?' she whispered.

He touched her hand. 'I think so. I know I can only live half a life without you, Abigail. Dear Abigail. I love you very much.'

Her smile was wonderful. It warmed him likc the September sun in Venice. She said softly, 'I could never have accepted your gift, my dear, if I hadn't suddenly been quite certain of that.' The smile became a laugh with a hint of mischief in it. 'After all, Mr Morrell, a lady never accepts a gift from a gentleman unless his intentions are strictly honourable.'

His breath caught in his throat and he reached for her. 'Oh, Duchess. I took your gift without knowing it – without recognizing it.' He drew her close to him and let her hair spill over his own shoulder. 'I didn't know you'd given me your capacity for happiness, my dear, until I was a thousand miles away. Then I discovered it was quite some capital investment. The interest came in so fast I could give it away and still have it.'

She drew back slightly to look into his dark face. Then she sighed with pure content.

'You really are a poet, Frank . . . Yes . . . we're both seeing very clearly.' She cupped his face with hands that trembled slightly. Carefully, like people long out of practice, they kissed each other. And then they were laughing and crying and holding each other as if they would never let go again.

THE END

RICHMOND HERITAGE

CHAPTER ONE

Charles told her the restaurant was newly opened and had been a buttery long before the Black Boar became a public house. Apparently lost among the rolling hills of Exmoor nevertheless it was full; Charles had had to reserve a table.

She followed his tall figure to a secluded lamp-lit corner smothering the now-familiar feelings of guilt as he pulled out a milking stool and settled her on it with unconscious gallantry.

'There are not many men Charles who could make a three-legged stool seem like a throne,' she said, letting her smile grow as he straddled his own stool opposite her. 'And in the next instant make it look like an unsaddled horse!'

His answering smile was slightly rueful. 'They're determined to keep the atmosphere at what ever cost to comfort,' he apologized. 'Are you all right Mary? What do you think of it?'

'Very nice.' She gazed around the softly-lit restaurant. The roof was unceilinged and dark with beams, the floor still stone-flagged. It reminded her vaguely of somewhere else. She searched her memory and came up with nothing. 'I've never been this far afield before – I wondered if I'd find it.'

'I'm sorry my dear, maybe I shouldn't have chosen a place so far from Milton Mains.' His dark eyes were suddenly serious. 'I had my reasons.'

Mary felt her heart contract. She held his intent gaze with difficulty. His face was quite still, the lines at the temples and mouth suddenly deeply etched so that he looked more than his forty-odd years. His dark eyes were unwavering.

'I wondered whether you'd come. I parked under the Black Boar sign – it squeaked horribly as it swung in the wind. I counted the squeaks. I told myself if I counted over one hundred you wouldn't come. I'd just reached ninety-three.'

Mary swallowed. 'Oh Charles. I shouldn't let you talk like this. I'm the mother of two grown-up children. And Jim—'

He said with unaccustomed violence, 'Jim doesn't know you're there Mary! And the children . . . as you say, they're grown-up.'

Instinctively he avoided criticism of Julie and Brian. Mary was grateful for his sensitivity. She might admit to herself that she had lost all contact with her children as well as her husband, but she couldn't have borne to have heard such an admission voiced by Charles.

His hand covered hers as it lay clenched on the table. Its warmth made her realize how cold she was. He gripped her hard as he spoke in a lower voice.

'Darling Mary. We can't go on like this. Pretending we're just good friends. Meeting further and further from Milton Mains in case we're recognized. It's not our way my dear.' His face lifted in a smile trying to reassure her, to lighten the atmosphere. 'You can't sit there on that wretched stool looking like some Elizabethan chatelaine and tell me you *want* to go on meeting me clandestinely—'

'Charles!'

'Face up to it Mary. That's what we're doing.' His grip became almost painful. 'You've got to make up your mind my darling.' He drew a breath and whispered urgently, 'Mary. Leave Jim. Leave Milton Mains. Jean Butler will take over the house-keeping and when old Mr Richmond comes out of hospital there'll have to be a trained nurse in attendance anyway. You won't be missed. You know it.'

'Yes,' Mary murmured and unexpected tears pressed behind her eyes. Twenty-two years of marriage and she wouldn't be missed. Oh, superficially perhaps, but in a year the scar of her departure would have sloughed right away. Julie and Brian might even be pleased to have a Mitchell of Mitcheldean for stepfather . . . well, Julie anyway. She remembered when she had met Charles at the Annual Farmers' Ball how delighted Julie had been. Mary had protested. 'He took pity on me Julie. Because your father wanted to talk cows with John Adams and that other man . . . he simply asked me to dance . . .'

But it hadn't been quite like that. Charles Mitchell was something of a recluse socially. Milton Mains, Jim's farm which had been in the Richmond family for centuries, was a five-hundred acre corner in an angle of the enormous Mitcheldean estate. Yet Jim had only met Charles half-a-dozen times when boundary fencing had to be discussed; Mary hadn't met him at all. When Jim had said they ought to go to the Annual Ball for once, Mary had had no illusions. She knew Jim wanted to talk about modernizing now that his father was in hospital. He'd only asked her to go with him because it would have looked odd to go without her. Charles, also attending for the first time, rescued her from a sticky evening; though he insisted afterwards that the boot was on the other foot.

She remembered his smile of relief as he came diffidently into the enormous ballroom and spotted the familiar face of his neighbour. He had been well aware of the effect of his arrival on the unattached female contingent that night.

'Ah Richmond—' he joined Jim eagerly. 'How is your father these days – I don't see him behind his beloved Shires any more.' Adam Richmond – known even to the children as 'Old Adam' – was recovering slowly from a stroke. Charles looked sympathetic and suitably concerned at the news. 'But you're keeping his horses, if only for show? It would break the old man's heart if you let them go.'

Jim had introduced Mary. Charles had smiled at her warmly, feeling safe with the wife of such a near neighbour.

'No, I haven't had the pleasure. I'm afraid I live a hermit's life Mrs Richmond . . . I wonder, would you care to dance? That is, if you do the old-fashioned kind of waltz I'm used to!'

Mary remembered laughing, moving away from Jim on Charles Mitchell's arm as if he weren't a stranger at all but someone she had known for years . . .

He was speaking to her again, his low voice breaking into her thoughts gently.

'Mary. I love you. And I think you love me.' He paused. She didn't speak but returned the pressure of his hand. 'Darling, I need you and Jim doesn't. It's as simple as that.'

She still did not speak but her eyes, darkly blue in the dim light, acknowledged that this was the heart of the matter. Surely all women needed to be needed? And it was true that Jim no longer needed her . . .

The waiter came and Charles released her hand and sat back to order for them both. Mary tried to relax, to sort out her own thoughts. She would have to give Charles some sort of answer; he was right, their meetings – so innocent at first – were becoming more and more clandestine. And it wasn't their way. And she couldn't go back – she couldn't tell Charles this was the end and she wouldn't see him any more. Charles had been her salvation this past year. Yet the alternative – actually *leaving* . . . packing a case, writing a note . . . other people did that sort of thing. Not Mary Richmond. Not after twenty-two years.

She looked around the new Buttery Restaurant trying to calm her suddenly beating heart, and unexpectedly the vague familiarity of the place slotted a vivid memory into her mind. Hadn't she and Jim stopped somewhere like this on their way to the coast twenty-two years ago? Yes . . . they had been married at mid-day – at the end of March to beat the tax-man – and the reception had gone on and on. It had been almost dark when they got away and they'd known they would never make their hotel in time for dinner. So Jim had pulled in somewhere before Plymouth. The Lobster Pot. She could even remember the name. She had been nineteen, not much slimmer than she was now, her pale hair – perhaps a little brighter – in curls on her shoulders. She had been wearing a tight-waisted two-piece, not unlike the sort of things Julie wore these days, and Jim had whispered, 'You're beautiful Mary. My Mary. My Mary Richmond . . .' What had happened to that young couple? Jim so ardent and adoring . . . She looked down at her hands as they lay on the skirt of the dress that did in fact look 'period' with its square embroidered neckline and full sleeves. Not a young girl's dress. Not a young girl's hands. Even the wedding ring which had been thick and embossed twenty-two years ago, was smooth and thin. Like an emblem of her marriage.

Yet who was to blame for the empty shell which was left them after so long? Surely she had done her best? And Jim . . . he had gone on loving her until long after Brian's birth hadn't he? She couldn't remember any more. She was certain it was a long time since he had needed her.

The pattern for Jim's wife had been set long before Mary came to Milton Mains. Jim's father – Old Adam – had inherited the farm before the First World War, and the Victorian ideas of *his* father along with it. He had refused to mechanize and the sight of Old Adam ploughing behind his team of shires was a common one – together with the huge open log fires in the farmhouse and the Christmas sheep roast. Most Victorian of all was his attitude to women. Until Jim's mother died she had enjoyed everything the comfortable income from the farm could buy for her. She preserved and pickled and ran the Women's Institute. But more than that she did not do. The farm was man's work; the house women's concern.

Mary arriving in the fifties seemed to get the worst of both worlds. With no Victorian servants to help her she found being a housewife a full-time job, so that at first there was no spare time for she and Jim to grow . . . interdependent. Then, later, when the children were older, she found no place by his side.

And it hadn't been Old Adam's fault entirely, either. She remembered vividly when it became obvious to her that Jim's attitude was exactly the same as his father's in that respect. Brian had been twelve and Julie fourteen when Richmond Queen, the shire mare most beloved by the old man, had foaled. It was a difficult birth and Jim and his father had taken turns to sit with the sweating animal, talking to her, encouraging her. Mary was a little nervous of the huge beasts with their enormous feather-trimmed hooves, but she had offered eagerly to take her turn. As she'd gone into the stable with coffee for Jim she'd felt an unexpected thrill of sympathy with Queen, sensing the same nervous anticipation in those eyes that she herself had felt as she lay waiting for Julie's birth.

'Do let me stay,' she'd said to Jim. 'I'm sure I could help her.' It had sounded girlishly naïve and she had rushed on, 'Adam need never know – I'll wake you in a couple of hours.'

Jim had sounded impatient as he'd taken the coffee. 'Don't be silly Mary. This isn't your place.'

Yes, he'd put it *that* concisely. Something that had been tacitly accepted ever since she arrived. Out of doors – or in the farm office – was not her place.

No . . . it was no good blaming Old Adam. When he'd gone into hospital six months ago she'd thought things might change. He wasn't desperately ill, a stroke had served as a warning and he'd gone into St Jude's for a complete rest. But he'd never be able to pull his weight on the farm again and Mary wondered if this might be her chance. Julie had started to train as a model, Brian was waiting to go to University and meanwhile was out all day in the sports car Jim had bought him . . . Mary had endless time on her hands. But Jim seized his opportunity to buy a tractor and he took on a young boy to see to the shires and the sheep.

And that was that. Except that Charles Mitchell literally bumped into her in the village and asked her to help him choose a new writing desk for his office. Which meant going to Mitcheldean to see where it was to stand. And she had stayed for tea . . .

She was roused from her thoughts by Charles' voice.

'Mary. Drink your soup while it's hot darling. You're shivering.'

It was true. In spite of the warm atmosphere in the new restaurant she was cold. She tried to smile at Charles and felt her mouth tremble.

'I'm sorry Charles. It's just that what you're asking seems such an enormous step. Yet I know you're right when you say we can't go on like this. And I could never return to the absolute emptiness of my life at Milton Mains. Even this evening . . .' she stopped.

'Go on Mary,' Charles said quietly. 'Tell me. You're not being disloyal.'

She tried to shrug. 'It was nothing really. Just that Jim was going to see his father and I asked if I could go as well. But it seems they want to talk business. Tony Elliot is to be in attendance.' Tony Elliot was the Richmonds' solicitor. 'Brian was out in that car of his. And Julie has gone to Paris on a thin promise of some work for *Parisienne* . . . so there I was.' She laughed. 'And then you telephoned.'

There was a long pause. Then Charles said, 'You see?'

She nodded. 'Of course. You've rescued me from an impossible situation Charles – made my life worth living again. It's just—'

'Such an enormous step.' He echoed her words with a smile and in an attempt to lessen the tension again, began on his soup. 'Come on darling, get cracking. I agree with you, but we've got to be sensible and make a few plans.' He looked at her consideringly. 'Would the big step be easier if you did it in two shorter strides?'

'How do you mean?'

'Supposing you left home. Took a holiday somewhere. Got used to the idea of having actually left Milton Mains. And then join me?'

She thought about it. Perhaps that was the answer.

'I'd have to be honest. Tell Jim I was leaving for good.'

'Of course.'

'I could go to Janice. My sister.'

They stared at each other. Mary felt as if she'd already gone. She was breathless, light-headed.

'It'll be all right darling. I'll make it all right,' Charles said urgently.

'I know.' She took his hand again. It was warm and reassuring. She thought: he *does* need me . . . I'll never be lonely again . . . he'll make up for my failure. She stared at him. He had given her something to live for and her heart suddenly swelled with gratitude. She loved him.

Later as she took the track to Milton Mains that led off the Minehead road, she told herself yet again that she was doing the right thing. Charles was a good man. He could so easily have suggested a sordid long-drawn-out affair of week-ends and days spent at Mitcheldean. But he hadn't. This last suggestion – leaving Jim and going to Janice for a time – would make the break so much easier. She felt her face grow warm as she considered the alternative:

packing her case and walking over Long Acre field to Mitcheldean. Moving in next door.

She negotiated the familiar double bend and noticed with annoyance that the five-barred gate to the yard was wide open. So Brian was home and, typically thoughtless, had left the gate unlatched. A cardinal sin in a farmer's son. Yes, his cream sports car was already in the car-port. She nosed alongside it and switched off. There was no sign of Jim's old Rover. She glanced at her watch by the interior light. Half past ten. Late for hospital visiting so he had probably gone back with Tony Elliot for dinner and more business-talk.

She stood still for a few moments in the darkness and let the sounds and smells of the farm settle around her. Softly, through the wall of the stable she heard the whinny of Princess, Richmond Queen's six-year-old daughter; then an answering snort from the Queen herself. Across the yard through the drifting rain she could hear the bleating of the sheep in the home field. The house, solidly Georgian, loomed behind her. This was her home. Milton Mains. She sighed sharply. She would miss it but not with real pain. Milton Mains had seen the end of her marriage.

She fished for her key in her bag and let herself in through the back door switching on lights automatically. Jim's gumboots and sou'wester were in the entry. The kitchen was warm and even more quiet for the big clock ticking above the modern range. Everything was just as she had left it three hours ago.

'Mother!' It was Brian's voice calling from the drawing-room. Long gone was the time when he would run to greet her. Now he just called. 'Is that you?'

'Yes.' She crossed the hall and went into the room still full of Mrs Richmond's beautiful rosewood furniture. 'Hello dear. No news from your father?'

'No.' He lounged in a button armchair in a way she

found vaguely insolent. 'He's not with you then?' His eyes were dark like Jim's. They looked up at her expressionlessly, then away to where the fire she had left this afternoon was settling in its own embers.

'No. He went to see Adam. They wanted to discuss business.'

'Uh-huh. Farm business I suppose. Exciting stuff.'

'Of course. It's our way of life after all.' Automatically she ranged herself along with Jim and Old Adam. If she was indeed leaving, Brian – and Julie – would have to know but somehow . . . if it was possible . . . she must preserve a vestige of family loyalty. Surely the civilized way of admitting incompatibility avoided complete disintegration of the family? She swallowed wondering whether divorce was civilized anyway.

Brian grinned as if he found her quick defence amusing. Then he said with that upward glance again, 'Where have you been mother-mine?'

She paused fractionally. She hadn't mentioned Charles' name for some time. 'I thought I'd try the pottery class at the new craft centre,' she replied casually. 'I – I've got rather a lot of time on my hands lately. And no outside interests.'

'Jolly good.' He stood up and leaned against the mantelpiece his back towards her. 'Did you enjoy it?'

Already wishing she hadn't lied she said too enthusiastically, 'Very much.'

He said almost inaudibly, 'I bet you did.'

She wondered if she had mis-heard him; in any case it seemed best to ignore such an obviously provocative remark. She fussed around the room plumping up cushions, stacking books, wondering aloud how Julie was getting on in Paris, what time Dad would be home, how Old Adam was. Brian made no response at all.

She straightened her back and looked at his downbent

head with tightened lips. 'Coffee, Brian?' she asked shortly.

'No thanks.' He didn't move.

'Then I'm going to bed.' She turned at the door but he still stared into the fire. 'Good night.'

' 'Night mother-mine.' It was a parody of affection. She left him and went upstairs with the sense of failure heavy within her again. If she'd needed proof of Charles' indictment of her marriage, she had had it in that little encounter with her son.

She stopped on the landing and looked into Jim's room. Jean Butler had cleaned upstairs today and it was immaculate. He hadn't been back since he left for the hospital at five-thirty. She went next door into her own room, bigger than Jim's because until three years ago they had shared it. Jim had had an attack of insomnia following a heavy cold and had moved into the old Victorian dressing-room. As far as Mary knew the insomnia had gone but Jim had never returned to their old-fashioned four-poster.

She stared around the empty double room with its new cream wool carpet and old-rose curtains and bed-cover. Jim had spared her nothing in the way of luxury. She must remember that.

She crossed to the telephone and dialled Charles' number. He answered so quickly she knew he must have been waiting by the phone.

'Ah. Hello Mary,' he said formally in case she was not alone. 'You're safely home.'

'Yes. Thank you Charles.'

'Thank *you* my dear. Mary?'

'Yes?'

'I love you. Remember that. Good night darling.'

'Good night Charles.'

She looked at herself in the long pier glass wondering why Charles had fallen in love with her. Even in her evening dress with her pale hair caught in a chignon on her neck she was so . . . ordinary. Her eyes were dark blue but not over-large in her round, school-girlish face. Her mouth drooped at the corners. And there were lines . . . plenty of them. Yet he loved her and in the face of Brian's sullen silence and Jim's unexplained absence, he had lifted her up again on his love. She smiled slightly at her reflection and lifted her skirt to kick her shoes free. Then stopped.

She put a hand to her mouth. Of course – the dress. That was why Brian had behaved with such veiled rudeness just now. She would hardly go to a pottery class in a dress like that.

For a moment she considered going back down and telling the truth. After all she had done nothing wrong . . . so far. But then . . . after she had gone to Janice's – wouldn't he put two and two together and find her departure a betrayal?

She bit her lip, trying to see the whole thing as simply as it had seemed earlier. Yes – she would let it go. Tomorrow, as soon as Jim was out on the farm she would be writing a note, packing up, going for good. To start making excuses now – and to her son – would be petty.

Exhausted, she undressed and climbed between the sheets. She intended staying awake until she heard Jim's car, but somehow she missed it during one of her cat-naps. She woke properly at five as usual, and went downstairs to make tea. She felt unrefreshed and her head ached. She had a vague memory of dreaming that she was searching for Jim in a dark wood and when she found him he turned round and it was Charles.

Only Stan Butler, the stockman, and Robbie the boy, were in the milking shed. Stan, fixing milking tubes without haste, said he had had no word from Jim.

'Not to worry, Mrs Richmond. He did say while he was in town he'd spend some time with the Elliots.'

Mary was not particularly worried. If she had needed

anything to stiffen her determination to leave, this was it. Apparently Jim thought it necessary to warn the stockman of his possible absence – naturally, because of the milking. But not his wife.

Her anger did nothing to buoy Mary up. It was a sad cold pain across her chest, a feeling of finality. Like an automaton she made tea and took it out to the men, then drank some herself; went back upstairs and had a bath instead of going back to bed as usual. She looked through her window and saw the sun, a half-disc on the Long Acre field. It was going to be a dry day at Milton Mains. And she wouldn't be here to see it.

At eight-thirty she telephoned her sister Janice in Cheltenham and asked if she could come for a few days. Janice asked no questions, it was as if she had been expecting the call.

Mary packed a case with slow deliberation and then sat down to write the note to Jim. It was strange how little there was to say. 'Jim—' not even 'Dear Jim'. '—there doesn't seem to be anything left, does there? I'm sorry but I can't stay any longer. You have the children. Perhaps my leaving like this will shock them into a closer relationship with you – I hope so. I really am sorry Jim. I suppose this is what true incompatibility is. I'm staying with Janice for the time being. Mary.'

She took the note into his tidy bedroom and put it in the traditional place on his pillow. She wondered how he would look when he read it. Would he remember their whirlwind courtship and those first few years?

There were sounds from below. She hurried to the head of the stairs but it was only Jean Butler arriving. She bit her lip – she'd forgotten all about Jean and she didn't really want her around this morning. Everyone would know sooner or later of course, but in all fairness Jim must be the first.

'Ah. Hello Jean. You're nice and early.' Thank goodness

she had done upstairs yesterday and so wouldn't see the case or the note.

'It's nine-thirty m'dear. Stan tells me Mr Richmond isn't back from town yet?'

'No.' Mary came halfway down the stairs. 'And Brian and I haven't made much mess so you can give us a miss for today.'

Jean smiled upwards. She was typically Devon with her round plump face and sky-blue eyes and heart-warming cheerfulness. She and Stan were closer to Milton Mains than Mary herself; they'd lived at the Lodge since Julie was born and looked on the Richmonds as their own.

'Not worried are you m'dear? You could always telephone Mr Elliot.'

Mary came down the rest of the stairs and held the newel post tightly. 'I'm not a bit worried Jean. Now you get off and put your feet up for once—'

'I'll not do that Mrs Richmond.' Jean laughed her whole-hearted laugh. 'I'll be glad of the chance to go into town myself. Is there anything I can get you?'

'Oh . . .' Mary thought quickly. 'I could do with something for the men's sandwiches—' she broke off suddenly. She would be doing no sandwich-cutting today.

'Yes? A nice bit of liver sausage?'

They'd have to have sandwiches. And Jean wouldn't mind doing them. It occurred to Mary suddenly that Jean ought to know she would be taking over the household.

She hesitated. 'Er . . . yes all right. Thank you Jean. Half a pound then.'

Jean's wide blue eyes were curious but she said no more. Perhaps she guessed. Perhaps everyone knew that the Richmonds had come to an end.

Mary went back upstairs and put on her outdoor things. She considered waking Brian, then decided against it. They had nothing to say to each other and she might break down. Slowly she carried her case on to the landing.

Then she stopped.

The sunshine was full out now and shone through the coloured glass in the hefty old front door. Colour splashed over the mosaic tiles in the hall, gleaming on the mirror, high-lighting the brass, the crystal chandelier; turning the white paint into a rainbow of reds and blues. And sitting on the hall-chest, his head in his hands, was Jim.

Gently she put her case at her feet and stared down at him. For an instant in the strange light she had thought this was a recurrence of her dream and it was Charles sitting there. Then she recognized Jim's turtle-necked sweater and suede car coat. She remembered him saying – was it only yesterday afternoon? 'Suit? Why on earth should I wear a suit to visit Dad? He wouldn't recognize me . . .'

She began to go downstairs and still he didn't move. The stained sun turned the white hair above his ears to fiery red and made his cupped hands ochre-brown. She recognized his attitude; it bore the marks of the cold finality she had felt earlier this morning. Still felt.

'Jim?' She spoke softly wondering if he had fallen asleep sitting there. 'Has something happened? Is Adam worse?'

He lifted his head very slowly and met her eyes. His own were black and stunned.

'Adam's dead Mary. He died at two o'clock this morning.'

'Jim. I'm sorry.' She was. Adam, behind his shires, ploughing the Long Acre field. Adam Richmond, part of the tapestry of Milton Mains. It was the end of an era.

'Yes.' He spoke blankly. His hands hung between his knees now, pale white in a trick of the light; useless. 'Yes. He's gone. But it was painlessly, in his sleep. He just stopped breathing.'

'I wish you'd sent for me. Why didn't you come home straight afterwards?'

'I slept for a couple of hours at St Jude's. Then I went to see Tony.'

'I see.' It was typical. It wouldn't occur to him to let her know. She thought of her case on the landing, the note on Jim's bed. Her heart lurched. 'Come on in the kitchen Jim. Let me make you a hot drink.'

He stood up obediently and followed her. In the normal light of the kitchen he still looked ghastly. She urged him into a chair and he immediately put his head in his hands again. His voice emerged, muffled.

'Mary. I don't know what to do. It's not the way you think . . . not the way any of us thought.'

She was bewildered. Had Adam eventually died of some awful undiagnosed illness?

'Here. Warm your hands round this.' She put a cup of steaming coffee in front of him. 'You're freezing Jim.'

'It's the shock.' He looked up. His dark eyes were blank but he took the coffee and cradled the cup with hands that trembled slightly. 'Mary. D'you remember Adam making a deed of gift of the farm and all its contents?'

'I realized that's why Tony came that week-end a couple of years ago. You never actually told me about it.'

'No. You know how Adam hated you to be bothered . . . well, anyway. It seems he left it too late. The gift has to be made seven years before death.' He focused her properly. There was a kind of pleading in his eyes. 'We have to pay death duties Mary. And Tony estimates them in the region of ninety thousand pounds.'

She stared at him, horrified.

'Can we find that kind of money?'

He shook his head numbly. 'We've used what the farm gave us – there seemed no reason not to.'

It was true. The house, the children, the cars . . . yes, they had lived lavishly for small farmers. Their riches, their inheritance, had been in the land. And now . . . Mary let her gaze slide over Jim's head and through the kitchen window. The watery April sun made everything look clear and sharp. Old Adam would never see it again; the farm he had loved perhaps more than his wife. And because he had stubbornly hung on to it for so long he had run them into this terrible debt.

Jim seemed to follow her thoughts. 'I suppose he thought he had another ten years at least. You know how his mind ran – he thought he was immortal!'

Mary bit her lip. Yes, she knew how his mind ran. He had been frightened that if anything happened to Jim, she would eventually own Milton Mains. A woman in charge of the farm. It would be unthinkable to Old Adam.

So, in a way, it was her fault that Jim was faced with this debt. She felt her thoughts jumping crazily . . . she had said just now, '—can *we* find the money—' yet on Jim's bed there was a note telling him he was on his own now.

She said abruptly, 'Jim, drink your coffee. I'm just going to fetch a cardigan, I'm cold myself.'

He said again, woodenly, 'It's the shock.'

She went slowly upstairs. Bath water was running in the bathroom so Brian was up. He would have to be told. She went into Jim's room and picked up the note. '. . . there doesn't seem to be anything left . . .' She drew a sharp breath. The full realization of what had happened dawned on her. There literally would be nothing left. Milton Mains would have to go.

She held the note against the front of her dress. How could she leave now? Perhaps later – a month – six months. But not now. Charles would understand – surely Charles would understand – that it was impossible for her to leave Jim and the children when they were facing up to the twin blows of Adam's death and the loss of their home.

She walked to the window and stared again at the Long

Acre field where Adam had ploughed each year behind his shires.

'Oh Adam,' she breathed. 'D'you realize what you've done? You might well have lost Milton Mains to the Richmonds. But you're keeping me.'

Her eyes flooded with tears as she remembered the proud, upright old patriarch. 'They're going to need me Adam. Your son is going to need me . . .'

She unpacked her case as methodically as she had packed it and telephoned Janice to tell her about old Mr Richmond.

'I'm sorry Mary . . .' Janice's voice was hesitant. 'But it doesn't really change the basic situation does it? You'll come in a few weeks?'

So Janice *had* been expecting a call for help.

Mary said, 'I – I don't know. I'm not certain. I'll keep in touch. Jim is taking it hard.'

Janice said slowly, 'I see. He might need you then Mary. At least for a while.'

'Yes.'

Mary replaced the receiver thoughtfully. Of course. She mustn't let sympathy run away with her. Jim would only need her for a while.

She slipped a cardigan over her shoulders and hurried back downstairs and into the kitchen. Jim was sitting exactly as she had left him.

She said briskly, 'I'm going to make you some breakfast, then we'll talk. We're going to manage somehow Jim. Don't worry.'

She busied herself at the fridge fetching eggs and bacon. Jim watched her in silence until the familiar frying smells seemed to rouse him.

'You know what it means don't you Mary?' he said at last.

She turned, the palette knife still poised over the pan. 'I'm afraid I do. At least – I'm not well up on the farm business of course—'

'Milton Mains will have to be sold,' he said abruptly as if he thought she might be reproaching him.

She put the gammon and eggs on a hot plate and carried it to the table. 'Yes. I thought it might have to be that. But Jim, it's not the end of the world—' he gave a short bitter laugh. 'But it's *not*,' she insisted. 'There are other farms. Small-holdings if you like. Places we could work ourselves without any paid help – oh our standard of living will have to come down.' She stopped suddenly realizing how her words were ranging her alongside Jim, making them into a partnership. And an hour ago she had been on the point of leaving.

He said slowly, 'Would you be willing to . . . start again?'

She wondered what he meant and decided to take his words at their face value. 'We've been well off but I've worked hard until the last few years. I can do it again. Money doesn't matter that much to me.'

She looked into his eyes willing him to snap out of the mood of dead despair and he stared back at her . . . she remembered Charles' warm gaze. Charles who loved her. Then a faint flicker came into Jim's dark eyes.

'No . . . maybe you're right Mary Richmond.'

It didn't mean anything of course. He probably didn't remember calling her 'my Mary Richmond' in the Lobster Pot all those years ago. But she found herself smiling.

'I might be,' she said.

His hand moved across the table. He might have been going to take hers but the door opened and Brian came in.

He still wore the strangely closed expression of last night and Mary got up quickly and went to him.

'Brian. Your grandfather died in his sleep last night. Dad was with him.'

'Old Adam?' The boy looked startled, the aggression gone from him. 'Oh no . . . Oh God . . . I'm sorry.'

He sat down and glanced at his father.

'Dad?' Jim managed a turned-down smile. Brian looked across at Mary. 'Well . . . what are you going to do?'

It was a strange question. Mary frowned. Jim raised his eyebrows at her and started on his breakfast; she spoke for him.

'You mean about the farm? You realize about the death duties then?' Brian looked completely bewildered. 'Of course you couldn't know. There's been a legal mix-up Brian and we have to pay a vast amount of death duties. Your father and I have just been talking and we think it likely we shall have to sell Milton Mains and move into something smaller.'

Brian stared at his father and then back to Mary. The curtain of hardness seemed to come slowly down over his face again.

'I see.' He paused then added almost brutally, 'Shall I have to sell the car?'

Mary felt sick. She saw Jim flinch, then he stood up and said jerkily, 'We must see. I have to go upstairs – excuse me a moment.'

He left the kitchen. Mary looked angrily at Brian.

'What's got into you?' she asked. 'Your father's had a terrible shock Brian. He's lost his father and his home in one fell swoop and all you can say is—'

He interrupted her almost savagely. 'Well, there's not much time for grief is there?'

'That could be his salvation, don't you see? If we make plans straightaway – contact the house-agents today – this morning even – we won't have time to think about our position—'

'*We* contact the agents?' His voice was a cruel mime of hers. 'What have you got to do with all this sordid selling and buying mother-mine? You won't have to get rid of your car will you? Or lower your standards—'

'Be quiet Brian, I've no idea what you mean—'

'Yes you have. It's easy for you to be noble isn't it? All that talk just now, as if you're going to save the family fortune!' His young mouth curved into an ugly sneer. 'Oh yes. I was at the Black Boar last night – I saw your car there. I'm surprised you didn't see mine – you're always so hot on me drinking and driving. Who were you with mother-mine – in your new dress and hair-do? I didn't think much about it then. Not until you lied to me later. Then this morning when I practically fell over your case up on the landing, I put two and two together. They add up to four quite nicely, don't they?'

Mary felt as if he had slapped her across the face. She stared at him, frozen. Then a movement caught the corner of her eye. Somehow she turned her head. Jim was standing in the doorway.

CHAPTER TWO

The three of them stood for a long five seconds while Brian's words seemed to echo among the china on the dresser. Mary's mind was blank except for the one urgent thought: Jim must not know she had intended leaving him this morning. If he did, any kind of working relationship they might have over the next few weeks would be inhibited right from the start. Just as she had felt that now he was in trouble she must stay and try to help, so he would feel that – for the same reason – he could not stand in her way. It would be an impossible situation.

Somehow she summoned up a shrug and an impatient glance at Brian.

'What a stupid fuss. I *was* going to spend a few days with Aunt Janice if you must know – I telephoned about half-an-hour ago and cancelled it.' She made no reference to last night and Brian's defiance crumbled before her dismissive words.

Jim came on into the kitchen.

'How dare you speak to your mother in that tone Brian.' Anger absorbed some of his despair and he looked more himself. 'Your whole attitude this morning is – unco-operative to say the least.'

Brian slumped into his usual hangdog stance. Mary wondered whether he would pursue the question of her visit to the Black Boar but he merely muttered something and turned as if to go. Mary felt suddenly guilty, knowing his accusation had been justified and in any case had stemmed from his basic insecurity.

'Don't go Brian—' she pulled out two chairs from the big kitchen table. 'Have some breakfast and let's discuss what we have to do first.' She plugged in the toaster. 'Coffee? Toast?'

Jim and Brian sat down together reluctantly. Glancing at them over her shoulder Mary found herself wishing for Julie's whirlwind approach. Julie was just as selfish as Brian, but she was completely open with it. It was Julie who had said enthusiastically, 'Charles Mitchell actually danced six times with you Mummy? Wheee . . . you're in! He's stinking rich. Don't forget your little daughter when you're living it up in marble halls, will you?'

Mary poured coffee and thought how ironic it was that between them the children held the truth about her, yet really understood her not at all. Perhaps it was only Charles who could ever really understand. She carried the breakfast tray to the table and sat down with a determined little smile.

'Adam wouldn't want us to sit here moping you know.' She turned her face towards Brian but his eyes were dark and expressionless again.

Jim said heavily, 'No. We must decide what to do. The agents I suppose . . .'

'Yes. Can you do that Jim? And I'll see to the – the other arrangements.'

'Would you?' Jim looked grateful. 'He's still at St Jude's of course. I don't quite know what happens next.'

'The undertakers will bring him home. And the vicar will see to the service – an announcement in the *Gazette* – I'll do it. And Brian,' she looked at her son. 'Will you try and get a message to Julie. The pictures are for *Parisienne* but I don't know her address in Paris.'

Brian picked up a piece of toast and began to eat, looking more normal. 'I can probably get hold of her through the Agency. Yeah. OK.'

Mary relaxed slightly realizing how tired she was after the unremitting strain of the last twelve hours.

She was glad when Jim said wearily, 'That's about it then isn't it? I'll use the phone now Mary, then go out and see Stan and Robbie.'

'And then try and get some rest, Jim,' Mary put in. 'I can give Stan a hand outside if necessary.'

He looked up, surprised. Then he said, 'Yes, I suppose you can. Thanks Mary.' He pushed his chair back from the table and went into the hall. The telephone pinged and his voice came to them, 'Can you get me Blewett and Harrison in the High Street?'

Brian finished eating and clattered his cup and saucer on to his plate. 'I think I'll go for a drive before lunch.' He felt her unspoken disapproval. 'Well, I can't use the phone for a while can I? And I might as well enjoy the car while I can.' He stood up defiantly. 'Anyway I promised Mike Stelling I'd meet him at Lower Brook.'

Mary took the breakfast things to the sink telling herself it was only natural the boy wanted to get out of the house, wishing he would stay and help Jim. He paused by the door.

'Who was it last night Mother? Who was it made you look so starry-eyed?'

She forced herself to stay where she was, not even look round at him. He was trying to hurt her because he was hurt himself. That was all it was.

'Don't be ridiculous Brian. I met an old friend for a meal. That was all.'

He hovered for a moment; she could almost feel him wanting to be convinced. Then he laughed a hard little laugh. 'But we must keep it from Dad mustn't we? Now that this has happened—'

She said quietly, 'Get out Brian.'

The door slammed behind him and she found she was gripping the edge of the sink and shivering slightly. That little exchange smacked unpleasantly of . . . of what? Warning? If Brian knew she had been planning to leave then he must also realize she had shelved the idea. Why had he found it necessary to remind her of the situation unless it were merely to taunt her? She shivered again.

The week-end was crowded. Old Adam came home and his open coffin was put in the little-used dining-room. He looked patriarchal and strangely boyish at the same time. As if at the last he had known what would happen and it had struck him as amusing.

Mary put a notice in the *Gazette* and telephoned the vicar to arrange the funeral for Tuesday. Early on Monday morning, the flowers began to arrive. They piled them around the mahogany table which was Adam's solid and familiar catafalque. The table legs were completely hidden by the massed freezias, lilies, daffodils and the huge sprays of early gorse brought by the village children because it was Adam's favourite flower.

Jim, looking at the spiky branches murmured, 'Determined, stubborn, prickly. Like he was himself.'

'And happy too,' Mary added. 'He could be happy, like the gorse flowers.'

'Yes, he could,' Jim admitted. He touched the sleeve of her dress. 'You don't hate him?'

She looked at him, horrified. He still wore the lost expression of last Friday; she thought suddenly it would be good for him when they had sold up and gone.

'No, I don't hate him,' she answered. 'And you shouldn't either. Maybe he's given us something more valuable than Milton Mains.'

He said nothing to this. Mary wondered why she had said it; almost as if she were suggesting a second chance.

She was glad when he let her sleeve go and bent his head to sniff a spray of lilac. 'Blewett seems to think Milton will be difficult to sell,' he said. 'We're too small for the big farmers and not quite small enough for a family concern.'

'Agents are always pessimistic.' Mary moved away from the flowers and stood in the window. It was icy cold in the unheated room and outside a light rain was beginning to fall. She wondered if it would delay Julie's arrival. 'This makes a marvellous family home. And it's provided a living for us – a good living.'

'The rooms are so big to heat and furnish. Blewett was horrified when I told him we had no central heating.'

'Well that can be installed.' Mary turned her back on the window. 'Jim, I was thinking about the furniture actually. We shall never get your mother's big stuff into a smaller farm. And it wouldn't seem right to move it out of Milton.'

'You mean sell it with the house? It's an idea. A good idea.' He put a hand to his head. 'Oh God. It's all got to go hasn't it?'

Instinctively she started towards him, then stopped herself.

'We could keep one or two things if you like.'

'No—' He stood up and took a deep breath. 'No. If we're to make a fresh start we must do it from scratch. It's just that—' he stared at his father's dead face. 'I can't help the feeling that Old Adam has taken everything with him.'

She was appalled at the desolation in his voice. She found she could not offer the usual comfort – 'You've got the children and me—' it was too pat and he would know it. Jim was too intelligent not to realize how superficial was their family relationship.

Then there was the sound of a car outside.

Mary said thankfully, 'It's Julie – at last.' She glanced at Jim. 'Shall we—?'

It was unusual for them to greet the children together. Normally Jim was outside and Mary was the one to go to the door. As she walked by his side and stood in the porch she wondered whether Jim was conscious too that this was just one more fresh start.

Julie looked thinner than ever, almost gaunt. Mary told herself it was natural. She had recently heard about her grandfather and had waited around at Orly airport for six hours, picked up her car at Bristol and driven most of the morning through the light April rain that would make a mist of spray around each vehicle on the motorway. Yet there was more to it than all of that. Julie was normally impatient, eating low-calorie meals standing up, but she was full of nervous energy. There was a lethargy about her this time and an irritability that erupted in tight little remarks.

She greeted the news of the proposed sale of the farm with a comment almost identical to Jim's yet with none of his very real grief.

'I see. Well . . . it looks as though Old Adam has defied all the rules. He really has taken it with him, hasn't he?' And she laughed without amusement.

'We'll still be living somewhere on the Moor Julie,' Mary said quickly, avoiding Jim's eye. 'You can go on living at home and commuting to your free-lance jobs – just as you have been doing.'

Julie examined her nails. 'Thanks,' she said briefly.

Mary sighed. Just when they needed Julie's energy it seemed to have gone. She looked at her young daughter and saw herself at twenty years old. Julie had more elegance; she wore her clothes with aplomb, but her fine blonde hair swinging like a bell around her shoulders, her violet eyes and schoolgirl face were a younger edition of her mother's. But so much of Julie's life was a secret. Mary knew she worked for an Agency in London, yet she called herself free-lance and jobs seemed few and far between. At seventeen she had demanded to go to a modelling school and since then they had seen less and less of her at Milton Mains. Young men telephoned but Mary rarely met them. Her only comfort had been that at least Julie still lived at home – or at any rate slept there four nights out of the seven.

It was a typical April day on Tuesday, sudden blustery showers chasing the weak sun behind low black cloud.

When Mary took the tea in to Stan and Jim in the milking shed she could guess how it would be by the warm moist air blowing straight from the south-west. The funeral service was to start at two o'clock; some time during the walk through the old graveyard there would sure to be a shower. How it would amuse Old Adam to see the village fineries being blown about beneath umbrellas.

Jean Butler arrived at nine-thirty to help cut sandwiches and make sausage rolls. She had been unusually subdued since returning last Friday with the liver sausage and hearing of Adam's death. Whether the news of the death duties had filtered through to the Butlers Mary could not guess. If so, perhaps Jean had looked ahead as they all had, and seen a time when the Butlers and Richmonds would no longer work together. Mary watched her as she moved capably around the big kitchen. Yes, the Butlers were something she really would miss from Milton Mains.

Some time during that long morning Julie and Brian appeared in the kitchen. Julie was already dressed in a grey skirt and tight-waisted black velvet jacket with a beret to match. She looked too smart for a funeral. Brian was bundled up in his dressing-gown and looked sick.

'Make yourself some tea,' Mary suggested. 'And Julie – have something to eat. There's still an hour before lunch—'

'Oh stop *fussing* Mother,' Julie snapped. 'All we want is coffee. And Brian will have his black.' She gave her brother a stony stare as she took two mugs from the dresser.

‘Does that mean—?’ Mary stopped herself; they could not bicker in front of Jean today of all days.

‘It means that Mike and I stopped for a drink on the way home last night,’ Brian said with a world-weary air which might have been funny in different circumstances. ‘At the Black Boar as a matter of fact.’

Mary felt the colour rush into her face. Julie raised her eyebrows.

‘Then you shouldn’t m’dear,’ Jean glanced at Mary and went on roundly, ‘If you want to risk your life and limb, so be it. But ’tis disrespectful on your grandfather’s funeral day—’

‘Not quite Jean. I was in the house before midnight.’ But he looked at her with a rueful smile and his tone was quite different from the one he used on his mother. ‘I was drinking to him actually. Rough cider – his favourite. That’s why I’m feeling a bit off I expect.’

Jean shook her head at Mary. ‘Always an answer,’ she commented. But she had successfully diverted a petty argument and Mary was grateful. Though it hadn’t made Brian’s aggressive attitude towards her any easier to bear.

They ate a scratch lunch at mid-day. Mary’s sister, Janice and husband arrived from Cheltenham and Julie talked to them in the sitting-room while Mary and Jim changed. By then Tony Elliot and his wife Anne had arrived from Taunton and the Butlers were waiting uncomfortably in the kitchen.

The hearse drew up outside the Georgian porch just after one-thirty. Mary stood in the hall and watched as the men fastened the coffin lid over Adam’s carefree face. Her heart was beating fast and she had a light-headed feeling as if this were all another dream. Then Old Adam left his home for good; the family divided themselves up in the three cars following the hearse and the last bumpy journey began down the track to the Minehead road.

After that, the dream-like quality of the day intensified. Small snatches of memory remained for Mary to examine afterwards; the endless centre aisle of Frinlode Church and the Vicar's voice intoning: 'I am the resurrection and the life . . .' The sudden shock as she realized that the Church was full, packed to overflowing with extra chairs in the aisle and the Sunday School benches cramming the Lady Chapel. And that people were crying. Crying for Old Adam? Or for the young Richmonds left with nothing? Then there was Adam's favourite hymn – O God our help in ages past – and Brian staring ahead of him with burning eyes. And the walk back down the aisle and through the church-yard to the Richmond plot.

'Dust to dust . . .' said the Vicar. And someone threw a posy of wild primroses with the first clod of earth. And the wind suddenly shook the new beech leaves over their heads and it began to rain. Just as Mary had known it would.

On the way back to the cars, she noticed Janice and her husband Bill, just ahead. Janice was holding Bill's arm. Such an ordinary sight. Then as Bill opened the car door for her, he slid his hand into the small of her back and gave her a small and gentle pat. It was a gesture of friendship and affection. It seemed to say, this will soon be over and we'll be home and can relax together. It was the sort of thing Charles might have done. Not Jim. Mary felt a rush of pure loneliness sweep over her; she paused and looked around at the slowly moving umbrellas and bent heads. And as if responding to some silent cry from her someone looked up. It was Charles. For a split second they stared at each other then he gave her a slight smile and moved on.

Mary was conscious of her heart again; it beat strongly and steadily against her ribs as if Charles had given her a secret strength. She turned and saw Jim coming along the path with the Vicar. Julie, like the model she was, held her skirt above her black boots. Brian slouched with his hands in his pockets. Mary thought with a pang: we have no comfort to give each other. Jim and I walked behind Adam side by side, but there was no contact between us.

'The Reverend Elmley is coming back to the house with us Mary,' Jim said in a low voice. 'Charles Mitchell will give him a lift. Will you go on ahead with the children?'

'Of course.'

Mary settled herself in the first car. The news that Charles would be at Milton Mains made her feel warm again. Perhaps she would have a chance to talk to him and explain how she felt.

The house was unexpectedly full. Jim must have asked a lot of Adam's old friends back; it was a tradition of Milton Mains that no-one left an occasion there without plenty to eat and drink. Even a funeral.

Mary and Jean were kept busy making and pouring tea and passing sandwiches. Jim dispensed sherry from the sideboard. The atmosphere gradually lightened and many of the mourners checked sudden loud laughs as they remembered why they were here. Mary noticed that Julie had annexed Charles. Typically. He was standing with his hand on the marble fireplace inclining his head towards her attentively as she told him some story with lots of graphic gestures. He was smiling almost indulgently. Mary felt a sudden yearning to be with him, looked after by him, loved and cherished.

Janice was at her elbow.

'Darling is it all right if Bill and I slip away now? Bill hates driving in the rain and I can see I'm not going to have a chance for a natter with you—'

'Of course Jan. You get off when you want to. I'm sorry about the mix-up on the telephone. I really did want a break, but . . . well, I couldn't leave now.'

'No.' Janice glanced at Jim. 'But you'll have plenty of time on your hands quite soon won't you?'

'I'm not sure. Things have happened Jan. I'll try to get it all down in a letter. We might well leave Milton Mains.'

Janice's eyes opened wide. 'Leave Richmond Park—' it was an old joke of Janice's, but Mary could only raise a small smile now. Janice put a hand on her arm. 'Darling. You're serious. But why? The place is thriving in a medieval sort of way—'

'Death duties,' Mary said briefly trying to look as if she and Janice were still discussing the weather.

'Oh my God. Poor old Jim. Oh Mary . . . still, I don't know. It'll be no great loss to you Mary. It's never been your home, has it?'

It was true. Yet it brought no comfort. It was just yet another aspect of the failure of her marriage.

She temporized. 'The children were born here . . .'

Janice hugged her arm. 'Cheer up darling. Something will turn up. Come to Cheltenham any time you want to. Or send the children. And keep in touch.' She kissed her sister lightly on the cheek. 'I refuse to see this as a tragedy Mary. It could be a good thing. Nobody can live in the past.'

Jean Butler came up with an empty tray. 'More sandwiches needed Mrs Richmond. Shall I—?'

'No Jean. I'll see my sister away and go into the kitchen for more.'

She felt a distinct sense of loss as she waved goodbye to Janice and Bill. Their togetherness emphasized her strangely solitary state in the midst of all her family and friends. She was glad to get into the warm familiarity of the kitchen – her special domain – and have something really practical to do. She had wanted Charles to come to the house, yet now he was here she realized that her decision to stay and help Jim through the next few weeks or months meant that she couldn't possibly see Charles too. Hadn't he himself said they couldn't go on meeting clandestinely . . .

The kitchen door opened and there he was as if once again she had summoned him with her thoughts. He closed the door carefully behind him and stood for a moment looking at her. Mary was afraid she might cry. She gave a small hiccuping laugh.

'I didn't think when I came in here . . . I mean, I didn't intend you to seek me out—' she swallowed. 'How did you get away?'

'I just said – excuse me – and walked out. I had to see you. You didn't telephone or write—'

'Charles I'm sorry. But in any case we weren't going to get in touch for a while were we? And the last four days have been so awful—'

'Mary—' he crossed the kitchen and wrapped her in his arms. It was the first time anyone had offered her comfort since she'd seen him four days ago. She pressed her forehead hard against the dark blue of his suit.

'It's all right. Really. Don't be too nice to me Charles else I'll howl.'

He said nothing, but his arms tightened. Mary squeezed her eyes tight shut then took a deep breath and drew away.

'I'm all right now. Thanks.' She turned to the table and began to put slices of sirloin between bread and butter with a kind of feverish haste. 'I'm glad to see you for other reasons besides . . . that.' She gave him a watery smile. 'I'm not going to Janice's for a while Charles. I – I have to stay with Jim for a while. You see—'

'I know. I heard about the death duties Mary.'

She was startled. 'How? No-one knows outside the family—'

'Stelling from Lower Brook Farm told me.' He jerked his head towards the door. 'Most of the people in there know. That's one of the reasons so many of them came back. A sort of farewell for them too.'

'Stelling?' She sat down. 'Of course. Mike Stelling. He's Brian's friend. They went out together on Friday and last night.' She said wearily, 'Not that it matters. Not really. Everyone would have known soon anyway.'

Charles straddled a chair near to hers. 'Darling, I'm sorry about it all, of course. Jim must be shattered. But what does it mean to us? You and me?'

She shook her head. 'I'm not sure. Jim might not even want me. But if he does, I'll have to stay. Can you understand?'

'Only too well.' His mouth turned down ruefully. 'I knew how you'd feel immediately Stelling told me. But how long will it be Mary?'

'Until Jim has sold and bought something else. And then . . . well until I feel I *can* go. I'm sorry Charles.'

He said nothing for a long time then he reached for her hand. 'On Friday I thought it was going to be you and me Mary. I wasn't even jealous of the years you'd had with Jim. Now, suddenly, I'm frightened. There are depths of loyalties—' he bit off his words and shook his head. 'Sorry darling, I'm not making it easier. Look. Can we go on seeing each other? Just occasionally. Like we did before—'

'No.' She stood up again pulling her hand away. 'No Charles. We've already decided against that. Besides—' she went back to the sandwiches, trying to sound matter-of-fact. 'It isn't fair to you. Keeping you hanging about.' She kept her eyes studiously on the bread-board. 'I want you to promise me Charles you won't shut yourself up and just . . . wait for me. You might need someone who is free and can give you so much more – children and—'

'Mary—' he stood up and caught her hands gently in his. 'Please stop talking like that. You're distressed and I don't want to add to your distress. So – for the time being – I won't try to see you or get in touch. But you know it will make no difference. I love you. Nothing can change that.'

She was silent, not even looking at him.

After a while he went on quietly. 'I'll be at Mitcheldean if you need me Mary. Will you ring me if there's anything – anything at all – I can do?'

She had no strength to argue. She just nodded.

'Thank you my dear.' He drew her to him again and she did not resist. 'I'll re-join the others now.' He kissed her without passion. The sort of affectionate kiss that Bill might have given Janice. They were drawing apart when the door flew open and Brian stood there.

'Oh—' He stared at them with the curiously blank look he seemed to reserve for his mother. 'Sorry . . . Dad wanted some more sherry—'

Mary felt colour flood her face. Furious with herself she said, 'You know where it is.' She tried to say naturally to Charles, 'Goodbye then. I'm sorry you have to go so early.'

Charles picked up a plate of sandwiches. 'I'll collect Mr Elmley. Goodbye Brian. – Goodbye . . . Mary.'

Brian did not answer. He disappeared into the larder and emerged holding a bottle in each hand. He was smiling tightly.

'So, Mr Charles Mitchell of Mitcheldean I believe?' he said to his mother.

Mary tried to sound brisk. 'Obviously. Don't be too clever Brian. Mr Mitchell came to help me with the food—'

'I saw. And give a little comfort on such a sad occasion?'

Mary flinched at his insolent tone. 'I admit I was upset. Now take the sherry in to your father. And stop making mountains out of molehills.'

Brian flushed angrily and looked like a schoolboy again. He started to say something and then changed his mind. Mary followed him slowly across the hall. Her hands holding the tray of sandwiches, trembled slightly.

That evening all four Richmonds sat together in the

sitting-room for once. Stan had left a big basket of apple logs in the hearth and Jim sat in his father's armchair and threw one on idly every now and then. Otherwise there was silence in the big room. Julie and Brian had been playing a half-hearted game of cribbage and now Brian shuffled the cards while Julie lay back with her eyes closed. Mary was darning the thick socks that Jim still wore beneath his boots for outdoor work.

Jim had been doing some sums on a piece of paper and now he leaned forward and addressed Mary. 'We might clear twenty thousand when everything's settled. That's if we sell slightly above market price. And we ought to do that by including the furniture as you suggest. I'm a bit old for a mortgage but if I can raise another ten thousand we should be able to get something in the region of a hundred acres. We can refurnish from the salerooms—'

Julie's voice interrupted him. She didn't move or open her eyes.

'Sounds charming. Pastoral. Grass roots and all that sort of thing. But I don't think it's quite my scene somehow.' She opened her eyes and raised herself languidly. 'I've been thinking. A friend of mine offered me a flat some time ago. I gave him a ring earlier this evening. The offer's still open. So I'll take him up on it next week. One less for you to worry about.'

Mary stuck her needle into the sock she was darning. 'But Julie will you be able to afford it? Where is the flat – Bristol?' She told herself sternly it was only natural for a girl of Julie's age to want her own home, yet if Julie lived away that would be the last tenuous link with the family gone.

'Good Lord, no.' Julie got up impatiently and perched on the fender. She looked ridiculously young. 'London – naturally. The Surrey side, but near enough to be available.'

'You've never needed to be so instantly available before,'

Jim remarked grimly. 'Milton Mains has been accessible for your other jobs.'

'Jobs in the West Country, yes. And only because you've kept the car going for me. Now . . . well, it's obvious you can't manage that any more.'

Her tone was not conciliatory and Jim flinched.

'This modelling – it's not serious—' he sounded angry now. 'Remember you asked me to do your income tax so I know what it brings in. I did think – now – especially with Brian going to University next September – you'd want to help out. Pull your weight.'

Julie flashed irritably round on him. 'Stick it out with you and Mother d'you mean? Grub around in some rotten little small-holding while you two are studiously polite to one another?' She snorted scornful laughter. 'No thanks. Why should I when I've got the chance of this flat?'

Brian started a slow clap.

Jim snapped, 'Shut up Brian!' He leaned towards Julie. 'This friend of yours . . . are you moving in with him?'

Mary drew a quick breath and looked at Julie. She wanted to cry: He didn't mean that – he's hurt – make allowances . . . She said nothing.

Julie smiled, unperturbed. Then, her voice full of meaning, she said, 'What do you think Dad?'

Jim's face suffused with colour. 'I'll tell you what I think. I think it's the only way you could afford to live in London on the pittance you earn. And I think rather than face a few hard times with us you'd pay that kind of price. You're not quite twenty-one Julie and I forbid you to live away from home.'

Julie stood up. She flipped her hair off the collar of her sweater casually but from the ramrod stiffness of her back Mary knew how furious she was.

'Sorry Dad,' she said lightly. 'It's eighteen now. Remember?' She glanced at Mary then at Brian, a faint smile on her mouth. 'Well. What an exciting day. Old Adam laid to rest and the daughter of the house a kept woman!'

Brian burst out laughing and Julie moved gracefully towards the door.

'Good night one and all,' she called gaily over her shoulder.

'Brian – please!' Mary bundled her mending away looking anxiously at Jim. His face was set and from crimson anger had turned dead white. 'Look – she's right. It's been a terrible day. Let's not do any more talking. Brian stop it. It's not funny—'

Jim said abruptly, 'I'm going to bed.' He hardly seemed to see them. Mary was reminded of Old Adam. Yes, Jim was Victorian enough to take this seriously and for it to be a body-blow. 'Good night.'

The laughter died in Brian's throat. He said good night almost meekly and followed his father out after an uncertain glance at Mary. It worried her. Jim must indeed be looking distraught for Brian to go to bed before eleven.

She tidied her work-box and put the guard around the fire. It had been an exhausting day for them all but more so for Jim. She recalled him seeing to the drinks in the dining-room where two hours previously his father had lain . . . the small mechanical smile on his face . . . his voice saying, yesterday, 'It's all got to go hasn't it?'

She switched off the lights and went upstairs and into Julie's room. Julie was sitting up in bed creaming her face; her eyes were very bright.

Mary came to the point. 'Your father jumped to conclusions just now Julie but you shouldn't have egged him on. It's been a rotten time for him and I'm afraid that was the last straw.'

'Oh what a fuss!' Julie looked unbearably exasperated. 'Does Dad think he's got to take over where Adam left off? Half the girls I know live with men . . .' she stared defiantly at her mother for half a minute then drooped like a sulky child. 'But as a matter of fact Derek would be my landlord. He's buying this crummy old house and letting out flatlets. Well, bed-sits actually. Honestly Mummy I'm not deserting the sinking ship or anything. Most girls of my age live away from home – you'd married Daddy before you were twenty – it's just not fair.'

'All right. Calm down. Of course you can be independent – if you're able. Just tell Dad how things really are—'

'I'm not apologizing—'

'And he'll accept the situation,' Mary went on blandly. 'And in two or three months' time when you're having to make ends meet, try and put yourself in his place as he was today.' She crossed to the dressing table and straightened the silver-backed brush and comb set that had been old Mrs Richmond's. 'Now I'm going to bed. Good night Julie.'

'Good night Mummy.' Julie grinned unwillingly. 'Sorry about the row. But *you* know how maddening Dad can be. I couldn't resist letting him think . . . sorry. I'll make it up tomorrow, don't worry.'

Mary felt a funny little lift of her heart. She returned the grin. 'Good night horror.'

Julie said sleepily. 'You know, you're different. Since I came back from Paris I've noticed a distinct change. It's good.'

Mary closed the door quietly and stood outside it. She felt encouraged. And with the encouragement came a renewed sympathy for Jim. He wasn't going to get much sleep tonight.

On an impulse she crossed to the dressing-room door and knocked tentatively. There was no reply. She turned the handle and peered around the door. In the light from the hall she saw the bed was empty. She stood indecisively, frowning a little, then she hurried downstairs and went through into the kitchen. The light was on in the entry. She took Jim's anorak off the hook and went outside. The night air was startlingly cold; it was black and starless. She stared blindly around the yard waiting for her eyes to grow accustomed to the dark; there was a snuffle and a stamp from the stables. Then Jim's voice, 'All right there my beauty. Steady now.'

She walked slowly across to where the shires stood in their stalls. Richmond Queen, her daughter the Princess, and Squire, the gelding.

'Mary!' Jim met her at the stable door. 'It's cold out here – go on in. I'm just checking.'

Mary passed him and went inside. The storm lantern cast shadows everywhere and glinted on the brasses hanging against the walls. The horses snorted at the sight of her. They hadn't enjoyed their day; the constant coming and going of cars had made them uneasy and Stan had been late getting them in. And they missed working with Old Adam. Perhaps they knew he was gone.

Mary said softly, 'We could keep *them* Jim. That would be no extravagance. They could work for their keep.'

Jim said, 'I was just wondering whether to get out of farming altogether. Get an office job – or a representative—'

'Don't be silly Jim,' Mary said calmly. 'You're a farmer.'

'Yes.' It came out like a sigh of despair.

There was silence. Jim fondled the Princess. He seemed to relax slightly.

Mary said, 'Julie was just being annoying you know. She isn't going to live with this man. He'll simply be her landlord.'

'I see.' He gave a short laugh. 'I suppose she thought it amusing to needle me.'

'Her nerves are stretched too Jim. I wondered whether the Paris trip was a failure. She seems very irritable.'

He didn't answer that directly. After a while he said, 'Both the children have grown away.'

'They're growing up. It's natural—'

'We live under the same roof. That's all.' She was silent, watching his square capable hand caressing the horse. He drew a sharp breath. 'Your visit to Janice on Friday . . . how long was it to be?'

'I hadn't made plans Jim—'

'You can still go now. There's nothing here to keep you.'

She flinched and averted her head. 'Naturally I don't want to take a holiday now. Besides there is a lot to do—'

'So you're staying to help out? Is that it?' His voice was unutterably bleak.

'Jim please – my place is here—'

'For how long Mary? I'm sorry but I must know. How long will it be before you go to see your sister?'

She turned to him impulsively hoping to soften the cold hardness of him. 'Jim – I'll stay as long as I'm needed . . . as long as you want me to stay—' she sensed his feeling of isolation – Brian's rudeness, Julie's desertion and the sudden realization that his wife had been going to leave. And the loss of his heritage. 'Jim you're not alone – I'm your wife—'

'Yes you are.' His voice was tightly controlled. 'And you promise you'll stay—?'

'Of course.' She said it gladly thinking that at last he was expressing a need of her.

He turned from the stall and took her arm in a hard grip. 'I'll hold you to that Mary. It's a bargain.'

Mary felt her heart sink. Jim's eyes were darkly unfathomable but there was no affection in his touch. Then, without saying more, he held out his hand. Mary took it. It was icy cold and pity stirred in her again.

It was a strange way for a married couple to seal a bargain. Outside the moon raced from behind a cloud and lit the yard. They stood there bathed in its light, still clasping hands.

CHAPTER THREE

The next three weeks proved trying for them all. Jim was in Taunton a great deal working out the complete specifications of Milton Mains for Blewett and Harrison; looking for a cheaper farm somewhere in the County; meeting Tony Elliot to discuss ways and means of paying off Adam's death duties. Mary was not sorry to be alone at the farm to carry on the endless task of sorting and packing. Jean Butler was a strong right arm as usual, but nowadays a very silent Jean. Jim had spoken to Stan and told him that he would make certain the new owners kept on both the Butlers. Indeed with the present shortage of labour any buyer would be delighted to have experienced help. But that wasn't what worried Jean. Mary knew how she felt. The thought of housekeeping in some strange farm without Jean's cheery presence within call made Mary feel as lost as Jean looked.

Julie patched up her quarrel with her father and sold her car two days after Old Adam's funeral. Casually she left the cheque for three hundred pounds on Jim's desk, but he returned it to her telling her gruffly she would need something to set up her own flat.

She glanced at him, her blue eyes bright and still defensive.

'Thanks Dad. At least you'll be saving quite a bit with me off your hands.'

It was slightly more graciously said than before and Jim accepted it – with the offer of the cheque – as a peace offering.

'That's for certain,' he said with a ghost of a grin.

Julie spent another two days wandering aimlessly about the farm and the house. It wasn't until after she had gone that Mary realized she had been saying goodbye to her old home. Julie would not be coming back to Milton Mains.

Brian continued to spend most of his time racketing around the countryside with Mike Stelling and a group of older boys who drove hotted-up bangers they used in scrambles. Mary understood only too well that Brian, suspecting her relationship with Charles Mitchell could hardly bear to be in the same room with his mother. She felt completely powerless to explain and only hoped that patience and understanding would eventually prove to Brian that she had a right to some personal happiness with someone else. Meanwhile his A levels were coming up and he wasn't working.

She tried to point this out tactfully one morning while he was eating one of his late breakfasts and Jean was out of the way upstairs.

'Work? For my exams? What's the point?' He stood up and went to the sink. 'No money for University now, is there?'

He filled a glass with water and drained it in one long draught. Mary looked at his up-thrust head, the exposed throat that was nearly a man's.

'Of course there'll be enough money Brian,' she said buoyantly. 'The County will allocate you a grant and we'll manage somehow.'

'That's the key-word, isn't it mother-mine?' He rinsed the glass and upturned it on the draining board. 'I'm afraid I can't "manage" . . .' he went towards the door, then turned at her involuntary protest. 'Does that shock you? Admitting I can't scrimp and save?' He gave one of his short laughs. 'Well you see, I haven't been brought up to it – have I?'

He was through the door before Mary could make any

kind of reply. She went to the window and watched him cross to the car port. The next minute his car skidded round in the mud of the yard and he was gone. She felt a wave of loneliness engulf her. Three weeks ago at Old Adam's funeral Charles had somehow given her enough strength to comfort Julie, even reassure Jim. But since then nothing had really changed. Jim never consulted her, Julie had gone, Brian was even more difficult. And Charles – Charles had kept his promise and dropped out of her life. Still staring unseeingly through the window she remembered with incredulity that only four weeks ago at the beginning of April, she had been on the point of starting a new life.

After Jean left she had an early lunch and then took a pile of newspapers into the dining-room and began carefully wrapping Grandmother Richmond's exquisite china dinner service piece by piece. She had almost finished when the telephone rang. It was Jim.

'Mary?' His voice was carefully impersonal. 'Good news at last. Blewett's had an offer for Milton. A good offer. I've accepted of course.'

Mary studied her free hand. It was stained dark grey from the newsprint. Once again she had her job in the house and Jim had his.

'Of course. Do you know the buyer Jim?'

'Yes. Our neighbour. Mitchell from Mitcheldean.'

Mary felt her face contract. 'Charles Mitchell? Are you sure?'

It was a stupid question and he treated it impatiently.

'Of course. I'm with Tony now – Mitchell's due within the hour. We can both sign the contract on the spot and cut a lot of corners. He knows every inch of Milton so the legal searches will be a mere formality. We should be able to leave in four to five weeks.'

Mary found she was gripping the receiver so hard her fingers ached. If Charles was doing this for her sake it was impossible . . . impossible. But how could she tell Jim?

She made the only objection she could think up. 'But we've got nowhere to go – we can't sell until we've found another farm.'

'That's what I rang about.' Jim paused and Mary could hear other voices in the background. She was stupidly hurt that he hadn't even called from a kiosk where they could have spoken in private. 'As soon as I've seen Mitchell I'm going to view a small place down by the coast.'

'Jim—' Mary felt desperate. He couldn't be this high-handed. 'Jim, wait a minute—'

'Yes?' He had only half his attention on her – she heard him murmur something away from the receiver.

'Nothing . . . not really. I just wondered . . . what's the name of this place you're going to see?'

Jim's voice was faint. 'Tony – what's the name . . .?' He returned to Mary. 'Caryford. It's called Caryford, Mary. About a hundred acres. Sheep at the moment but run right down. We might get it below market price.'

'Caryford . . .' Mary repeated the name without enthusiasm. She had no sense of it being her new home. The coast was forty miles away. There would be no chance of bumping into Charles in the village.

Jim sounded brisk. 'I must go Mary. Don't worry if I'm late.'

She forced herself to say, 'Good luck.' Then the receiver sang emptily in her ear. She said aloud, 'Oh Charles . . .'

She hesitated indecisively for a moment, then she dialled the Mitcheldean number. He had told her to ring him if she needed any help . . .

'Charles?' She almost gasped with relief as she heard his voice. 'I thought you might have already left for Taunton. Charles, Jim has just telephoned to tell me you've made an offer for Milton Mains. My dear – you can't. Please withdraw. You must see it's impossible—'

'Mary.' His voice was quietly reasonable, but pleading. 'Let me come and see you. We should talk—'

'No. I'm sorry Charles but I couldn't bear it.' She knew she sounded on the edge of hysteria and tried to add a laugh.

Charles said quickly, 'All right. All right darling. But listen to me – will you listen Mary?'

She drew a deep breath, determined to put her view before he could talk her into acquiescence. 'Charles, don't you see, not only does it tie you down – and I don't want that – you promised . . . but it's almost, well it's almost as if you're buying me.'

'Mary darling. Please stop it. This isn't like you. Of course I want to help Jim to get settled because I know that brings you closer to me. But I've wanted Milton Mains ever since I took over Mitcheldean from my father. Ask Jim. I've tried to buy it before – not a hope of course. Your Long Acre field cuts right into my estate Mary. Check it on the Ordnance Survey. I can put a farm manager into the house and he can run the whole of the dairy here from that west side.'

There was a pause.

'So you won't withdraw?'

'It's not a question of won't my dear. Surely *you* can understand?'

She said wearily, 'I know how Jim will see it later. If you and I—'

'Not *if* Mary. When. When you and I get married. Is that what you mean?'

She paused fractionally. 'Yes.'

'And will it matter then? If Jim chooses to misunderstand a perfectly logical transaction, will it matter?'

She thought of asking him what logic had to do with it. She remembered Jim's dark despair that night in the stable. Then his quick hard bargain with her. Maybe it was only she who reasoned emotionally.

She stiffened her spine, 'No. No of course it won't matter. Not then.'

There was another pause then Charles said, 'Can you tell me when that might be Mary? I mean, can you see your way more clearly now?'

She thought of her promise to Jim. But she could hardly tell Charles about that.

'Well, things will move now I expect. Jim is viewing another farm down by the coast after he's seen you.'

'The coast? I'd hoped you would be nearer.'

'Yes. Perhaps it will be easier though Charles. I feel I must be . . . whole-hearted about this.'

'Oh darling. I suppose if you didn't have such a conscience I wouldn't love you, but it makes things difficult at times.'

She managed a proper laugh at this. 'Seriously Charles. This had better be goodbye for the time being.'

'You'll get in touch if there's anything . . .?' She promised and he wished her good luck huskily and waited for her to put her receiver down. She hesitated then did so with sudden decision and went briskly back to the dinner service. But as she moved the tea-chests into the hall she knew she wasn't at all happy about Charles buying Milton Mains.

It was almost dark when Brian came in. He raised his brows in mute enquiry as he saw the crowded hall.

'Dad's sold Milton,' she told him as she strained the first of the broad beans from the garden. 'So I thought I'd better get cracking.'

He came slowly to the table. With a child's disbelief of anything unpleasant he said, 'So. It's really gone. I never thought it would actually happen. Who's the buyer?'

Mary swallowed. 'Charles Mitchell.' She put a knob of butter in the beans and tossed them vigorously.

There was a silence. She could almost hear Brian digesting

the implications of Charles buying the farm. Very nearly she repeated his own justifications for it, then decided any kind of explanation would sound like an excuse.

At last he said, 'So where are we off to then?'

She almost sighed with relief that he too let the subject lie.

'Probably a place called Caryford. On the coast.'

'Oh Lord. The back of beyond. What am I supposed to do there?'

'Well you might be able to work. Your exams will be over but there will be reading for your first term at Exeter.'

He made no comment on this either and after supper he announced he wasn't going out that evening.

'I'd better catch up on revision I suppose. And—' he looked at her sheepishly. 'I've got another car and it wants a bit of attention. I don't think it would get me very far this evening.'

'You've what?' Mary looked at him aghast. 'Oh Brian—' she hurried to the window and in the last of the evening light saw a decrepit old Ford in the car port. 'You've bought one of those wretched bangers – you can't mean to start scrambling at a time like this—'

'Calm down mother-mine!' Brian was smiling, and not one of his bitter smiles this time. 'I did a swop. I've got to have something to get me into Taunton this term haven't I? And now you haven't got a car . . . well, I wondered if you'd share the expense with me. You can use it in the evening – you'll want to get around saying goodbyes and so forth, won't you? Anyway I got the Ford *and* a cheque for three-fifty. So I did better than Julie!'

His face was flushed and he looked exactly as he'd looked on his twelfth birthday when he'd saved his pocket money for four weeks and bought her some 'pearls'.

Mary felt herself relaxing imperceptibly. 'Oh Brian, you did well. And of course we'll share the running costs. I shall be pleased to have some transport again.' Though she could have walked to the village to say her farewells to the few families she knew there.

She felt almost happy as she sat up waiting for Jim. As she heard the Land-Rover pull into the yard just before midnight she went to the door forgetting for a moment that he was just a polite stranger. He was coming slowly across the yard and she saw with a pang how the last month had aged him. Though it was dark, the old Jim would have looked round him, automatically checking that the farm was safe for the night. Now he walked with bowed head, his hands hanging at his sides.

'Mary!' He was surprised to see her. When was the last time she had gone to meet him like this? 'Still up? I didn't think you'd wait this long.'

She took his coat and hung it in the entry.

'How could I go to bed?' she tried to sound light. 'I had to know how you got on. What did you think of the farm – Caryford?'

He didn't answer immediately. His weariness reminded her of the day in April when his father had died. He sat down at the big kitchen table and rubbed his eyes as if to clear his head.

'Caryford?' He didn't sound very interested. 'Oh yes. I've bought it. Just a few legal details for Tony to tie up. Searches and so forth. But it's as good as ours.'

Mary paused in front of the oven, cloth in hand.

'You've bought it? Were there others after it then?'

She carried the casserole to the table.

'What? Good Lord no. It's completely run down – been on the market for months. That's why it was so cheap.'

'But—' How on earth could she protest at him settling it without her? Yet surely even business partners consulted? 'But, what was the hurry?'

'There's nothing else going at our price. And we must

get in before the summer's over. There's a lot to do.'

She stared at him dumbly. 'Yes. Yes of course. I just thought . . . nothing.' She spooned vegetables on to his plate. 'Stan brought the beans in this afternoon.' She wondered whether she was going to cry.

'Good old Stan.' Jim began to eat without appetite. 'I could do with him at the new place. I'll need to plough some of the land and he could have coped with the sheep.'

She swallowed determined not to offer her help again.

'One thing,' she said brightly, 'Charles will keep the Butlers on here all right.'

He glanced up. 'Yes. Yes of course.'

She felt herself flush. She rarely spoke of Charles at all let alone used his christian name.

He changed the subject abruptly. 'Any news?'

She remembered her pleasure at Brian selling his sports car. It seemed a long time ago. She told Jim.

'The cheque is on your desk,' she said. 'And he insists that you keep it. He says it will pay the removal firm.'

For the first time since he had come home Jim smiled.

'Yes. All right. It might make him feel he's pulling his weight.'

She began to clear up his meal, expecting him to tell her something about the new farm but apparently that subject was finished.

'Leave the washing-up Mary and get to bed. You look all-in,' he said instead making for the hall door himself. 'Good grief – no wonder.' He surveyed the tea-chests with surprise. 'You've been busy.'

'Yes.' She took his advice and left the sink. 'You see Jim—' she snapped off the kitchen light and crossed the hall to the stairs. 'I like to feel I'm pulling my weight too.'

She didn't look round but long after she had settled down for the night she could hear him moving around downstairs. Wearily she closed her eyes. There was still no real partnership between them . . . yet, inexplicably they had the power to hurt each other. It didn't make sense.

The next few weeks sped by. They went on living their lives separately. Brian immersed in last-minute work and then exams; Jim up early and late for the milking and spending his days between Mitcheldean, Tony Elliot's office and the new farm; Mary packing and buying the bare essentials of furniture for Caryford. Pride forebade her to ask Jim if he would take her to see the farm, but in the end she was forced to enquire the size of the rooms.

'Small,' he told her briefly. 'The usual – two receptions, kitchen, three bedrooms. Sloping roofs so don't get any wardrobes. The bathroom's downstairs. Sort of tacked on to the kitchen.'

'We could take the oak chest from the hall,' she suggested. 'That would do for our clothes . . .'

'There's storage space under the eaves, so we won't need bedroom furniture,' Jim said carelessly. 'Get the absolute minimum of stuff. None of ours will do – too big.'

She bit her lip, angry and upset that she was unable to take any real pleasure in furnishing her new home; hurt that Jim had no conception of the enormous effort involved in clearing out a large family house and tailoring her ideas to such frugal limits as Caryford appeared to offer.

Julie telephoned and showed an unexpected interest in the new place.

'There seems to be plenty of work for me down here – I'm surprised really,' she said, then added with unusual frankness, 'But, to be honest, I'm missing Exmoor. It was nice to get away from people each evening.'

Mary noticed wryly she didn't say she missed her family.

She said, 'Well, you can always come to the new place. We shall keep the Land-Rover of course and I could meet you at Barnstaple.'

'What's the new farm like Mummy?' Julie asked. 'Is there a room for me? How big is it?'

'There are three bedrooms apparently.'

'Oh.' Naturally Julie knew her parents occupied different rooms. 'Well you could have a bed-settee downstairs perhaps. How does it strike you? Is it pretty?'

Mary sighed. 'I haven't seen it yet. Dad isn't very good at describing things as you know.'

'Oh,' Julie said again. Then – 'Poor Mummy.'

Mary chose to misunderstand. 'I don't mind leaving here too much. It's not my home as it is your father's. And yours and Brian's of course.'

'I hadn't thought of it like that. In any case it really belongs to Old Adam doesn't it? The past.'

Mary wished Jim could have heard those words. As June blazed its way through cloudless skies he seemed to withdraw more and more into himself. Twice when she called him for supper he was with the three Shires. When he should have been sorting Adam's papers he was staring through the office window as if he could imprint the view of the familiar fields on his mind.

Then the twenty-third dawned grey and cloudy yet breathlessly hot. The two enormous pantechnicons which were to take their things the forty-odd miles to Caryford arrived. Stan and Jean were on hand to help with the loading; the one van was for farm equipment the other for household stuff and the sheep would arrive in trucks the next day.

Jean was frankly upset and kept pulling a handkerchief from her sleeve and blowing vigorously.

'I never thought to see this day m'dear,' she said repeatedly to Mary. 'The Butlers and Richmonds . . . well, we're like an institution. I d'remember walking over they fields with Brian when he was just two year old. He's like my own.'

Yes, Jean had never had children of her own and she had shown unexpected firmness with Mary's. Neither Brian nor Julie were ever rude to her.

'He'll miss you terribly Jean,' Mary said. 'You must come and see us as soon as you can. And as often. You know you'll always be welcome.'

Jim and Stan said a tight-lipped farewell through the window of the Land-Rover. Neither of them were used to much speech – a look, a nod or a jerk of the thumb were the kind of signs they used for communication and now they had no words. Young Robbie saved the day by thrusting his hand into Jim's.

'Bes o' luck Mis'r Richmond. Hope you does as well there as you done 'ere.'

They were off. They passed the lumbering vans after they left the lane. Brian followed close behind in his Ford. The enormous horse-box containing Richmond Queen swayed smoothly behind them. Jim would have to make two more trips before nightfall to collect the Princess and Squire. Once more Mary would be alone to settle in as best she could.

It took them nearly two hours to reach the tiny hamlet of Carybridge. The lanes twisted and turned on themselves across the high moor and down through the deep valleys and the cloud ceiling was so low it cut their speed to a minimum. The River Cary was a small rushing stream that came from the top of the moor cutting itself a combe over thousands of years till it reached the sea. Half-a-dozen houses, a post office, a pub and a church huddled around a stone bridge that gave the village its name. Further down the combe where the river widened, there were stepping stones and a footpath across two fields. Jim drove over the bridge, however, and approached the farm along a stony track hemmed in by dry-stone walls sprouting foliage and flowers of all descriptions. Then there was a five-barred gate propped open. And the farmhouse.

Mary never forgot her first view of her future home. It was built in the middle of a saucer-shaped field, presumably to protect it from the prevailing south-west winds, but which made it seem almost an underground dwelling with its roof and chimneys at eye level. The saucer had a lip on the west side and here she could see the footpath across the fields and the river shining in the distance studded with the stepping stones and boulders. There was some poor quality orcharding behind the house and an acre of tilled ground straggled with the yellowing leaves of field peas. Then the moor swept upwards, wooded and wild and lost in cloud.

Mary could think of nothing to say. 'It's – it's well sheltered,' she faltered at last.

Jim smiled grimly. 'What you mean is – there are no views from the windows. The front rooms on the north-west side aren't too bad but I'm afraid it's very dark inside.'

He drove slowly over the tussocked field. Behind them the Queen whinnied quietly as if she knew this was home and Brian bounced and jolted his old car past them and drew up first outside the front door.

'Where are the stables? And the cow sheds?' He called getting out and staring at the house with an expression of distaste.

'The Shires will be all right outside through the summer,' Jim said tightly. He went straight to the box and let the Queen down the ramp and on to the pasture. 'It's not good grass I'll admit. I'll have to buy feed.'

The huge horse nodded graciously seeming to approve all she saw. They were forced to laugh and, for a moment, Mary thought they were like any family arriving at a new house.

'But Dad . . . there's just *nothing*!' Brian took up again. He was peering around the small house genuinely appalled.

'Where's the stock? And look at the state of the land!'

'I know. Why do you think it was cheap?' Jim fitted the key into the front door and led the way inside. 'I'll switch on water and electricity Mary. D'you think you could rustle up some tea before I go back?'

'Of course.' Mary had packed tea-things in a picnic basket and she followed Jim through a narrow passage and into a dark kitchen at the back of the house, holding the basket in front of her. She stared around her in dismay while Jim fiddled with a spanner beneath a shallow stone sink in the darkest corner. The walls were lime-washed brick which had flaked a miniature snow-storm over the stone-flagged floor. There was a fairly good electric cooker next to the sink and a single bulb dangling on a long frayed flex from the ceiling. That was all. She had expected shelves, maybe even a modern unit.

She put the picnic basket on the floor and unpacked the kettle.

'The pantry is through here,' Jim went through the back door and disclosed a large pantry to the right of the porch. Mary breathed a sigh of relief. 'This—' he pointed to the left of the porch. 'Is the old wash-house. There's a copper with its own furnace. And beyond it is the bathroom. That's modern anyway.'

He looked so miserable she couldn't make it worse.

'It'll be marvellous Jim. This kitchen is bigger than I thought. Maybe I can put the fridge and washing machine out in that place and we could eat in here.'

He shrugged. 'I'll leave that to you. Do whatever you like.'

He went back through the passage without noticing Mary's exasperation. She heard him ask Brian to give him a hand with the carpets. They had hoped to lay them before the furniture arrived, but, wrinkling her nose Mary decided the floors must be scrubbed first. She made tea and forced herself to hum a tune as she did so. Caryford wasn't *that* bad . . .

By the end of the day her optimism had all gone. The floors were scrubbed and the carpets laid, Brian had connected the fridge and made up two beds and gone into the village for milk and bread. Mary had cleaned the pantry and lined it with fresh paper and stacked most of her food and utensils. But there were a lot of snags. The new table and four chairs completely filled the kitchen and would have to be moved into the tiny dining-room. There was nowhere for Grandmother Richmond's china. The storage space in the eaves upstairs was full of cobwebs, so clothes lay everywhere, over beds, even in piles on the floor.

When Jim returned for the last time it was gone nine o'clock and the heat had reduced them all to an exhausted stupor. Mary threw a plastic cloth over the tea-chests of china and dished up scrambled eggs and tea. They ate without speaking, each occupied with their own thoughts.

Later Jim said, 'The sheep will arrive some time tomorrow. I shall have to make some kind of pen. I see there's willow fencing stacked at the back of the house. The other people must have used that – probably made it themselves too.'

'Brian will help you,' Mary said, glancing swiftly at her son.

'Sure.' She couldn't tell if he was being sarcastic. He had worked hard himself and was exhausted. And she knew that the sight of the cramped and decrepit farm had brought home to him their plight properly at last. 'It's a bit primitive isn't it Dad? Willow sheep pens went out with ox-ploughing—'

'Old Adam ploughed behind Squire and the Queen,' Jim said roughly. 'And I shall do the same. They must pay for their keep somehow and I can't afford them and the tractor.

Anyway what was good enough for the old folk is good enough for us.'

Mary wondered if this philosophy included Old Adam's attitude to women. Surely the pattern wasn't going to be repeated all over again? She thought desperately of the help she needed in the house: storage units, a hatch through to the dining-room. Jim could have done it easily on wet days and she could have pitched in and helped him outside when the weather was good.

She said wearily, 'It's unbearably hot. I'm going to bed before the storm breaks.'

'Same here,' Brian stretched and yawned prodigiously.

'If it rains I'll put the horses under the kitchen window. They'll be protected there.' Jim stood up. 'No milking tomorrow. At least we can sleep in.'

He didn't look pleased and Mary knew he was thinking of the steady, tranquil routine at Milton Mains . . . Stan in the milking pit with the cows gently working their way through five to a side . . . early morning tea by the first light . . . breakfast after you'd earned it. She could find no words of comfort. It was only as she was sliding between the sheets that she remembered Brian hadn't put up a bed for Jim. She had intended telling him matter-of-factly that he would have to share the double bed for one night, but she had simply forgotten. Surely he would take it for granted . . . she sat up in bed listening. No sound came from below.

Impatiently she got out of bed and drew on her dressing-gown. It was ridiculous to feel so inhibited – Jim was her husband. Softly she opened the bedroom door and crept down the narrow stairs. The sitting-room light was on and she pushed the door open casually, a prepared speech on her lips. Then she stopped. Jim had shoved together the two small easy chairs she'd bought in Taunton and was uncomfortably asprawl on them, fast asleep.

She looked at him for a long moment before she returned to bed. The difficulties of the long day seemed to rise up in her and this was the last straw. Jim would prefer an uncomfortable night on two chairs rather than share a bed with his own wife.

She was at last falling into an uneasy doze when a flicker of sheet lightning lit up the sloping ceiling above the bed. Automatically she counted the seconds until the thunder. It came softly, a long low rumble from the top of the moor almost immediately followed by a single splat of rain against the open window. One of the Shires whinnied nervously.

Mary sat up again listening for Jim. There was complete and creaking silence throughout the house. Then another enormous and heavy rain-drop. And another.

Mary padded to the window and looked out. It was completely black but a sudden stamp of hoof against turf told her the horses were about twenty yards away staked halfway up the saucer around the house. Lightning played over the moor again and there they were, heads up.

'All right – I'm coming,' she breathed.

She didn't stop for dressing-gown or slippers, the rain would come in earnest at any moment. The sheep-bitten grass was soft against her bare feet and the air electrically warm on her arms. She ran over to the horses, murmuring endearments, gathering up the tethers and pulling the stake free. They crowded around her, nuzzling her gratefully, blowing into her neck. It was the first time she had led the three of them together, but she felt no fear. She was almost to the house when lightning and thunder struck together; the sky seemed to crack open and hurl rain down the combe with terrifying violence. She was instantly soaked, her nightdress clinging to her, her long hair dripping on her shoulders.

Squire stopped with a suddenness that nearly jerked her

arm out of its socket; his whinny sounded even above the drumming of the rain.

'Come on – come on my beauty—' Mary tugged at the rope, dashing water from her face with her other hand. 'You'll be all right next to the house – come on.'

Squire dragged on his rope. Princess, thoroughly uneasy now, jerked her head and stamped one of her huge feet.

Mary sobbed encouragement to them. She was terrified they would pull away and thunder off into the darkness. She could imagine them breaking legs against the boulders in the swollen river . . . slipping over the cliff into the sea.

Then a path of light cut through the darkness from the house and Jim's voice came to her.

'OK Squire – where are you? It's all right—'

'Here Jim!' Mary screamed. 'Over here by the house! Quickly – oh quickly—'

She felt the tethering ropes taken from her and Jim's voice, stern now, admonishing Squire to stand still. He was in pyjamas, already saturated like she was. In the light from the house she could see the powerful muscles in his neck knot as he struggled with the frightened horse. She drooped where she was, uncaring now of the deluging rain, rubbing her arms, thankful to see him.

They were in the lee of the house, the jutting eaves protecting them from the lashing storm; Jim was staking the horses again, rubbing them down with a sack, talking to them as if they were naughty children.

Mary pushed her hair from her face and scooped it behind her neck.

'Jim, I'm sorry. You were so tired I didn't want to wake you—'

If she was expecting thanks she was disappointed. The kitchen light reflected from his eyes; they were darkly furious.

'You must be mad – thinking you could manage these beasts in a storm like this—'

'It hadn't started Jim. And I *could* have managed them if it had held off for a few seconds more—'

'Get in the house! You're soaking wet!'

'That doesn't matter. So are you.'

He caught her wrist suddenly in a grip that hurt.

'I'm used to it and you're not. Will you do as I tell you!'

She stared at his white face knowing once again she was being put in her place – and that this time Jim was justified. Her own anger rose to meet his, but it was a blind anger, trembling and near to tears.

'I – I hate you!' She sounded even to her own ears like a petulant child. 'I've been doing what you tell me for the last twenty-two years—'

His grip tightened and she gasped into silence.

He said tensely, 'Why are you here then? I gave you a chance to back down – clear out and go to Janice's. Was it for the sake of the children? Or because you were sorry for me?' His face was running with water and he wiped it with his pyjama sleeve. She was reminded of Brian as a little boy. Tears ran with the rain down her face. This man was her husband . . . they had two children . . .

'I came because I wanted to! I wanted the Richmonds to be a family again – helping one another – not separated by high walls! But you wouldn't understand that. You think that any kind of dependence on another human being means weakness – don't you?' She was crying uncontrollably, almost choking on her own tears.

The grip on her wrist loosened and she felt Jim's arm across her shoulders, piloting her round the house and through the front door, down the passage and into the kitchen. She couldn't stop crying; exhaustion and strain had caught up with her. She made a token protest as he wrapped her in towels and rubbed at her hair. She hardly remembered climbing the stairs and getting into bed. But as the light went out and she felt the empty place beside her, the tears came afresh.

The last thing she recalled before she fell into a sleep that was near total unconsciousness, was the scent of the rain-fresh turf through the open window, the rushing of the swollen Cary and the more distant sound of the sea. Backed by the percussion of the snort and stamp of the horses. And somewhere beneath the unhappiness, her mind seized on a positive thought. Caryford was going to be her home . . .

CHAPTER FOUR

Mary awoke knowing it was late. The sky was grey through the open window and the air was much cooler. She rolled over in bed and picked up her watch from the floor. It was nine-thirty. Her head throbbed and there was a pain in her shoulder where Squire's rope had pulled at her arm. The room looked terrible, choc-a-bloc with heaps of linen and piles of boxes. There was so much to do . . .

She got out of bed, stifling a groan, and went downstairs, clutching her dressing-gown to her. No-one was about. She peered into the sitting-room. The chairs were back on either side of the fireplace. The bathroom was empty. Going back upstairs to dress she knocked on Brian's door and went in when there was no answer. He too had disappeared.

She dressed hastily in jeans and a shirt and hurried outside. Both cars were parked on the gritty grass at the side of the house and the horses were loose and enjoying the fresher pasture at the top of the saucer as if last night had never happened.

Mary frowned. Jim and Brian must be working together somewhere out there. She couldn't remember the last time Brian had helped his father with the work of the farm.

She made herself busy for the next two hours. The kitchen was definitely too crowded so she pulled the table into the dining-room and laid it for a late breakfast – or early lunch. Then she went upstairs and tackled the cobwebs in the eaves. By mid-day all the upstairs cupboards were clean and the linen and clothes stacked away. She looked into the third bedroom. Julie's bed was stacked against the wall and a minute dressing table stood under the window. It was a tiny room immediately above the kitchen. Hard to imagine Jim managing in here.

She heard voices downstairs and for some reason looked at herself in the mirror smoothing her hair back into the elastic band on the nape of her neck. She noticed her colour was high and put her cool hands to her cheeks for a moment wondering what was the matter with her.

'Mary!'

She went out on to the landing. Jim was standing inside the front door.

'Ah, there you are.' He sounded relieved. 'We didn't think we should be so long otherwise we'd have left a note.'

Jim leave a note? She ran down the stairs and went into the kitchen as if something was boiling urgently on the stove.

'I was going to do eggs again. But as it's lunch-time shall I open a tin?' She filled the kettle and put it on the cooker avoiding his eyes. 'I've moved the table into the dining-room to make it a little less cramped out here.'

'Yes, so I see. It's fine.' Jim cleared his throat and then called heartily, 'Brian! Your mother's been moving the furniture again.'

A groan came from the sitting-room and Mary looked at Jim at last, her wide eyes asking a question.

Jim grinned more naturally. 'The lorries with the sheep rolled up at eight o'clock. It was too wet for them down here after that rain so I got Brian up to help me drive them on to the moor.'

'D'you mean to tell me I slept through all the unloading?' Mary was aghast at the thought of the turmoil she had missed.

'Stan was with them. You know how good he is with sheep. He had them practically holding hands in a crocodile—'

'Oh dear – I missed Stan too,' she said with regret.

'I made him tea. He had to get back straight away. There's plenty to do before Mitchell's man moves into the house. He and Jean send their love.'

'I can't get over it. I haven't slept like that since . . .' she had been going to say 'since our honeymoon'.

'No.' He walked to the sink and rinsed his hands. 'I looked in. You were well away. I didn't want to wake you . . . after last night.' He dried his hands, his back towards her. 'Are you all right?'

'Of course.' She realized they had actually held a conversation – stilted perhaps but much more than their usual exchange of remarks. The memory of the angry things she'd said last night returned to inhibit her again. Somehow she forced herself to say, 'I'm sorry. But the horses seem all right this morning.'

'They're fine. Absolutely fine.' He was using his hearty voice: he wanted to forget last night. 'Brian's been a big help this morning,' he went on half-humorously, then added – genuinely surprised – 'And I honestly believe he enjoyed himself.'

Mary caught his eye and they exchanged smiles, half-rueful, half hopeful for the future. She turned back to the stove immediately with a small shock. It was a long time since she had communicated with Jim except in anger.

After a scratch lunch they went out immediately to start on the sheep pens. Such unaccustomed exercise was telling on Brian and he looked weary, but he followed his father outside without protest.

Mary took her shopping basket and walked the two miles into Carybridge to see what the local shops had to offer. She was surprised to find that most of her household needs could be bought in the two or three local stores which clustered around the village green. What was more, vegetables, meat and fish were delivered once a week with the groceries.

The Postmistress, Mrs Westbrook, informed her what she needed was a deep-freeze.

'I did used to tell Mrs Curtis – what was at the Ford before you – if you got yourself a nice deep-freeze you could pop in a couple of those sheep, a box of fish and all the veg and fruit you could grow and there wouldn't be hardly nothing to buy.'

'It's an idea Mrs Westbrook,' Mary conceded. 'But at the moment we don't know how our money's going. And then there's space. The kitchen is rather small—'

'Oh not the kitchen my lovely. That wouldn't do at all. But 'twould go a treat in the wash-house. Specially if your husband took away the copper.'

It seemed Mrs Westbrook knew Caryford intimately together with the lay-outs of most of the houses in the district.

'Now over at the Watling-place, Mr Watling's thrown the wash-house into the kitchen and they've got a lovely breakfast room out of it. But of course all these farms along the coast have got their kitchens at the back which makes them cold sort of rooms I d'say.'

Mary smiled as Mrs Westbrook went on with her re-planning. Her avid interest in her neighbours was like Jean's and never bordered on mere curiosity.

'Now m'dear,' the little post mistress concluded. 'Being as how you're not on the telephone, if there's any messages come through for you, I'll come straight out on my bike and deliver them. I don't want you to feel cut off. We're all one big happy family down here y'know.'

'That's nice,' Mary said, meaning it. 'I don't think anyone will want to get in touch urgently. Unless it's my daughter. And even she . . . no there's no-one. But thank you very much Mrs Westbrook.'

She came away with a loaded basket feeling that the village was ready to take them in via Mrs Westbrook.

Already they were less isolated – the thought that Julie could get in touch with them easily made her feel part of the world again. She acknowledged with surprise how very much she was missing Julie.

The walk down the combe was gay with flowers and after the rain the scent was heady. She took the short cut across the stepping stones and paused in the middle of the river to gaze out across the grey sea in the direction of Wales. If they worked hard and saved hard they could make Caryford . . . something. It was a far prettier place than Milton Mains and in two or three years perhaps they could afford to build on to the house. She checked her thoughts suddenly. Two or three years? She wouldn't be here then, would she?

Determinedly she went on across the rest of the stones and crossed the fields to the house. No need to think of that now. She had quite enough to do in the present without worrying about the future.

She prepared a beef casserole for supper and swept up yet more flakes of whitewash from the stone floor. Then she put on some gardening gloves and went outside. Jim and Brian were still hammering and wiring the willow fencing into a pen on the sheltered side of the house. Jim cut holes in the turf for the stakes, hammering them home with a mallet while Brian fastened each section together with wire. After a while Mary picked up the wire cutters and began cutting the wire into twelve-inch lengths. Brian took them from her with muttered thanks. His hands shook with tiredness.

She waited until she was certain Jim had accepted her presence, then she touched Brian's arm.

'Go on in Brian. I'll take a turn here. Try and rest before supper.'

He did not protest and she took the wire from his scratched hands and bound it round the next two willow stakes, twisting it tightly and pushing the ends into a loop. It was the first time she and Jim had worked together – unless she counted last night. Remembering last night she suddenly smiled seeing it in her mind as an outsider might have seen it – two scantily clad people quarrelling in the rain.

Jim rested his arms for a moment on the close-woven fencing. His own face lightened into a half-grin.

'As Brian said, it's primitive. But . . . I don't know – there's something about the place.' He hesitated searching for words. Under the low sky the little house looked squat and huddled, the orchard and field peas simply scruffy. It was hard to find a good word to say for Caryford.

Mary nodded encouragingly. 'I feel at home here,' she said.

His smile widened. 'I can't go as far as that. Milton Mains is still home to me. But I feel . . . fit. Younger somehow.'

Mary remembered her headache and sore shoulder. They had gone, the shoulder a mere twinge to remind her of last night. And last night was no longer an entirely unpleasant memory.

'Yes,' she agreed wonderingly. 'Perhaps it's the air.'

He looked at her. 'Perhaps it is,' he said. Then he lifted his mallet again and Mary went on cutting and twisting wire.

That night Brian helped his father get the sheep fastened securely into the pen against the predators of the moor, and for the next two weeks he more than pulled his weight only taking time off at week-ends to meet Mike Stelling halfway between Caryford and Milton Mains. The work was hard and unremitting and Mary took her share most days. They picked the straggly field peas and managed to sell them to a quick-freeze plant. Jim cleared the field and put in winter greens. He ploughed some more land for winter wheat too looking exactly like Adam had looked walking behind the shires. Brian and Mary started a vegetable garden near the house for family use and in spite of her determination not to look into the future Mary found herself considering a deep-freeze in the old wash-house and wondered whether Mrs Westbrook knew a local electrician . . .

The work still piled ahead of them mountainously. They needed a dog for the sheep, a cow for their own milk and butter, fertilizer for the thin soil. Mary would have liked to suggest keeping poultry too, but she couldn't ask Jim to give his time to making hen runs. And the house needed paint and paper . . . It was frightening to realize they were living on their meagre capital until next Spring's lambs.

Then, in their third week at Caryford a letter came from Jean Butler.

'Dear Mr and Mrs Richmond, not forgetting Brian,' she wrote in her round schoolgirl hand. 'Stan and me hopes this will find you as it leaves us. Missing the old days. But fit and well. Mr Mitchell is a good master. He leaves us alone and tells us he wants Milton Mains run as if the Richmonds was still there. We have two men over from the estate to help with the milking and Robbie and Stan finds plenty to do in between times. The house is still empty. This is what we want to see you about. We want to see you anyway but this makes it urgent. Will Sunday be all right? Mr Mitchell says he would like to come too. We send our love and are really looking forward to seeing you again. Yours, Jean (Butler).

Jim laughed. 'Who else could it be? Good old Jean. It'll be great to see them. And at one time I thought I wouldn't want to see anyone from Milton ever again.'

'That means you're beginning to be proud of Caryford.' Mary smiled above the letter which she had just read aloud. Her heart was beating uncomfortably at the mention of Charles' name and she avoided Brian's eyes. 'I wonder what the mystery is?'

'Something to do with the house. Mitchell wants to alter it drastically for his manager probably and the Butlers are objecting.' Jim tried to speak lightly.

Brian cleared his throat. 'Don't you know mother?'

Mary said, surprised, 'No. How should I?'

'I just wondered if you ever rang Jean. Or anyone else. When you go to Carybridge for the shopping.'

Mary said quietly, 'I would tell you if I did. I imagine your father is right. The Butlers' loyalty would compel them to consult us—'

'Oh quite.' Brian stood up impatiently. 'And Charles Mitchell would come along for the ride.'

Mary felt her face flush. Luckily her back was against the window.

Jim said, 'That's why I think the alterations must be drastic. Probably some basic reconstruction work . . . we must try not to mind. Milton Mains is nothing to do with us now.'

Brian walked out of the dining-room and Jim stared after him.

'I didn't realize it went so deep with him, Mary. I've been terribly wrapped up in my own sense of loss.' He turned and stared at her face his brown eyes clear and vulnerable in the morning sunshine streaming through the window. 'You too my dear. It was your home as well. I'm sorry.'

'Don't be, Jim. I like it here – I really do like Caryford.' She reached out a reassuring hand and he took it between both of his. It was a repeat of the starry night at Milton when they had made their bargain. But now it was morning and everything was subtly different.

After a moment he dropped her hand and stood up, almost embarrassed.

'Well, I must get on with the ploughing. Can you and Brian see to the sheep?' She nodded and he went to the door. 'Thank you Mary,' he said.

She stayed sitting by the window for a few minutes watching him cross the saucer towards the Shires. A tremulous joy seemed to be starting at her finger-tips. She touched Jean's letter and looked down at it lying on her lap. Charles was coming. That must be it. He would see for himself how well they were managing down here and he would know that the long time of waiting was coming to an end.

Sunday dawned another pearly day in that wonderful summer. Mary let Brian and Jim take the sheep to the top moor while she prepared the lunch. She had given a lot of thought to the day's arrangements, wanting – almost desperately – that Caryford should make a good impression. As she looked around the cramped dining-room she came to a sudden decision. They would eat outside, al fresco. The view from the front of the house was ideal; the splashing river, the ford itself and then the flat expanse of the sea. Eagerly she up-ended the table and manoeuvred it through the door and the narrow hallway. Then the chairs. If she left the windows wide open she could serve the meal from the deep window ledge. She spread a cloth and put an earthenware pitcher of wild flowers on it; buttercups, daisies, tall fronds of cow parsley, a solid centre of dazzling forget-me-nots. It looked Arcadian. The meal itself was almost frugally simple. Mrs Westbrook had gleaned a chicken from the 'Watling-place' and Mary had roast and glazed it. There were hard-boiled eggs, green salad. Plain water to drink. A fruit cake worthy of Jean's own baking; cheese.

She surveyed her arrangements with pleasure. Nothing to be ashamed of here. The Richmonds had changed their role to pastorale. They had certainly not 'come down in the world'.

Mary smiled at her own unexpected partisanship. Then

she told herself it was for Charles' sake and she ran upstairs to do something about her own appearance. It was hard to know where to begin. She gazed at her reflection with a rueful smile remembering her appearance the last time she and Charles had eaten together. Now her long pale hair was bleached and crisp from three weeks' sunshine and occasional swims in the sea. Her skin too showed the results of her outdoor life; it was darker than her hair, shiny across the forehead and on her cheekbones. Her hands and nails were past redemption. On the other hand she was definitely thinner.

After trying on three of her old summer dresses, she decided they were no longer her. She dragged on clean jeans and one of Brian's shirts, brushed her hair smoothly behind her ears and into its usual rubber band. She would put on no airs. Like Caryford itself she would be natural. Earthy if need be.

Jim obviously approved her decision and what he described as 'the picnic set-up'. Brian glanced at her in surprise.

'I thought you'd want to get dressed up,' he commented. He sounded pleased that she hadn't. She smiled at him, thankful that his old attitude had been diverted. He had worked so hard these last three weeks, immersed himself in the place; as they all had.

They arrived at mid-day in Charles' discreetly massive Bentley bumping incongruously over the field. Jean and Stan at first ill-at-ease in their Sunday best, gradually relaxed in the informal atmosphere; Charles continued to hold himself a little too erect, to listen too attentively to every remark Jim let fall. He produced a bottle of sherry from the glove compartment but it did nothing to put him at ease. When they drank water with their meal he glanced at the half-empty bottle obviously wondering whether it was interpreted as patronage. Mary found herself leaning over backwards to include him in the gay badinage going between Brian and the Butlers. Treating him like a guest. Which of course, he was.

Stan said, 'Well. Your dad's making a farmer out of you after all Brian-boy? You'll be my rival where sheep's concerned I do hear.'

Jean chipped in. 'I did always know it. D'you remember Mrs Richmond when he was just a baby how he did answer the bleating lambs?'

Brian lifted his dark head and called raucously, 'M-a-a-a-a . . .' The Butlers rolled about laughing. Brian said more seriously, 'There's something in that actually. I reckon it's my Ma that's got me farming at long last.' Mary looked her surprise and Brian grinned again. 'Precept and example mother-mine.'

'You mean you do some of the outside work Mrs Richmond?' Jean asked.

Jim answered her. 'We all have to dig in here Jean. The Richmonds are pulling together.'

Jean's clear blue eyes rested momentarily on Charles. 'I'm glad to hear it,' she said.

Charles' smile was strained. 'And how is Julie getting on?' It was as if he were looking for a gap in the Richmond front. Mary frowned; he had found it; Julie had not written since their arrival at Caryford.

Jim said quickly, 'Making a name for herself in the modelling world probably.' He smiled across the table at Mary and she realized he was reassuring her. 'We'd soon hear if things had gone wrong.'

'Miss Julie will always be all right,' Stan maintained. 'I've never forgot the time she tried to ride Bluebell – that Jersey heifer – you remember Jean . . .?' They reminisced some more and there was even more laughter. Brian glanced at Charles his eyes bright. He saw, as Mary did, that the new owner of Milton Mains was completely excluded from all things Richmond.

They sat for a long time at the depleted table and it was Jim who finally questioned the real reason for their visit.

'Not that we're not delighted to see you. You know that.' He looked at Stan and Jean. Charles crumbled some bread. 'But your letter sounded very business-like Jean. Come on, what's it all about?'

Jean glanced at Stan and Stan passed the look on to Charles. 'I reckon it's Mr Mitchell should tell you. 'Tis his idea and a kind and generous one it is. But Jean and me – we said we had to see you first. If you'd any objection we'd turn it down flat. But—' he stared earnestly at Jim then across to Mary. '—we'd not be usurpers. Just caretakers in a manner of speaking. Caretakers of the Richmond heritage like.'

Jim looked helplessly at Charles. Charles said abruptly, 'I want Stan and Jean to move in to Milton Mains. Manage the farm. Make their own day-to-day decisions and have a say – the biggest say – in the policy of that side of the estate.'

Jim looked a question at Mary. She said hesitantly, 'It sounds a marvellous idea—'

'It's great!' Jim leaned over the table and clapped Stan on the shoulder. 'Absolutely great. I couldn't wish for a better successor . . . the Richmond heritage. I like it Stan.'

Brian hugged Jean looking like a very young excited schoolboy. 'I'm so glad you'll still be there Jean. It's as good as us still being in residence.'

'It's much too big for us of course,' Jean demurred, her cheeks like polished apples with pleasure. 'But we're going to have three students from the Agricultural College and in the holidays I can have my sister's girls.'

Everyone was talking together again. Yet the man who had arranged it all, sat silent.

Mary spoke quietly under cover of the general babble. 'Charles it's good of you. You must have realized how it would please Jim and Brian. Thank you.'

His smile was instant. 'I actually did it to please you Mary.'

'Well it has. Bless you my dear.'

'Mary I'd like to talk to you. Can you make an opportunity?'

His eyes were pleading, his face wide open. If Jim had seen him now he must have guessed . . . she glanced swiftly around the table but no-one was looking at Charles. She stood up unobtrusively.

'Help me clear the table,' she said in a low voice. 'And for goodness' sake smile.' But Jean had seen her and rose too. In a moment Mary had five willing helpers jostling each other down the narrow passage to the kitchen. '*Please—*' she begged in a sergeant-major voice. 'Everybody outside. This can wait until you've gone back to your demanding cows!'

There was more laughter and Jim suggested everyone should help him choose a site for a stable instead. They trooped to the back of the house and Jim and Stan soon became absorbed in measuring out stalls and a harness room on the dry grass.

Jean said, 'How far is it down to the sea Brian? Is it near enough to take a swim most days m'dear?'

'Sure—' Brian crooked an arm at her. 'Come on, I'll show you. Lend you a pair of trunks if you like and you can take a dip.'

'We'll come too,' Mary said. 'Jim and Stan will be happier on their own. I'll make sure he doesn't push you in Jean!' She walked alongside the giggling Jean and Brian leaving Charles to follow. She knew the exact point – level with the ford – when she would drop behind with Charles. It seemed obvious that they must be alone for a few minutes to discuss plans, yet now that she had organized it she felt strangely reluctant to leave Jean.

They came to the ford and Mary moved away sideways and studied the clear water coursing between the stones. Charles joined her. Brian checked his stride but Jean went on towards the beach taking him with her. Mary knew with a sick heart that Brian guessed at her ploy; the easy atmosphere of Caryford seemed suddenly disturbed by the old tensions of Milton Mains and now she had Charles to herself there was nothing to say.

He jumped in front of her on to the first stepping stone, laughing naturally, conscious too of Brian's lingering presence. Then he turned a few yards off.

'Thanks Mary,' he said in a low voice. 'It's been so awful hasn't it?'

She realized that the lunch *was* sticky for Charles; now she saw he meant their total separation since Adam's funeral and her more recent isolation at Caryford. She suddenly felt guilty. She had missed Charles – she must have missed Charles – yet at the same time she had found a curious content over the past three weeks. Was it because Brian was happy, Jim at least resigned? Which meant that the way was clearing for Charles and herself?

She reached over and clasped his helping hand impulsively.

'Dear Charles. It's so good to see you. You . . . you're a rock.'

He pulled her over to his boulder and for a moment they stood together closely his eyes searching hers. Then she leapt on to the next stone fearful of Brian's critical gaze. Charles stayed where he was.

'That didn't actually answer my question Mary,' he said slowly. 'Let me put it a different way. Have you missed me?'

Again she spoke quickly, horrified at the thought of hurting him. 'Yes – yes of course I have Charles. But . . . well, you can see that things are going well. That –

that's pleased me. Because of us.' She spoke in bursts as she went from stone to stone, Charles following her at a discreet distance.

She reached the opposite bank where distance and the noise of the water lent a certain privacy. She looked back to where Jean and Brian were standing on the shore-line. Jean was trying unsuccessfully to skim some of the flat stones from the beach and apparently urging Brian to teach her the right way. Mary waved to him and he put up his hand in acknowledgement and then at last turned away and bent to pick up a pebble.

Charles said, 'Yes. I see things are going well.'

'Doesn't that please you?'

'If it means you will feel free to join me, yes.'

'We agreed that I should go to Janice first,' Mary reminded him quickly. 'I couldn't possibly leave Jim *for* you, Charles. Not after you bought Milton Mains. He would imagine we'd arranged it all between us. So that I could live there again.' She began to walk upstream feeling unduly agitated. Charles strode after and took her arm.

'Mary – I explained all that at the time. It was the logical thing for me to do—'

'Charles, it has nothing to do with logic. It's an emotional thing.' To her annoyance she felt tears starting in her eyes. Jim would be so bitterly hurt . . . all the good she had done in coming here would be worth less than nothing . . . better had she left him straightaway . . .

Charles said desperately, 'Darling, please don't cry. Let's sit down. Brian can't see us – sit here—' a rocky outcrop made a natural bench and she subsided unwillingly. He sat by her and put an arm around her shoulders and immediately she relaxed against him. It seemed so natural. He was the familiar friend and comforter; she had wept before and he had held her gently, asking nothing, bolstering her confidence.

He went on in a low voice, 'It's going to be all right Mary isn't it? I can see your loyalties are being torn even more than before but – the situation is the same surely? Jim and you . . .?'

She shook her head against his shoulder answering his unspoken question. Jim didn't love her. There had been opportunities for affection and he had given her none. Charles was quite right after all, the situation was the same.

'Then please stop crying.' She felt his lips on the top of her head. 'Of course it's rotten for you here my love. Completely cut off from everyone and everything you've ever known. But you've certainly done a good job – I agree. Perhaps in the autumn—'

'Not until after Christmas Charles.' She pulled away to look up at him pleadingly. 'Forgive me my dear, but I must be here for Brian's first vacation. And Julie will come for Christmas . . . I can't possibly leave until after then.'

'I see.' Again he gave her that searching stare. 'And how long will you be at Cheltenham with your sister?'

'I – I'm not certain. Oh Charles I am sorry. Somehow I don't want to make any decisions – I don't even want to think—'

He smiled. 'That's all right Mary, I can wait.' He hesitated then asked abruptly, 'But you still love me, do you Mary?'

She said sincerely, 'Of course I do—' how could she help love Charles? When everything became unbearable he was always there. 'Dear Charles. Don't doubt that for an instant. It's just that I'm such a coward—'

He held her tightly. 'Not a coward. Never a coward – a coward would have been at Mitcheldean with me right now.' He released her and looked into her eyes again. His own were suspiciously bright. 'Mary d'you realize you have never before told me you loved me? I've known we were friends – that there was a certain physical attraction. But you never actually *said* . . . not even before Adam's death when we made our plans—'

'Charles I'm sorry—'

'Don't say that again—' As before when tension ran high between them he sought to bring it down to normal. 'Come on. Let's get back.' He stood up pulling her to her feet. 'Stop worrying Mary – I'm not going to badger you. Everything's just the same, I promise.' He grinned trying hard to look devilish. 'I have even kept my promise to look around. I took Cecily Adams out to dinner last week.'

She smiled at him gratefully. 'To the Black Boar?'

'Of course not,' he drew her arm through his and began to walk back to the ford. 'Would you have minded?'

'No. In a way I'd have been glad. She's young and energetic and—'

'Shut up,' he said amiably.

She was suddenly too tired to argue. Only the sight of Brian halfway across the stepping stones galvanized her to action and she pulled her arm free and ran to meet him. He waited until she reached his stone.

'Are you all right?' he asked and looked past her to where Charles was negotiating the first boulder.

She forced herself to say gaily, 'I'm fine darling. Shall we go back now and have a cup of tea? Where's Jean?'

He hesitated, then he turned and began to go back. 'She's already had that idea. Wanted me to help her.'

Mary leapt to the bank behind him. She wondered just what she had achieved by that conversation with Charles. Except Brian's renewed suspicion.

She said, 'Race you back to the house! Loser washes up.'

She ran easily up the saucer towards the squat house basking in the afternoon sunshine. It looked like a haven. Brian lagged deliberately behind her determined to keep himself between his mother and Charles. She felt as if she were running from a problem. Instead of towards one.

CHAPTER FIVE

During the next few days Mary felt as if she were watching Jim go through some magical rejuvenation process. Seeing and talking to the Butlers again, knowing they were going to live in his old home, realizing that they – and their landlord who was, after all, a land-owner to be respected – were impressed by his new farm, gave him a new lease on life. If before, he had been slowly coming to terms with the reversal of his fortunes, now he seemed to take a positive pleasure in them. He whistled tunelessly about the place, talked to the sheep as well as the Shires and joked easily with Brian. His attitude towards Mary changed slightly too. Sometimes he was still the polite stranger, almost embarrassed by their proximity; there would be moments of closeness too as there had been before; but occasionally she would catch him staring at her as if he were struggling to put a name to someone he half recognized. Seeing her through other eyes perhaps . . . Jean's or Stan's . . . or even Charles'.

Brian, who started the week tightly defensive, relaxed too under such geniality. He and Mary were working at the interminable job of clearing the buttercups from their precious vegetable garden one afternoon when he straightened suddenly and massaged the small of his back.

'Mother . . .' he stared towards the sea striving to sound casual. 'Did you know Charles Mitchell was coming on Sunday?'

There was no insolence in his young voice, rather a note of pleading. Mary drew off a glove and wiped a sticky hand on her jeans.

'Jean told us in the letter of course. Otherwise . . . no. Nothing was prearranged if that's what you mean.'

He smiled a little uncertainly. 'I suppose that's what I meant.' His black eyes, so like Jim's rested on her momentarily. 'Thank you.'

Mary said nothing. She recognized that Brian was trying to overcome his uprush of bitter jealousy and work things out for himself. She replaced her glove and went on weeding feeling a return of the guilt from which she had run on Sunday afternoon. Should she try to warn him for the future?

He didn't return immediately to his work. After a bit he said with difficulty, 'I'm sorry Mother. It's just that . . . well, you're still so darned attractive and I know Dad and you . . .' his voice trailed away in embarrassment.

She wanted to stand up and thrust the weight of guilt away from her physically. If only Charles hadn't come on Sunday; they could have jogged on nicely each of them in separate compartments so that no irrevocable hurt would have followed when she eventually left . . .

She said with more vehemence than she intended, 'Your father and I – you couldn't possibly understand Brian, so please don't try. We're here, aren't we? Working together. That must be enough.'

'It is – oh it is—' eagerly he crouched beside her, a little boy again, trying to reassure and protect. What a curious mixture he was of child and adult. 'If he lets you alone it'll be all right – I know it will.' She wondered in bewilderment whether he was still talking of Jim. Then he said, 'If he pesters you Mother – let me know, won't you?' And she realized he had meant Charles.

'Oh darling . . .' she wanted to hold him in her arms again but the guilt was still there, the knowledge of what she was going to do. 'Don't take your responsibilities so seriously. Please.' She tried to smile. 'We must all be responsible for ourselves. You, Dad, me . . . Julie, making her own way in London. We all have to live our own lives.'

He laughed then. 'You sound like I used to sound. Like a student.' He sat back on his heels and went on reflectively, 'You know I've changed haven't I? Oh I still enjoy going out – I admit I have a drink when I meet up with Mike and the boys. But I don't . . . well, I don't sort of want to break out any more. D'you know what I mean? I want us to be a – a unit. It's this place I suppose. It's like working on a co-operative isn't it? Grass roots. That sort of thing.'

She said in a low voice, 'Yes. Yes, it must be the place.' She followed Brian's eyes around the beginnings of their garden. They had planted late beans and the rows of crossed sticks hid the house from view. The sea and the wild country behind it looked untamed and untameable. She shivered a little. It needed a unit to stand against such raw Nature. One man on his own . . . as Jim would be when Brian was at University, Julie in London, herself – where?

Brian said, 'You're surely not cold? Let's go in and make some tea.' He pulled her to her feet. 'Tell you what. Shall we walk into the village this evening and ring Julie? It's about time we heard from her. You must have written half a dozen letters since we arrived.'

She smiled ruefully. It was almost a relief to have something so concrete to worry about. It was natural for any mother to look a bit strained over an errant daughter.

In the end they all walked into Carybridge that night and while Mary had an unsatisfactory conversation with Julie, Mrs Westbrook expounded her ideas about a deep-freeze to Jim.

Julie said for the second time, 'So everything's working out down there for you?'

'Yes darling. You know that from my letters. What we want to know is – how is it going for you?'

'Fine. Just fine. I'm keeping myself anyway – the car money Dad gave me is still intact.'

It sounded like one of Julie's typically frank replies yet Mary sensed evasion somewhere.

'And apart from the job? Surely you don't work all the time yet you haven't managed to fit in a letter—'

'Mummy, I *never* write. You know that. I kept in touch by telephone before and now you're not on the telephone—'

'Julie. Is something wrong? Or – rather – not quite right?'

'Oh Mummy do stop it!' The irritability was still there. 'I'm tired that's all. If you must know I have to work hard being awfully gay and witty each evening in order to get a job next day.'

There was a humming silence. Mary said, 'I see.' Then – 'Darling, listen. Why don't you come down for a holiday? Just a week-end.'

'That's when it all happens. The parties, the punting, the picnics.' The telephone transformed her gay laugh into near-hysteria. 'Sorry. I might manage the Bank holiday—'

'That's six weeks away!'

'But I can't promise anything. Besides from your description of the hovel there's nowhere to lay my head.'

'You know we'll always find room – Julie please come – oh dear there's the pips—'

'Don't have any more time, Mummy. Someone's just called for me. Take care of yourselves darlings. Love to Dad and Brian.' She was gone and Mary hung on to the dead telephone for a moment indecisively, wondering whether to ring her back and insist on her coming home. But what good would it do really? She would hate Caryford and its isolation and Jim would have to go back to the two chairs in the sitting-room . . .

Behind her Jim said, 'Has she gone? You might have let me say hello or even goodbye.'

Mrs Westbrook laughed. 'We women never realize how much time we use in gossiping. And Mrs Richmond – stuck in that inconvenient house with two men for company – you must miss your daughter m'dear.'

Mary smiled uncertainly still thinking of Julie, and Jim said quickly, 'Is everything all right?'

'Yes of course.' She forced her smile into focus. 'She's doing well. But so busy. No hope of seeing her just yet.' She looked round the Post Office. 'Where's Brian?'

'Waiting outside.' Unexpectedly Jim took her arm. 'Mrs Westbrook has been telling me we should have a deep-freeze in the wash-house—'

The floodgates of advice were opened again as the Post-mistress told them of the electrical warehouse in Stapleford where they could buy freezers at wholesale prices. 'That's with a trade ticket m'dear. And you're very welcome to mine. You'd really need a freezer when you're cut off like we are down here. And if you're growing all those vegetables like Mr Richmond's been telling me—'

'Let's have a look at the wash-house Mary.' Jim drew her towards the door. 'And maybe we'll take Mrs West-brook up on her offer this Saturday. Would you like a trip to Stapleford?'

She looked at him disbelievingly. It would be four weeks since they moved and she hadn't been further than the moor with the sheep or Carybridge for the shopping. And she hadn't been out with Jim since the Annual Farmers' Ball last year when she had met Charles.

'Can we spare the time Jim?' she asked. 'The sheep—'

'We'll be back by mid-afternoon. They can look after themselves until then.' He was laughing down at her, sweeping away her objections as he'd done years ago. 'We'll take Brian to chaperone us,' he added roguishly.

She felt herself blushing. 'Well it would be a nice change,' she said sedately.

Mrs Westbrook clapped her hands delightedly. 'The Pannier Market is on Saturday too. They have some marvellous bargains – remnants, things like that—'

'There you are Mary. We're going.' Jim hugged her arm against his side. 'You can wear a dress and we'll have lunch out somewhere.'

Brian looked up in surprise as they emerged from the Post Office both laughing. He was sitting on a bench outside, shredding a dandelion methodically like a child playing 'She loves him, she loves him not . . .' and the eager response on his face as they told him of their plans seemed to confirm the result of the game. He took Mary's other arm as they swung back down the lane and she wondered whether the warm pressure of his hand on her wrist was significant.

That night she stood by her open window watching the moon sail serenely across the moor, listening to the horses snuffling and stamping below and she made a pact with herself to live just for the present.

'I won't worry about Julie. And I won't worry about Charles. And I won't worry about what I'm going to do next Christmas,' she whispered into the scented darkness. 'Somehow – here at Caryford – we're in between the awful things that have happened and the awful things that must soon happen. It – it's a breathing-space. And I can enjoy it in that way surely?' She drew a deep breath. 'I *will* enjoy it,' she concluded almost defiantly.

The next day Jim took the pick from his store of tools and started hacking at the old brick furnace in the corner of the wash-house. Brian levered the copper free during the afternoon and rolled it outside the front door and Mary shovelled it full of earth and planted it with primroses and clumps of wild lupins blooming late along the cliffs.

After their evening meal they walked together up the saucer to fetch the sheep home. The sun was turning the sea ruby red and the gulls swooped and called their good nights along the pitted cliffs. The sheep pushed and bumbled down through the bracken herded by Brian and Jim both armed with sticks. It was a scene straight from a Hardy novel and Mary, walking behind to round up stragglers, knew that she had won another day from the threats of the outside world. It was as if here, at Caryford, they were all encapsuled in a protective bubble. They penned the sheep and staked the horses and went down to the beach for a swim before bed-time. Mary was a timid swimmer and stayed in the shallows floating over the swell while Brian and Jim struck out energetically for an off-shore rock. She watched them race back. If Julie had been here it would have been nearly perfect . . . and maybe Caryford could restore Julie too . . .

Saturday was cooler. A day of high cotton-wool clouds shredded across the sky by a light breeze. Jim looked unusually formal in a jacket and Mary slipped a cardigan over her blue cotton dress. Brian swung himself into the Land-Rover in his usual garb of jeans and garish tee-shirt, merely grinning when Mary asked him whether he would be warm enough.

It was strange to leave Caryford. The Shires watched them go unconcernedly apparently reassured by their constantly reiterated – 'We'll be back soon.' The bumpy two miles to the village which seemed to cut them off so effectively from civilization, was reduced to a mere jolting ten minutes; another five in low gear and there was Carybridge far below them, a scatter of toy houses around a match-box bridge. The farm itself was invisible in its saucer of living green but they could place it by the mouth of their little River Cary bubbling into the sea through its fringe of boulders. Then the moor humped a protective shoulder towards the horizon and it was all gone. They drove gaily on towards Stapleford.

The tiny town based around the ancient wool-market had widened in the last twenty years into a residential sprawl around the river even extending to a trading estate where the electrical warehouse was situated. Jim drove straight there and only just found a space in the enormous parking lot already shimmering with heat and exhaust fumes.

'Business first,' he said in response to Mary's and Brian's dubious expressions. 'Let's get the freezer settled then we can go into the town and enjoy ourselves at the market.'

'If we can find somewhere for the truck,' Brian warned. 'It's tourist-time, remember.'

They had indeed forgotten. The oily concrete was hot through Mary's thin sandal-soles and in spite of much-vaunted air-conditioning the enormous warehouse accommodation smelled thick and stuffy. It was incredible that holiday-makers should choose to spend their time in such a place, yet it was crowded with blistering, sun-hatted visitors peering at electric blankets and hair-dryers. Bargain signs were everywhere, yet Mary was appalled at the prices; at Milton Mains she had never had to think of money-values in a personal way and since Caryford she had spent money only on food.

'Jim. Can we afford this?' she said in a low voice. 'We can easily manage without it and it seems a terrific outlay all at once.'

'It's all right Mary. It will save us money in the long run. And we still have some capital from the sale of Milton.'

She wished Jim had changed sufficiently to include her in money matters. It was difficult to know where economy ended and meanness began. However he insisted she choose one of the larger models – 'to take at least two of our wretched sheep' – and wrote a cheque without any apparent qualms. But when Brian suggested they should think about storage heaters because Caryford would be cold and draughty in the winter, he shook his head.

'We're surrounded by wood Brian and there are grates in all the rooms. We must live off the land as much as we can.'

Well, they had always heated their homes by open fires. But there had been plenty of help outside to fetch and carry fuel. Mary shut her mind against the picture of Jim on his own coping with the endless task of sawing wood.

Around the old Market Hall in Stapleford the panniered donkeys stood patiently, heads hanging in the noon-day sun, while visitors milled around them, children stroking their dusty coats, adults turning over the goods on the open stalls. The Richmonds clustered around a lorry housing a portable forge and festooned with harness and gleaming brasses. Jim fingered the latter lovingly. This year it was to have been the Princess' turn for the Autumn Agricultural Show but such events seemed incongruous in the frugal setting of Caryford. They moved on to the farm implements. Then the market stalls.

Brian said, 'You know, we could expand into poultry. Free-range eggs have a good market and there's the orchard and the big area around the house.'

Jim nodded but Mary remained silent unwilling to commit herself to something that would mean more work for Jim in the future. Of course, if she stayed she could manage poultry herself . . .

Jim leaned forward to speak against the incessant babble around them.

'Mary. I want to order fertilizer and seed. Will you carry on round and see if you would like anything? It's hopeless to try and stick together in this crowd.'

'Yes. All right.' She had five pounds of the housekeeping money in her handbag and wondered whether she was at liberty to spend that on herself. 'What about you Brian?'

'I'll be at the farm machinery stand.'

'OK.' Jim stared around. 'Hopeless to try to meet up here again. Let's make it the Red Lion at one o'clock.'

Brian nodded and began pushing his way through the crowd. Jim grinned. 'See you,' he said. Then suddenly leaned over an intervening shopping bag and kissed her nose. 'Buy yourself something Mary. Something useless.'

She laughed and turned away immediately to hide her feelings. The kiss had been the kind of salutation Bill might have given Janice, intimate and friendly. She smiled, wrinkling her nose where it had landed. She felt different. Special, conscious of her bare legs beneath the blue flowered dress, her slim waist.

She dawdled along the line of stalls. There was nothing she needed, nothing she particularly wanted, but she was determined to buy something for Jim's sake. For a long time she fingered diaphanous nighties on the underwear stall and then she moved on. In different circumstances it would be a provocative present to buy herself; with things as they were it might well have precipitated a renewal of their married life. Her face grew warm at the thought and she picked up a chain and pendant and examined it closely. That wouldn't do either, somehow jewellery would be too insignificant; she was suddenly frightened of giving Jim the wrong impression.

Then she came to a stall displaying a heap of multi-coloured silk scarves giving a touch of an Eastern bazaar to the rural English scene. They seemed just right. And she needed a scarf for her hair when it was windy and the neck of that rather scratchy jumper she wore in cold weather . . . She picked up a russet and orange square and held it outside the awning of the stall in the full sunlight.

A voice said, 'It's absolutely right for the lady I had in mind. I'll take it.'

She looked up startled. Charles stood before her, laughing, apparently unsurprised at finding her in the midst of this throng. He wore a corduroy jacket and an open-necked shirt and the carefree atmosphere of the market seemed to have affected him too; he looked younger, surer of himself. Nevertheless some of her happiness dimmed at the sight of him.

'Charles! What on earth are you doing here?'

'I wanted cattle feed. And Jean Butler needs curtains for Milton Mains. So I drove her in. It's marvellous seeing you like this – I spotted Brian looking at the tractors and thought there might be a chance you were around.'

'Did he see you?' she asked quickly.

'I don't think so. What does it matter – I've a right here surely?'

'You know how it is with Brian.' She stared worriedly over Charles' shoulder. 'He'd never believe this was coincidence—'

'Oh come on Mary. Both Julie and Brian live their own lives now – just as you will soon live yours darling.' He took her hand. 'I've thought such a lot about our talk last Sunday darling. You made me so happy Mary – so happy—'

'Charles please – people will see—'

He dropped her hand. 'Sorry. It's just that . . . well, I've realized since seeing you that it won't be long. Christmas is five months away. Just five months—' he took the scarf from her fingers and brandished it at the stall-holder. 'We'll have this one please.'

'Charles – really. I was going to buy it myself. There's no need—' she fiddled with the clasp of her handbag but the scarf was already paid for and being wrapped in tissue. 'Charles I can't accept this. Honestly.'

'I've never given you a present my dear – sorry but I insist this time. A fairing. To remind you of me.' He shook it out with exaggerated gallantry and draped it around her neck. She felt stifled and impatient, irritable with herself and Charles. She tried to smile gratefully.

'Thank you. Look, I really must go. I have to meet Jim and Brian for lunch. I'm sorry Charles.'

'Oh dear.' His face fell. 'I was going to suggest we give them all the slip and drive for the Black Boar but I suppose that's impossible.'

'Quite impossible.' She glanced around and her eyes widened. 'Charles here's Brian. My dear – forgive me – please go away. Believe me if he sees us here it could spoil everything.'

Her frantic voice convinced him. He looked startled for a moment and then gripped her hand urgently. 'Please telephone me Mary. I know we agreed not to get in touch – but please ring soon. Tomorrow if possible. Goodbye darling.'

He was gone. But Mary knew immediately that Brian had seen him – had probably seen him by the tractor and followed him here. In fact he swerved as if to follow him again, then hesitated and pushed his way towards Mary.

'What's going on?' He was white with anger beneath his tan and the resultant colour made him look sick. 'He sneaked off when he saw me over there—' he gestured behind him with a shaking finger. 'Now he hops it again. Did you tell him we were coming to Stapleford today?'

'Of course not.' Mary tried hard to sound light which was difficult in the face of Brian's obvious distress. 'He bought Jean over to choose some curtains – he just spotted me and thought I'd like to know. That's all.' She began to walk back towards the High-street. 'Come on Brian. We're going to be late—'

'Hang on—' He peered above the heads of the crowd. 'I'd just like a word. One word.'

'Brian – please—' she was thoroughly upset by the intensity of his resentment for Charles. 'He's got to get Jean back to Milton Mains. Don't make a fuss – it was simply a chance meeting.'

He looked down at her reluctantly and let her draw him away and gradually they edged and pushed themselves into the comparative calm of the Red Lion's medieval courtyard.

'We shall never get a table,' Mary said as she led the way into the lounge bar. But Jim, signalling from a corner, had booked a place by the window on the first floor dining-room overhanging the crowded market-place. They took their drinks there straightaway and sat recovering slowly, looking from the menu to the motley scene beneath them, talking about the delivery of the fertilizer and then the freezer. Mary smiled reassuringly at Brian and told Jim about the surprise appearance of Charles Mitchell and that Jean Butler was also in the town somewhere. At last Brian smiled back, a rueful turned-down smile that acknowledged and laughed at his own Victorian attitude. Their meal arrived, scampi for Mary, more traditional plaice for the men, and they were in the midst of it when Jim asked a casual question.

'Did you buy yourself something Mary?'

She looked up smiling, fingering the brown and orange silk at her neck. 'The scarf. Do you like it?'

'Very much.' He reached across and felt the fine silk. Like the kiss, it was an intimate gesture, almost a caress. 'A memento of a very pleasant day.'

She dropped her eyes. 'Yes. Thank you Jim.'

On her right Brian sat silent for a moment, then he pushed his plate away. She looked at him inquiringly and was horrified to find him staring at her his black eyes accusing. And then she knew. Brian had followed Charles from the farm machinery stall so of course he had seen his unmistakable gesture as he tied the scarf around her neck.

She said quickly, 'Brian—'

'It's all right mother-mine.' His voice was light, sneering. 'I can't quite manage the fish. The heat I expect.' He pushed his chair away from the table. 'I'll meet you at the Land-Rover.' He made for the door, lumbering blindly against a chair. Mary gestured to Jim to stay where he was and followed Brian. She caught up with him at the top of the stairs.

'Brian – wait, please—' she caught his arm and he stood stock still, his back to her. 'Listen. I intended paying for the scarf and Charles came up and took the matter out of my hands. I would still have insisted on paying for it but you came along and he left. I'd honestly forgotten – I know it sounds incredible but it's true. I chose the scarf as a present from your father and that was uppermost in my mind.' She stopped speaking and dropped his arm. He stayed where he was, then someone came up the stairs and they both had to move aside. His profile was towards her; it was still yellowish and set.

He said, 'It's all right. I *do* understand.'

'Then come back and sit down—'

'No,' he jerked away from her. 'No, I can't sit there and be a party to pulling the wool over Dad's eyes. Sorry mother. Take your time – I'll have a walk around before I go back to the car-park.'

She watched him go down the narrow stairs wondering whether he intended searching for Charles again. She had a sinking feeling that a showdown of some kind was imminent; the one thing she was trying to avoid.

She rejoined Jim at their table.

'Is everything all right Mary?' he asked half-standing to peer through the window for Brian.

'He'll go the other way through the courtyard,' she said. Then she smiled. 'He's restless that's all. All the people

– the noise – it's given him a taste for more people and more noise.'

He grinned at her. 'He'll want to play the transistor tonight then?'

'I expect so.'

She forced herself to finish her scampi. Brian was right. She was deceiving Jim every day, every hour she was with him. It did not help to tell herself that she was doing it for his sake.

CHAPTER SIX

Surprisingly the journey back to Carybridge soon after their lunch was as cheerful as the one coming. Brian had run into a couple of 'the boys' near the river at Stapleford and they had spent a happy hour examining one of the hotted-up bangers used in local scrambles.

'He did all the work himself Dad. Evenings, week-ends – you know. As long as the suspension's OK you can use any old car off the scrap-heap—'

'They jolly soon go back there too, lad,' Jim laughed, pleased that Brian seemed recovered. Mary felt the same, though again she wondered at the strange mixture of child and adult in her teenage son. Apparently all worries about Charles were put from him completely and the nearer they got to Caryford the more secure Mary felt. She said as much as she got them a cup of tea when they arrived soon after four o'clock.

'It's been fun. And I'm thrilled about the freezer. But it's better here.' She moved a jug of moon-daisies from the table. 'I wouldn't want to make a habit of going into Stapleford, especially in the holiday season.'

Jim said with mock seriousness, 'All right. I promise I won't take you out again for a long, long time.'

'That's good of you,' she grinned.

Brian slumped into a chair. 'Oh I dunno . . . I feel . . . I feel I'd like to *do* something tonight. Something crazy, terrific—'

'Like fetching the sheep? Having a swim after? Maybe I could give you a game of chess?'

'Oh Jim—' Mary laughed and even Brian grimaced at his father.

But it was obvious a sense of anti-climax dogged him for the rest of the afternoon. Mary started on their evening meal and did some baking for the next day; Jim went on with the store shed he was building by the side of the house ready for the fertilizer and seed he had ordered. Brian could settle to nothing. He didn't seem to want to be alone with his mother, yet after a few half-hearted attempts to hold timber for Jim he drifted away and returned at supper time with an armful of drift-wood which he tried to light in the sitting-room grate. It smouldered sulkily.

'It's too warm for a fire,' Mary protested from the doorway. 'And you need kindling and paper first.'

'I thought I'd try the grate.' Brian looked disappointed. 'We could sit round tonight . . . I mean it gives a focus point—'

'It's supper time. The dining-table is quite a good focus point.'

He followed her in and hunched on a chair staring at the platter of rissoles without interest. Mary sighed as she went to call Jim. It was plain that Caryford was failing to comfort and protect Brian as it protected her.

They had just finished their evening meal when a curious rattling and bumping sound came through the window and they looked up to see Mrs Westbrook riding her bicycle over the turf like a sedate cow-poke managing a bucking bronco. She waved gaily as she saw their peering faces. 'Nothing to worry about m'dears!' she called in greeting as she dismounted and leaned her bicycle carefully against the side of the house. 'A mysterious message – I thought it might be urgent.'

Mary's smile froze as she hurried to usher in their visitor. She could only think of Julie and as they'd been in touch only three days before it was unlikely to be good news. Unless she was planning to come down . . .

'Sit here Mrs Westbrook—' she pulled out her own dining chair and the Postmistress sat on its extreme edge. 'You must be exhausted cycling from the village and across the field.'

'Not a bit – not a bit m'dear.' However she alternately fanned herself and patted her heart taking her time while her busy eyes went around the dining-room. Mary calmed her impatience; this was how Mrs Westbrook got her architectural titbits, a small price to pay for the service she gave.

'Now . . .' the Richmonds almost leaned forward in their eagerness. 'How did you get on about the freezer?' Mrs Westbrook beamed around her. 'Did you manage to fix on something?'

Jim glanced at Mary and produced the trade card with thanks. Mary told her briefly about their day.

'Very nice. Very nice.' Mrs Westbrook pursed her lips. 'I been thinking about it all m'dears. What you want to do is to have that wall down—' she jabbed a finger at the kitchen wall. 'That would make you a decent kitchen you could eat in and you'd have twice as much light—'

Jim said, 'Could you give us the message Mrs Westbrook? I'm afraid my wife is worried that our daughter is in some kind of difficulty.'

'Of course m'dear.' Mrs Westbrook produced an old envelope from her cardigan pocket. 'That's what I'm here for isn't it?' She fished some spectacles from another pocket. 'Now . . . I wrote it down exactly as it came because it didn't seem to make no sense of me. So here 'tis . . .' She looked over the spectacles and pronounced slowly: ' "Tell him 'tis scrambling tonight and we've entered the Ford" . . . that's all there is to it Mr Richmond. Does it make sense?'

It was another complete anti-climax; Mary and Jim stared

at each other blankly. Then Brian said, 'It was for me Mrs Westbrook. Yes, it makes sense.'

She tucked away the envelope and removed her spectacles, well satisfied. 'Well that's all right then m'dear. Nothing unpleasant I hope – no? Well now, as I was saying, about that wall—'

'It makes no sense to me lad,' Jim said curtly. 'Does it refer to your old Ford? And are you proposing to drive it in a scramble tonight?'

Brian flushed. 'Yes to both questions Dad.'

Mary said, 'Thank you so much for coming over Mrs Westbrook. Would you like a cup of coffee or tea before you go back?'

The Postmistress stood up reluctantly. 'No thank you Mrs Richmond. Can I telephone a reply for you?'

Jim shook his head before Brian could speak. 'No thank you. We've troubled you enough. It's very good of you to come out especially.'

'Only ten minutes on my trusty steed,' trilled Mrs Westbrook over her shoulder as she went back down the passage. 'And such a pretty ride. Now don't forget that wall. It would open the place up towards the sea.' She mounted her bicycle with a funny little skipping jump and went off down the lane waving to the horses who lifted their heads in mild surprise.

Behind her Mary could hear Jim's voice suddenly grim. 'You fixed all this up in Stapleford I suppose? When we thought you were feeling ill?'

'I didn't say I felt ill Dad,' Brian's voice was loud with a sense of injustice. 'I didn't do anything behind your backs if that's what you mean. Like I told you, I met a couple of the lads and they said there was scrambling tonight and I could bring the Ford if I wanted to.' He looked up as Mary came back into the room and then added defiantly, 'And I want to.'

Jim said with finality, 'The Ford's not up to one of those hill courses, it would split in half. And those lads are rather thoughtless aren't they? Telephoning messages through to the post office and expecting that old girl to come all out here on a fool's errand—'

Brian's voice was still loud, resentment adding to the sense of injustice. 'How else can anyone get in touch with us in this godforsaken place? We're stuck out here – nowhere to go – working all the daylight hours and you object to—'

Mary said quickly, 'You'll be off to Exeter in another two months Brian. And nobody's objecting to you going out. We're objecting to you risking your neck . . . though it is rather late—'

'Late?' he rounded on her, his mouth lifting in the horribly familiar sneer. 'It's not eight o'clock yet mother-mine. Just about the time we used to go out for the evening back home, isn't it?'

She knew what he meant. The date with Charles at the Black Boar had been for eight-thirty. She flushed and moved to tuck her chair beneath the table.

Jim glanced at her and turned back to Brian, coldly decisive.

'You're not to drive the Ford in any scramble Brian. It's simply not safe.'

For a moment father and son stared at each other, Brian on the edge of mutiny. Then he said tightly, 'And am I allowed out as a spectator? As I'm eighteen. And as I've done exactly as you asked me since Old Adam died. Working my guts out here—'

'I'm grateful Brian.' Somehow Jim was reining in his temper in a way he had failed to do three months before with Julie. Mary realized it was a sign of his renewed confidence. 'But we've all worked hard—'

'And I've lived it up at week-ends with Mike Stelling and

two glasses of cider,' Brian went on heedlessly. 'Oh and a free lunch in Stapleford today. Big deal.'

Mary said as normally as she could, 'Stop bickering you two. Off you go Brian. And please be careful.' They both broke off and looked at her the crescendo of their anger temporarily halted. Mary began to stack plates and after a moment Brian slouched outside. They heard the Ford start up and begin to cough its way towards the lane.

Jim said, 'Thanks Mary. I don't know what I'd have said to that last comment about the free lunch.' Automatically he joined her in clearing the table. 'I thought Brian had turned over a new leaf.'

'This is only temporary. The trip to Stapleford unsettled him.'

'I really can't see why.' Jim followed her into the kitchen with a loaded tray. 'It was ordinary enough heaven knows.'

Mary began to wash up remembering Brian's impassioned assurance just now that he hadn't gone behind their backs. No, it was she who was still leading a double life. It was no good telling herself that she was safe at Caryford – that they were all safe. Outside Charles was still waiting for her and she – she was still waiting for him wasn't she? They might not be meeting clandestinely but their whole situation was clandestine. She took a pan of boiling water off the cooker and poured it into the sink immersing herself in steam. She felt that Jim must see her guilt.

But he said equably, 'We really ought to see about some kind of hot water system before the winter.'

She thought, surprised: the subject of Brian is closed. Jim's not furious, not even put out. And he was holding a tea-towel.

'There are rather a lot of things to do before winter. The stable is first priority, surely?' She rinsed cutlery and stacked it in a jug. Jim took it and started to dry it.

'I suppose so. But so much can be done with this house Mary. Mrs Westbrook's idea was darned good—'

She looked round then. 'You were listening? You mean the wall between the kitchen and dining-room coming down?'

'Yes. I couldn't help but listen could I?' He grinned as he put away the knives. She couldn't remember the last time he had helped her to wash up. 'We took her advice about the freezer. She's obviously given these old farmhouses a lot of thought.'

They both laughed. Mary suddenly felt wonderfully relaxed again. Brian was bound to have teenage tantrums. If it hadn't been about Charles it would have been about something else. It was quite normal. And here she and Jim stood, discussing alterations, washing up together. Yes, it was marvellously normal.

She said gaily, 'Actually it was quite a good idea I suppose.' She held dripping hands above the sink and turned to stare around the little kitchen. 'We should get the light from the dining-room window of course. And it would be nice to look out on the sea from here. Would it be much of a job?'

'I'm not sure. We'd take a line of bricks out I suppose and support the ceiling on a beam. I'm no builder but Stan would come over and give me a hand once the harvest is in.'

'It would be nice to have a proper farm kitchen again. That *is* something I miss from Milton Mains.'

'Nothing else Mary?' Jim said quietly.

She dried her hands not meeting his eyes. 'Not really. Not for myself. Of course Julie—'

'Ah. Julie.' Jim went to the open back door and stared up the saucer towards the horses. 'We lost her with Milton didn't we?'

'No.' Mary shook her head decisively. 'If we have lost

her, then we'd lost her long before we sold Milton. She misses it. But she would have gone anyway.' She didn't want Jim to lose his happy mood. 'I miss Jean and Stan of course. But it's good to know they're at the old place.'

He straightened and smiled again. 'You're right there Mary. And we shall see plenty of them too. We can visit them without—'

'Without tears,' Mary concluded for him as he hesitated. Then she said briskly, 'Come on, let's get the sheep down. We're getting sentimental.'

They didn't talk much as they walked up the moor together. Far below them the sun was just dipping into the sea making a fiery pathway across the water. There was a little breeze and as they reached the high ground Mary slipped off the rubber band securing her hair and shook it free over her shoulders.

Jim said seriously, 'You haven't changed much in twenty-two years Mary.'

She looked round at him ready to accept the compliment laughingly and then the smile on her face died. He was looking at her as if at last he recognized her. And in the same instant she saw him. Really saw him. Jim Richmond. She felt her face grow warm and she walked on hurriedly towards the huddle of sheep.

'Outward appearances don't mean much Jim. I'm not really the same as I was at nineteen.'

He waited until she stopped. Then he said, 'Of course not. We've grown up – we've grown apart. We both know that. But the Mary Richmond I'm talking about . . . she was in love with me.'

She stood where she was staring down at the glittering sea below the cliffs. So her efforts to bring the Richmonds together again had been more successful than she intended. They had come to this. Her heart beat irregularly. In a strange, contrary way, she was angry with Jim.

She said over her shoulder, 'Yes. She was. And Jim Richmond was in love with her. But as you pointed out Jim, they grew apart.'

He was behind her, his hands on her shoulders. 'They're still there Mary. Maybe they got buried under . . . events. Happenings. Everyday details. But Jim and Mary Richmond are still there—'

She moved away from him. 'I don't think so. I think they are stifled by those everyday details.' She turned to face him. 'Don't let's be fooled by our – our isolation here Jim. By the setting sun and the sea and nostalgia.'

'Mary—'

She interrupted him brutally, 'Jim – do you remember the name of the restaurant where we ate on our wedding night?'

He looked utterly bewildered. 'Do you mean the hotel?'

'No. We stopped and ate on the road. Before Plymouth.'

'So we did. I'd forgotten.' He shut his eyes then opened them and shook his head impatiently. 'I can't remember what it was called. What does it matter? What does it prove?'

'Just that you've forgotten. Jim Richmond is still buried.'

'For God's sake Mary. So I can't remember the name of some roadside café—'

'Oh it's not just that.' She spread her hands helplessly. 'That's just a symbol I suppose. It's . . . you used to share everything with me in those early days. We talked. Really talked—'

'We're out of the habit. Lots of married people lose the knack of conversation. And look how we've shared things since we came to Caryford.'

'Yes. It's been different here. We've got a good working relationship. But you let me help only because you have to. That first night you were angry because I tried to help with the horses—'

He was angry again at the memory. 'You damned near lost us the Shires. I was entitled to be a little annoyed.'

She laughed suddenly and unexpectedly. Her laughter was near tears but in a way it was funny that Jim thought he could sweep away the last few years of complete coldness by resurrecting their younger selves and then lose his temper over the memory of that first foolish night in the thunderstorm.

'Oh Jim, I'm sorry. But don't you see, we can't go back. We *are* different. We've got to start from now. Even the night of Old Adam's funeral – in the barn – you claimed my help simply because I was your wife. If you want anything more than a working partner, then we have to start from scratch—'

'All right.' His dark eyes were unfathomable. 'All right we'll do it that way. Partner.' There was a silence. Then Mary turned to skirt the edge of the field and get behind the sheep. He watched her and when she was in position he called out, 'So it's just a working arrangement is it Mary Richmond?'

She didn't answer. She recognized it as a challenge and knew that if it hadn't been for Charles she would gladly have accepted it. As it was she felt bewildered by the sudden turn of events. Loyalty and fidelity . . . they were words she had used to spur her into coming to Caryford and they had applied to Jim. Now they seemed to apply to Charles. Charles was waiting for her . . . trusting her . . . and she had told him she loved him.

They did not go swimming that evening and as they sat together in the sitting-room there was a new tingling awareness between them. It had been there occasionally since the night of the storm, but had been immediately submerged, unacknowledged. Now, in spite of their casual talk about the farm and possible alterations, it was there between them in the open. Mary had difficulty with her breathing.

Just before midnight Jim said, 'It's no good waiting up for Brian any longer. He might stay at Lower Brook with Mike. Or even sleep in the car. Just to show us he's independent.'

'I suppose so.' Mary longed for Brian's return for many reasons. 'If only we were on the phone—'

'No.' Jim stood up and stretched. 'That's an improvement we don't want. It would . . . break in on us.' He relaxed and stared down at her. 'Come on my dear. Stop worrying about him. We shall have to get used to being without him when he's at Exeter.'

She thought of the long winter months alone here with Jim. '*If* he gets his A levels,' she said quickly. 'He didn't do much work before the exams—' she got up as casually as she could and moved towards the door. 'We should hear soon.' She started up the stairs. 'Good night Jim.'

'Mary.'

She stopped and then turned and looked down at his face knowing what he was going to say. She could put him off no longer even if she had wanted to. And her pounding heart told her she did not want to put Jim off. She tried to remind herself of Charles, tried to conjure up his solidity, his emotional security. With Jim there was no emotional security. With Jim she was walking a tightrope . . .

He waited, his foot on the bottom step.

She said, 'Jim – I don't know – it's been so long—'

He reached up and took her hand. 'And we've changed. You've been at some pains to point that out to me my dear. But if we'd met for the first time today . . . there would be something between us wouldn't there?'

He came up a step so that their eyes were on a level. His were very dark, almost black. He cupped her face with his work-rough hands.

'Wouldn't there?' he insisted.

She tried to laugh. 'Even so . . . it would be rather sudden—'

'Ah . . .' he kissed her lightly and she didn't move. 'But that's the best part of it Mary. Because we're married.' He kissed her again. Then he put one arm around her and she felt her heart pounding against his. 'You're my wife Mary.'

The words had an uneasy familiarity. She didn't quite relax against him. The inner battle was no longer between Charles and Jim. It was between Jim and . . . and Jim. His mouth on hers seemed to claim her and part of her wanted to be claimed. The other part . . .

She twisted her head suddenly. 'Someone's coming—'

It was true. A car engine was hiccuping as it took the bumps in the field much too fast. Jim went on holding her for a moment while they both listened. Then he muttered, 'Young fool . . .' and relaxed his arms slightly. Mary realized how cold it had gone.

'It isn't Brian,' she said. 'That's not the Ford.'

'No.' He listened again. 'What's happened . . .' he looked at her and for an instant his arms were close again. 'Mary, I'm sorry.' Then he left her and went to the front door. She shivered wrapping her own arms around her shoulders. In the instant before he opened the front door she thought: he never said he loved me.

Then the door opened and in the light from the hall the black and white of a Panda Police car gleamed. Somehow Mary was down the stairs and Jim was holding her again, only this time it was different.

A young policeman got out of the car and came over to them taking off his cap. 'Mr and Mrs Richmond?'

Mary made a small moaning sound of assent and Jim's arms tightened.

'It's all right madam,' the policeman said quickly. 'There's been an accident but your son is alive.'

'Thank God.' It was all that mattered. She could cope with any kind of injury, but not his death. Somehow she straightened her trembling legs. Jim barked out an incoherent question and the policeman spoke in more formal tones.

'I'm afraid I have to tell you that your son has been taken to Taunton hospital with fractured ribs and lacerations following a car accident—'

'He's going to be all right you say?' Jim asked.

'That's my information sir. Have you got transport? I can take you into Taunton if you would prefer.'

'No. We'll go immediately. Mary—' he turned to her. 'Can you manage it?'

'Yes.' She forced herself to stand up straight without his help. 'I'll fetch my coat and bag while you start the Land-Rover – is there anything you need?'

'My jacket. On the bed. My wallet is in there.' Jim ran past the Panda, calling thanks over his shoulder. The policeman said something but Mary was halfway up the stairs. She switched off the lights on her way down, slammed the front door hard. Somewhere behind the house the horses whinnied . . . then the roar of the Land-Rover's engine filled the night.

She remembered bargaining with fate about living in the present. She remembered thinking that Caryford was inviolable. And she knew she had been living in a bubble. And the bubble had burst.

CHAPTER SEVEN

The forty miles to Taunton were the longest Mary had ever driven. Jim and she exchanged hardly any words; once as they flashed through a village he asked her to look out for a signpost; another time she drew his attention to a diversion sign which loomed out of the darkness and then was gone. In the few lights that were still burning she had occasional glimpses of his face. It was set and old.

At last they were in the outskirts of Taunton and the hospital sign came at them out of the darkness. St Jude's. Here was where Old Adam had died and changed the course of their lives. Jim peered out of the car window and then parked close to the lighted Casualty entrance. They stumbled up some stone steps and then someone was telephoning a Sister to come and meet them and someone else was pointing to chairs by the reception desk. And at last the royal-blue uniform of the Sister glided down the corridor . . .

'Your son returned from the operating theatre an hour ago. One of his fractured ribs was pressing on the lung. However, no damage has been permanently done.' She smiled suddenly. 'He is a very healthy young man.'

Mary thanked God for the last few weeks' regular meals and hard outdoor work.

'When may we see him?' she asked, her voice loud in the padded silence of the hospital.

'Immediately if you like.' The Sister began to walk down the corridor and they followed. 'He is unconscious of course but he may come round – partially – in an hour or so. I will call you again if that happens.'

They went through a door into a small single room. It was very hot. Brian lay on his back, his arms at right angles to his body. The bed-clothes were tucked around his waist and a complicated tracery of bandage covered his chest. His face was relaxed and boyish. Mary saw again how long his black eyelashes were, how full his mouth. Tears rushed into her eyes. Jim stood by the bed looking down and repeating, 'Thank God . . . thank God.'

The nurse turned and led the way out.

'I have his clothes and watch in my room . . .' she walked briskly down another corridor and somehow they followed. Mary remembered later that she was clinging to Jim's arm but whether to support him or herself she never knew. The Sister handed over a polythene bag through which the jeans and shirt Brian had worn to Stapleford looked heart-breakingly familiar.

She said, 'The man who brought your son in is still in the waiting-room. Apparently he is a friend of the family. Mr . . .' she consulted a note. 'Mr Charles Mitchell. You would probably like to see him before he goes.'

'Charles—?' Mary put a hand to her throat. Her mind jumped frenetically to try to fit Charles into all this. 'How do you mean?'

Jim said, 'Brian was on the other side of the county – a scramble—'

Sister said briskly, 'I don't know about that Mr Richmond. I understand Mr Mitchell found him in his car which was upturned in a ditch on his land. His hands were through the windscreen and his body was depressing the horn. Otherwise he would not have been found until the morning.'

Mary heard Jim's breath whistle sharply; to her dilated eyes the objects in the room – the Sister herself – appeared very far away and as they receded so sounds grew louder.

Jim's voice reverberated in her ear. 'We'd better go and see Mitchell, Mary. I simply don't understand . . . Mary are you all right?'

'Yes. Yes I'm all right. It doesn't make sense.'

'Sit down Mrs Richmond.' A glass of water appeared. 'Drink this my dear. Your son is going to be all right.'

'Thank you.' Jim was crouching before her. 'I'm all right Jim. It's just that . . . Sister it sounds as though Mr Mitchell saved Brian's life.'

The Sister said gently, 'Together with the ambulance driver and the surgeon of this hospital.'

'Of course . . .' She didn't want to owe Brian's life to Charles. How could she think of such a thing now? But she didn't . . . and she didn't want to see him either.

But they were trailing after the royal-blue uniform down yet another corridor. Everything kept moving away from Mary as in a nightmare. All the corridors and doors were the same and she was quite certain she would never find Brian again. Only Jim's hand, warm on hers, anchored her to reality.

The waiting-room was an annexe of the Casualty Ward and the bustle and noise though horrific in its own way, was matter-of-fact. As Charles rose from one of the canvas-backed chairs she was even able to smile as if this were a normal occasion. And then she remembered this morning and the scarf and Brian's sick face as she lied to Jim in the dining-room of the Red Lion.

Charles seemed to have his own worries. His face was tightly drawn and his eyes seemed to have sunk far back into their sockets. The hand he put out to Jim trembled slightly.

'Mitchell.' Jim urged him back down into his seat and they all sat down in a tight little circle. 'What on earth's happened? We just don't understand this.'

Charles looked at Mary. 'I'm sorry. So terribly sorry.

He's going to be all right is he? They said he was but he looked . . . oh Mary—'

She said, 'He's going to be all right Charles. He's sleeping now. He looks peaceful—' she felt Jim's eyes on her, sensed his puzzlement. 'We thought he was at Stapleford. Scrambling. But Sister says he was on your land.' Her voice sounded stronger than she'd imagined possible. He looked away from her at last; down at his hands.

'I don't know about that. All I know is that Stan rang me from Milton Mains. He said they could hear a car horn from beyond Long Acre field. By the time I got there he and Jean had found Brian.'

Mary put her head in her hands suddenly. Jean had been with Brian. Jean who had walked him up the Long Acre field as a baby. Jean and Stan . . . second parents to Brian. She felt a wave of gratitude. Jim put a hand on her shoulder and gripped hard knowing how she was feeling.

'You got the ambulance and came in with him? And presumably gave the police our address. It was good of you Mitchell. Thanks.' There was a little pause then he said slowly, 'So the mystery remains. You've no idea at all why Brian was driving his car across ploughed land?'

Charles shook his head without speaking or looking up. Mary felt the first stirrings of a new fear.

Jim went on, 'He must have driven through the yard at Milton Mains. Maybe – maybe he was drunk and wanted to visit his old home.' Mary made no protest. 'But I still do not understand why he went on like that. Over the Long Acre. Towards Mitcheldean.'

Mary said faintly, 'So long as he was found. And he's going to be all right.' Jim continued to frown and she said directly to Charles, 'The car – it's no good I suppose.'

Charles shook his head wearily. 'I don't know. It seemed to be in one piece.'

Jim cleared his throat. 'The weather's been so dry –

ground would be hard enough to take it. Not that it matters.' He sighed sharply. 'He must have been drunk.'

'I could arrange to tow it out. Phone a garage.' Charles looked up eagerly. 'And Stan's got a couple of days off. Would it help if he spent them at your place? He might be useful if you're tied up here.' Mary thought: he feels responsible just as I do. But there's nothing I can do about it. Nothing. And she imagined Brian drunkenly angry, driving crazily across ploughed land to warn off the man he saw as a threat . . .

'What do you think Mary?' Jim was looking at her and the frown was still in his eyes.

'Yes please,' she said simply. Someone would have to look after the horses and the sheep. Who better than Stan and Jean?

There was nothing else to say. They sat for some time in growing discomfort. Mary knew she should try and have a private word with Charles and could not. She could find no words of consolation for either of them, it seemed to her as if – sitting there with Jim – they were both branded with guilt. She hoped he would make no effort to speak to her directly and when at last he stood up and excused himself she felt only relief and gratitude.

Jim too was silent after Charles' departure. He clasped his hands between his knees and stared at them as if deep in thought. Someone came and sat near them nursing a fractious baby. Later still there were drunken shouts from the treatment room and a nurse hurried across the waiting-room and spoke into a wall phone. Jim took no notice and Mary watched it all with unseeing eyes. It seemed like eternity before the blue uniform of their Sister appeared at the glass doors and beckoned to them.

'Brian is semi-conscious now and is calling for his father,' she said permitting herself a smile. 'You can both go in for a few minutes but he won't remember this when he comes round properly later today. He will probably talk a lot of nonsense – don't let it worry you please. We are quite satisfied with his condition.'

Mary glanced at her watch as they went back down the maze of corridors. Four o'clock. She could hardly believe her eyes. Only four hours since she and Jim had been on their way to bed. She glanced at him but he was still wrapped in his own thoughts. This time they walked separately behind Sister.

The little room seemed hotter than ever. Brian lay as before spread-eagled on the clean white linen but now his eyes were wide as he stared at the ceiling. They moved closer to put themselves in his line of vision.

'Is that you Dad?' His voice was loud and high. 'Dad? . . . I don't want to see Mother. Don't let Mother come in. Please Dad.'

Mary stopped dead in her tracks, appalled. Jim went forward hurriedly. 'It's all right old chap. You're quite presentable – nothing to worry about—'

Brian's voice cut across his, stridently insistent. 'I don't want to see her. I can't see her—'

Mary looked at Sister her wide eyes asking a question. Then at the helplessness she saw there, she turned and stumbled out into the corridor.

The professional voice said, 'Don't be hurt my dear. He'll probably call for you in a moment. He's ashamed and cannot face you just yet. Meanwhile we mustn't excite him – his respiration—'

'It's all right. Quite all right.' Mary managed to sound reassuring and after another pat Sister rustled off to her room. The corridor was very quiet again. Very warm. Mary subsided against the door jamb resting her forehead on the white paint, letting the pain of Brian's rejection sweep over her in an agonizing wave. She told herself she shouldn't be surprised; he had been rejecting her for a long time now.

His subconscious was saying frankly what his sneer had said covertly over and over again. Yet these last weeks . . . these last few precious weeks at Caryford protected by their own special bubble . . . she had hoped so much that everything was somehow magically going to come right.

The door wasn't closed properly. Her weight pushed it open an inch and as she instinctively drew back Jim's voice reached her, very firm, very matter-of-fact.

'That's silly talk Brian – be quiet now. Of course your mother loves us. Listen to me son. If she didn't love us would she still be at Caryford now? You've got it all wrong about Charles Mitchell. I can promise you that.'

Mary moved away from the door and subsided on the chair Sister had placed for her. The import of Jim's words did not immediately reach her though her quick reaction in leaving the door confirmed that they were dynamic. She sat very still controlling her breathing and seeing the words as if they were written before her. So . . . Brian had told Jim about Charles. It didn't matter. Had he also told his father that he had been driving to Mitcheldean to have it out with Charles? Perhaps even that wasn't so bad. Brian was all right and maybe his drunken midnight escapade had provided him with some kind of catharsis.

The impact – the reason for her laboured breathing – came with the word love. 'If she didn't love us would she still be at Caryford now?'

She put her head in her hands. It was true. She had meant to see Jim through the move and the bargain they had made in the barn at Milton Mains would have meant nothing by now if she had really loved Charles. But she was still at Caryford and planning to stay until after Christmas. She thought: all my talk tonight, all my resentment for the years of neglect – it doesn't mean anything. Jim's right. There is something between us.

She dropped her hands and stared at the opposite wall.

It seemed faintly ridiculous to discover that she was in love with her husband now. Any time during their day together – at Stapleford – on the high moor when they collected the sheep and then later tonight when she had tried so hard to avoid Jim – any of those times she could have seen and understood. She could have shown Jim her love, made a bulwark against which doubts about Charles would have foundered instantly. But now . . . now that Jim knew . . . saw what Brian had suffered . . . now it might be too late. She knew Jim's stiff-necked pride of old.

Five minutes later he emerged from Brian's room. His face gave nothing away; he looked at Mary briefly and shrugged.

'He seems barely conscious. Ashamed of what he's done I suppose. Anyway he wants to see you now.'

'You told him he had to see me. Jim he's been talking about Charles – I know – I heard—' she tried to speak levelly but her voice trembled on the verge of desperation.

'Be quiet!' He sounded unutterably weary. 'Now is not the time to quibble over our marital affairs. Go and see the boy for God's sake—' he broke off and then went on quietly, 'He just wants to forgive and forget now. Make a fresh start. Put his mind at rest. That's all you have to do.'

'What are you going to do?' Whether she meant at that moment or in the long term she had no idea. He took the question at its face-value.

'Go back to the waiting-room and telephone Stan. They'll be up now for the milking.'

'All right. Jim . . . it'll be all right. It's going to be all right.' She tried to smile at him but he turned away quickly. Sick at heart she went into Brian's room.

Already his eyes were glazing with sleep. She took one of his upflung hands and murmured reassurances and he pressed her fingers.

'Mother . . . I'm sorry. So sorry,' he whispered.

'It's all right darling. I understand.' She leaned over him and said more clearly, 'There's nothing to worry about Brian. Try to believe that.'

He actually smiled then and his lids drooped. 'I know. Dad told me. I've been a bloody fool.' He closed his eyes and gradually the pressure on her fingers relaxed. She watched him for another few minutes and then let go his hand and straightened her back. Yes . . . Brian was going to recover fast. He had got over his emotional crisis, literally knocked his pent-up anger out of his system. Very carefully she kissed him and then left the room.

Jim was still on the wall-phone when she at last found her way back through the corridors to the waiting-room. He replaced the receiver carefully.

'I've just rung Anne Elliot,' he said shortly. 'Tony's coming to collect you for the rest of the night.'

'I can't possibly leave Jim. There might be a change in Brian's condition – anything—'

'I'm staying here and I can telephone you immediately if anything happens. Stan and Jean will be at Caryford for breakfast. Everything's under control.'

She recognized that he had taken the reins in his hands. There was to be no showdown, no discussion. He would make decisions for them all as Old Adam had taught him. She shivered. But there was no strength left in her to fight him. And she could no longer borrow strength from Charles. At least this night had shown her that very clearly. She had leaned on Charles and inexcusably mistaken her reliance for love. She recalled his taut face and sunken eyes. Had he known too that this was the end of the road for them?

She felt completely weak like a cork tossed on water and when Tony Elliot arrived ten minutes later in his sleek car she let herself be tucked into it and driven away from Jim and Brian although her every instinct rebelled against the Richmonds being split up at this time. When they reached the Elliots' comfortable detached house on the outskirts of Taunton the sensation of living in a dream helped her to behave almost normally. Anne Elliot was making coffee in her beautiful modern kitchen looking like a model in a dark-blue Victorian dressing-gown . . . it was all so different from Caryford. Mary was able to smile gratefully and tell her the encouraging news about Brian, even sip at the coffee. Really, she told herself as she got into the pristine bed in the Elliots' guest room, there was nothing to feel quite so awful about. Brian could convalesce at Caryford until the University term started and they could return to the life of hard work and long dreamless nights . . . she found she was crying.

She must have eventually slept because it was broad daylight when she next opened her eyes. The flowered curtains were partially drawn showing a rather grey sky in between flowering cherry trees. Anne Elliot stood by the bed smiling down at her and holding a tray. She was dressed in a linen suit.

'Anne, I'm so sorry – it's late – are you going out?' Mary struggled up in bed her head throbbing painfully.

'I'm dressed for Church. But we don't have to go Mary.'

'You mustn't think of changing your usual routine Anne. Please. I'm feeling such a nuisance as it is.' She took the tray neatly laid with thin bread and butter and a tiny silver dish of marmalade. 'Oh my dear, how kind of you.'

'Now stop being all grateful Mary. You'd do the same for me.' Anne went to the window and drew the curtains fully back. 'Not a very nice day I'm afraid.'

'I gather there's no news?' Mary said anxiously trying to push her hair into some kind of order.

'Nothing extra. He's sleeping peacefully. Jim says you're not to worry.'

Mary smiled. Tony and Anne had no children.

'All right. Just so long as you don't let me get in your hair. Look – I'll enjoy this breakfast and then get over to the hospital.'

'There are no buses and it's miles to walk. So that's out.' Anne looked mysterious. 'Besides you'll be having a visitor shortly. Take a leisurely bath and get dressed and make yourself some coffee – use the house as if it were yours.'

Mary was grateful and alarmed at the same time. She hoped very much her visitor would not be Charles.

She had in fact just finished dressing when she heard someone come into the empty house and cooee. Unmistakably a female cooee. She went halfway down the stairs and peered along the hall. Then she descended the rest in a rush and was holding Julie to her in a way quite unlike their usual calm selves.

It was really Julie. Not so soignèe as usual but still something very special in jeans and denim jacket with half her hair in a topknot and the other half floating around her face. Mary could not believe it. She held her away and then clasped her again.

'Mother – it's OK . . . OK.' So strange to hear Julie in the role of comforter. 'I've been at the hospital for an hour and Brian's comfortable and Dad's going to have a sleep in a little room next door and they'll telephone immediately if there's any change.' Julie paused and took a breath. 'Come on now. It could be so much worse. This isn't like you.'

Mary realized her face was running with tears. Try as she would she couldn't check them.

'It's been so awful,' she hiccuped. 'Oh Julie – thank you for coming – it's all my fault—'

Somehow they were in the kitchen and Julie was finding

her way around Anne's things and making strong coffee for them both. Mary found a corner of her thoughts to be surprised at her neat-fingered efficiency.

Then Julie was smiling and trying to make her mother laugh.

'First of all I'm woken in the middle of the night – well, five thirty – by the landlady saying I'm wanted on her phone and would I please not make a habit of early morning calls. Then Dad says Brian's seriously ill after an accident, so I borrow my flat-mate's car and drive like mad. Only to find Brian looking like an innocent cherub fast asleep and Dad absolutely as usual. So I come here for coffee and a quiet chat with my calm mother . . . and what do I find!'

Mary somehow managed a smile. 'Julie I'm sorry. Really. Oh darling you've grown up so much. Is it only six weeks since we saw you?'

'Longer. Obviously it's gone slower for me than for you.' She paused looking down into her coffee. 'Is it really so awful at this new place?'

'Caryford?' Mary recalled her greeting to Julie. 'No. It isn't awful at all. I didn't mean that.'

'What did you mean Mummy? And why are you blaming yourself for Brian's accident? Dad says he went off in a fit of boredom and rolled the car at Milton Mains when he was drunk. I really don't see how you can blame yourself for that.'

Mary sighed. Julie was possibly the only one who could understand Mary's feelings over the past few years. But she knew Jim would see it as a further disloyalty if she confided in her daughter.

'I didn't . . . understand . . . his boredom I suppose. I've been so content at Caryford. It meant getting away from Milton Mains. It wasn't entirely my home Julie.'

'No. I think I knew that. Especially after Old Adam

died.' Julie frowned trying to sort out her own feelings. 'I mean, when it was our grandfather's home – well it was ours too in a way. But after he was dead it just seemed to go with him. And in any case it was different for you Mummy. You weren't born there or anything.'

'It's strange you should say Adam took everything with him. Your father said that just before the funeral. It's not strictly true.' Mary shook her head tiredly. 'Ah . . . never mind now. Whatever the reason Julie, I think Caryford is sweet. Oh, it's cramped and right down on its beam ends. But because of that it has terrific possibilities. But it's tough on your father. Tougher still for Brian I suppose. There was a stupid row. He must have been upset – he couldn't have known what he was doing . . .' the tears overflowed again.

Julie took her mother's cup from her trembling hands and put it in the sink, then she crouched before her and shook her gently by the shoulders.

'Look. Will you kindly stop it. I refuse to change places with you and mop up your tears and worry about you getting run down in this new place. That's your job, not mine. Understood?'

Mary managed a watery smile as she nodded. She looked into her daughter's blue eyes – so close – so like her own. She thought wonderingly; we're not fencing, or bickering . . . at last, at long last, we're talking.

Tony and Anne came back soon after that and Anne prepared an early salad lunch. Mary protested that she ought to rejoin Jim at St Jude's but she was talked down and found herself sitting in the Elliots' elegant dining-room with french doors open on to a shaven lawn, actually coping with iced soup and stuffed tomatoes. Julie told her that Stan had telephoned from Mrs Westbrook's and everything was all right at Caryford, so there was absolutely nothing for her to worry about. She was amazed at herself. Brian was ill, Charles must be miserable and Jim doubtless hated her, yet she sat here meekly doing what she was told. For the moment she knew she was a broken reed.

After lunch Julie drove them both to St Jude's. It was Sunday visiting time and Mary was suddenly conscious that she was still wearing the jeans and shirt in which she had helped Jim round up the sheep the night before. Just the night before.

A different Sister sat in the little office at the end of the corridor. She told them that Mr Richmond was still sleeping but if they would like to wake him now—?

Mary said quickly, 'No. No, he could only have had three or four hours. There's no point—' She hardly admitted to herself that she did not want to face Jim. 'If we could sit with Brian for a little while?'

'Certainly Mrs Richmond. You will see a definite improvement.' She smiled dismissal and then added as an afterthought, 'Mr Charles Mitchell telephoned to inquire your son's condition this morning.'

'Oh.' Mary felt her colour high. 'Oh, that's fine. Thank you.'

Brian was lying as Mary had seen him last night with his eyes closed but they flew open immediately at the sound of the door. Mary wondered whether he remembered what he had said at four o'clock this morning or if there would be resentment now and she manoeuvred herself in front of Julie until she could see his expression. But the smile he turned on her was completely unshadowed. It reminded Mary of Brian as a young boy.

He said weakly, 'Hi there mother-mine. And Sis too. This is a great honour. I'm not going to die am I?'

'Idiot,' Julie said shortly, unawed by bandages and those crucified arms. 'You're not so easily got rid of.'

Brian's smile became a grin. 'Don't sound so regretful Ju . . . what brings you here then if it isn't to weep by my bedside?'

Julie fetched a chair for Mary and settled herself on a corner of the bed.

'I've come to be with Mother if you must know,' she said. 'Nothing to do with you.'

'Good old Ju.' The dark eyes turned on Mary. 'You're taking this badly Mother-mine?'

Mary felt the treacherous tears again. Brian had used that affectionate term only sneeringly before, now there was a tenderness in his voice that made her heart swell dangerously.

'Naturally we were worried,' she said. 'But you're doing so well—'

'Yes, I'm going to be OK. I can tell.'

There was a little pause while they went on smiling rather foolishly, then Brian said, 'Look. Did I dream last night? Did we decide to forgive and forget? Start all over?'

'We did.'

'Then . . . we don't have to talk about it do we?'

'Of course not.'

'The police—?'

'We'll sort all that out. Later.' Mary wondered exactly what would happen. After all Brian must have been drunk.

Julie said, 'Look on the bright side. You injured no-one save yourself.'

'I hope not.' Brian looked at Mary. 'Dad seems to understand pretty fully. And you—'

'I understand too.' Mary did not dare think of Jim. She said quickly, 'Have you any pain anywhere? What about the breathing?'

'I've got a bit of a headache and my hands are smarting. That's all. A therapist came round just before you arrived and gave me a short breathing exercise. Apparently I'm a strong, healthy lad!'

'Yes, so they told us last night. So Caryford has done something for you.'

He looked serious. 'Caryford's all right. Which reminds me – where is Dad?'

Julie started to say, 'He's sleeping—' then stopped as the door opened and Jim came in. He needed a shave but his hair was combed and he looked much as usual. Mary gave him a swift glance then looked away.

He spoke in the jovial voice he often used to Brian.

'Quite a family party. Did I hear my name mentioned?'

'Yes.' Brian was beginning to sound tired. 'I wanted us all to be here. I want to say something and it's better if you all hear at once. Perhaps if you talk it over afterwards you'll be able to understand how I feel.' But his eyes never left Jim's face.

Jim said, 'Save it Brian. You're tired. We'll be here this evening.'

Mary felt her heart beginning to beat with slow, hard strokes. Was Brian going to insist on having everything in the open? Obviously Jim did not want that.

'Let him speak Jim,' she said in a low voice.

Brian smiled at her. His breathing was suddenly short and shallow.

'It's all right mother-mine . . . it's about Exeter.' He closed his eyes momentarily and took a chestful of air. 'I don't want to go. That's no whim. I've not wanted to go for ages. But there was nothing else to do. Now there is.' He stared at Jim again. 'I've enjoyed working at Caryford Dad. It's not like Milton Mains where everything had been jogging on for hundreds of years . . . it's like pioneering.' His eyes turned to Mary. 'That's how you feel too isn't it Mother?' He coughed a little and then went on. 'I want to work there eventually. Help you make the new Richmond place.'

Mary felt the treacherous tears again. It was so exactly how she had felt and not even realized . . .

Jim cleared his throat. 'Nothing to stop you doing that son. *After* University.'

Brian's head turned wearily. 'Dad I could spend those three years learning things that will be useful to Caryford. If I could enrol at the Farm Institute – be a student for a year . . . you know how it's done.'

'Yes, I know.' Jim had taken students over the years in spite of Old Adam's affronted reactions. 'Have you thought who would take you?'

Brian grinned. He knew when he had won a battle. 'Mike's father is thinking of applying for an agricultural student this year.'

'Oh I see. A deep-laid plot.' But Jim was smiling and Mary could guess that he was as much thrilled at the thought of Brian wanting to follow in the family tradition as he was disappointed at him giving up his University place.

'Well son, we'll do as you suggest. Think it over.'

Julie said, 'About time he did *some*thing . . .' and stuck out her tongue at her brother.

They left the tiny ward smiling; outwardly close. The new Sister was effusive; people turned to look at Julie so casually elegant; they admired Jim bronzed and dark. Mary trailed behind almost frightened of their strength. Yesterday . . . or was it this morning . . . she had wanted to talk to Jim. To explain. Now she had no strength to explain anything; no right to talk to Julie; and Brian wanted to forget . . .

Jim turned to look for her. 'Come on Mary.' He put his hand under her elbow as if he thought she might run from him. 'We've got a lot to discuss.'

Mary walked docilely across the car-park.

CHAPTER EIGHT

They stood by the Land-Rover suddenly undecided about where to spend the time until the evening visit.

'Don't let's go back to the Elliots'.' Julie urged. 'We can phone them and then go and have tea along the river somewhere.'

Jim fingered his stubble doubtfully, but eventually agreed. 'I don't really feel like being sociable. I can leave the Rover here and we can use that car you've borrowed Julie.'

Mary, who would have preferred the neutrality of Tony and Anne's found it impossible to demur. She said, 'If there's a shop open anywhere could you stop? I'd like to get some fruit juice for Brian.'

They managed to buy some at the little tea-house they found among the trees on the banks of the Tone. The weather was still overcast but it was warm and they sat at one of the white-painted iron tables a few yards from the water. They had late strawberries and Devon cream and endless cups of strong tea. Gradually Mary relaxed a little. She sensed Jim was doing the same. Julie, not realizing that the unease between her parents was anything new, kept a stream of chatter going about her London life. Mary thought sadly that perhaps it was just as well Julie had not shared their happiness at Caryford. As far as she was concerned the situation was normal.

'So you're doing well Julie?' Jim asked, rousing himself from a smiling torpor.

'Not bad.' She grinned at her father. 'I've still got the

money from my car intact. And I've added to it. So I can afford to take a week or two off.' She looked across to Mary. 'That is – if there's room for me at Caryford.'

Mary hesitated and it was left for Jim to say, 'Of course there is. Your room is a bit cramped – I speak from personal experience – but it's a room.'

'But—' Julie, in spite of being a modern miss, turned slightly pink. 'What about – I mean if you've been using it—'

'Look.' Jim put his hands on the table and leaned over them. 'Let's make a few plans while we're together. If you really can stay for a week or two Julie, I suggest that you and your mother go back to Caryford tomorrow. Wait a minute—' he held up his hand as Mary began to protest. 'Naturally that depends on Brian's condition. But he's strong, he should be all right. The thing is, Stan and Jean will have to get back to Milton and I'll have to stay here for a while. And the sheep and Shires aren't going to take care of themselves.'

Julie looked curiously at her father. 'Well, that's all right with me. But are you going to trust a couple of women with your new farm?' She spoke banteringly but her eyes were serious.

Jim said tersely, 'Your mother can manage, if you help her. She's done everything there is to be done on the place.'

Julie's gaze switched to Mary. There was a little silence while she digested this information then she repeated, 'Well of course that's OK. We can use Maggie's car. Anytime. But—' she frowned slightly. 'I don't want to put any spokes in any wheels Dad but I would have thought Mother and I would be more suited to the hospital visits.'

Jim said, still in the same brusque voice, 'I shall have to see the police Julie. Brian was drunk in charge of that old Ford. Also while I'm here I can visit the Farm Institute and see John Stelling – try to fix Brian up at Lower Brook as a student.'

'Oh.' This was the father Julie knew and she sat back in her chair. 'So it's all decided.'

Jim did not look at Mary. 'The life suits him. It could be the making of him. Yes, I think it's decided.'

Mary clenched her hands in her lap. As clearly as if he had spoken aloud Jim was telling her to keep out of Brian's life from now on.

Brian seemed to have improved by the evening visit and the next morning his breathing was almost regular and he did not get so exhausted when he spoke. He listened to his father's plans and nodded agreement.

'It's the only thing to do Mum,' he said, reverting to his schoolboy name for her. 'You couldn't cope on your own, but with Julie—'

'Oh, so I'm not quite useless in your estimation?' Julie asked in mock amazement.

'You've got a car, so you could drive along to dear old Mrs Westbrook and send a message couldn't you?' Brian said sarcastically.

'Is that the Postmistress who rides a bike?' Julie smiled. 'It all sounds peaceful after London.'

Jim cleared his throat. 'The thing is, Stan has to get back to Milton Mains tomorrow and I know your mother isn't going to want to leave you so soon.'

'Mum for Pete's sake! What can you do here? Besides . . .' his face flushed. 'You'll only get upset if there's any trouble with the police and it would make it all worse.' He looked at her pleadingly. 'Please go Mum. Let's get back to normal as soon as possible and try to forget this whole . . . business.'

Mary wondered if that was possible. Would a return to Caryford make anything better? She had certainly wanted Julie to sample its recuperative powers. She smiled at Brian. 'We can see when we're not wanted,' she capitulated.

'But you promise to do exactly as you're told young man. All right?'

'All right Mum.'

Jim said stonily, 'Now that's settled may I suggest you leave this afternoon? You'd have to go tonight anyway and I don't fancy either of you driving across that moor in the dark.'

Mary shivered remembering the nightmare ride on Saturday night, but this afternoon seemed so soon. However she was the only one to think so. Brian pointed out she would miss the evening visit anyway and Julie said she wanted to see Caryford as soon as possible. In the end Mary dropped a kiss on Brian's forehead and said she would drive in for the day on Friday to see him.

Once out of the ward it seemed pointless to wait through lunch before setting out so they left before midday, waving goodbye to Anne who was impeccably dressed in another linen suit for a meeting in town. Jim was intending to move his few things into the Elliot guest room but meanwhile he went straight to Tony's office to talk over the legalities of Brian's accident. Mary was not sorry to be spared a proper farewell to him. In her present mood of weakness she felt unable to speak directly to Jim.

Her spirits began to revive a little as they drove along the twisting lanes of the high moor. They stopped and had bread and cheese at a tiny pub apparently miles from any customers and pressed on immediately. It was two o'clock as Mary directed Julie over the bridge and along the flower-hedged track to where the saucer of turf held the house in its cupped hand. Julie stared silently.

'It's all right,' Mary laughed. 'I hated it when I saw it first. It was unbearably hot – we had a terrific thunderstorm our first night – and it looked so lost and shabby.'

Julie said, 'It's like a house in a fairy-tale. The roof seems to come right down to the ground somehow.'

Mary was pleased with this reaction and as they bumped over the turf she pointed out the stepping stones, the sea, the gorse covered cliffs with a certain pride. 'It's so small after Milton,' she said. 'But perhaps that's its attraction.'

Stan and Jean had not been expecting them, nevertheless Jean had been baking all morning to fill the larder against their return and the smell of hot biscuits and raspberry buns completed the storybook illusion for Julie. Especially when Jean appeared at the open doorway wearing her old-fashioned starched apron, closely followed by Stan in his smock and what he called his 'cider hat'.

It was a heart-warming reunion. They talked until it was time to bring the sheep home. Stan was happy to be with sheep again and Jean was at ease in the tiny kitchen among Mary's familiar utensils and china. And they were both deeply happy to be able to help out at such a time of crisis.

They all walked up to the moor together. Jean and Mary lagged behind while Jean told how she had pillowed Brian's head on her dressing-gown and told him over and over again, ' 'tis all right m'dear.' She stared out to sea. 'I wasn't just saying that to comfort him Mrs Richmond. I had a feeling it *was* all right – from that very moment. There's a lot of talk about the youngsters making their protests and I reckon that's what Brian did on Saturday night. Got it out of his system like.'

Mary was amazed at how closely parallel Jean's feelings were to her own.

She said, 'Brian resented . . .' she faltered, wondering how much explanation she owed Jean.

'He's resented a lot of things m'dear,' Jean said quickly. 'But most of all the break-up of his home. He needed someone concrete to hate – his grandfather was dead and he loves his parents – so it had to be poor Mr Mitchell.'

'Yes. Yes, that was it Jean.' And it was – so simple put in Jean's every-day phrase. 'I wish you'd explain it to Julie.

Nobody has told her exactly what happened and I think she's wary of asking.' She smiled mistily at the homely face. 'I have great hopes of Caryford relaxing her. Helping her to get her priorities straight.'

'I shouldn't be surprised m'dear. Look at her now.'

Julie, ahead of them, had stopped and was gazing at the sun drowning in the sea and stretching her arms towards it in a gesture of surrender. She looked over her shoulder and saw them.

'You know—' she called. 'I've got a feeling this is the life.'

Unexpectedly Mary's eyes filled with tears . . .

Stan and Jean did not leave the following day. A message came from Mrs Westbrook in the morning to say Charles would fetch them on Wednesday afternoon. A sense of holiday infected them all. With the fine weather and four pairs of willing hands they were not overworked and when Mary mentioned Brian's suggestions for keeping poultry, Stan began to knock up a hen-house from some old doors he found stacked behind the new bathroom. He also put up some shelves in the kitchen and confirmed that to knock down the dividing wall to the dining-room would be a fairly simple matter.

On Tuesday evening Mary and Julie walked into Carybridge and telephoned Jim. The news of Brian was encouraging and Jim had got things moving in other directions. John Stelling would be willing to take Brian as a student if he was accepted by the Farm Institute and suggested that he should spend part of his convalescence at Little Brook simply observing. His place at the Institute depended on his A level results and his year's practical work. But it was fairly certain he would get a place there.

Mary, sharing the receiver with Julie, made sounds of approval and left it to her daughter to ask the questions and reassure Jim that everything was fine on the farm. When Jim asked abruptly, 'Are you all right Mary? Yourself?' she said 'Yes, of course. And you?' 'Yes . . .' a pause then he said, 'I was hoping to see Stan. To thank them both myself. But it's doubtful.'

Julie took up again, 'I think they've enjoyed it in spite of the reason for them being here. The weather's marvellous. Mind you it will be a pot-hole full of mud in the winter.'

Mary moved away. Jim's spurious closeness over the telephone wire made her want to see him. Very much. But first there was Charles. Tomorrow she would see Charles and explain that it was finished. And then – then perhaps the way would be clear for her and Jim . . .

On Wednesday morning she felt a heavy sense of dread at the task ahead of her. It was going to be difficult to convince Charles that even if her marriage eventually collapsed and she left Jim, it could never be to go to Mitcheldean. It was less than two weeks since he had been here before and she had told him she loved him.

However Charles was not alone when he arrived. The Bentley bounced up to the front door like a sedate duchess and Julie and Mary both weeding in the garden had to knock the dry soil from their hands to be introduced to a sandy, thick-set young man. Charles introduced him easily.

'Michael Sandford. Our new vet.' Mary wondered whether he had brought him as protection. 'He's only recently qualified and has joined the local practice.'

Michael Sandford shook hands awkwardly. 'I was at Mitcheldean this morning and Mr Mitchell suggested I accompany him. I hope you don't mind Mrs Richmond.'

'Not at all.' Mary smiled though she wondered how this would affect her talk with Charles. 'It's a good idea to meet possible clients and get to know both ends of the

County . . . This is my daughter Julie. And I expect you've heard that my husband and son are in Taunton.'

'Yes. Mr Mitchell mentioned about the accident. I'm so sorry Mrs Richmond.' He took Julie's hand as if it were a lifebelt. 'I'm pleased – delighted—' he looked into Julie's eyes and seemed to forget what he was saying.

Julie rescued her hand. 'Did you take a look around Milton Mains Mr Sandford?' she asked, her eyes very wide and blue. 'It's our old home you know.'

Michael Sandford nodded. 'Yes. I understood that the Richmond herd did in fact take their name from you.'

Mary and Julie looked a question at Charles and he explained smoothly, 'I thought it only right that your father's and Old Adam's careful breeding should be remembered. And the "Richmond herd" has quite a ring to it.'

Julie flushed suddenly. 'Oh – oh that was good of you Mr Mitchell.' She turned impulsively to Mary. 'Dad will be so pleased.'

'Yes.' Mary didn't look at Charles. Stan and Jean had said nothing about the 'Richmond herd' so it was probably a very recent idea. To make amends?

Julie was smiling at the new vet and making good use of her long lashes. 'We've still got some stock we can be proud of Mr Sandford. My grandfather's Shires came with us to Caryford.'

Mary suddenly realized Julie was trying to make an impression on Michael Sandford. She said gently, 'Would you like to see them? They are grazing just over the rise. Julie will take you while I make a cup of tea.'

'That would be very . . . nice.' The new veterinary surgeon developed a colour rivalling Julie's. 'If you could spare the time Miss Richmond?'

Julie was unexpectedly gauche. 'I suppose so,' she said ungraciously. 'And for goodness' sake call me Julie.'

It didn't sound a friendly invitation but he immediately responded. 'And my name is Michael of course.'

They went off, Julie talking in a high affected voice quite unlike her usual self.

Mary said unthinkingly, 'My goodness. That was quick.'

Charles laughed naturally. 'Yes. It would be an interesting combination. Glamorous Julie Richmond and workaday Michael Sandford.'

Mary said quickly, 'Julie isn't just glamorous you know Charles. She's good in the house. And I've been amazed at how she's turned her hand to things outside since we arrived on Monday.'

'It's pretty amazing the way you're coping my dear,' Charles said. 'I was surprised when Stan told me of your plans to stay here alone. For one thing I didn't think Jim would permit it.'

It was upon them. The explanations. Mary felt her heart sink.

'No. He never would at Milton Mains of course. It's different here. Charles I'm sorry – I should have known before. It's quite different here.'

He said nothing for some time, staring down at the dusty grass and moving a pebble gently with his toe. Then he sighed.

'Let's go down where we were before Mary. We must talk.'

'Stan – Jean – wait a minute I'll ask Jean to make a snack or something.'

Jean was already spreading the cloth in the dining-room.

'I'll lay up a good proper tea m'dear and call Stan in half an hour. You go and have your chat.' Then unexpectedly she added, 'And go easy with Mr Mitchell. He's a good kind gentleman.'

Mary nodded. Jean understood so much. 'I'll try Jean.'

The ford was shallow today after two weeks of dry

weather. They wandered past it and followed the river on to the small beach. The tide was in and lapping quietly around the rocks from which they swam. Mary sat on one and stared into the water.

'You know what's happened, don't you Charles?' she began without preamble. 'I'm so sorry. I feel I've cheated you . . . yes I *have* cheated you—' this as he automatically began to protest. 'But I didn't know I was. I relied on you so terribly Charles and it seemed like love – last April at the Black Boar I didn't think I could live without you—' he sat down by her and took one of her gesturing hands. '—I don't think I *could* have lived without you then my dear. But it was because somehow you gave me back my self-respect . . . oh Charles I can't explain it now.'

'Exactly.' Charles managed to smile at her spate of words. 'You can't explain it. You've thought of nothing else since Brian's accident and you're in a hopeless muddle. You think it happened because of us—'

'You think so too Charles. Be honest.'

'I was . . . shocked. I had no idea it went so deep with the boy. When I saw him there I realized instantly he had been trying to get to me . . . who knows what was in his mind?' His hand gripped hers and he bent his head. 'Yes. It was awful Mary. But we can't take sole responsibility darling. Jim . . . and the boy himself—'

'He was innocent,' she said sharply. 'If you can't see that what's the use of discussing anything?'

'Mary please. Don't be angry. You might say something irrevocable. Can't we leave it as it was? Brian's crazy action hasn't changed the basic issue surely? You say it's different here at Caryford and obviously you're helping – you feel part of the place. But can't you see my darling, Jim has no choice at the moment?'

Mary stood up with her back to him. He tried to retain her hand but she freed it and clasped both her hands in front of her. 'Charles, forgive me—' she spoke with difficulty. 'But Jim and I – that doesn't matter any more in relation to us. Yes, I am in a hopeless muddle about him. I admit it. But I know how I feel about you my dear. There's everlasting gratitude and there is a very deep affection. But . . . if I leave here now it will be to start a new life on my own.'

His hands on her shoulders were gentle. 'I couldn't allow that Mary. I'd want to look after you. It would be enough – I wouldn't ask anything of you unless you wanted to give it. Surely you couldn't refuse me the happiness of comforting you?'

She put her hands over her face and felt the tears.

'Oh Charles, it *wouldn't* be enough. Perhaps it would have worked before. Not any more. Jim knows about us – Brian told him that night – and it would kill him—' she broke down completely.

Charles turned her to face him and held her against his shoulder stroking her hair. After a while she was still, leaning against him, feeling as she had so often felt, borne up, supported by him.

At last he said slowly in her ear, 'Mary. You still love Jim.'

It wasn't a question and Mary did not answer. She seemed to hear Jim's voice overlying Charles' as he'd used similar words to Brian in that small hospital room. 'If she didn't love us would she still be at Caryford?' She was revealing her love every day she stayed here . . . even Charles saw it; and Jim must have seen it for a long time, yet since that night he had not even held out a hand to comfort her.

Tears overflowed again and she hung on to Charles almost desperately. It was complete confirmation.

'It's all right . . . all right my dear. I'll still be at Mitcheldean. I can help somehow. There are ways—'

'Charles—' she raised her head. 'You must not do anything – please – don't get in touch – nothing—'

He smiled reassurance and she moved away a little trying to compose herself and there . . . unbelievably there . . . standing on one of the stepping stones, was Jim.

Mary stared at him over Charles' shoulder for a timeless second not hearing Charles' words of comfort any more. As if she was outside her own body she could see the scene through Jim's eyes, yet for that eternal second she was unable to move towards him or call or do anything at all. Held by the same sense of helplessness which had numbed her since Brian's blurted accusation in the hospital, she saw herself – Jim's wife – in the arms of the man who had already acquired Jim's home.

And then the second clicked on to the next and Jim turned abruptly away and trudged slowly alongside the river towards the farm.

Mary's tears had gone, she was frantic. 'Charles—' at last she pushed him away. 'Charles that was Jim. He saw us. He must have thought – oh my God.'

'I'll explain Mary.' Charles looked round but Jim was some way off. 'We've done nothing – I'll explain—' he put out a hand and leaned on the rock for an instant, almost blindly. Mary realized that his calm acceptance of the situation was a thin front. Charles had just taken a terrible blow. But she couldn't think past Jim.

'No. You mustn't see him. So much has happened Charles and this will look so . . . planned. He will suspect even Stan and Jean. And my dear I want to avoid a row at all costs. I'm sorry but I couldn't bear it. Could you make some excuse to Julie and take Stan and Jean off as soon as you can?'

He said slowly, 'I suppose so. Is it what you really want?'

'Really.'

'I wish there was something . . . all right Mary. Will you telephone?'

'No.' She tried to soften the flat refusal. 'I mustn't. You've got to forget me as soon as you can.'

He said flatly, 'Don't be ridiculous. I love you. And that's that. I'm stuck with it.'

She thought bleakly that it was the same for her. She was stuck with her love for Jim and the feeling he'd had for her seemed to have died.

They walked back to the farm. There was no sign of Jim or the Land-Rover so he must have parked on the other side of the ford and walked across the stones. The others were already finishing one of Jean's bumper teas and Charles drank a cup standing up saying he had just remembered an appointment. Jean nodded understandingly. In a short fifteen minutes they were in the Bentley and bumping gently back along the track.

Julie said, 'Well, that was quick. Not that I'm sorry. Michael Sandford was a bore didn't you think?'

She actually waited for her mother's opinion but for once Mary did not pick up her cue.

'Darling, can you start clearing up on your own?' She looked anxiously to the top of the field where the Shires should be grazing. 'Your father is somewhere – he came across the ford. He must be with the sheep or the horses. I'm going to look for him.'

Julie was unsurprised. Jim's comings and goings had been casual enough at Milton Mains.

'Don't worry Mum. If it was bad news of Brian he'd have come straight to the house. He didn't feel like being social.'

'Probably. But I'll go and find him all the same.'

She trudged slowly up the field wondering what she was going to say and why in fact Jim hadn't put in an appearance. He wasn't the sort to sulk and she had been rigid with fear that he would turn up before Charles left and order him off the property. Her heart quickened at the thought that Brian was worse and Jim simply hadn't been able to face her.

He was on the other side of the saucer standing with his head against Princess' neck. She ran forward.

'Jim – what's happened? Brian—?'

He didn't look up. 'Fine.' He reached up and felt the horse's velvet nose. 'When are you going?'

'Going?' She tried to control her breathing. 'Going where?'

He jerked round impatiently. 'To Mitcheldean. Stop trying to fool me any longer Mary for God's sake. When is it?'

'I'm not going to Mitcheldean Jim. That's what I was telling Charles when you saw us on the beach. Listen Jim please. I know Brian told you something about Charles and me when he was delirious, but there's never been anything to it—'

He looked at her and she saw that what she had mistaken for weary resignation was barely-curbed anger. There were dangerous sparks in his dark eyes and the hand that fondled Princess trembled slightly.

'Tell me this. Honestly if you can. Before Adam died – were you intending to leave me then?'

'Yes – but—'

'The trip to Cheltenham to see Janice—'

'I *was* going there. I couldn't make up my mind about Charles.'

'How typical. You can't make up your mind about so many things can you Mary? Tell me another thing. Did you come to Caryford as a permanent measure – or just a temporary one – to see me settled?'

'Jim – be fair! It sounds so awful the way you're putting it, but it wasn't like that at all—'

'And even that day in Stapleford you met him didn't you? Brian mentioned the scarf.'

'Oh Jim please!' Defiance gave her an unexpected strength. 'Yes, I did see him at Stapleford. And he paid for the wretched scarf too. But it was entirely accidental—'

'Nevertheless you found it easy to lie about it at the time. No wonder you put me off that night.'

She had been going to blurt out that she loved him. Now she was silent, choked by the cruelty of his words.

He went on tensely, 'And now Brian's crash has filled you with guilt and you've made a fond farewell of Charles Mitchell until the guilt wears off. Is that it?'

She stared at him, appalled. And yet – how nearly that was to the truth. Self-disgust swept over her taking the momentary strength she'd had, making her limp.

'No answers any more Mary? So let me tell you what's going to happen—' he left the Shire and she moved and stamped uneasily. 'You're *my wife* Mary. D'you understand that?' He gripped her arms suddenly and she swayed as if she would fall down. 'Mitchell's got my home. But he's not going to have you as well. You said that you'd stay here as long as I needed you and I need you – I can't run this place without you.' She staggered and he held her up. 'Are you listening Mary?'

She stared into his eyes and read his intention. Her one coherent thought was that if he kissed her it would be all right. He must love her. There would be no more need for confusing words.

Then his mouth came down on hers claiming her. His wife. His property. Let no man trespass. She closed her eyes, surrendering herself, waiting for his response.

There was none.

CHAPTER NINE

Mary stayed where she was with the horses for some time after Jim had left her. She supposed dully that, like him, she found comfort in their large, undemanding presence. They gave an illusion of permanence and security to everything – even the disintegrating Richmonds. She laughed a little at that thought and then put her hands to her burning cheeks. Never before had she felt so completely . . . powerless. When she had been ignored and useless before, Charles' love had stiffened her pride and made her feel – at least for a little while – that she wielded her own destiny and could go. Make a new life for herself. Now her pride was as nothing and Charles' love, still there in spite of everything, made her feel guilty and uncomfortable. She pushed the heels of her hands into her eyes as she remembered what Jim had said and what Jim had done . . . as if she were . . . she looked up and almost laughed again. As if she were one of the horses. That was it exactly. He would care for her because she was his and had been his for a long time. And in return she must do her share . . .

When at last she went back to the house it was gone seven o'clock; time to bring home the sheep. She half-hoped that Jim would have slipped away as unobtrusively as he had arrived leaving just a message with Julie. But he was munching one of Jean's sandwiches and discussing plans to knock the kitchen wall down; as if nothing had happened.

'Here's Mummy,' Julie greeted her. 'Dad's getting ideas about the house already.'

Mary smiled briefly and picked up a tea towel. She

remembered when Mrs Westbrook had first mooted the scheme and the way she and Jim had discussed it afterwards. It had grown between them. Now, it was Jim's scheme.

He said, 'We must get it done – and the stabling for the horses – before winter. They want Brian to go to a convalescent home on the South coast for two weeks before starting at Lower Brook. When he's gone I'll have a chat with Stan. See what we can arrange.'

'If you'd been in a sociable mood,' Julie said reprovingly, 'You could have seen Stan this afternoon. And met the new vet.'

Jim laughed at her without embarrassment. Mary dried up as if nothing had happened between them. It increased her feeling of weakness to complete impotence. Did Jim think by the seal of that possessive kiss he could take away her independence and free will? She shivered in the warm kitchen. Of course that was exactly what he had done. She had known she could never leave him for Charles. Now she could never leave him at all. And his complete lack of tenderness crumbled her self-respect to dust.

'Cold Mary?' She felt as if he were mocking her. 'Let's take a walk up to the moor for the sheep. It's a lovely evening.'

Mary shook her head quickly. 'It's been a long day. I think I'll have an early night.' She moved to the door as if she was afraid he might force her outside to share another angry intimacy. When he stayed where he was she asked hesitantly, 'Are you staying the night?'

'Yes. I thought I would. Brian is completely out of danger now and simply needs rest.' He smiled mirthlessly across Julie's head. 'It's all right, I'll take his room.'

Julie put away the last of old Mrs Richmond's crockery which Jean had had to unearth for the visitors.

'I'll come with you Dad. I want to hear about the gay city life and whether Anne Elliot ever wears anything but neat two-piece suits. Oh and I have to tell you about our new vet . . .' she chattered on with her usual blunt insouciance and Mary looked away from Jim's expressionless eyes and went upstairs.

She had been sleeping in Brian's bed while the Butlers were in the bigger double room and she tried not to think as she moved her things across the landing. But when she laid Jim's pyjamas out she saw that her hands were trembling. She stood up abruptly and went to the window. Jim and Julie were walking along the lip of the saucer, outlined against the dipping sun. It might have been Jim and Mary of twenty years ago walking there . . . if things had been different. If they'd bought Caryford then instead of going to Milton Mains. Yet – could things ever be different? Had Jim really changed?

She said aloud, 'If you had an ounce of pride you'd leave now. You'd ring Janice from the Post Office and get a lift somehow to Taunton and catch the first train . . .' But she knew she wouldn't. The pride that had carried her through the years of loneliness was all gone. She turned and looked at Brian's narrow bed. Then she sat down on it and picked up Jim's pyjamas and held them against her hot face, her easy tears flowing again.

The next day life slipped into its previous pattern as if nothing had happened. Save that Julie sat in Brian's place and talked far more than he had, it might have been possible to think everything was normal.

Jim informed them brusquely at lunch-time that he would stay until Saturday when he had an appointment with a Police Superintendent about Brian.

'Will it be all right?' Julie asked in the face of Mary's silence.

'I think so. He didn't hurt anyone else and it isn't as if Mitchell will complain about trespass.' He cut himself some cheese. 'The official line will be that he's been punished already.'

'Yes.' Julie frowned. 'Jean told me exactly what happened. I didn't realize poor old Brian took the old home so seriously.'

Jim's eyes flickered. 'No. Neither did I.'

Mary said breathlessly, 'If you're going to be home then it will be all right for me to go and see him tomorrow won't it?'

Julie laughed. 'You don't have to ask permission Mummy. Besides I could have managed quite well without you.' She began to clatter plates together noisily. 'Michael Sandford said he'd come over and give me a hand with the sheep if I was here alone.'

'Oh?' Jim grinned. 'Is that so?'

'Yes. I happened to mention that Mummy was going to Taunton on Friday and he offered immediately.'

'Then you won't be accompanying your mother?' Jim asked.

It was as good a way as any of letting her know she could go. Mary stood up. Communication between them was becoming difficult.

On Friday morning she kissed Julie goodbye and started slowly over the field in the borrowed car when Jim appeared from behind the house and walked quickly towards her. She stopped immediately and wound down her window.

He said brusquely, 'You'll be back before dark, won't you?'

She was thrilled as a schoolgirl at his concern for her. 'Of course,' she said.

He flushed, misunderstanding. 'Oh I know you'll come back,' he said. 'I'm not worried about that.' She flinched away from the hardness in his face. 'At least I trust you to keep *that* promise Mary Richmond.'

She started the car again with a jerk and bounced along the lane much too fast. Her face was burning. Did he really hate her so much?

It was a welcome change to go into the Elliot's calm almost opulent home again. Anne kissed her fondly; the last week-end had cemented a friendship that had never really got going over the years. Mary was amused to see she was wearing another two-piece and just had time for a coffee before going to address a Ladies' Convention on 'The role of professional wife'.

'Mary – before I forget—' they were in the immaculate drawing-room which Anne was pressing on her as a 'rest room' for the day. 'The man from Mitcheldean telephoned yesterday – the one who found Brian—'

Mary nodded. 'Charles Mitchell.' She was worried and flustered. Surely Charles wasn't going to try to see her yet again?

'Yes. He wants you to ring him. It was rather odd actually because I thought Jim would come back first so I suggested Mr Richmond could get in touch but he said would I please save the message for you.'

'Jean left something at Caryford probably,' Mary said, angry with Charles now. 'He has been so kind – lending us the Butlers.'

Anne was perfectly satisfied, perhaps a little disappointed. She left soon after and Mary lost no time in dialling Charles' number. She was lucky to find him in and spoke without preamble.

'Charles – I asked you not to get in touch. Please don't try and reach me through the Elliots again. They are well known in the town.'

'I'm sorry,' he said shortly. 'Naturally I've been worried Mary. What happened – how was Jim?'

It was impossible to explain. She reassured him as best she could but knew he could tell from her voice that everything was not as 'fine' as she repeatedly said.

'Look my dear—' he tried to sound his old matter-of-fact self. 'Please let me do something to show Jim a little friendship. Would he accept a couple of heifers from the Richmond herd?'

'No. Nothing Charles. I'm afraid there's only one way you can help at the moment.'

'Keep away,' he said slowly. 'Yes. You said that before.' There was a short silence then he said, 'Goodbye Mary.'

The receiver clunked dead against her ear and she was left knowing that she had hurt Charles as much as she had hurt Jim. It was such a mess.

To see Brian was instant reprieve. His arms were free again and in the week he had been in hospital his hair had grown into curls on his neck. He seemed to have shed all the sullen bitterness which had cropped up since Adam's death. Somehow his father's assurance when he had been semi-conscious after the accident had gone home. He was like a schoolboy.

He recounted his plans: two weeks at Exmouth, another two weeks at Lower Brook – four weeks convalescence in all. And then – as he put it – the 'nitty gritty'.

'How will you manage without me at Caryford Mum?' he asked grinning. 'Jean came in to see me yesterday and she said you were going to take on some pullets.'

'I hope so. There will be plenty to do.' Jim planned to plough more land and there would be the vegetable garden and the hens. It would be a blessing; they might be able to avoid seeing each other for hours on end. 'How was Jean?' she changed the subject.

Between the afternoon and evening visits, she drove into the town and bought Julie a blouse. On the next counter was a pile of cotton shirts, thin and cool. She hesitated, then almost defiantly bought one for Jim. She just had time for tea and cucumber sandwiches with Anne and then it was back to the hospital, her arms piled high with fruit and paper-backs for Brian.

'You'll write when I'm at Exmouth won't you Mum? And perhaps pop along to Mrs Westbrook's and give me a ring?' He grinned in case the words sunded too emotional. 'I must know how Ju gets on with this Michael Sandford character and I know she won't write.'

'Of course I'll write. And phone. And I'll come over to the Stelling place and see you in just over two weeks' time . . . Will you be all right now Brian?'

'I'll be fine. Take care of Dad.' He laughed self-consciously. 'It's quite a shock to a boy of my tender years – discovering his parents are in love you know.' He looked up and saw her face fiery-red. 'Oh dear. Have I put my foot in it? You've both got it bad haven't you?'

'I don't know what you mean—'

'Well. Dad breaks out in a light sweat every time he mentions your name. And now you're blushing like a schoolgirl. I know the signs Mum. I did human biology at school.'

She wondered how he would feel if he knew why his father reacted as he did. Somehow she returned his grin.

'That's the trouble with teenagers. They never see their parents as human beings.' She patted his hand. 'I must go. I promised to be home before dark.' She ignored his loud laugh and kissed the top of his head. 'Goodbye darling – take care.'

Somehow it was a long and lonely drive back across the moors to Caryford. Half of her longed to be home, to see Jim again and hear his voice. The other half trembled and hid from the thought of his contempt. She rehearsed things she could say; safe, anonymous conversations about Brian or the performance of Julie's borrowed car. Tomorrow Jim would be leaving again, returning to Taunton to see Brian on his way and sort out any difficulties with the police. If he called on Stan as well he would probably stay away all the week-end. Then he would be home for good. And Julie would be going back to London. And they would be alone. She shrank inside herself at the thought.

But when she drove across the bridge and along the bumpy lane the farm was still a hive of activity. Two lorries, one fitted with a ready-mix concrete drum stood behind the house and in the long red beams of the setting sun men were still working on some kind of construction.

Jim was nowhere to be seen but in the dining-room Julie was laying the table for supper and kissed her mother excitedly.

'Isn't it marvellous? It's a pre-cast concrete building firm or something. They rolled up this morning out of the blue to erect a stable! Dad was working of course, so I looked at the order and naturally assumed he'd put it through as he was talking about stabling for the Shires. Anyway I said go ahead.' Julie giggled, she was positively fizzing with good spirits. 'They'd already laid the concrete foundation when he came in at mid-day and – guess what? He hadn't ordered it! He went all white and funny and I thought he was going to tell the men to get off the place. Then along comes your dear old Mrs Westbrook with a telephone message from Stan. He met a man in a pub and heard about this special offer and got in quick. Dad still looked a bit odd but he had to accept it of course . . .'

She rattled on. The firm guaranteed to erect a building in twelve hours so tomorrow night the Princess and the Queen would have their new stable . . . the floor would be completely set by then . . .

Mary thought back quickly. She had telephoned Charles at eleven and he had never really told her why he wanted to speak to her. And she had told him to keep out of Richmond affairs. And at twelve-thirty the message had come through from Stan. Was this Charles' doing? Had he seen his mistake and gone straight to Milton Mains to enlist Stan's help? Her heart beat uncomfortably hard. If she could guess at this, so could Jim.

However the new stable was certainly a topic of conversation that evening, if not entirely safe. The four workmen stayed to supper and were quick to sing their own praises. And even Jim had to admit a grudging pleasure that his beloved horses would be safely housed from now on.

After the meal Mary busied herself with the mountain of washing-up leaving Jim to speed the workmen and walk up to the high moor for the sheep. Julie was nowhere to be seen. She came in after dark dripping wet. She had been swimming fully clothed. Just because she felt like it. She laughed at Mary's astonishment.

'Haven't you ever wanted to do something completely mad when you're happy?' she asked. The question filled Mary with unbearable nostalgia.

The next morning she found herself unexpectedly alone with Jim while Julie walked into Caryford for the week-end supplies. She was making coffee for him before he left; it was suddenly a mammoth task.

'Did Michael Sandford call in yesterday?' she asked desperately. 'Julie was expecting him and she seemed rather excited last night—' she dropped a spoon and bent down flustered, to retrieve it.

'Yes. Bit young for a vet I thought. I wouldn't want him near the Shires.' He sounded abrupt. 'Don't bother with that Mary—'

She went no doggedly, 'How did he and Julie seem together? I mean—'

'I know what you mean. They barely spoke. Julie went on and on about some bloke in London who takes her everywhere – she's never mentioned him before. Young Sandford just nodded and that was that.'

'Poor Julie,' Mary said sincerely. She put a mug of coffee in front of him wondering how two people could so misinform each other. Jim took his wallet from his jacket and opened it. Before she could turn away he placed a piece of paper in front of the coffee cup. It was a bill for sixteen hundred pounds. With a sinking heart she realized it was to do with the new stable.

Jim was watching her face. 'Yes. Very reasonable isn't it? For a three-stall stable and harness room?'

She said nothing.

'One of those do-it-yourself concrete garages wouldn't be much less than that,' Jim went on inexorably. 'So I would think some kind friend has contributed towards our stable. Probably half the cost. What do you think?'

She turned her back and tried to speak normally. 'I know what you're getting at of course. All I can say is – I know nothing about it.'

'I wish I could believe that. I realize this is a long-standing order but it seems odd you planned to be away the day of delivery. I expect you and Mr Mitchell had a good laugh yesterday imagining my surprise at his lovely present didn't you?'

She closed her eyes and lowered her head. 'You know it wasn't like that. I know absolutely nothing about the stable. It was as much a surprise to me—'

'Did you see Charles Mitchell yesterday?'

'No—' Before he could continue his interrogation she went on desperately, 'I telephoned him. He'd left a message with Anne asking me to. Perhaps he intended telling me about the stable – I've no idea. I just told him to keep away from us all. I was telling him the same thing on Wednesday.'

There was a silence. She could hear Jim breathing.

'And he won't – is that it? He keeps pestering you – harassing you—'

'Stop it!' She turned to face him furiously. 'He wants to make amends. To help us out. To gain our friendship – *our* friendship Jim! Try to put yourself in someone else's place for once – how d'you think he feels finding Brian like that? Guessing why he was there – on his land in the middle of the night? Charles is a shy reserved man who wouldn't hurt anyone.'

He stared at her glinting blue eyes for a long moment. Then he said curtly, 'We're not accepting anyone's charity anyway. I'll go and see him.'

'By all means. But—' she was surprised and elated by her own anger. 'Remember what I said Jim. If you and he brawl like a couple of animals over me, then it's finished. I'm *me* – Mary Richmond – d'you understand that? I belong to myself and I don't go to the highest bidder or the strongest fighter!'

He went on staring and she stared back. At last she stood straight before him without any guilt. She felt gloriously . . . self-possessed . . . in the best sense of the word.

At last he turned on his heel and left the kitchen. She heard the engine of the Land-Rover start up and chug away, then pause as he met Julie returning from the village and stopped to say goodbye to her. Defiantly Mary went over to the packing case and picked up his cooling coffee and drank it down. She was not going to feel down-trodden any longer – not even to the extent of throwing away unwanted coffee.

They spent the rest of that day getting the stable ready for the horses. A neighbouring farmer – the ubiquitous Mr Watling – had promised straw and Julie took the car and fetched it and they laid down a decent carpet of it in the stalls. Then the brasses and harnesses were fetched from the boxes and cupboard in the eaves and polished to eye-straining brightness and hung in the harness room. The two old hurricane lamps from Milton Mains were placed strategically and the Queen's rosettes pinned above her stall.

As if sensing that all this activity was on their behalf the Queen and her daughter moved slowly towards the house, grazing as they came. Laughing at their diffidence, Julie led them in to see their new quarters.

'You needn't pretend you're not as curious as any old human being would be,' she said to them. Then, turning to her mother, 'Isn't it strange? Squire's not half so bright as these two ladies – look he's just standing up there. Hasn't even realized anything new has arrived.'

Mary frowned. 'Actually that isn't like him.' She took a walk up to the saucer's edge where Squire stood impassively apparently gazing out to sea. He wasn't grazing, but he seemed all right and whickered a greeting to her as she ran her hand under his mane. His coat was slightly rough.

'All right old man?' Mary said. He snuffled and bent his head as if nodding. Mary remembered it was Squire who had reacted so nervously to the thunder on the night of the storm. Perhaps he mistrusted the new stable and would refuse to use it for a while.

The other two seemed to thoroughly enjoy their new home however. Ridiculously Julie and Mary took their supper out and ate it with them in the stable.

'A real celebration party for you – you spoiled babies!' Julie told them as they hung their lugubrious heads over the stalls and almost smiled. 'Now Caryford is a real farm – it's got its own stable and a champion shire inside it.' She gave them both sugars and then took a handful and trudged up to give it to Squire. But when she returned she had to tell Mary he had refused the delicacy.

'His coat feels rough and he's drinking a lot. D'you think he might have a temperature?' she asked worriedly.

Mary said, 'I know so little about the horses. You know

how possessive Adam was with them. Mr Hopkins came and checked them before we left Milton.'

'Maybe we should call Michael in to look at him,' Julie suggested.

Mary hid a smile at such an obvious ploy. 'We'll see how Squire is tomorrow. Don't worry him to use the stable. It's very warm and he'll be all right.'

When she went to bed she found her presents for Julie and Jim still lying on the chest of drawers. She took the blouse in to Julie straightaway. Apparently it was just the thing – the height of fashion. Mary had chosen it because it reminded her of the peasant blouses she had worn when she first met Jim. The wheel had turned a full circle.

'I should go to a party in this,' Julie said regretfully. 'One of the Young Farmers' things. I could wear that long cotton skirt . . .'

Mary left her trying on combinations of clothes in a belated attack of femininity and went into Brian's room with Jim's shirt. Any present-giving in that direction seemed out of the question now. She opened a drawer and slid the shirt between others.

The next morning Squire seemed no worse, certainly not bad enough to call in a vet. Even Julie had to admit that. It was the first Sunday in August, another beautiful day. After tea, Julie suggested they walk into Carybridge for the evening service at Church.

'You want an excuse to wear your blouse,' Mary teased.

Julie turned slightly pink. 'Not at all. But I've been home just over a week and apart from the workmen on Friday – oh and Jack Watling who let me have that straw yesterday – I've seen no-one.'

'You've seen Mrs Westbrook at the Post Office. You've been in most of the village shops. And of course you've met the new vet.' Mary said dryly.

'I hope you're not getting any silly ideas mother?' Julie asked with as much dignity as she could muster. 'And what have you got against going to Church?'

'Nothing. I'd like to go,' Mary grinned.

It did them both good to escape from the farm for an hour. They were conscious too that they created quite a stir in the club-like atmosphere of the old Saxon Church. Mary had wondered whether she was prejudiced in thinking that Julie had a special quality about her, something sterling that had nothing to do with her face and figure. Now she saw that other people recognized it too. They smiled welcomingly at the two women and from comments afterwards it was evident that Mrs Westbrook had put it about that the Richmond women were managing the Caryford place alone.

Among those who spoke to them in the porch after the service was a red-faced man who pumped Mary's hand and offered her 'any help I can give'.

'Mr Watling, Mother,' Julie introduced him. 'He was kind enough to offer the bales of straw when he saw the stable going up.'

'Ah – and if Mr Sandford 'ud known you'd be in Church tonight young lady, he'd have been here.' Mr Watling said to Julie with a twinkle in his eye. 'Did you know our young veterinary surgeon is staying at my place for the week-end Mrs Richmond?'

'No, I didn't,' smiled Mary. No wonder Julie had been eager to fetch the straw yesterday.

Julie walked fast to the ford. 'You need not think I wanted to go to Church to see Michael Sandford,' she remarked haughtily as she jumped from stone to stone. 'He's rather dull actually.'

'Yes dear.' Mary watched her daughter crossing the water much too fast. 'Mind you don't fall,' she warned ambiguously.

The next day Mary felt on edge wondering whether Jim would come home or not. Squire had moved nearer to the farmhouse and did not move or attempt to graze all morning. Mary went across to him a dozen times to talk to him. His coat was still rough to the touch but otherwise there seemed nothing wrong with him.

She said to Julie, 'If your father's not home by tea-time, you'd better slip into Carybridge and ring for one of the vets.'

Julie did not look pleased at the minor triumph. She knew as well as Mary how it would affect Jim if anything happened to one of Old Adam's horses.

But she temporarily forgot Squire when an ancient station-wagon bumped down the lane during the afternoon and Michael Sandford got out.

'Er – hullo,' he called at the open front door.

Mary and Julie were screened from view behind the foliage of the kidney beans and Mary stayed where she was letting Julie go forward to greet her visitor alone.

Julie gave him an off-hand 'Hello.' There was an hiatus then she went on without warmth, 'Did you want anything special?'

Mary thought wryly how unlike her real self Julie was when she was in love.

'Well, yes. As a matter of fact . . .' Michael's tongue seemed to get in his way. '—there's a dance tonight. A hotel near Ilfracombe. I happen to have two tickets and I wondered if you would come with me?'

There was another pause, much longer this time. Then Julie said in a more normal voice, 'I'd love to. Thank you very much Michael.'

'Oh good. I'm so glad. I wasn't a bit keen – I don't know anyone yet . . .' he sounded suddenly relaxed too. Mary smiled to herself recalling how awkward Jim had been with Janice and her parents until he was certain how she felt. Julie was just about the same age as she had been then . . .

It was naturally assumed that Michael would stay to tea. By which time there was still no sign of Jim. Mary bit her lip remembering what he had said about trusting the new vet with the horses. At last she said she must telephone Milton Mains and see what had happened to Jim. Julie made a face thinking her mother was being heavy-handedly tactful but Mary just shook her head and started up the borrowed car.

Mrs Westbrook was washing up and left the switchboard immediately she had connected Mary with the Butlers for which Mary was surprised and grateful.

'Jean? Have you any news of Mr Richmond? I was expecting him home today and he hasn't arrived yet.'

'Oh . . . Mrs Richmond?' Jean sounded oddly evasive. 'Is that you then m'dear? What some weather we're having aren't we? Second hay-making we'll be having at this rate I reckon.'

'Yes. I expect so. Jean is he with you?'

'Who – Mr Richmond? Well he was m'dear. Him and Stan are around somewhere . . . that is, I'm not certain—'

'Jean,' Mary said tersely. 'Tell me what's happened.'

Jean sounded like a broody hen yanked off a set of eggs. 'I dunno what you d'mean m'dear. Mr Richmond naturally called in to see Stan about a certain matter—'

'The stable,' Mary said. 'Then I suppose he went over to Mitcheldean. You might as well tell me Jean.'

'Oh dear. He told me not to say a word d'you see and now he's off somewhere with Stan. It's typical of men—' Jean was vexatious. 'The truth is Mrs Richmond there was a bit of a rumpus but Mr Richmond was very anxious you shouldn't know about it. He thought he'd stop here till Wednesday or Thursday – till his eye's better—'

'His eye?' Mary's voice was sharply anxious.

'Just a bit bruised m'dear. Nothing to worry about. To tell you the truth I think both of them were spoiling for a fight and it's done them good. They had a drink after as friendly as could be—'

Mary felt her temper rising. How dare he? After what she had said. Neither of them were hurt obviously so there was nothing to worry about. But plenty to make her furious. And she was furious. She felt sick with fury. To be brawled over . . . like one of the Shires . . . and then to be all hale and hearty and masculine and shake hands. As if something had been settled with their fists. And him . . . hiding behind Jean's skirts . . .

She said tightly, 'Will you tell him something please Jean. Will you tell him to stay until Thursday at Milton Mains. Stay with you just as he'd planned. That will give me time.'

'Time? Listen m'dear – what do you mean? Don't you go and do anything hasty now—'

'It's all right Jean. Mr Richmond will understand. Just tell him that. Goodbye my dear.'

She put down the phone. She was trembling all over. She'd done it – she was free of the Richmonds at last.

CHAPTER TEN

Mary hardly registered the return of Mrs Westbrook and she accepted the enormous bunch of early chrysanthemums the postmistress had picked for her with automatic gratitude. She could find room for only one thought in her mind and even the necessary actions that would bring it about raced around the periphery of her brain meaninglessly.

She had her freedom. She had given some kind of ultimatum to Jim – exactly what had it been? Anyway he had broken it and released her from the promise she had made at Milton Mains. Their marriage had become a kind of bondage for her and she was free. She said the word soundlessly as she got into the car again. Free. She was herself again, belonging to nobody. Her responsibilities towards Charles . . . Brian . . . Jim – even Julie who was in love – they were all at an end. Finished by two men scrapping like undignified schoolboys.

Mrs Westbrook said, 'And how's the boy? Coming home soon I hope?'

'Home?' she almost laughed. 'No. Actually he's going to the Farm Institute to learn to be a farmer.' She wondered fleetingly if learning to be a farmer meant acquiring this frightening sense of property that Jim had. That Old Adam had had. 'He's getting better. Thank you Mrs Westbrook.'

It sounded stilted. She hesitated wondering next whether she should go back to the Post Office telephone and ring Janice. Today was Monday and she must be gone by Wednesday. There was time . . . let Julie have her Farmers' Dance this evening and then tomorrow she would talk to her. Try to explain. Julie would be able to hold the fort at Caryford until Jim got home . . . with the help of Michael Sandford.

She drove back very slowly trying to still her thoughts and absorb peace from the countryside. The sight of the ford and the glittering sea and the little low house made a lump come into her throat. And then she saw Squire, standing alone at the edge of the saucer, his head drooping. That's why she had gone to Carybridge – to ask Jim if he would allow Michael Sandford to look at Squire! And she had forgotten all about it.

It ought not to have mattered any more. She was free . . . no more responsibility for anything at Caryford . . . but she couldn't leave Squire another night in obvious discomfort. She went up the field and talked to him and he raised a heavy head and looked at her but he made no sound in greeting. His big brown eyes were dull.

She walked determinedly back to the house. Julie and Michael were making a long job out of the washing-up and she asked Michael immediately if he would take a look at Squire.

'My husband won't be home until Thursday and the horse can't go on like he is,' she said. 'If you could just help us to get him in the stable—'

'I'll have a look at him up there first of all,' Michael said. 'No need to disturb the old fellow if he's just off-colour.'

He dried his hands and rolled up his shirt sleeves looking so ridiculously young that Mary felt renewed qualms about her decision. But he became completely different – competent and assured – when he went out to make his examination. Mary and Julie stood back almost respectfully as he ran his square hands over Squire's coat and then carefully down each leg, talking to him gently the whole time.

'He's a grand horse Mrs Richmond. But there's certainly something wrong . . . that's the way old chap—' he said as Squire leaned down and blew in his ear. '. . . his coat is very rough. He's eating nothing and drinking too much. There's an infection somewhere.'

Mary felt Julie's eyes on her, suddenly alarmed. They both knew how quickly a horse could succumb to illness.

'He hasn't used the stable you say? It could be a stoat bite – something like that. You haven't heard a squeal?'

Mary shook her head. 'The workmen were making quite a bit of noise all day Friday. I suppose it's possible—'

Michael grunted and stayed where he was on his knees, running his hands again down the off foreleg.

'Something here. Just above the knee – can you feel it?'

Mary knelt beside him. Sure enough she felt a hard lump where his fingers guided hers.

'It's a blood swelling. A haematoma,' Michael explained, standing up and caressing Squire's nose. 'Some damage was done and the skin healed too quickly. The poison and a sort of tangle of blood clots are trapped in that lump. He's pretty bad Mrs Richmond. With your permission we'll get him into his stall and I'll lance and drain it immediately.'

Mary felt her mouth go dry. If Jim lost one of the Shires . . . yet Michael sounded as if he knew what he was talking about and he looked both efficient and sensitive when he worked. She bit her lip, glancing at Julie. There was no doubt in those blue eyes.

Julie said in a low voice, 'I don't think you've got much choice Mummy. What will happen Michael if you don't lance it?'

He shrugged. 'I can inject massive doses of penicillin and hope for the best. He's strong. But if I deal with the haematoma he'll be better by the morning.'

Mary said, 'Come on. Let's get him into the stable.'

Michael nodded briefly. 'OK. Julie will you fetch my bag from the station wagon. And put some water on to boil.' Julie the independent, ran obediently ahead of them.

By the time Michael had got the big Shire into his stall and found an upturned bucket for himself to sit on, Julie was back. He opened his case and selected several lethal-looking instruments.

'I'll need this sterilized Julie,' he said turning again quite naturally to her as his assistant. 'Boil them up in a large pan, then drain the water away and bring them here in the pan. May I wash up in your bathroom Mrs Richmond?'

It took about fifteen minutes to get ready. Already the long summer evening was beginning and Mary lit both hurricane lamps and held them high so that their light fell directly on Squire's foreleg. The horse seemed to know he was in good hands and stood patiently while Michael clipped the hair around the swelling and made four injections of anaesthetic in a square around it.

'There.' He sat back on the bucket. 'We wait a moment for that to take effect and he won't know I've even started.' He smiled suddenly and reassuringly at Julie. 'He won't be able to dance like we will tonight. But by tomorrow—'

She smiled back confidently. Mary looking at them in the pattern of light and shadow recognized their togetherness. Julie was doing what every woman longs to do, helping the man she loved. Mary knew it should make her feel even freer but somehow it didn't. Desolation and anxiety vied for a place in her heart.

Then Michael said, 'Scalpel please,' and Julie put it into his hand as if she'd been assisting at operations all her life and stood unflinchingly while he made an incision about four inches long across the swelling.

As the pus and blood spurted out Mary turned away for a moment, then forced herself to look back thinking that she must be able to tell Jim exactly what this new young vet had done.

'Forceps,' Michael said extending a wet hand.

He removed the rest of the blood clots quickly and

cleanly. Squire's ears moved and Mary whispered encouragement. Otherwise it was very still inside the stable. Around the lamps a moth began its dance of death and from the moor an early owl hooted a greeting.

'Sutures,' Michael said. He was dusting the clean wound with a powder. 'That was penicillin,' he said, glancing up at Mary. 'And now I'll do six nice big blanket sutures and we're almost finished.' He worked steadily. 'Can you make a big pad of cotton wool Julie? I stitch it on to the outer skin to protect that little lot. Then it's just a couple of shots in the neck. Penicillin and anti-tetanus.'

He went on smoothly and unhurriedly, occasionally thanking Julie or asking Mary to move the light slightly. Squire did not move.

'There,' he said at last, rubbing his hand over the injection punctures in the neck. 'All done.' He looked at Mary's trembling arms. 'You can relax now Mrs Richmond. In fact we all can. How about a coffee? Then I'll go back to the Watling place and have a bath and put on my glad rags—' Julie smiled at such a dated phrase, but her smile held no scorn.

She helped her mother make the coffee while Michael cleaned his instruments.

'He's not dull, is he?' she asked soberly. 'Or a bore.'

'No darling, he's not,' Mary agreed. 'I think he's rather special.'

Julie's eyes sparkled into renewed life. The long hour's work in the stable had taken nothing of her energy, yet Mary felt drained.

'So do I.' She giggled. 'I told you that blouse was meant to be worn to a dance didn't I?'

Mary forced herself to laugh back. 'All you think about is clothes,' she said and realized with a shock that a few short months ago she would have meant that. Now, Julie insisted on fetching the sheep home before she got ready for the dance, helping to get the Queen and Princess in their stalls, making the last-minute check of Squire.

'Are you sure you'll be all right?' she asked her mother repeatedly. 'Shall I miss the dance – there'll be plenty of others—?'

'You certainly will not!' Mary said decisively. 'It would make Michael think you had no faith in his veterinary abilities. He has assured us that Squire will be all right – and you can see that for yourself—'

'OK, OK.' Julie twirled in her long cotton skirt. 'It's just that you seem all tense and anxious. And I can't bear anyone to be even the littlest bit unhappy tonight. Especially you.' It was uncharacteristic speech for the down-beat Julie. Mary forced another wide grin and found it wasn't too forced after all. It was hard to stand against the effervescent happiness of her daughter tonight.

However, after they had gone she felt a return of the mixture of worry and emptiness that had visited her in the stable. She tried hard to rekindle the invigorating anger that had upheld her immediately after speaking to Jean but it was gone. She stood by the front door looking towards the dark sea and told herself she should pack and start a letter to Janice, but she went on standing there aimlessly feeling lost . . . as if she were adrift on that sea.

A snuffle from the stable at last roused her from her torpor and she ran round the house and shone the torch on Squire. He was standing very still in his stall – but so were they all. She whispered a few words to him and his head moved lugubriously in her direction.

'Are you all right old chap?' she felt his nose; it was warm and rough. Why on earth hadn't she asked Michael what kind of good and bad symptoms to look for? She was again overwhelmed with anxiety and wondered what was the matter with her tonight; she felt a bubbling cauldron of emotions one moment and practically comatose the next.

'Jim will never forgive me if anything happens to you Squire,' she whispered and then stopped biting her lip. What did it matter how Jim felt about her after she'd gone? Perhaps her worry was nothing to do with Jim – just the horse? She told herself firmly that this was so. And it was only natural after all. She had been conditioned to be concerned for them . . . her memory recalled Princess' birth again and Jim's all-night vigil in the stable at Milton Mains.

Would he sit up with Squire now? He might well do so . . . she switched on the torch again and frowned at the three enquiring heads. Then she made up her mind; Michael would bring Julie home in the early hours and could check on Squire's condition then; meanwhile she wouldn't sleep and she might as well sit out here in the night-scented air as lie on her bed.

She took the lamp into the kitchen to light it and made herself coffee. Then she made several trips back and forth with a folding chair, a book; even a pen and paper to make some sort of coherent list of things she must do before she left . . . this time there would be no note to write for Jim. He must have known when he went to Mitcheldean – when he actually struck Charles – he must have known that it was the end. She tried not to imagine him actually beginning to fight; she knew Charles would never make the first move. Jim's temper had only just been contained when he left on Saturday, if it had been simmering all through Sunday it would have reached explosion point by Monday. The pictures that flashed through her mind to be instantly suppressed made her feel physically sick. She shifted her position in the chair and opened her book tipping it determinedly towards the glow of the lamp. It was all behind her now. She was free.

For a long time she read the print in front of her without taking in a word. The horses were silent except for sudden blowing sighs and the night-sounds – sounds she was completely used to – seemed magnified and mysterious through the top half of the stable door. She was conscious of the high empty moor soaring invisibly behind the stable, of the sea lisping below. Carybridge was a mere two miles away and the Watling place no more than four miles in the other direction, yet she felt isolated as never before. Probably this was the first time she had ever been alone in a house . . . she thought back to her childhood . . . yes it was. At Milton Mains either Jim or Old Adam had been there and even on the night of Old Adams' death Brian had been in the house. And in any case Milton Mains had never seemed cut off; Jean and Stan were in the cottage along the drive and other farms surrounded them.

Mary drew a deep breath and heard it vibrate in her throat. She told herself she wasn't nervous, yet even as she read another page she was trying to identify the curious screech which echoed regularly from the cliffs, to isolate it from a background reverberation which must be a plane.

It came again, a long-drawn-out cry; a rabbit in a snare or a badger. If only the engine-note wasn't so loud she could tell whether it was far or near, in pain or merely calling to its mate. And then she realized that the engine note was loud because it was nearer. She stopped listening to the animal and concentrated on the mechanical noise. It was a car coming this way.

Her heart pounded in her throat as she glanced at her watch. Unless something was wrong it wouldn't be Julie and Michael yet; it was only one-thirty. If it was Charles she couldn't stand another scene. He might know she was leaving Jim and he might think that meant she would turn to him . . . for a horrified instant she imagined Jim deliberately leaving the field clear . . . and then she knew it was the Land-Rover bouncing down the lane. It was Jim coming home.

There was a feeling of blind panic in the stable; the

horses sensed it and snorted nervously. Mary leapt up and blew out the hurricane lamp not knowing why she did so. Illogically she imagined that if he thought the farm was empty he would turn and go away again. She only knew one thing: she could not bear to see Jim now – maybe in the morning with Julie back in the house and the sun high in the sky. But not now in the middle of the night when her nerves were like wires and she was so utterly alone.

The Land-Rover took to the turf much too fast; it sounded like a speed-boat when its screw leaves the water; the engine raced and then bit and then raced again; and was suddenly dead. Jim had switched off outside the front door as usual. She could imagine him sitting there surveying the darkened house. The next instant the front door closed quietly behind him. Naturally he assumed that his wife and daughter were asleep in bed; he had no idea that so much had happened this evening.

She stayed where she was, pressed back against the solid wall of the house facing the half-open stable door, hardly breathing. The meeting was avoided; Jim would go to bed in Brian's room not knowing that she was below him in the stable. Their interview would take place tomorrow . . . it would be all right. She let her breath out slowly and shudderingly, trying to raise a smile at herself. How ridiculous – how Victorian – to be hiding from her husband in the stable! It would amuse Old Adam.

Then, with shocking suddenness, the patch of grass outside the stable door was illuminated with a square of light. She stared at it, her eyes distended. It was her bedroom light. Jim had gone into her room and switched on her light. She pushed herself against the wall until the old stone-work bit into the flesh beneath her thin shirt. It was the first time he had gone into that room since he had helped move the bed into it . . . no, he had put her into the bed that first night of course . . . Not since then. He was looking for her; he intended to see her immediately; and now he knew she was missing.

In a moment the night became lighter as all the lights in the house were switched on. Then the front door crashed shut and she heard him coming round the house to the stable. Naturally the stable was the first place he would look. And she was going to be caught in here hiding like a schoolgirl.

She moved quickly away from the wall galvanized into sudden action which again had no basis in logic. She felt for the picnic chair and sat down in it. Torchlight stabbed brilliantly outside the door; she hung her head limply forward and forced her arms and hands to relax; the beam of the torch shone whitely on her closed lids for an instant and then was extinguished.

She heard Jim lift the latch of the lower door-leaf very gently and felt his presence inside the stable as an increased air pressure. Then he scuffed on a piece of straw and one of the horses whinnied a greeting. She feigned a bewildered waking.

'Squire—?' she moved deliberately in the chair and immediately Jim's voice broke the soft silence reassuringly.

'It's me Mary . . . it's only me.'

She wondered how she should react . . . how she *would* have reacted if she'd roused herself from a sleep to find Jim unexpectedly there.

'Why are you here?' Where was her anger, her proud independence now? She clenched her hands trying to force outrage into her voice. 'Why are you *here*?' she repeated loudly.

'I'll tell you in a minute. First why are you out here – sitting with the horses?' She could see him in outline now. He was standing with his back to the Queen; a good yard from her chair.

She told him as concisely as she could the events of the evening and Michael's sterling help with Squire.

'They will be back about three,' she concluded. 'And he'll take another look at the leg of course. But I'm practically certain he's all right. Take a look at him.'

He said again, 'In a minute.' The torch shone out again and flickered on her face; she flinched and it went out. 'When Jean told you I'd . . . assaulted . . . Charles Mitchell, did you mean to leave me?'

She held on to the arms of the chair. 'Yes.'

'Were you planning to go to Mitchell?'

She was struck by the hopelessness of explaining. Wearily she said, 'I told you how I felt about Charles. I was going to Janice.' She swallowed. 'I *am* going to Janice. I'll talk to Julie tomorrow and leave in the afternoon.'

'Why?'

'Jim – I can't talk now. I'm too tired.'

'All right. Then don't fence any more. Just tell me why.'

She put her head down on her hand. 'I can't be fought over Jim. I'm not a piece of property. I tried to explain yet you went straight to Charles and started a fight. I felt – maybe wrongly – that you were releasing me.'

'No. I wasn't releasing you Mary. I just couldn't help it. I resented him so much . . . his proprietary attitude towards you last week down on the beach – it was unbearable to me.'

There was a silence. He didn't move towards her and when the horses leaned over and nudged him he ignored them.

She said on a sob, 'I'm sorry.'

'Yes. So am I. For so very many things Mary. But we can't go on being sorry. That was one of the reasons I hit Mitchell. Probably it was one of the reasons he hit me back. It probably sounds primitive to you but it set us free from each other. I'm not apologizing any more Mary. I want to start again.'

'Jim – tomorrow—'

'No. Not tomorrow. Tonight. Now. You see, I love you Mary.'

She gasped. There was silence and she found she was gripping the metal arms of the picnic chair as if she might fall off.

He went on inexorably, 'And I think you love me. And that's enough . . . the past . . . everything that's happened . . . nothing matters. We start from now.'

Somehow she pushed herself upright with some idea of running.

He said urgently, 'Don't go Mary! The only reason you could go to Cheltenham tomorrow is because you don't love me.'

'Jim, we've been through this. Before Brian's accident – I told you how I felt—'

'No you didn't. Maybe you would have done if the police hadn't come. Do you love me Mary?'

'No!' she almost shouted the monosyllable at him. 'You've come back tonight just because you thought you might be losing me – just as you'd have rushed back if you'd known about Squire—'

'Damn Squire!' He took a step towards her and grabbed her arm. Furiously she shook him off and started towards the door. 'I wasn't going to come back till tomorrow – with flowers and chocolates like any kid in love for the first time—' his voice rose too and the horses shifted unhappily in their stalls. 'But then I came as soon as I remembered because it seemed too urgent to leave it even a few hours—'

She remembered the way he had rushed to her room. Her heart lurched. 'Brian?' she whispered stopping and turning towards him.

'No. Not Brian.' She could see his face now, white in the darkness. His eyes flashed. 'I remembered something. I remembered the name of the café where we stopped for dinner on our wedding night.'

She stared at him saying nothing, hardly breathing, as if her whole future depended on him being right.

He took a step towards her. 'It was the Lobster Pot,' he finished quietly. 'And you were right about things changing. You are more beautiful. And I love you far more than I did then.'

Everything was still crazily illogical. Jim and Charles fighting . . . her own personal freedom . . . the horses . . . Julie and Michael . . . yet, inexplicably, a tide of warmth flowed outwards from her heart at Jim's words. If he had arrived tomorrow with flowers and pleas for forgiveness she might still have reached for the desolation of independence. But he had come tonight, at midnight, because he remembered where they had eaten on their wedding night.

He said, 'Mary? You wouldn't have sat by Squire all this time if you'd hated me . . . even if you'd been indifferent—'

She said in a thread of a voice, 'I've known I love you for some time. I thought you knew.'

His arms were warm around her; she leaned her head on the familiar shirt front and heard the familiar heart-beat.

'Jim I'm so tired,' she whispered.

'I know my darling.' He kissed her. 'Let's go to bed, Mary Richmond.'

CHAPTER ELEVEN

Mary woke very early. Her watch had stopped but the sun had the pearly brightness of a summer dawn and through the open window she thought she could still smell the dew.

She propped herself on an elbow and looked at Jim's sleeping face with the same shy curiosity she'd felt as a bride. Ridiculous to feel self-conscious with her own husband. She reminded herself of the countless times she'd woken to find him beside her before the mere staleness in their relationship had turned sour and they'd slept separately. But it hadn't been quite like this. There had been the early milking; Old Adam and Stan in the kitchen talking of yields and silage and acknowledging her presence only as they took their tea from her.

Here it was different. She had a stake in Caryford. She could manage it alone if need be . . . just for a time . . . while Jim attended sales. She recalled the last three days alone. And Squire. And then after . . . her face grew warm.

Quietly she slipped out of bed and pulled on jeans and a shirt. Jim did not move. He looked completely relaxed. She crept downstairs amazed to smell coffee and find Julie up.

'Don't tell me you've only just got home?' she whispered looking at her daughter's uncreamed face and hair still in its last evening's chignon.

Julie smiled blissfully. Having run out of the clothes she'd brought from London she was wearing a pair of Brian's old pyjamas, patched and faded. She looked about fifteen.

'I couldn't go on sleeping,' she said. 'I'm too happy and it seemed such a waste of time.'

Mary smiled back. She had been constantly surprised during the last two weeks by likenesses between herself and Julie. She had never wanted to sleep when she was very happy and this morning was no exception.

'Don't avoid the issue,' she insisted. 'When *did* you get back last night?'

Julie glanced at her watch. 'Four hours ago,' she discovered. She looked up at her mother. 'The blouse was just right. And – and Michael Sandford *is* rather special.'

'I thought he might be.' Mary could feel Julie's tremulous happiness like an electric current, intensified because of her own. Julie was feeling as *she* had felt when she first knew Jim; as she felt right at this minute. Yesterday she might have warned Julie to be careful, not to let herself feel too much. Today it was different. Everything was startlingly different. She remembered her terrible sense of failure where her children were concerned – where her marriage was concerned. Yet somehow, even through the barren years, Jim and she had given them this heritage, this capacity to love. Hadn't Brian's very unreasonableness, his bitter drive through Milton Mains, proved that? And now Julie, perched on the packing cases, her hands around a mug of coffee as if in prayer; so obviously, so heart-rendingly in love.

As if acknowledging the parallel closeness of their feelings, Julie said tentatively, 'I saw the Land-Rover. So Dad came home.'

'Yes.' Mary poured herself some coffee. 'It was late – I'm not certain of the time. I was sitting in the stable.'

'Idiot,' Julie said – almost fondly. 'Squire was fine. And I checked him this morning. Michael's a brilliant vet.'

'It wasn't that I didn't have complete faith in Michael. It was a wonderful job he did last night. I was just over-anxious.'

There was a short pause. Both women, no longer separated by years, sipped their coffee companionably. Then Julie said, 'Dad didn't sleep in Brian's room.'

Mary felt her face warm. She considered explaining to Julie about her father's insomnia and the early mornings when he had to start milking long before it was light. But Julie was a woman in love.

So she said very simply, 'No.' She looked into Julie's blue eyes. 'I – I don't think he'll be using Brian's room any more.'

Julie cleared her throat but her eyes still overflowed with tears.

'Well . . . that will be much more convenient when Brian comes home for week-ends,' she said in a wobbly voice.

'Yes.' Mary wondered how much Julie knew or guessed. 'Dad and I have had our difficulties darling—'

Julie jumped impatiently off the packing cases. 'Oh Mum – did you think Brian and I didn't understand the situation at Milton Mains? Time somehow stood still there – the Richmond tradition I suppose – and it split you and Dad didn't it? You need not pretend now.' She stared through the window at the summer sky. 'I always thought you had a rotten deal. Well, that's why I always seemed to be having rows with Dad and tried to make a career for myself.' She laughed without bitterness. 'I was determined I'd never be dependent on any man!' She turned and made a wry face at her mother, begging forgiveness. 'I simply didn't understand Mummy.' She sighed sharply. 'Anyway . . . for some reason Brian had it in for you – I could never understand why. Men sticking together I suppose. But we could both see what was happening.'

Mary looked at her daughter mistily. She was so independent, so strong-willed. Rather than stay at home and 'take sides' she had decided to go away. And Brian . . .

Brian had never told his sister about Charles. How fiercely loyal they both were.

She said softly, 'Brian understands now. We talked . . . on Friday.'

'I'm glad.' Julie touched her mother's sleeve much as she had as a child asking for reassurance. 'And it will be all right now. Will it?'

Mary said, 'Yes. Yes, it will be all right.' She felt the soaring confidence of the woman in love and loved in return. 'There will be setbacks – rows perhaps. But we shall manage darling. Don't worry.'

Julie hugged her mother quickly and then swung back on to the packing cases. 'It's Caryford. The air or something down here. I don't know . . . it's terrific.' She poured another cup of coffee. 'Which brings me to something I want to mention. Something I've had in mind for a long time now. About me.'

Mary relaxed against the stove recognizing that their emotional closeness was over and that now there was a different bond between them; a kind of intuitive understanding.

She said, 'I can probably guess.' She grinned. 'You want me to teach you how to cook. Or maybe even darn socks—'

'Among other things.' Julie grinned back and then stuck out her tongue. 'Seriously I want to ask you—' There was a sound on the stairs and Julie looked towards the hall door. Mary felt her heart pound suddenly. Her assurances had been so confidently given just now, but was it really going to be all right? How much was the magic of last night going to mean in the bright light of this morning?

Jim appeared in the kitchen doorway. He glanced at Julie sitting on the packing cases swinging her legs, then at Mary as she leaned against the cooker. He too had pulled on jeans and a shirt and his need for a shave was all too evident. His dishevelment gave him an air of uncertainty, of diffidence. Mary saw with a pang that he too was unbelieving of so much happiness.

'Is there room for me?' He came into the kitchen tentatively and touched her hand as it lay on the cooker. It was a question asked. She turned her own hand palm upwards and held his fingers warmly.

'Yes—' her voice wavered suddenly. 'There's always room for you Jim.'

Julie rolled her eyes. 'Do you two want to be on your own?' she enquired. 'I've got lots of things I can do—'

Jim smiled into Mary's eyes. 'We've got lots of time . . . we can spare her a few minutes can't we?'

It was a new Jim, and Julie's laugh, echoing Mary's was astonished. He turned to her. 'You were going to say something just now Ju. Go ahead. I'd like to hear it.'

Mary said warningly, 'Julie, your father hasn't even met our new vet remember—'

Jim's arm encircled her waist and held her hard against his side.

'Let her do her own talking, woman. I know the new vet is responsible for Squire's leg. As far as I could see last night he'd done a good job.'

Mary glanced up at him. He hadn't even looked at Squire last night and there had been no time this morning. Then she saw and understood. If Michael was a rotten vet and Julie loved him, that was all right with her father. Mary wondered how she could ever have thought Jim put the horses before his family.

Julie made one of her ghastly faces. 'Proper little matchmakers aren't you?' She grinned suddenly. 'It's nothing to do with Michael as a matter of fact. Although perhaps it is. I don't know – I'm afraid everything is something to do with Michael from now. He's a marvellous person.' She was terribly serious now. 'It's . . . look if I told you I wanted to give up modelling and come and work here –

at Caryford – would you be horrified? I mean could you stand having me around all the time? And could the farm afford it – I know we're horribly hard-up. But I'd pull my weight. Poultry has been mentioned – I could take that over. And I could work on the vegetables too – we could easily grow enough for market produce. And that would leave you two free to start a new herd if you wanted to. I mean, Dad's really a dairy farmer isn't he?'

Jim held up his hand to stop the flow. Mary was laughing beneath her breath with sheer happiness.

Jim said, 'I think we could manage an extra hand, don't you Mrs Richmond? At least until Brian finishes his agricultural course. And as that lasts for three years—'

'I might be around for much longer than that,' Julie said soberly. 'All right, I'll be honest with you. I'm in love with Michael. I've been in love before but it's never been like this. If he – if he doesn't feel the same way, you'll have me on your hands for the rest of my life. Because there'll never be anyone else.'

'Oh Julie,' Mary reached across to the packing cases. 'Darling, don't worry. I'm sure he feels the same.'

'I hope so. I think he might.' Julie put down her coffee cup and stretched hugely. 'Oh I feel so marvellous – isn't it wonderful to be alive?' She jumped down and aimed kisses at her parents. 'I'm going to get dressed and go and talk to the horses. Michael will be calling to see Squire later on and I want to be on the spot.' She paused in the doorway and said almost shyly, 'I'm glad about you two. And I'm sorry I've been a bit of a nuisance in the past. I'll try to make up for it.'

Mary and Jim said nothing. They stood silently and listened to her going upstairs, singing in her bedroom and then clattering down again and out through the front door.

Then at last Jim said, 'It must be catching.'

Mary twisted her head to look at him. 'What?'

'This business of falling in love.'

'It wasn't a dream then? Last night.'

'No Mary Richmond, it wasn't a dream.' He put both his arms right round her and held her protectingly. 'It really happened.'

'And—' her voice was muffled by his shoulder. 'When we talk . . . will it all go away? Will the wall still be there?'

'I don't think so. But we need not talk if you don't want to darling. This can be a completely fresh start – no questions—'

She shook her head unwillingly. 'That would do for a while. Then our minds would ask questions which we couldn't voice. That's how it started – we never talked.'

They were silent for a long moment, clinging together as if indeed they were surrounded by invisible dangers.

Jim said in a low voice, 'You don't have to tell me about Mitchell, Mary. It might be better if you didn't.'

So Charles *was* still one of the dangers in spite of the fight. She leaned away from Jim forcing a smile.

'Well. That proves that I do have to tell you . . . come on Jim, let's walk the sheep up to the top . . .'

It was more difficult than she had anticipated. The beginning of the story implied a criticism – an indictment – of Jim which she was now unwilling to make. Later, the stolen meetings sounded sordid.

She tried to excuse herself. 'When I knew about Adam's death – when I made up my mind to stay if only for a while – I didn't want to see Charles at all. I couldn't split my loyalties down the middle even though you needed me solely as an extra hand—' Jim made a sound of protest there but she was insistent. 'Be honest darling. That night in the barn – after the funeral—'

He sighed. 'I'm sorry Mary. All I knew then was that I needed you desperately and you were considering going to Cheltenham – maybe for good. I just used what weapons came to hand and the only one I could find was my legal claim on you.'

'Oh Jim . . . anyway I must be honest too. I could find no comfort in you then my dear and though I must have known right at the beginning that when Charles bought Milton Mains it was over between us, when he turned up here with Jean and Stan that Sunday I accepted the comfort he offered. I'm sorry Jim. I can understand myself up until then. But that afternoon I wronged you and I wronged Charles.'

She went painfully on. The chance meeting at Stapleford, the stupid business with the scarf, Brian's reactions.

'When we talked that evening Jim, I must have known I loved you. But Charles was still in the way. I felt I owed him a loyalty somewhere. Then Brian's accident ended it. It just finished Jim. I felt a terrible regret for his unhappiness and for my part in it, but nothing else. When I heard you tell Brian that I must love you all to stay at Caryford, I knew the truth. I was almost irritated with Charles for his desperate attempt to help us. When he came – was it only last Wednesday – I tried to tell him gently that it was over. He was convinced only when he saw I was in love with you . . . and then I broke down and he mopped me up.' She stopped and turned to face him. 'Jim . . . even if I had left – before Adam died – I really believe I'd never have gone to Charles. I thought you were indifferent and it hurt my pride so much I was glad for Charles' obvious admiration. I was flattered that he left his big estate to see me. But once I'd got away I'd have seen things in perspective and realized I didn't love him.'

He took her hand and held the palm against his face. 'I believe that now too Mary. But I might not have done before I hit him. So you see there is a certain value in my temper.'

She cupped his face with her other hand and kissed him. There were no questions. He had accepted the bitter fact of Charles.

She said gently, 'Darling I think you might have a black eye later today—' showing him that she too had accepted the fight.

He grinned irrepressibly. 'He'll have a worse one,' he said.

They walked on until Caryford was lost in a fold of ground and the sea and wild country seemed to belong to them alone. Jim tried hard to find words for what he called the 'automatic existence' they had slipped into after the children were born.

'If we'd bought our own farm . . .' he frowned with concentration as he stared back into the past. 'If Adam hadn't been such a strong character. I don't know Mary. I suppose we were strangled by tradition. Life had gone on like that for so long – women in one compartment, men in another. Perhaps our marriage wasn't so different from many others – can't you see Tony and Anne treading the same path? The thing is, we've got a second chance. Jean said that.'

'Jean?'

'Yes. She told me about Brian's accident. She thinks he was using Mitchell as a scapegoat but that his real anger was against Old Adam for letting Milton go to someone else. Apparently as she cradled him in her arms she whispered to him, "Your grandfather gave you something more precious than the farm Brian. He gave you a second chance." Maybe he heard her with his sub-conscious.' He smiled. 'He's certainly made a miraculous recovery. Anyway, when she told me that, I applied it to myself. I stopped being angry with my father – yes, I'd been angry with him Mary. I saw that a second chance was exactly what he'd given me.'

'Yes.' Mary remembered staring up the Long Acre field in the April sunshine on the day of Adam's death. 'Yes, I saw it like that too.'

Jim picked a piece of grass and studied it. 'Well . . . there was still Mitchell. That blasted stable. I decided to go and see him – I didn't want to embarrass Stan by questioning him.' He split the grass with his thumb-nail. 'At first he was evasive. Then he admitted he'd ordered the stable, paid half, then cancelled the order and put Stan on to it. He was a bit pompous and said a lot of things about friendship and helping. I interrupted and asked what right he had to help. And he went all hot under the collar and said he thought I knew his special feeling for you . . . I couldn't take it Mary. I just went for him.' He threw the grass away and looked at her. 'What surprised me was when he picked himself up he came over and gave me this,' he touched his eye. 'I didn't know he had it in him.'

Suddenly Mary started to laugh. She lay back in the grass overcome with the sheer humour of the situation. It was the same when she and Jim had quarrelled fiercely in the pouring rain . . . enormous and awful while it was happening; ridiculous and laughable afterwards in retrospect.

He leaned above her. 'You don't mind too much darling? Not now?'

She reached up. 'Not now. But oh Jim, I'm so glad you remembered about the Lobster Pot . . .'

They walked back down the saucer holding hands. The stable was a new blister behind the weathered house; Julie emerged from it leading the Queen and Princess. Michael's old station-wagon was parked by the front door.

'We'll make a decent yard in that angle between the house and stable,' Jim murmured. 'Something we can swill down in the winter—'

'The new kitchen-dining-room first, please,' Mary begged laughing. 'Oh and another hen house. And cattle sheds if we're going to start the Richmond herd again.' She caught his hand. 'Jim, aren't you excited?'

He said, 'It's so much better than when we first started out.'

She said solemnly, 'Everyone should start married life with two grown-up children and a run-down farm mortgaged up to its leaking roof.'

Like a gentle dove their new-found happiness stayed. Cherished, never taken for granted, it spread its wings over them all and the rest of the summer sped by. Julie disappeared for a week in the middle of August. She took the borrowed car back to London, gave up her flat and was collected by Michael, the wired space at the back of his car piled high with suitcases and polythene bags of luggage.

Brian finished his convalescence at Exmouth and settled in at Lower Brook farm after a brief week-end at Caryford. He looked fit and well and even more like Jim in his sudden maturity. He informed his parents seriously that he did not wish to be known as a farmer but as a conservationist; because conservation was what farming was all about. Jim and Mary nodded with equal seriousness. Jim mentioned later that 'Farmer Richmond' was less of a mouthful than 'Conservationist Richmond'. Brian considered, then at last he said with assumed reluctance, 'All right. I give you permission to shorten it to Connie Richmond.'

Mary knew that such small exchanges were the very fabric of a close family life. They had been missing from the Richmond family for a long time.

Autumn came. They attended Harvest Festival at Carybridge church and Tony and Anne Elliot came for the day. The financial news was good and on the strength of it Jim went ahead with the kitchen alterations. The new dining-room, rush-matted and furnished with a pine dresser from Stapleford Pannier market on which glowed Grandmother Richmond's china, was a vast improvement. The twin windows, back and front, filled the long room with light and Mary could stand at the sink and watch the sea. She felt all the thrilled satisfaction of a housewife who had been forced to manage in cramped inconvenience and is suddenly given scope for her talents.

'Let's have a party!' Julie said, arranging a brass jug of chrysanthemums she had grown herself. 'We ought to celebrate – it's been such a wonderful summer.'

Mary and Jim looked at each other. Yes, they had cause to celebrate.

Michael said suddenly and gruffly, 'Tell you what. Let's have an engagement party.'

There was a little silence. Julie stayed completely still bending over her flowers. Then she said lightly, 'Who's getting engaged?'

Michael said hoarsely, 'Stop being coy. We are . . . aren't we?'

Julie turned and looked at him. She was smiling but her eyes were full of tears. 'I thought you'd never get round to asking,' she said.

Mary knew that to be ignored like this . . . not ignored, included in a proposal of marriage . . . it was the greatest compliment Michael could have given his future in-laws.

They decided to hold the party the following Sunday. Jim fetched Brian for the week-end and Michael brought a sleeping bag. The young people spent the afternoon with the horses. Julie had talked her father into letting her enter the Princess in the Autumn Agricultural Show and she insisted on grooming all three – 'So that no-one will feel left out.'

Jim helped Mary to prepare the meal and lay the table.

'This is the first time I've made iced soup,' he joked as he sieved vegetables with exaggerated care.

Mary said, 'And I've never cleaned out a stable until we came here.' She placed a Richmond silver candelabra in the centre of the cheap deal table. 'It's a good mixture, isn't it?'

He stared at the heavy silver and then up at his wife's animated face.

'It's the only way for us Mary-mine,' he said.

The party was a great success. Mrs Westbrook had supplied Mary with fresh lobsters – 'from a special friend in Barnstaple' – and she had made the sort of salad Old Adam had enjoyed in the days of Milton Mains.

After Michael's short and impromptu speech of thanks, Jim stood up to give the toasts.

'First—' he glanced at Mary and then longer at Brian. 'I give you Old Adam.'

He paused and Julie protested. 'Honestly Dad – I don't want to be rotten but why Adam first?'

Jim held his glass at eye level. 'Because if he hadn't hung on to Milton Mains so grimly – if he'd made that Deed of Gift years ago when you children were small – we'd never be here now. Brian wouldn't be training to become a farmer – sorry old man – a conservationist. You wouldn't have met Michael Sandford, promising young veterinary surgeon. And Mary . . .' he stopped speaking and immediately Julie raised her glass and they all said fervently, 'Old Adam.'

Mary looked at Jim across the table. She knew what he had been going to say. If it weren't for Old Adam, she wouldn't be here now. For an instant she let herself remember that night in the Black Boar Buttery restaurant with Charles.

Jim was speaking again. 'And I'd like to propose a toast to you all for the parts you've played in getting Caryford really started. Because it has started. The sheep we sold last month fetched a good price. The vegetables are going steadily. And the eggs.' He smiled around the table. 'Brian was here in those first gruelling weeks when there was everything to be done at once. Then Julie and Mary came into their own. Michael probably saved Squire. So this is . . . to us!'

They raised their glasses again. 'To us!' they shouted boisterously and almost in unison. And as the laughter died away the sound of a car came through the window.

Mary raised her brows. 'Stan?' she asked briefly. They had wondered whether to invite Stan and Jean to the party so closely had the Butlers' destinies been caught up in theirs. But sheer lack of space had discouraged them from writing or going into Carybridge to telephone.

'Sounds more like Tony and Anne,' Jim said. 'That's not Stan's old truck.'

A curious premonition seized Mary even before she went to the window. She had sat at a table like this wearing this same dress only just over six months before. It was a moment of 'déjà vu'; she felt a physical squeezing of her heart.

Jim said, 'All right. I'll go—' she watched him push back his chair and go into the hall. Brian was saying something to Julie and Michael was laughing but above their voices she could hear Jim's, suddenly constrained. 'Oh . . . hello. No – it's all right. Do come in. Mary will want to see you.'

She had already seen the Bentley bouncing across the turf but it was still a shock when they came through the door together. The man she loved and the man she had thought she loved. Charles.

For a timeless second she stared at them hearing again Jim's greeting – 'Mary will want to see you.' Did he really think that? She looked at him; it was all right, his dark eyes were warm, they seemed to be trying to tell her something.

'Come on, sit down Mitchell,' he drew out a chair and Charles sat down uneasily. Brian had dried up. He was staring at his plate. Charles was still a danger.

Charles said, 'I – I'm so sorry. I've come at the wrong time—'

Julie interrupted gaily, 'Not at all Mr Mitchell. You're just the person we were going to toast next—' Mary stared at her. 'We'll always be grateful to you.'

What on earth was Julie saying? And yet . . . wasn't it true?

Julie lifted her glass. 'Here's to the man who brought the future Mr and Mrs Sandford together!'

They drank automatically. Brian hesitated then lifted his glass. Jim was laughing, filling a glass for Charles. And then Mary understood. She might not want to see Charles, but she needed to see him again. In the midst of her family and taking his rightful place as a kind of benefactor. Because if they turned their backs on Charles . . . if *she* turned her back and refused to see him again . . . he would become an unfinished chapter. There was the danger.

She sipped her drink and smiled. Yes, she was grateful to Charles Mitchell. She caught Brian's eye and let her smile grow confidently. He grinned back.

Charles cleared his throat. 'Too kind . . . I'd no idea. May I congratulate you both? I hope you'll be as happy – as happy as your mother and father obviously are Julie.'

Brian said a loud, 'Hear, hear!' and Jim said quietly, 'Thanks Mitchell.'

Charles stood up. 'I really must go. I thought you might like to know . . . Stan entered the Richmond bull in the Agricultural Show. It won first prize and Stan had a replica of the cup made for you. I have it in the car.'

Julie was ecstatic. 'What could be nicer? How marvellous of you to bring it over Mr Mitchell – today of all days – thanks so much.'

Charles made some deprecating noises. 'You did all the work before you left Milton Mains. The Butlers are absolutely delighted of course. They – they send their love.'

Michael said unexpectedly, 'You've done what you hoped then sir? I remember the first time you showed me Milton Mains you said all you wanted to do was keep up the Richmond tradition.'

There was a little silence. Charles was brick red. He made a move towards the door. 'I'll get the cup.'

Jim said swiftly, 'Why don't you go with him Mary? I know you'll have all kinds of messages for Jean. Cheerio then Mitchell – so good of you—' he looked round at Mary's doubtful face. 'Go on darling. Only you can help him now.'

Mary went down the narrow passage after Charles, marvelling and grateful for Jim's trust and understanding. She didn't know what she could say to Charles, even if she could say anything. But just to leave Jim's sheltering presence and step out to join him was a gesture of friendship.

He kept steadily on to the Bentley parked some way from the house and lifted a cardboard box from the passenger seat. She took it from him and then placed it on the ground.

'We'll see it later Charles. I can take it with me when I go back. Let's walk up here for a moment. That is – if you would like?'

He fell into step beside her without a word and they climbed up the slope of the saucer away from the sea and the ford where they had talked before.

At last she stopped and turned. The sun was dipping into the sea and below them the farm was small and still pathetically poor.

She said, 'You've helped me Charles. More than I can ever tell you. When I hit the low spots you were there. And now I'm happy . . . I have everything—' she swept the horizon with her arm. Yes, it was true, love had given her the whole world. Jim had given her love. And Charles could never have done that. 'I'm sorry Charles. It seems you have so little.'

He did not try to reassure her. He put out his hand and she laid hers in it. Together they stared at the panorama beneath them.

'I'm glad you're happy Mary. I won't pretend to be happy myself because that would mean I felt only friendship for you. And I still love you.' She jerked her hand protestingly but he held fast. 'There is one thing however. Before I knew you I wouldn't understand what you meant when you talked about having everything.' He smiled suddenly. 'I would look and see that all you had was a poor hill farm and a staid marriage.'

He was silent again. Then he said, 'Yes, I've changed Mary. You've changed me. I was stiff . . . reserved. I couldn't imagine any woman would think much of me. But for a time you relied on me – you leaned on me – you made me strong.' His smile widened into a grin. 'I even fought for you Mary. Did you know?'

'Yes Charles,' she remembered her disgust. 'Thank you.'

'No. Thank you my dear. I've come out of it with a kind of confidence. Not entirely empty-handed. Am I making sense?'

She said slowly, 'I think so. It isn't so difficult from how I felt about helping Jim is it? We all need to be needed Charles.'

His grip on her hand tightened. 'Perhaps it's as simple as that Mary.'

She didn't carry it further by suggesting that one day there might be someone else and after a moment they both began to walk back down to their everyday world by common consent. And then he left her to pick up the box containing the cup and to drive along the track and over the bridge connecting Caryford with the outside world.

She watched him until his tail light disappeared. It wasn't satisfactory. Until Charles found someone he could love and marry perhaps she would always feel a needle of guilt at the thought of him. But it wasn't all bad. He would heal and meanwhile the way was open for him to call and see them . . . talk to Jim.

At last she turned and looked at the farmhouse. It was rosy-red in the setting sun and the windows twinkled with the frail light of the candles in the dining-room.

She said aloud, 'This is our home. Our Land. Our heritage. And we are together.'

And she ran down the springy turf to re-join her family.

THE END